The Thyme Bank

by

Pauline Morphy

Best wishes
Pauline.

The Conrad Press

The Thyme Bank
Published by The Conrad Press in the United
Kingdom 2025
Tel: +44(0)1227 472 874
www.theconradpress.com
info@theconradpress.com
ISBN 978-1-916966-58-1
Typesetting and Cover Design by: Levellers
The Conrad Press logo was designed by Maria
Priestley.
Printed and bound in Great Britain by Clays Ltd,
Elcograf S.p.

Chapter 1.

Frances gazed across the Thames at a tiny beach, revealed by low water. On the oily mud lay an abandoned boat, more skeleton than body, fringed with acid green weed. A touch of burnt orange was provided by a rusty bucket dangling from the stern, and a more garish orange by a stranded buoy, to which the boat was attached. On a broken slab of iron-spiked concrete sat a hunched cormorant. Always such gloomy-looking birds, she thought, but worth drawing, then a hand touched her shoulder, startling her.

'Sorry, Fran,' said a beautiful West Indian girl, putting a tray on a low table beside her chair. 'Milk-no sugar. I remembered.'

'Thanks Alida,' said Fran, smiling up at her. 'I'm impressed you always remember.' She reached sideways to lift the cup and saucer.

'My boss's influence. He remembers everything about his clients so, his secretary should at least know their drink preferences.'

Nor does she mind providing them, thought Fran, watching the slim, elegant girl walk away. Almost level with the reception desk, she half turned.

'Sorry again. Mr Thomas says he won't be long, but you take your time to finish your coffee.'

'Mr Thomas isn't keeping Miss Shaw waiting,' said a tight, very different voice from behind the reception desk. 'Pharoah Publishers are strict timekeepers. Miss Shaw arrived rather early.'

'I did,' Fran said, receiving a cold stare from the super-efficient Naomi. 'I tend to arrive early. I expect I've a neurotic fear of being late.' And risking your wrath, she thought.

No response came; the receptionist's attention was now entirely taken by a new arrival, a tall man in a dark coat.

'Dr Fellowes? Mr Brooks is expecting you. He won't be long. Tea or coffee while you wait?'

Naomi's tone was honeyed. Intrigued that someone had elicited her approval, Fran took a second look. Wow! Black hair, a cheekbone that could cut paper, straight nose – he was pure Greek god. His coat was slung around his shoulders, revealing a grey roll-neck sweater and darker grey cords, all expensive-looking yet casual. His reply to Naomi's offer was too quiet to catch.

Fran leaned back in the deep chair and sipped the coffee, again looking at the river but with her mind elsewhere. Was the man a well-known author, highly valued by Pharaoh? What sort of doctor? Medical? Academic? She grinned: not like her to be interested. Men hadn't featured much in her life so far, and at present not at all – not since her first brief relationship that led to disillusionment – well, if brutally honest, to revulsion. At least she could now look back on that experience with wry humour. You'll just have to put it down to experience. Clichés have their place eventually, but she could have hit Alison, the first person who had told her that (as much a self-styled counsellor as a friend). It was she who had told her that in her first year at university she was known throughout the campus as The Ice Maiden. Anyone who hadn't paired off at the Freshers' Ball, or soon

4

afterwards, was likely to be labelled frigid or gay. Her secret crush on a fellow student, who had been occupied elsewhere until the night of their graduation, had not led to the exultation she had expected. Mike, President of the Students' Union and campus sex symbol, arrived unexpectedly at a party at Fran's shared flat, high on euphoria at achieving a First and on a combination of stimulants. Fran, probably equally high on euphoria and an over indulgence in Australian wine, stumbling passively with her head throbbing, had allowed him to lead her over the mountainous range of packing cases, books and clothes to her narrow bed.

Around two a.m. she'd abandoned any hope of achieving sleep in the few inches of bed available. A hot shower was more attractive than proximity to the snoring mound beside her. In the bathroom, shuddering at finding the water tepid, she'd dissolved into tears of disappointment.

A week after she had left the students' flat he phoned. She had no recollection of giving him her number. He was coming to London so could they meet? She'd made a firm excuse and hadn't heard from him since.

But they'd only had sex, hadn't they? Or had they? Fellow graduate Alison had quizzed her. He hadn't handcuffed her to the bed or made her dress up as a schoolgirl? Although laughing, Fran's reply had been firm. Another time, if there were another time, she'd rather be with a gorilla. At least it would be warm and furry, not sweaty and hairy.

The stirring of the cormorant out of its catatonic pose became more interesting to her than her reverie. Its wings half-lifted, head craned around, it looked like someone outraged by intrusive or loutish behaviour; clumsily it lifted its wings and took off, disappearing downriver into greyness that was unrelieved by any hint of sunshine.

Again, Fran heard the receptionist's honeyed tones: 'Would you like me to page Mr Brooks, Dr. Fellowes?'

'No, please don't trouble. He wouldn't be delayed without a good reason.'

Lovely voice. A slight drawl – bored, perhaps?

'No, you're right, Dr Fellowes.'

The honey positively oozed now and Fran nearly laughed as she recalled her first encounter with the power-dressed, perfectly made- up receptionist. Not for her that tone of voice when she'd arrived, looking every inch the art student, clutching a portfolio, and humble with gratitude that an art editor was favouring her with an interview. 'Well, you'd better take a seat', was the greeting she got and, turning to do as instructed, she'd collided with Mr Thomas, the very man she was going to see. By the time they had retrieved the contents of her tatty portfolio both were giggling and, on the road to becoming good friends, for which, it seemed, Naomi had never forgiven her.

'Mr Thomas will see you now, Miss Shaw.' The now tight, formal voice brought her back to the present. She picked up her bag and portfolio and stood up.

'You know the way,' said Naomi, unnecessarily.

'I should, by now,' said Fran, keeping her voice as pleasant as possible. Looking straight ahead, she walked beyond the reception desk and opened a door leading to a corridor, not doubting that a cold stare was following her.

A second pair of eyes watched her leave. Dr. Fellowes saw a young girl with tawny brown hair pulled into a ponytail and a face, only glimpsed, that was pure Burne-Jones. The rest of her was concealed by a brown shawl with a fine gold thread running through it and a fawn velveteen skirt that skimmed the top of small brown boots. He smiled. Maison Oxfam, possibly, but worn with style. She moved beautifully. So many women were ruined by their posture and way of walking. Was she an artist? A student? She was refreshingly natural-looking, making the effusive Naomi about as alluring as a shop window dummy.

Had he not been feeling maudlin, as he often had in the eight months since his mother's death, he might have reacted to Naomi's obvious message. It would have amused him to see her response if he'd feigned appreciation of the jacked-up bosom and endless legs, visible behind the ridiculous Perspex type desk.

Picking up a copy of The Illustrated London News he leafed through it with scant interest, his thoughts on the main reason for his trip to London – not a cheerful one. And why the sudden compulsion to visit his birthplace and his sole remaining relation – at least, the only one he was aware of? He loved his bright, funny, abrasive grandmother but where was she? Certainly not discoverable in the frail, angry yet sometimes, frightened woman, being slowly destroyed by Alzheimer's disease. If his planned visit stemmed from a sense of duty, wasn't that misplaced? It was unlikely she'd even recognise him. She was safe – in a Home – the best he could find. She was even in a house she'd long admired, a Victorian mansion, skilfully converted for its present use. But she had no idea where she was and, perhaps, that was a blessing. The Streatham she'd come to as a young wife had suffered a number of changes over the years.

He grinned wryly, remembering the visit three months ago when he'd retraced familiar paths across South London's parks and commons, once trailed by a posse of Red Indians, led by him – their natural leader. But that day he'd seen no unaccompanied children, no bow and arrow wavers, no ten-year-old spy-stalkers creeping through fringing woodland; the only stalkers were daytime hookers, one of whom had punched the nearside window of his car to get his attention, and then had snarled obscenities at him as he'd driven away.

At least, today, he had a protracted lunch to look forward to and a couple of nights of Charles's expansive hospitality and, as that thought raised his spirits, his friend erupted into the room.

'Sorry, but we've been embroiled in a tricky contract. Great to see you.'

Simon stood up and the two men embraced like continentals, then, with a backward wave to Naomi, Charles led the way through glass doors to the lift area.

'I've a cab waiting. Langan's okay for lunch?'

'Fine, but I wouldn't mind a whelk stall; it's the company that counts.'

'You might get a bit of that tonight. I've some fun lined up for you.'

'Female fun, Chas?'

'No, you randy goat, a party; something a bit different, even for you.'

As they reached the ground floor, Simon's mood was lightening. Trust Charles to get it right – to provide some light relief.

*

Forty minutes after entering his office, Fran gave Ken Thomas a hug and left with a commission to illustrate a book on wetland wildlife in the Somerset Levels. It was perfect: an easy drive from her Exmoor studio and no need to produce anything before late July. Back at home she declined the lunch offered by her aunt, Miranda, having, at Ken Thomas's insistence, shared his sandwiches.

Miranda enthused about the commission. 'That's great, darling, and fitting so well with our plans.' She poured coffee for them both, carried it to a low table at the comfort end of the kitchen where they both flopped onto a large sofa. After a few sips, Miranda said, 'You'll come to Bernie's party, won't you? He and Fallada are so keen to see you there.'

Fran had been gazing through the large French windows at the sun-enhanced colours of the flowers in the long, sloping garden. A walk would be lovely.

'Sorry, what did you say?' she asked.

Miranda repeated her request, and Fran responded a bit reluctantly.

'I feel awkward about meeting them socially. In a way Bernie's my boss, being a director, and you know what people might say – I get work because he knows you.'

'He doesn't, at least only through his wife. He didn't even know you sometimes work for Pharaoh and why should he? It's a huge company and his

9

involvement is largely with the American side. Honestly, Fran, you do take your scruples too far – there's no question of favouritism or...'

'I know that,' interrupted Fran, 'but others might not.'

'Do they matter whoever they are? Anyway, it's not a staff party. Bernie holds other directorships, and this do is about fostering international relations.'

Fran groaned. 'Even better reason for not going. Can't think of anything more boring. Anyway, shouldn't you get an early night before a journey and not go gallivanting?'

Miranda burst out laughing. 'I'm not yet in my dotage - not quite ready for you to take the parental role. I shall go anyway, but Fallada will be disappointed not to see you again. She wants a few young people to be there to give a bit of light relief and she's longing to show you her amazing house. You might even have fun – you haven't had much these last months.'

'I'll come,' said Fran, grinning, 'but to see the amazing house, not to be light relief. Promise we'll leave early?'

'As early as we decently can,' said Miranda. 'More coffee?'

'No thanks. I'd better finish packing. It's a bit hard deciding what to take and what not to. Two months! It's such an age to be away.'

'You don't have to pack everything for two months. There are shops on Greek islands.'

Fran drained her cup and stood up. 'Right: shorts, tee shirts, trainers, underwear and a toothbrush.'

Miranda laughed. 'Good start, but we're not exactly backpacking.'

In her bedroom, Fran picked up the phone and dialled the number she was most familiar with next to Miranda's. It rang and rang. It would, of course - why would anyone be in on market day? She replaced the receiver, grinning at her mistake and her childish need to be reassured that her beloved dog, Beamish, only delivered to his best friends two days ago, had settled in happily. Right now, if with Fred and Norah in Barnstaple, he was probably nosing along a row of sheep pens or, if left at home, returning resignedly to his basket, having been unable to fathom how to answer the phone.

She laughed aloud looking around; was it this room that turned her into a child again? It had changed a little bit over the years: pony posters exchanged for images of film and pop stars, and the china horse collection safely stored in the attic to make way for half the contents of the Body Shop. The Laura Ashley curtains and duvet cover had replaced My Little Pony patterns only a few years ago, probably for her sixteenth birthday. Photos of departed guinea pigs, a white rabbit and Beamish's predecessor still hogged the windowsills. On the bedside table was just one silver-framed photo from which a beautiful bride and handsome groom smiled joyfully. It was positioned so it was the first image she saw on waking – her late parents.

She forced herself to get on with the packing and wished she could do so with more enthusiasm. It was largely her fault they were embarking on this lengthy holiday. 'Time you resumed your island hopping now I'm a big girl,' she'd said on her last birthday and Miranda had enthusiastically agreed, saying that what she resumed Fran should commence.

She could hardly refuse when she heard the proposed trip was to be so special, evoking memories of her aunt's carefree years of wandering the Greek islands year after year, until she became the legal guardian to her brother's orphaned child.

Miranda had given up so much for her that Fran felt the least she could do was to offer her companionship. For years she'd put her needs second to Fran's, taking only vital trips to do with work and enduring the sort of holidays that delight a child. She'd always welcomed Fran's friends to the house but what a relief term time must have been, affording her set hours of peace.

Fran wondered what she could wear to the party as it wouldn't be like a Students' Union thrash. And what memories that evoked. She grinned, seeing again the garish flashing lights, hearing the monotonous beat that carried from one piece of music to another, relentlessly. Was that the fun Miranda was sure she was missing? She hoped not.

Chapter 2

'You are at your usual table, Sir,' said the waiter, leading the way.

'Great you could fit us in at short notice, Raymond,' said Charles.

'Oh we always try to oblige our regulars, Sir.' Simon was amused at the deference shown to Charles. Once seated and perusing the menu, he asked, 'Has this place become a habit, Chas?'

'A bit, as American clients like it.'

'And they don't get chucked out – if their faces don't fit?'

Charles grinned. 'That was ages ago. I recommend the spinach soufflé or the mushrooms with herbs and....'

'And it's on me as I'm not a client,' interrupted Simon.

'You are for today. I insist. After all you are an author.'

'Hardly of airport reading.'

'Bloody cheek. We do publish serious stuff as well you know. Now, the lamb noisette is a good main course.'

After they had ordered their food the wine waiter appeared and suggested, 'We've a good St Emilion, the one you like.'

'Okay for you, Simon?'

'Fine. I trust your palate, Chas.' Simon spoke without irony. Both had belonged to an old established wine club at Oxford and, when it suited them, were discerning drinkers.

13

When the waiter moved away Simon commented, 'Thank God for a bit of relaxation. Probate and everything's completed.'

'I still can't believe it.' said Charles. 'I'm so glad your mum was at our wedding. She looked wonderful, but she always did and that was just two weeks before died.'

'That's what was so hard, Chas - the shock. And she wasn't quite fifty-three.'

'So she was nineteen when she married, twenty when you were born and alone again at twenty-three. She always seemed young but I thought that was just in comparison with Mum.'

The waiter returned and, as Simon watched Charles go through the scenting and tasting ritual, he remembered how enduringly middle-aged Sheila Brooks had always seemed. Being married to Marcus must have aged her. He was a know-all, particularly when addressing women. He always had to draw attention to himself, had to be different from the other men even at his son's wedding. The cravat he wore, a hideous pink brocade, left him with no neck at all and with the addition of a top hat he looked like a Tenniel cartoon character. 'Thank goodness Charles takes after Sheila', Simon's mother had whispered. 'He's her son but with all the spirit she no longer has, poor woman.'

She'd loved the wedding. She would never have dreamed of saying anything coy but from the way she kept giving him meaningful smiles he knew she was seeing it as a rehearsal for the really important one – her son's.

Simon's glass was filled and they both drank then, with commendable swiftness, their food arrived.

'Is yours all right?' asked Charles, after a minute. 'These mushrooms are really good.'

'Excellent, thanks. Bit different from canteen nosh.'

They ate for a while then Charles asked, 'Any contact from your father? I wondered if he might have read your mum's obituary?'

'No, thank God. I bet he only reads The Sun. Mum never heard a thing after the divorce. Never knew if he married the girl when she reached sixteen. He could be dead by now for all I care.'

'You've never wanted to know him, have you? I remember at school you said you hoped you'd never set eyes on him.'

'I still feel the same way. I've no curiosity about him. When I was clearing the house, I found a photograph of him. He'd written 'To my darling wife, Liz' on the back. He's the only person who ever called her Liz, so she steadfastly became Betty after he left.'

'Have you got the photo?

'No, I burnt it. All I've kept as proof of his existence is the marriage certificate, decree absolute and my birth certificate. If I'd found that photo years ago I'd have dyed my hair blonde, up-staging you. Mum used to say he only gave me one thing – his looks. If that's so at least I haven't used them to seduce a fifteen-year-old.'

Charles was grinning broadly. 'Ah, as we've shifted onto underage sex, remember that assistant matron at school?'

Simon laughed. 'Steady, I was nearly seventeen. I reckon she deflowered half the sixth formers before moving on to higher things - Repton, wasn't it?'

'No idea. I wasn't party to those excesses.'

15

'Hm - zits, was it? Never mind Chas, you made up for it at Oxford. Remember that May Day when we were hauled off to the nick? I really thought we were for it that time. Considering we were pissed we did pretty well.'

'You mean you did with your Oscar winning act of contrition. I don't know how anyone else would have got us off with just a verbal reprimand.'

'Desperation, Chas. Even for Oxford we'd been a bit extreme, daubing ourselves with that awful green slime and leaping off Magdalen Bridge, starkers.'

Two well-groomed and hatted women at a nearby table collapsed into girlish giggles, then disappeared behind their menus.

'If they were ten years younger, I'd ask them to join us,' said Simon, quietly.

'Or ten years older,' suggested Charles. 'They can be okay.'

'Good God, you're not into infidelity already, married five minutes.'

'No, definitely not. I can't believe my luck. And Anna is much easier to live with than you were. I love being married. Anyhow, what about you? What's this move to Exeter about? Is it Margot's idea?'

'God no, she doesn't feature. She's going back to Aberdeen soon.'

'You're splitting up?'

Simon shook his head. 'Nothing to split, never was. By the way, before my new job starts, I'm taking a break in Kenya.'

'No need to say more. You'll be seeing sexy Caroline. Ah, here's the main course.'

Again, they concentrated on eating for some while then Charles said that Simon's life was due for a major shake-up.

'Really? According to the Oracle or astrology?'

Charles grinned. 'Neither, just simple homespun psychology. Your significant parent has died. It's like the severance of the last strand of the umbilical cord. You may laugh, Simon, but it happens like that – men get jolted into making major changes: jobs, partners, countries – some even get married.'

'You managed that without a prior bereavement, Chas. How do you explain that?'

'Natural progression in my case.'

'So is my job change. It's a better salary, pleasant surroundings, low crime rate. Exeter's attracted me for years. Mum took us there, remember? On that first camping holiday at Salcombe? And I never intended staying in Manchester forever.'

'I never understood why you ever went north of London. Was it an ancestral pull?'

Simon gave an exaggerated shudder. 'Far from it. Once Gran's parents died there were no links and....'

'But who knows what goes on in the subconscious,' interrupted Charles.

Simon grimaced. 'And who'd want to –I don't. Yet I'm always asking my students to consider what makes a writer tick as seen by his outpourings; so now they regard someone of the likes of Gerard Manley-Hopkins as a shrink's joy more than a serious poet.'

'I don't doubt it, Simon. Although I'd say his usefulness is in the area of speech therapy.'

'Chas, you're a literary stain, but this food is excellent.' Simon helped himself to more tiny, buttered potatoes and *mangetout*. 'What pulled me north? It was the kudos of being at Manchester for my first permanent job. And it was a chance to see life with a bit more breadth to it. We had it pretty easy, didn't we? Supportive families, ambitious for us, willing to make sacrifices.'

'True in your case, Simon, but I doubt if Dad would have given anything up for me. Mum made the sacrifices.'

'But he sowed the seed of Oxford for us, Chas.'

Topping up their glasses, Charles shook his head, grinning his disbelief.

'It's true,' Simon continued. 'I was staying at your place and Marcus was in one of his picky moods, complaining we lacked ambition and were wasting our public-school education. Our responses were pretty vague so he got really cross. He said if we weren't aiming for Oxbridge we might as well aspire to be shelf-stackers at a supermarket. He was so angry I believed him.'

'Yes, you sly beggar, getting fixed up at Magdalen while I was still agonizing over A levels.'

'Not my duplicity, Chas: Mum did her research and suddenly I was off on a round of exams and interviews. Whatever we think of Marcus, we've got him to thank for our most enjoyable and scurrilous years.'

Charles laughed. 'I suppose you're right. Working class people of his generation had only heard of two universities that counted, and his roots, now middle class, are pretty shallow. That's why he was so status mad for me.'

Raymond, the waiter, arrived offering the menu for puddings. They settled for coffee.

'And how about a brandy?' suggested Simon.

'Better not. Got a tricky meeting at three with an author who doesn't want to cut a potentially libellous passage. I've got to seem sharp, at least. What will you do, visit your gran?'

Simon was thoughtful for a moment then shook his head. 'No, I've probably had enough driving for today.' He glanced at Raymond who was hovering. 'Just the one brandy, please.'

Charles felt in his inside jacket pocket and took out a key.

'Take this and let yourself in. Come and go as you like. Help yourself to anything you fancy. Anna has changed a few things since you last came – making the house more hers, or should I say, ours.'

Grinning Simon pocketed the key. 'Is it genuinely fifty-fifty, or Anna's insurance policy in case you split up?'

Charles laughed. 'You old cynic. It's an outright joint gift from her parents. Just shows what confidence they have in me.'

'Or they're senile. Bit tough on Marcus, seeing a valuable piece of real estate coming from the other side, as it were, and he's in the trade.'

'It rankled. Anna and I expected nothing like it from either side. We could have put a roof over our heads, albeit a lot more modest than the one we've got, and with a thumping mortgage. I can't get over such generosity. And speaking of houses, you'll see an amazing one tonight, Bernard Howard's.'

'So, it's his party?'

'Yes. His wife invited me. She drops in at work occasionally. I declined, saying you were coming to stay so she insisted you should come too. She's really keen to meet you.'

'Why? Is her marriage on the rocks? Is she wanting a virile young...'

'Youngish,' interrupted Charles. 'And she's happily married with teenage kids. She's heard of you.'

Simon grinned. 'In what capacity?'

'A respectable one. She read that book review in the Guardian, the one about Auden and was impressed. She's spotted one or two more of your contributions and she likes your light, satirical touch.'

Simon was amused to see the hatted women, who had been looking towards the walls that offered a rather puzzling display of eclectic paintings, had resumed their interest in them.

'No doubt,' he said, glancing at them, 'when I was trying to be really deep and serious.'

'Oh, she's no fool,' said Charles, following his gaze.

'Clearly not. Sounds a discerning woman. I can't wait to meet her. I've travelled lightly by the way, so if it's a black-tie affair you'll have to help me out.'

'It won't be. It'll be any sort of dress or undress - totally cosmopolitan and...'

Charles was cut short by the ringing voice of a tall, blonde girl, slinking panther-like between tables.

'Charles, angel – see you at the party. You'll introduce me to your friend, won't you? Can't stop now.'

The girl left the restaurant with a following of two braying young men

'Who was that?' asked Simon. He had noted the girl's superb figure, moulded by a tobacco-coloured catsuit.

'Nobody. She's something in the rag trade. Susie Hall-Spencer. She featured in a fashion book we published. What's funny?'

'You...she...everything. Once you'd have been drooling.'

Half an hour later Simon entered the terraced house, the sort estate agents term 'bijou'. Not a bad wedding gift – a bit of real estate in Chelsea! He mounted the stairs and found the door of the spare bedroom was ajar. He smiled to see a welcoming jug of flowers on the dressing table, the bed made up and a top corner of the duvet turned back. Good old Anna, the perfect hostess. He dumped his bag on the floor and sat on the bed looking through very clean glass onto an exquisite tiny garden within a mellow brick wall hung with wistaria. The top pane of the window was open just an inch, enough to allow the passage of birdsong into the room. Extraordinary! No cacophony of traffic noise yet Kings Road was only yards away.

It would be so easy to give himself over to the peacefulness, to kick off his shoes and stretch out on the duvet. He had no doubt sleep would engulf him and why not? He glanced at his watch – three twenty. If he drove to Streatham now he'd be snarled up in the rush hour traffic on the way back – be late, maybe, for the party. No, he'd indulge his sleepiness, partly induced by the brandy, and be on form for tonight as Charles would expect him to be.

Chapter 3

Fran stared, amused and amazed. It was as if an enormous jelly mould had been attached to the entire back of the house. Outside, dark trees grew up to it and above it, just leaving a slip of sky visible through the dome. Inside it was the Day of the Triffids: great tropical plants, ferns, palms and vines were artfully arranged to form arbours and avenues. Colourful birds flew about, apparently unconcerned that their vast aviary had been invaded.

'I must be tripping,' said Fran. 'Is it real?'

Miranda laughed. 'I knew I hadn't done it justice describing it. It has to be seen to be believed. And you've seen nothing yet.'

Fran grinned, eyes widening. 'But just the hall is amazing. How did they create a semi-circular, oriental-looking room from a Georgian rectangle?'

'It's partly illusion,' Miranda said. 'A clever use of marble pillars, vast mirrors and all those wonderful rugs and wall-hangings, and the great Ali Baba vases.'

A waiter appeared, immaculately turned out, and holding a silver tray bearing champagne flutes.

'Thank you,' said Miranda, taking one for each of them. The waiter nodded politely and moved on. After sipping for a moment, Fran and Miranda exchanged satisfied smiles.

'Not sorry you came, Fran?'

'No, sorry I moaned. This is fun.'

'Fun and a bit of glamour never harmed anyone. It's good to see you sampling both. Ah, here's our hostess again.'

Miranda smiled at the approaching woman, and Fran noted their similarities: both in their fifties, tall and Junoesque. Fallada Howard, half American and half Egyptian, wearing a strapless turquoise sheath was more revealed than Miranda in her black and purple silk dress. Fallada's jewellery was spectacular; chunky diamonds sparkling from neck, wrists and earlobes while Miranda's was comparatively modest: bangles and necklaces of Indian silver. Fallada's hair was the colour of mahogany and hung in great sausage-like ringlets, not showing a sprinkling of the grey that Miranda grumbled about then ignored. What was most alike about them, Fran decided, was a natural confidence and charm.

She glanced down at herself, wondering if she should have dressed up a bit. At home the scoop-necked, semi-fitting cream dress had looked fine, but here, in the company of exotic birds and glamorous women, it must look pretty drab.

Arriving beside them Fallada said, 'Fran, dear, I love your hair like that – loose. You look charming.'

The warmth and sincerity of her tone reassured Fran who smiled and returned her unexpected hug.

'Aren't the young lucky, Miranda? No need for fine feathers.' Fallada touched the amazing jewels at her neck with a throwaway flick of her fingers and continued, 'Fran, it was sweet of you to come. It's a bit dull for you with all these middle-aged business types but I am expecting a few younger people.'

'Don't worry,' said Fran. 'I'm loving seeing your house. Is that a spiral staircase over there? It's so entwined with greenery I can't tell.'

'Yes. It's one way to our little art gallery on the top floor of the house. Now that might interest you. We've collected paintings on our travels from all over the world. Go up if you like. Miranda's seen it, so may I monopolise her for a bit?'

Miranda smiled. 'See you in a while. You'll really enjoy it.'

She and Fallada were right – the gallery had plenty to interest and please her. She lost track of time as, quite alone in the large, converted attic, she examined paintings from China, Japan, the Philippines, India, South America and the Seychelles. They ranged from primitive to sophisticated. Many had a refreshing naivety, and these held her attention the longest. She guessed those artists were untrained, painting from the soul as one of her favourite tutors would have said. Fallada and Bernard had a good 'eye' and how refreshing that they spent their obvious wealth on present day artists who, probably, were mostly poor.

A pang of hunger finally drove her back to the party but slowly. It was amazing to look down from the stairs onto a scene that reminded her of visits to the tropical house at Kew gardens. Not that visitors to Kew would be attired like Fallada's guests. Flashes of colour moved under the screening foliage but there was more black and white as men far outnumbered women, and no woman could outdo the brilliant plumage of a parakeet that flew, screeching, past her ear.

The spiral staircase was steep – she hadn't noticed that on the way up. Holding the handrail she descended cautiously, unused to wearing high heels. A few steps below her four men were standing on a small viewing platform.

'Nasty touch of déjà vu for anyone surviving the Burma campaign,' said one, white haired and slightly stooped. He was rewarded with guffaws from the others.

'I'm tempted to shout 'fire',' said another, and then all were convulsed with laughter as, below, a woman shrieked and held up her glass, watching the contents turn cloudy.

'God, a bird's dumped in her drink,' said the first speaker. 'What other wildlife are we going to contend with – snakes, d'you think, in those vines?'

'Only human ones,' came the dry response from the tallest of the men.

There was something familiar about his voice. As Fran reached the platform he spoke again, 'Look chaps, down by that little fountain, an amazing-looking woman. Half a silver foundry around her neck and...'

'Bit old for you,' said the older man.

'They're often the best. Usually grateful.... Oh, sorry.'

In response to Fran's icily delivered, 'Excuse me,' the tall man who had been speaking, moved aside allowing her to continue down the stairs. In seconds Fran had realised two things: he had been talking about Miranda and was the Doctor Fellowes she had seen in the reception area at Pharaoh.

At ground floor level there was now no sign of Miranda. Fran looked for her, pushing aside giant leaves and entwining vines, apologising to groups of businessmen smelling as strongly of scent as their overdressed women. Rounding a scratchy fern she collided with a dinner-jacketed man clamped to a large phone.

'Look where you're fucking going,' he said, then into the phone, 'Not you, darling. I'll give you a ring later- from home, as long as the coast's clear.'

Glaring, Fran walked on. At last she saw the waiter. She described Miranda to him. He smiled at once.

'Ah, Miss Shaw. She's on her way to the dining room. Come, I'll show you.'

Fran beamed at him: at last, in the jungle, was a decent human being. She followed him to another amazing sight, a much-reduced copy of a room in Versailles and there, about to help herself from the buffet, was Miranda. Fran picked up a plate and joined her.

'How was it? Did you approve?'

'I loved it. Nice to think there are people who bring things back from holidays other than seashells and paperweights. What have you been doing?'

'I learned a lot about this house – how it was left a derelict shell after the war then, eventually, Berni and Fal managed to buy it. As long as the front was faithfully restored in Georgian style they were given carte blanche with the rest. Sometimes parties of schoolchildren, students of architecture, even minor royals, visit. It's the most eclectic mixture of styles and periods. There's a Chinese boudoir, a Victorian bathroom....'

'Stop,' said Fran. 'I can't take in anymore, except some of this amazing food.'

She looked along the buffet table, struggling to make a choice.

'Their chef was trained at Claridges,' commented Miranda as they moved along.

'Surprise me,' said Fran, laughing.

They carried their plates to a long dining table and were surprised to find two empty chairs together. Sitting down Fran commented, 'Where is everyone? Maybe dealing comes before eating.'

A swarthy-looking man, sitting next to Miranda, said, 'There's a second dining room upstairs – Edwardian and only finished last week.'

He and Miranda fell into conversation while Fran concentrated on eating. Sharing dear Ken Thomas's sandwiches seemed a long time ago and the lime and spiced chicken was delicious.

'Pudding?' she suggested, a while later.

'Please. You know what I like, Fran.'

She was sure Miranda gave her the merest hint of a wink as she stood up. Her companion hadn't stopped talking, except to overfill his mouth.

Fran walked across to the buffet and considered the array of puddings. She started to spoon tiny profiteroles into two glass dishes then was distracted by a high- pitched female voice. Glancing in its direction she saw the tall, dark-haired Dr. Fellowes entering the room with a blonde girl in a shiny gold-coloured dress, hanging onto his arm. The girl spoke again and now the whole room could surely hear her, even above the diners' squawks and guffaws.

'Charles says you were notorious at school and Oxford. Are you still? I hope so – I love naughty men.'

Whatever his response was it didn't seem to please the girl. He disentangled her arm from his and, with a fleeting smile, walked out of the room, leaving her staring after him. Had he been rude, making the sort of comment he'd made on the staircase? Fran grinned, finished spooning and picked up the dishes, then noticed that the girl was already talking to another man and running her hand up and down his arm. He was an older man, the one who'd been so rude to Fran in the conservatory. He was facing the girl squarely, giving her his full attention. Business and sex, sex and business – what a combination!

'What are you grinning about?' Miranda asked, as Fran sat down.

'Oh nothing. Can we go soon?'

Miranda glanced at her watch. 'It's twenty past nine. Fallada knows we're off in the morning so I suppose we can. We'll skip coffee but I'll have to find that Victorian bathroom, how about you?'

'No, I'm okay thanks.'

Minutes later, when Fran got up, Miranda's companion was still yacking and she was looking a bit wan.

'Don't be long,' Fran said quietly. 'I'll wait for you in the conservatory, doing a bit of bird watching.'

She looked everywhere as she crossed the hall. Paintings, wall-hangings, ornaments screamed for attention. If the Howards bought paintings from talented unknowns to hang in their gallery, the reverse was true here.

'Oops, sorry,' said a familiar voice and a hand touched her arm. 'We were about to collide. Oh, I've seen you already today, haven't I?'

Startled, Fran found herself looking up into the most dazzling blue eyes she'd ever seen on a man. His smile was so disarming she had no option but to respond pleasantly, smiling and nodding.

'Yes, at Pharaoh.'

'Hi, I'm Simon – Simon Fellowes.' He held out his right hand.

'Frances Shaw – Fran,' she said. His handshake was firm, dry and cool.

He gave a little laugh. 'I must admit I know that. Chas told me. You know him, Charles Brooks, one of Pharaoh's editors.'

'Only slightly. Is he here?'

'Yes, with his wife, Anna. I've lost them for a moment. It's such a scrum.'

Fran looked away for a second. Why had he been enquiring about her? What could she say that wouldn't sound too banal?

'It's an amazing house, isn't it?' she managed. 'A bit like a film set.'

He nodded. 'Unreal. Your first visit too? I'm only here by courtesy of Charles. Our hosts seem charming but I'm not too enamoured with international business types.'

His friendliness and charm were undeniable. Emboldened, Fran grinned and, as if hearing the words uttered by someone else, said, 'Are older women wearing silver foundries more amenable?'

He stared, momentarily disconcerted. 'You heard me - on the spiral staircase. D'you think I was rude?'

'Yes, very. You were talking about my aunt, Miranda.'

'Oh God! I'm so sorry. I wasn't meaning to be rude. She's wonderful-looking.'

He looked and sounded so contrite she gave a small laugh. His expression of relief made him seem less suave.

'Miranda - Miranda Shaw? Is she the Miranda Shaw?'

'Yes.' Encouraged by his revealing question, she asked, 'Are you connected with the Arts?'

29

'Loosely. I teach English literature at Manchester University. Ah, a drink?'

The friendly waiter appeared offering more champagne. Fran declined

'Better not. Must keep a clear head. Miranda and I have to catch a plane in a few hours.'

'You're not flying out of my life?' exclaimed Simon, taking a glass.' I've only just met you. And I was about to suggest doing something mad – being in Oxford for May morning although a while away.'

Fran smiled, looking down so her hair swung forward brushing warm-feeling cheeks.

'Tomorrow we're going to the Greek islands for a few weeks.'

'You'll roast. It'll be the hottest time, hardly bearable.'

Fran glanced up. He was looking really concerned.

'We know but don't care. It's the only free slot for Miranda this year and she's desperate to start island-hopping again. She just follows her whim. She's talked of the Cyclades and the Dodacanese - all new to me.'

'And when you come back where will you be?'

Again, Fran glanced down, sure that her face was growing pinker. Was this how sophisticated men were with women? Was such confidence part of the package that came with physical beauty and sex appeal way off the Richter scale? Her throat felt dry. Maybe she should have taken that champagne. Other parts of her felt odd too.

'So where will you be?' he repeated. 'In London?'

'No. Devon.'

'Devon!' Simon's exclamation caused several people to look round but he seemed oblivious of them.

'Why is Devon so surprising?' she asked.

30

'That's where I'm going to work - at Exeter University. Is your home in Devon?'

'Yes, and in London. I do most of my work at my cottage on Exmoor and Miranda's house is along the road from here but very different from this one.'

'You live with your aunt?'

'Not much now. She brought me up from when I was four. My parents were killed in Israel. My father was her little brother.'

'So we're both orphans - destined to meet. Your aunt's approaching. Will you risk introducing us?'

It was ironical that Miranda had heard of Simon: she had been discussing his work with Fallada. They shook hands. Their instant mutual approval was obvious.

'A while back I read one of your articles. How refreshing to meet someone whose subject is literature.' Miranda lowered her voice. 'I've been hearing about money flows and market trends and I've hardly understood a word. Delighted to meet you, Simon.'

For the next ten minutes Simon's words were addressed as much to Fran as Miranda but it was the latter's quick responses that fuelled the discussion. The size of Miranda's personality could be overshadowing but Fran had long learnt to cope with it. Now she was listening more to her own thoughts. Why had this man who could rival any Jane Austin hero, been asking Charles Brooks about her? Surreptitiously, she studied him: the shapely mouth and perfect teeth, amazing eyes, and hair, thick and straight – and so black! Celtic ancestry or Mediterranean?

31

Miranda was on a favourite hobbyhorse, traditional classical education. After a while she concluded, 'Better to loathe Milton and Shakespeare at eleven, then slink back and fall in love at sixteen, than never be introduced to them. There's a danger they'll seem overwhelmingly formidable if the diet is wholly modern literature. But what am I doing holding forth to you, Simon? Your turn to criticise sculpture.'

Simon laughed. 'That would tax me. The great joy of literature is its availability - it's a universal language...'

'And so it must be for future generations - ah, your friends are coming. Fallada introduced us a little while ago and told me of their connection to you.'

Miranda was beaming at the approaching couple, Charles and his wife. Within seconds of Fran being introduced to them, she was surprised to hear Miranda inviting them home for coffee. What about that early night, time for a few last-minute jobs and a bit more packing? Was this a ruse of Miranda's to give her some 'young company'?

Having said their farewells to the Howards, they all walked the few hundred yards to Miranda's house, Charles and Anna flanking Miranda and Simon walking with Fran. He was tall, six foot she guessed. She wasn't tiny – five foot five. Her height pleased her. She thought very short girls looked like toddlers trying to keep up with tall men.

'Chas was relieved to find a space in Bernie's drive.' Simon said. 'Even St John's wood isn't safe enough for his beloved old Riley. He's spending a packet renting a garage for it in Chelsea. God, the times I've had to push the old heap along the High.'

Fran laughed. 'So you go back a bit.'

'We met at prep school. I won a scholarship to Dulwich, then we were at Oxford together.'

Ahead Miranda half-turned. 'What a shame it's a bit late to see the garden. It's Fran's creation,' she said.

'So you're a gardener as well as an artist,' said Simon. 'Do you cook also?'

'Like a dream,' said Miranda. She walked up a short flight of steps and unlocked the front door. 'Would you like to see the studios while I make the coffee?'

All chorused their approval so Fran led them to the large first floor studio which, she explained, was used by students.

'So your aunt teaches as well as doing her own work,' said Anna, looking around at pieces of sculpture showing every stage of endeavour.

'Not teach exactly. She's available to discuss and advise, but give the students freedom to develop in their own way.'

'Where do they come from?' asked Charles.

'Everywhere and from all backgrounds. Miranda set up The Foundation for Sculpture six years ago. She runs courses for people interested in sculpture but not necessarily aiming to study it. Most of the attendees have jobs, some are unemployed, and a few come from a local centre for adults with learning difficulties.'

'That would be of interest to you, Anna,' said Simon, then looking at Fran added, 'Oh, I don't mean Anna has learning difficulties, but she works with kids who do.'

'A really worthwhile job,' Anna said. 'Best job for a teacher, not that Simon agrees.' She pretended to punch him.

'Come and see Miranda's own studio, next door. There's also one in the garden where the hard, dirty work is done, as she terms it.'

They followed Fran into another room where, above the marble fireplace, a large block-mounted photograph showed a youthful Miranda standing beside Barbara Hepworth. 'Wow, that's lovely. They look so happy,' said Anna.

'As a student Miranda won a national competition and the prize was a weekend working with Barbara, and they became good friends. Miranda was devastated when she died.'

'I've seen that photo reproduced in a book,' said Simon.

He, Charles and Anna stood looking around but stock still as if a bit overwhelmed.

'Miranda hates a hands-off, reverential approach to her work. Feel free to touch things. D'you know a piece called Felloweship? It went to America – to Virginia. It was a horse and donkey. I fell off it when I was seven and broke my arm.'

'So you were a tomboy,' said Simon. 'Are you still?'

Again, Fran felt the colour rise in her cheeks. She turned away, rested a hand on a strange-looking beast crouched on a chest-high plinth and announced, 'My first pet.'

Anna joined her and patted the animal.

'What was he?' asked Charles.

Fran grinned. 'A mongrel. My parents found him in Israel. He was in a dreadful state so they brought him home. Wasn't he beautiful?'

'Beautiful wood,' commented Charles, tracing the grain with a forefinger. Everyone laughed and Fran conceded he hadn't been a beauty.

'But he had a beautiful character and I loved him madly.'

'Lucky beast,' said Simon. 'And this is your work?

'With my aunt's help. You can see why I'm not a sculptor.'

Minutes later the smell of fresh coffee drifted into the studio, tempting them all down to the basement kitchen.

'What a lovely room,' enthused Anna. 'So cosy.'

Miranda smiled warmly. 'We like it. It's our family room. Scenes of homework struggles, tears, celebrations – they've all happened here.'

And there was plenty of touching evidence verifying her words. On the dresser between choice pieces of china were photographs of Fran at all stages, from infancy to graduation.

'Who is the child on the pony?' asked Anna.

'Me on Chuckle, an Exmoor pony,' said Fran. 'We still have him at home on Exmoor.'

'Ah, so Exmoor is home,' said Simon.

'Oh, certainly to Fran. She's in her element there with the wildlife and marvellous landscapes. And it gives her a chance to get away from here.'

Fran did not protest but exchanged a look of complete understanding with her aunt. 'Fran hates cities,' Miranda continued. 'Her father was the same. He endured Cambridge for the sake of getting the degree he wanted, but after that he became quite a nomad.'

'Which I'm not,' Fran protested.

'No, darling, but you could be.'

'I endured Leeds for the sake of getting the right degree, and Barbara Hepworth went to that Art School, so there's a similarity.'

'Was it so awful?' Anna asked.

Fran smiled and shrugged. 'Mostly I hated it, but there were fun times. Miranda thought I should leave London for a bit and broaden my horizon. I was a day girl at school here so I expect she was right. Anyhow, it showed me what I didn't want.'

'Which was - is?' Simon asked.

'Urban life,' she said with feeling.

'Aren't there compromises?'

'Yes, I s'pose that's what I have now. Sometimes in London, sometimes on the moor.'

'And shortly in Greece,' said Miranda. 'Dear, generous girl, foregoing time with her friends.'

Fran smiled. 'I'm depending on you to educate me. It will be my first visit.'

'Mine was a school trip,' Anna said. 'We all behaved atrociously, flirting at every opportunity.'

'I can't imagine it,' Charles exclaimed. 'I thought you were the Head Girl?'

'I was eventually. It was an all girls' boarding school, remember? Really unhealthy.'

Miranda laughed and admitted that she'd been to a boarding school. An hour slipped by unnoticed as easy chat prevailed about school and college days and first jobs. In the company of younger people, Miranda looked so relaxed and as if she'd shed twenty years

Simon, sitting next to Fran, accepted more coffee from her then put a hand on her arm.

'Frances, I'd like to spend time with you,' he said quietly. 'Is it impossible?'

'Trying to find us in Greece would be like looking for a needle in a haystack. Miranda follows her whim.' She looked at him directly. 'I'm not being difficult. It's been fun meeting you, and please - everyone calls me Fran.'

Suddenly, she had to jump up to rescue a pan of milk rattling on the Aga.

'I'll have a drop of milk,' said Miranda. 'It might absorb the alcohol and help me to get a few hours sleep.'

'Heavens, you've a 'plane to catch,' said Anna. 'We really ought to let you go to bed.'

'Don't worry. I'm a night hawk. A couple of hours will suffice.'

'But really I think we should go,' Anna insisted, instinctively thoughtful. 'Anyway, I have to get organised. My in-laws are coming to lunch tomorrow and I'm still sufficiently new as a daughter-in-law to be nervous.'

'Not of Sheila,' Simon protested. 'She couldn't be easier.'

'I agree but Charles's father terrifies me.'

Miranda looked surprised. 'He's very different from his son, then.'

'Oh yes,' Anna said, 'or I wouldn't have married Charles.'

'Don't worry,' Simon said, as they all stood up. 'His dad will direct any criticism onto me. We go back a long way.'

Farewells were exchanged, then, insisting that Miranda should sit down and rest, Fran accompanied everyone to the front door.

'Fran, where will you be on Exmoor? How shall I find you?' asked Simon, quietly.

Her eyes held his and, in spite of him being the elder and light years ahead in experience, he looked almost vulnerable.

'Everyone knows our cottage: Spring Cottage. Just ask in....' she paused, giving a little chuckle, 'Simonsbath.'

He laughed, recognising the deliberate mispronunciation −not Simmons, the Devonian sort. 'I hope that's some kind of omen,' he said and gently squeezed her arm then followed the others down the steps

'Thank you for a lovely evening,' she called quietly, polite as a child after a party but with adult sincerity.

Simon turned and blew her a kiss. 'Best one for me for ages,' he said. 'Hope there'll be lots more.'

Chapter 4

Simon drove across Albert Bridge and cruised along Prince of Wales Drive, passing the building that housed the second floor flat rented by Charles for six years. It had sheltered all and sundry but particularly him when he retreated frequently from the claustrophobia of post graduate Oxford. His thoughts veered to Anna, kind, funny and presentable. A bit 'Tory platform wife' with her neat hair and even features, good teeth and, as her legs weren't perfect, she had the sense to wear dark tights and simple shoes. Would she have suited me, he wondered. No. The outstanding feature of her character, for him, was her conventionality, and he found that unattractive. Margot, a fellow lecturer and current girlfriend, whatever her drawbacks, was certainly not conventional.

He was close to Streatham now and making good time until an accident in Poynder's Road created a tailback of traffic. Impatiently, he drummed his fingers on the steering wheel and wished he still smoked, a restriction imposed when Margot moved in with him. He reflected on their meeting sixteen months ago when she had told him he was the most attractive man on the campus and she'd do anything for him. Worried about a minor indiscretion with one of his students and its possible tiresome consequences, (she never took her eyes of him in lectures, and quoted sorrowful love poems at tutorials), he did not hesitate. Margot was pleased to hear that he had spent a year in the USA at Harvard, and that the theme of his PhD had been the American revolutionary influence on English romantic poetry. Her passion was American history and she was delighted to find they had an academic interest in common. Gradually she discovered he was an academic lightweight but with infuriating self-confidence, and he grew weary of her academic intensity, but neither tired of the other's body. Even he was impressed by her lack of sexual inhibitions

The traffic moved at last. Simon wound down the window. The polluted air was slightly tinged with Spring freshness as well as petrol fumes, and the streets were brightened by forsythia in narrow front gardens. He mused on where he might have installed his grandmother had he been rich. Perhaps, in a beautiful Georgian spa town where a visit would be a pleasure if only for the architectural elegance. In spite of his reviving melancholy, he lingered in the areas he knew well.

He pulled up and left his car outside the optician's shop that his mother had managed for years after the owner, Edward Turner, retired. A kindly, fatherly type he had been a mentor to Betty Fellowes. Simon was sure he'd be appalled to see that the business had been renamed Eye-to-Eye and that his once tastefully arranged window now displayed busts of Madonna, Michael Jackson and the Spice Girls, all gazing at by-passers through a variety of amazingly garish spectacle frames. Simon jumped violently as a heavy hand descended on his shoulder. He turned to find a black handsome face beaming at him.

'Lennie. Lennie Wint!'

'As I live and breathe. You look great, Si, but wouldn't your mum turn in her grave at the change in the shop?'

He jerked his head towards the large window then said, 'Sorry - that wasn't very tactful. I was really sorry to hear she'd died.'

'That's all right, Lennie. You're right, she'd be appalled.'

'What you doing here, Si? Aren't you still in Manchester?'

'Yes, I'm only visiting. What about you? What are you doing these days?'

Lennie grinned and pointed to a spick and span launderette across the road, under a flashing neon sign saying: Wash'n Nosh. 'That's me,' he said proudly, 'or rather - us. We've only had it for six months but it's doing well.'

'You're married?'

'Sure. My wife's the nosh bit. We've a small café at the rear. Come and meet her.'

Simon hesitated.

'You in a rush?' Lennie was clearly disappointed.

Simon said, 'I'm visiting my grandmother. She's in a residential home, The Hollies. She's got Alzheimers.'

Instantly Lennie understood. 'That's real tough. She was an amazing lady. Like her, you know, I'm a councillor. Yeah me, only two of us blacks on the council!'

'Which side?'

'Labour.'

Simon laughed. 'And you - a capitalist. How d'you get away with it?'

'T'other side would never have put up with me. Anyway, I truly believe in Socialism. One thing amazes me, my shop windows haven't been smashed.'

'That's easily explained, Lennie. You were a schoolboy boxing champion. You bloodied my nose more than once. Sometime, I'd like to meet your wife? Do I know her?'

'No. She was born in Brixton, taken to Jamaica when she was five then returned six years ago. We married in Cascade and were back there, visiting her relations, when your mum died so couldn't be at the funeral. Come any time, and meet our son, he's nearly one.'

'Lucky you. Right, I will next time. Remember the song, My Beautiful Launderette? So now you've got one.'

Both laughing they parted, reluctantly, but Simon was determined to make a small detour and it was a pity he did. Opposite his old home he sat in pained disbelief. Beside the gate a board announced the property was SOLD. For years his mother and grandparents had lived in hope of one day owning their beloved home. From time to time, they politely approached the owners (a substantial local family with property in several boroughs) and offered the full market price. Equally politely, the owners declined to sell. As they were conscientious and fair landlords it did not greatly rancour with the tenants but, later, it frustrated Simon that the owner could not see the golden opportunity offered them. Who else would decline such a price with controlled tenants in situ. Now he felt angry on behalf of his family and cheated out of a modest inheritance.

The irony of the situation dominated his thoughts as he drove away; the sudden death of an active woman in her early fifties, without prior illness to warn her that her heart was in the same sorry state as her father's, who had died four years before. The local newspaper had made a feast from a crumb, loving every bite.

`Mrs Betty Fellowes, well-known, local optician and daughter of Mrs Grant (Retired Councillor), dropped dead as she walked to her home in Abbotswood Road.'

The front-page article went on to extol the achievements of the retired councillor more than those of the dead optician. The editor had hoped for an interview but had received short shrift from the deceased's son.

The Hollies had been the family home of a nineteenth century shipping merchant. The front garden had all but disappeared under tarmac, relieved by a few grimy laurels and sad-looking flowers in plastic urns. To the right an ugly flat-roofed extension afforded entry to wheelchair users. Under the doorbell, which Simon pressed, a gleaming brass plate introduced the proprietors as Mrs H Lawson-Brown SRN and Mr B Lawson-Brown BSc. Only Mrs had been present when Simon inspected The Hollies and he learned she was normally an absent owner. This was just as well given her distinct Anglo-Indian accent. Gran was of the generation who abhorred interracial marriages while denying any hint of prejudice.

As a boy Simon had teased her for her views. Suppose a really nice family, like Lennie's, moved in next door, would she mind? Simon asked her this after that pertinent question had been tackled on her favourite radio programme, Any Questions?. Of course, she would not mind, provided they did not play that nasty tin music (`Steel, Granny') and cook curry with the windows open (`That's Pakistani's, Gran'), and leave broken old cars in the front garden (`Like English people, Gran'). Yet his grandmother had waged war on unscrupulous landlords who exploited immigrants; later to be disillusioned to find many of them were immigrants themselves.

Quick footsteps were approaching the door which was opened by the manager, Miss Symes, but always called Matron. 'Dr Fellowes, so nice to see you. Do come in.'

He shook her hand and entered the gleaming hall, with its white enamelled panelling and large gilt-edged mirrors. An embroidered screen concealed the fireplace. Stiff looking armchairs did not invite lingerers.

'Mrs Grant is really well. Of course, the confusion grows worse but we expect that. Have you had a good journey? Such a long way to come.'

'Yes, fine thanks,' Simon said, then followed her up the staircase to a gate, barring the way. Unlocking it, she explained, 'We can't take chances, some of our residents wander.'

'Not my grandmother, I hope.'

There was a moment's hesitation. 'She has some restless days.'

They stepped onto the landing then Matron turned into a corridor. 'Do you remember the way? It's along here.'

After a few steps a very bent old woman blocked their progress. She leaned on a walking frame on

44

which hung a tapestry-style knitting bag. A shapeless brown cardigan covered most of her shiny beige dress, and her stockings concertina'd over shapeless furry slippers. She seemed unable to look up and muttered that people were always getting in her way.

'Now then, dear, we don't want to be in your way, we just want to get past you.'

'I'm not in your way, you silly cow. You're in mine.'

Matron flushed. 'Mrs Johnson, we don't want bad language, not in front of our visitor.'

'Yes we do; we aint' all 'hoity-toity. I spect 'e's 'eard it all, ain't you, love?'

Grinning, Simon admitted he probably had. The woman then looked up at him sideways, and gave a parrot-like cackle. 'Nice lookin' chap. You a doctor?'

'Yes, but not medical.'

'This gentleman is Mrs Grant's grandson.'

'Oh, she's another one 'oos 'hoity-toity. Go on then if you must.'

They squeezed past her leaving her still muttering.

'We do have all sorts and conditions here, I'm afraid, Dr Fellowes. We do our best for all of them.'

'I'm sure you do.'

'Well, here we are,' said Matron, brightly.

A card in a brass holder bore the words: Councillor Mrs N Grant. Really this was overdoing it! She had retired from the council four years ago when the Tories were riding high nationally and she felt she could safely leave a floating, rather than sinking, ship. The best event in her life had probably been the arrival of the first woman Prime Minister.

Matron tapped the door once, then opened it. 'Here he is, safe and sound, all the way from Manchester.'

45

Nancy Grant was seated on an upright armchair, knitting a red garment on large blunt needles. Simon felt pleased that she could still knit. He sidled past Matron and bent to kiss her. She jerked her head away, sharply.

'He's your grandson, Mrs Grant, remember? Show him what you're knitting for our Bring and Buy sale.'

Immediately Nancy dropped the knitting into her lap so half the stitches slid off the needles.

'Oh dear.' Matron rescued the knitting, then found a space for it on the chest of drawers among the many photographs - nearly all of Simon.

'Look at these lovely flowers, dear. Isn't it kind of your grandson?'

Simon handed them over, suddenly ashamed of the unscented dozen in their plastic cone. They were obtainable along with newspapers, cigarettes and petrol. He did not even remember if she particularly liked flowers; it was his mother who had cultivated a variety in the back garden.

She sniffed, then pushed them away without comment.

'I'll see they're put in water,' said Matron, picking them up.

A television flickered in the corner by the window. Matron switched it off.

'She loves watching T.V. It's on all day.'

'Does she have any choice?'

Matron looked slightly affronted and forbore to reply.

Nancy glanced at Simon. 'You'd better sit down.' Her tone was imperious.

Hesitantly, because Matron was still present, he did so. 'Are you well, Granny?'

46

'Of course I am. I'm going home soon.'

'You are at home, dear,' said Matron, walking towards the door. 'I'm having tea sent up. Will you please excuse me, Doctor Fellowes?'

'Of course. Thank you.'

As the door closed Nancy turned to Simon with a puzzled but appraising look. She looked spruce in a maroon wool dress with white collar and cuffs. Her heavy gold chain bracelet clunked on her wrist and her Maltese Cross hung from beneath the crisp collar. Her hair was neatly waved and pure white, but so thin now he could see her pink scalp.

'What can I do for you, young man?' Her voice was strong.

'No, it's what can I do for you, Gran?'

'Mrs Grant, young man, if you please.'

He might have been an errand boy or the meter reader. 'Don't you know who I am?'

'No, should I? I feel I've seen you somewhere. Was it in hospital?'

'No. I'm your grandson, Simon.'

'Are you sure? I have a daughter. It's time she came to see me.'

'Yes, you do - did, I mean. She was called Betty and I'm her son.'

'Are you?'

'Gran, we all lived together. You, Grandad, my mum (she was your daughter, Betty) and....'

Interrupting, Nancy asked, 'Where was that then? I don't remember.'

'We lived at The Rowans, Abbotswood Road. I started school from there. You used to work at the primary school, particularly helping the slow readers.

47

I went to Dulwich on a scholarship, and I boarded eventually, but not 'til the sixth form.'

She shrugged, her face blank. He perused the photographs on the chest of drawers and selected one.

'Look, here I am in my school uniform.'

Nancy took the photograph from him and studied it for a minute. 'Hm, can't see a likeness,' she said, handing it back.

'I was very young then, nine or ten. I'm thirty-three now.'

'You don't look it.'

'Good. Look, here's a photo of all of us together in Dulwich Park.'

She held the photograph so it caught the light coming through the window behind her.

'Nice looking bunch.'

He grinned. That was more like her. She had been inordinately proud of her family's looks. 'Do you recognise Grandad? Your husband, Jim?'

'If you say so. Where is he now? In Oxford?'

'No Gran, I went to Oxford. Grandad died nearly five years ago.'

'Oh, in the war?'

'No that was Uncle Freddie, his brother.' He put the photograph back and picked up a book from the bedside table. He read the title, *Kingfishers Catch Fire* and the message on the fly leaf: *To dear Granny, with much love from Simon. Christmas '79.'* He then read the message aloud, the pleasure in his voice.

'You still like reading.'

'No. I can't get on with it. They choose such rubbish.'

'This is a Rumer Godden, Gran. One of your favourites. You never read rubbish. It was you, and Grandad, who set me on the right road.'

'Was it? I don't think so, young man. I don't know you, do I?'

As he patiently repeated his family history the door opened and a small tea trolley was carefully pushed into the room by a young girl in a green check overall.

'Here's your tea, Mrs Grant. So nice you've got a visitor. I'm Daphne.'

Simon introduced himself, shook her hand then quietly asked, 'Does my grandmother need a bit of help?'

'Yes. She has a special cup on the lower shelf. She spills things, you see.'

He noticed the lidded plastic beaker and, when Daphne had gone, poured tea into a china cup.

'Still no sugar and a drop of milk, Gran?'

'How do you know that? You seem to know a lot about me, or think you do.'

'That's because I'm Simon, your grandson.'

He helped her to sip her tea, and placed a linen napkin on her lap.

She looked up at him with pale, yellow-tinted eyes, once as blue as periwinkles.

'Very nice. You make a good cup.'

He wondered if more milky tea in that horrible beaker was her usual lot.

'Sandwich, Gran? Cucumber, I think, or egg'.

'Egg, please dear.' She smiled at him, really smiled for the first time. She held the plate in her lap and daintily bit into sandwich. Her teeth clacked, something she once would have found intolerable.

'Nice sandwich,' She commented a few minutes later and accepted a second one. Simon found a spare cup and saucer on the bottom shelf of the trolley. He hoped Matron was not planning to join them. If so, she could have the plastic beaker. He drank the tea then ate an egg and lettuce sandwich. 'My grandad, your Jim, liked these', he said.

'Who was Jim?'

'Your husband. He worked in the Town Hall in Lambeth.'

And again, with infinite patience, he ran through his recent family history. He wanted to ask about his great-grandparents. Would she remember them? Might he confuse and agitate her? Did she take after her father who survived a serious mining accident then set himself up as an ironmonger and was modestly successful. Was she more like her mother, a primary school teacher? Nancy was a natural leader. She had loved and respected her quiet dependable husband, but had dominated him.

The quiet striking of his grandfather's retirement gift clock aroused Simon. He glanced at his watch. Their times coincided. An hour had passed, surprisingly quickly.

Nancy seemed to have lost interest in him yet her face wore an expression of concentration. Slowly he became aware of a distinct, unmistakable smell. He felt a strange mixture of revulsion and compassion. That this neatly-dressed, still dignified old lady was incontinent appalled him. He looked around for the bell, and in reaching for it beside the bed knocked over a glass of water.

Nancy started and frowned.

'I'm sorry, Gran.' He mopped the water with a hand towel.

'Are you in the habit of breaking into people's rooms?'

He nearly laughed. 'No, I haven't broken in, I'm visiting. I'm Simon.'

'Hm, funny sort of visitor.'

The door opened and Daphne came in carrying the flowers in a heavy glass vase. Simon felt so relieved he could have hugged her.

'My grandmother seems to need some more help– a bit different.'

The girl gave him a look of quick understanding. 'That's all right. We know she has a little problem.'

She put the vase beside Simon's first graduation photograph then turned to Nancy.

'There now, Daphne's going to put you to rights, Mrs Grant.'

'Nancy, if you like, dear. Call me Nancy. Just you, not anyone else.'

Simon stared at his often autocratic grandmother who was smiling up at the young girl. She attempted to rise from the chair, but Daphne was swiftly at her side to help her.

'I'd better leave now.' Simon hoped his voice sounded normal.

'Oh, we won't be long. There's a nice comfy chair outside, just around the corner.'

'Thanks, but I must go. I'll come to see you again, Gran.'

'If you wish.'

He leaned forward and Nancy suffered a peck on her cheek, unsmiling.

51

'Thank you,' Simon said to Daphne then, as he closed the door, he heard, 'Dear, who was that young man?'

He sat in his car, hands gripping the steering wheel, engine silent. Somehow, he resisted an impulse to wrench the wheel round and flee to the warmth and sanctuary of Lennie's launderette, but what right had he to inflict him with his melancholy. Gradually he calmed himself by rationalising the situation. Gran was undoubtedly well cared for and, in her own way, happy. She was accorded status; was still considered `somebody', Councillor Mrs Grant. He could do no more for her, so why should he be troubled by irrational feelings of guilt? His only role was to provide the supplement that enabled her to have the deluxe level of care. She was no longer, to him, his loved, familiar grandmother but a tetchy, confused old woman. Quite reasonably the young carer now meant more to her than her own grandson.

A sooty, ragged cloud smudged the pale face of the sun and dissolved into rain. The windscreen became blurred.

Charles and Anna would be waiting for him; a drink offered, a meal in preparation. After dinner there would be a chance to off-load to Charles, who would nod and murmur but say little. Instinctively he would know that his ability to listen was all that was required.

Simon switched on the engine, then the radio. It was five-thirty and Radio Four told him he was listening to P.M. He found this absurdly comforting.

Chapter 5

'You've seen some of the finest Byzantine fortress in The Cyclades,' Miranda had announced, with as much pride and enthusiasm as a native. On the island of Santorini, Fran ran out of adequate responses. Exhausted after visiting three islands in five weeks, she was doubting the wisdom of accompanying her aunt around her spiritual home. They had looked at graffiti attributed to Lord Byron, had peered into the Cyclops's lair, walked on ancient marble pavements and watched the ominous bubbling of a volcano.

At the start of the sixth week, on the ferry to Sikinos, Fran felt tired and sick. She longed for Poseidon to do his worst, swiftly.

'So quiet it's hardly known to tourists,' enthused Miranda. 'Lovely people. Cheer up, darling, soon you'll feel fine.'

And as ever, she was right. Hours later, installed in a little stone house and served with an excellent, simple meal, they sat on the terrace above the flickering lights of the village, and Fran felt her strength returning. She smiled placidly, half listening to Miranda's accounts of piracy which here, at least, superseded the absurd activities of the gods.

'You don't regret coming do you? Not missing home too much?'

Miranda's change of subject surprised Fran.

'No, it's been interesting, but a bit tiring. A huge amount to take in.'

'I've overdone it – talked too much. It's my passion, that's the trouble. Sorry, darling.'

Miranda topped up Fran's glass, then her own. 'I was wondering if you regretted taking yourself away – right away – from your friends.'

'No, the gang might find me anyway. Half the old student mob are supposed to be visiting Greece this Summer.'

'I was really thinking about someone different: Simon. Fellowes You know I felt there was an instant affinity between you. He wanted to see you again.'

'I know, and I felt the same but....' Fran hesitated, sipping her wine, then continued, 'I felt a bit overwhelmed. An older man, so gorgeous and charming – I bet he can get any woman he fancies.'

'But he's in his thirties – Charles told me, and not married. He can't have met the right one yet.'

'And you think she could be me? Come off it! A scruffy artist, nine or ten years younger.'

'But would you like it to be you? You're still young, of course, with lots of time ahead.'

'I would like to be special to someone like that. He's the first one I've really thought about a lot. But what about you? With your looks you could have had anyone.'

Fran turned sideways to look at Miranda, attractive, and with a figure many twenty-year olds would envy.

'No. The only man I really would have given anything for was married so absolutely taboo.'

'Happily married?'

'Not terribly but I was not going to put it to the test.'

'How many people would think like that nowadays?'

'Too few. As far as I was concerned anyone else's partner was not fair game. One simply didn't allow it to happen. That was how I was brought up. Remember, my father was a clergyman.'

'You get on so well with men. I can't understand why there's been no one else. You've men friends, of course, but no one you could spend your life with?'

Miranda smiled and shook her head. 'Darling, marriage wasn't all there was in life for me. I had my work, reasonable success, and a gorgeous child I didn't even have to give birth to.'

'I didn't hold you back, did I? You didn't give up the idea because of me.'

'Certainly not. Your grandparents on both side were still alive and they helped a lot and I could afford daily help. Honestly, darling you were a joy, not an encumbrance.'

Fran stood up, moved behind Miranda and put her arms around her shoulders.

'My dad couldn't have picked a better carer for me.'

The next week was as physically and intellectually demanding as the previous ones. While marvelling at Miranda's profound knowledge of historical sites, myths and folklore, and of cultures inherited from multifarious inhabitants and invaders, Fran preferred to learn from her own observations.

'You've had thirty odd years to absorb all this,' she pleaded. 'My head is aching with so much information. The gods were a vicious rabble, raping and slaying and betraying. No wonder the Greeks are a political disaster. I suppose they can't sort out myth from reality.'

'What an enchanting thought,' said Miranda, laughing.

'Logic,' said Fran. 'It's why they're always having coups or juntas - whatever they're called. They're acting out the behaviour of their gods!'

Miranda found this so amusing Fran instantly regretted her churlishness. Without her aunt she would have had little chance of seeing islands off the tourists' routes. She would not have an automatic entreé into Greek homes, and the loan of donkeys and battered old cars. For Miranda a locked church was readily opened, a priceless icon or manuscript lovingly revealed, a caíque made ready to sail them to amazing sea caverns thick with stalactites. Even when her good knowledge of Greek failed her, when confronted with remote, ancient dialects, her personality won through. However overwhelming these experiences became for Fran, she acknowledged their uniqueness.

She revelled in the dramatic beauty of the islands. Attracted to stark, challenging landscapes far more than the gentle and tameable, she did not as easily accept the people hewn by such landscapes. People whose ancestors included Phoenicians, Venetians and Turks, whose heritage was about warfare and exploitation and every imaginable form of hardship. She noticed the cruel expressions on some of the lined and gnarled faces, the obvious subjugation of the women, and the tormenting of the physically and mentally impaired. A young herd boy, stoning his goats to hasten their progress. turned pale in terror under the scorching lash of her tongue, although he could not understand a word. Only Miranda's swift intervention prevented Fran from hitting him.

Yet, wherever they went they were met by friendly, welcoming smiles from Greeks who seemed genuinely to enjoy their presence.

'Times have changes,' Miranda said. 'When I first came here it was not unusual for a wayward woman to be stoned and hounded from a village.'

'So I could strip and swim?' suggested Fran. At their tiny, rented cottage, she was sunbathing on a flat roof, made into a balcony.

Miranda laughed. 'No, that would outrage the islanders. Change hasn't been that drastic.'

'If a helicopter flew over it would probably crash,' Fran suggested.

'I doubt if one has ever been seen here.' Miranda smiled, setting a jug of freshly made lemonade beside her, and pouring some into two earthenware mugs.

Fran drank deeply. 'Hmn delicious. How do'you make it?'

'Local recipe. I've written it down. Darling, do watch you don't burn. Shall I put some cream on your back. It's quite pink.'

Fran lay on her front while Miranda gently smoothed sun cream over her.

'Even with your skin you shouldn't take chances.'

An hour later Fran leaned against a tree and looked critically at her little sketch of olive trees backed by a crumbling wall. It lacked any hint of life. Her heart was not in it. The sun was immediately above her head and the leaves offered minimal protection. Her loose cotton dress and brief pants felt damp. She put her sketchbook down and pulling her dress up to her waist slid onto the dry ground. It felt cool against her bare thighs. Not a bleat, rustle or a human voice disturbed the silence. The lack of songbirds was uncanny, even for midday. How many had been culled in mid-flight as they headed for Exmoor?

She made a sudden and unchangeable decision: she would curtail her holiday by two weeks. While that would give Miranda some freedom, she could make a start on her commissioned work.

*

'Have you stayed here with Tom?' Simon asked the bronzed, slender girl who half lay, half sat, watching lizards sunning themselves on a low wall. She stretched a long, slim leg and stirred the surface of the azure swimming pool with scarlet painted toenails.

'Hmn, once or twice, but borrowing the house seems to coincide with his field trips.'

'He knows you're here now?'

'Of course.'

'And that I'm here?'

'I said you might be, along with one or two others.'

'And where are they?'

'Shut up, Simon. I hope you're not becoming a moralist.'

'Caroline, I just want to know what the form is in case Tom turns up.'

'He won't. He's miles up country. Lake Rudolph, I think.'

'You don't change. D'you remember we spent the night together before your wedding?'

'Of course. It had to last a long time.'

'Caro, why did you marry? Not just Tom - I mean why marry at all?'

She hesitated, feeling in the pocket of her towelling wrap for a cigarette. He picked up her lighter and flicked it open.

'Thanks.' She inhaled deeply. 'I wanted a bit of security. And Tom had been offered the post in Nairobi. I'd always wanted to live abroad, and there was no budging you.'

'Surely Tom knows you're unfaithful?'

She laughed. 'Old-fashioned term. If he does it doesn't worry him. He never questions me.'

'Maybe he's having a riotous time with his students. Doubtless they're the same the world over.'

'I don't think so. Anyway, students are risky. Even you draw the line there; don't you?'

'I've learnt to.'

Simon narrowed his eyes against the afternoon sun and watched a monkey slip along the high wall surrounding the garden. It was after mangoes.

'What about kids? You're still young.'

Caroline shrugged. 'If it happens that's okay. Neither of us is desperate. Anyway, what about you? I thought Margot was a fixture.'

'So did she.'

'So she's going back to Scotland - reluctantly.'

'Yes and no, I think it came as a relief in the end.'

'Do you shy from permanent relationships?'

'I suppose I have. I wouldn't if it seemed right. Chas has made out all right. Still, they have only been married five minutes.'

'Cynic. I think they're going to be all right. Nice of Chas to invite me and Tom to the wedding.'

Caroline shrugged her towelling robe off her shoulder, revealing, small, high breasts.

'Lord, I'll either have to take you to bed or plunge into the pool,' Simon said.

She rose to her feet. 'It's possible to do both.' She stood naked, poised like a figurehead, then dived expertly scarcely making a splash.

Catching up with her Simon encircled her with his arms, pulling her backwards against him.

She gasped. 'Oh God, it's marvellous, only don't drown me.'

'What a way to go.'

'What about the houseboy?'

'You mean you want him to join in?'

'He's gone home. I told him we're eating out.'

He relaxed back into the water sliding beneath her.

'Is it possible, out of one's depth, Simon?

'Caro, when were we ever out of our depth?'

Reluctant to leave the mingling scents of ylang-ylang and frangipani, it was hours later when hunger forced them to make the short drive into Mombasa. In the flickering candlelight at The Capri, Simon thought how extraordinarily beautiful Caroline was with her blonde-streaked hair, dark slanting eyes and rather haughty expression. Many eyes were upon them and the waiters were unusually attentive.

Caroline's expensive lime silk dress was draped on one shoulder, leaving the other bare and gleamingly bronzed. Her only jewels were a thin gold and ruby chain at her throat, a bangle and her wide wedding ring. Simon liked such simplicity. It reminded him of Fran's style. Her face hovered on the edge of his consciousness, distracting him momentarily from the excellence of the food and seductive company. He forced his mind into the present and concentrated on an enormous platter of mixed shellfish washed down with an excellent Chablis.

'Now for the ostrich steaks' enthused Caroline, whose size ten figure belied her appetite.

'Seems rotten now having seen them running about in the wild.' Simon grinned.

'Not that rotten. Are you okay? You seem a bit absent.'

Simon looked at her quizzically. 'Don't you feel slightly uneasy. As if Tom might suddenly appear?'

'You've said that already today. He won't turn up, and he really does know you're here. I think you're feeling insecure. It has nothing to do with Tom.'

Simon leaned back a little while the plates were removed.

'Caro, stop being the amateur psychologist.'

'No. You stop patronising me. It isn't amateur psychology, just common sense.'

'God! You sound like Chas.'

'Good. He's wiser than I thought, and knows you better than anyone. I can see a change in you, and it's since your mother's death. You're more reflective, more malleable and. almost, only almost, vulnerable.'

He shuddered, laughing too readily. 'Sounds dangerous.'

'No, could be the making of you.'

They waited while their main course was served and Simon ordered another bottle of wine.

'Mum liked you, Caro..'

Caroline smiled. 'Only because she didn't really know me. But we did have a rapport.'

'You must have. She let you cook in her kitchen. Even Gran was impressed.'

'Ah, now she was formidable. Saw through me like a sheet of glass.'

'Strangely, she is still formidable although her mind has gone.'

A diversion occurred with the arrival of two of Caroline's fellow lecturers from Nairobi University. They were a husband and wife who, like Caroline, rented a house in Mombasa for the longer vacations. They showed no surprise or curiosity at Simon's presence with Caroline. Pleasant though they seemed he regarded their arrival as an intrusion, and was relieved when they said that they were moving on to a nightclub.

'We could go,' suggested Caroline. 'It's worth a visit. Looks over the Indian Ocean.'

'We can do that from home,' Simon said decisively. 'Let's look at a bit of unpolluted night sky then go to bed.'

'Early night?' She grinned. 'Good idea. I've plans for tomorrow. I thought we'd go up the coast to Lamu, and don't worry, we'll leave a note for Tom.'

Chapter 6

Looking due west from the rim of the valley, Fran could see the high plateau known as the Chains, a great natural sponge of peat and heather. Here numerous tiny springs arise, the source of all the streams bisecting the moor. Of these, one alone becomes a major waterway, the River Exe. Once, however, long before Fran's birth, other streams assumed importance after prolonged heavy rainfall. The sponge became saturated and tiny waterways grew into rivers which converged to carry part of the unique, beautiful town of Lynmouth into the sea.

But on this dazzling day, nature offered nothing more menacing than a hovering buzzard in a cloudless sky. The sun relentlessly nudged panting sheep to retreat beneath overhanging banks or into little stony crevices. Even Fran, a sun worshipper, frequently had to seek the bit of shade afforded by the pony trap parked with its shafts resting on a slab of rock. Nearby, her pony grazed, indistinguishable from his `wild' relations apart from the head collar he was wearing, with its short, trailing rope to remind him he was domesticated.

Fran washed alizarin crimson from her brush then wiped it on the heather. She squeezed a little burnt umber onto her palette. Her dog sampled the paint water, too lethargic to walk a yard to his own bowl.

'Bad for you,' Fran told him. He thumped his tail and sank onto his haunches to scratch. Fran considered the painting before her with diminishing enthusiasm. She had stayed out too long and was sinking into lethargy beneath the afternoon sun. She took a flask from the trap and poured herself a mug of iced water, then gave Beamish a fragment of ice to suck. Together they sat leaning against the off-side wheel. In ten minutes she would make a move, provided she still could.

She dozed a little until a fly landed on her nose. Then she thought about the short work she had just completed for a local author and the work she had started for Pharaoh. She wondered, cautiously, if she could consider herself launched as a freelance illustrator so soon after graduating. Now she was able to pay her way. A trust fund had paid for her education, but it was unlikely it stretched to contribute to the lifestyle she had enjoyed with her aunt. At last she was able to reciprocate by giving Miranda impromptu treats: theatre tickets, a bottle of good wine, a newly published book, and a trip to the races.

Her somnolence was rudely shattered by Beamish whirling into a frenzy of barking. Reluctantly, she got to her feet, steadying herself against the trap.

A couple of hundred yards away stood a man looking in her direction.

'Stay, Beamish,' she commanded, and the dog paced on the spot, growling warningly.

The man walked slowly towards them. The sun was behind him making Fran squint a little, wondering if she recognised him. A hundred yards closer she knew him by the darkness of his hair, his height and easy walk.

'It's all right, Beams, a friend.'

The dog looked at her as if unconvinced, but did not bound forward.

To Simon Fran called, 'Don't worry, he's only guarding.'

Simon lengthened his stride. 'What is he? Finn McCool's Grey Dog, or a cross between an Airedale and an Irish Wolfhound?'

She laughed, delighted. 'Not many people recognise the Airedale bit.'

'We had one next door when I was a child.' Simon came close enough to pat the dog's head. 'Good chap, good fellow.'

'He's being extra protective because I left him for weeks,' Fran said.

'Was he in kennels?'

'No, with my next-door neighbours. How did you find me?'

'I asked at the post office in Simonsbath. A chap directed me to Spring Cottage where a tractor driver suggested you might be here.'

'That was my neighbour, Fred Yeo. Did you walk?'

'Not all the way. My car's over the ridge.' Simon surveyed the pony and trap with interest. 'Your sole means of transport?'

'No. Miranda bought me a Polo when I graduated. I still prefer the trap.' She began to gather paintbrushes together on a piece of cloth.

'I'm not disturbing your work, I hope?'

'No, it's too hot even for me. I've done all I can for now. The sun's really relentless.' Fran put her painting gear over the side of the trap then noticed that Simon was looking at her appraisingly. Her cheeks felt hot as she walked up to the pony and, talking to him, led him to the trap from which she produced his harness.

'Can I help?'

She smiled. 'I don't know. Can you harness a pony?'

'No, I've no idea, but I could learn.'

He watched her slip the collar over the pony's head. Chuckle stood like a rock while the rest of the harness was attached with Simon fastening straps under instruction.

'What next? Do we back the pony into the shafts?'

'No. We draw the trap forward.'

'Then how do you manage on your own?'

'By having a superb pony who doesn't budge no matter what I do. And feel the trap; how light it is?'

Simon lifted the shafts. 'Shall I start?'

'Yes please, very gently so the shafts run into those straps. Yes, that's excellent.' Fran beamed her approval.

'That's the closest I've ever been to an equine, except for a beach donkey,' Simon confessed.

'Well, never take it for granted they're all like Chuckle,' Fran said, pushing damp hair off her forehead. 'We've had him since he was seven months. For years he was my riding pony, then we taught him to pull the trap. I'll give you a lift to your car, then you can follow us down to the cottage. Would tea be in order?'

'Yes, please.'

Sitting in the trap highly amused Simon, and even more so when he swapped it a few yards later for his BMW. What a contrast!

The earlier glimpse he'd had of Spring Cottage had not prepared him for the enchantment of the thick-walled house. Approached from the lane, beneath an archway and into a cobbled, ancient courtyard, it looked encased with Virginia Creeper, pale lemon roses and a huge Gypsy Queen clematis.

'It's part of a really old farmstead,' Fran told him as she unharnessed the pony. 'Our neighbours have the bigger farmhouse and most of the land. The cottage was sold away from the farm before the last war and Miranda discovered it in a near-derelict state twenty-six years ago.'

The courtyard was protected from the lane by a high old wall sprouting clumps of deep crimson, pink and white valerian. The house, stables and a barn, beneath which Fran kept the trap and her car, bound its other sides.

'The barn was Miranda's studio years ago; now it's mine. She spent a lot of time here when I was small then her success forced her to be in London. I'm left to my own devices down here which suits me very well. Now, let's have some tea.'

Fran led the way through a narrow strip of garden bordered by low iron railings to the front door. She swiftly bent towards a flower-pot, spilling with salmon pink pelargoniums, and extracted a key from beneath it. Such low level of security surprised Simon but he reminded himself he was a town-dweller.

The interior of the cottage was cool with its flagstone floors brightened by Indian rugs. From the small hall Fran led the way to a sitting room where one wall was almost covered with bookshelves. The furniture, deep chairs and a sofa, was practical and a little shabby, as were the curtains with linings hanging a little below hems. Beyond the sitting room was a kitchen with a green Rayburn, and bunches of drying flowers and herbs hanging from dark oak beams. Fran filled an electric kettle from a brass tap

67

above a thick porcelain sink flanked by wooden draining boards.

'We've only had electricity for ten years,' she said. 'I hated succumbing, but Miranda felt she'd earned a few creature comforts. Before we had the little box room upstairs made into a bathroom, we used to have a tub in front of the inglenook. It was wonderful on wild rainy nights.'

Simon had no doubt. He reigned in his imagination and concentrated on the amazing view across the valley.

'I've only Indian tea, is that all right?'

'Fine. I can't get over this view.'

'Then see more of it. Go out through the French windows in the sitting room. There's a little terrace that goes the length of the cottage.'

He unbolted the door and walked on to the flagstones. The garden sloped gently downward and was bordered by a high hedge. To the left a smaller hedge and fence separated it from two paddocks. The lawn was intersected by flower beds bearing a great variety of colourful plants. Geranium, pelargonium and agapanthus, were types he recognised thanks to the enthusiasm for gardening shared by his mother and grandfather. Several fruit trees edged the lawn and beyond them, was a small vegetable plot, then a wild flower garden. The view across the moor seemed to stretch for miles, showing expanses of purple and subtle yellows interspersed with areas of green. The only sounds reaching Simon were birdcalls and the bleating of sheep from the neighbour's farm.

'It'll be cooler if we have tea inside,' Fran called and he returned indoors, almost reluctantly.

He carried a tray from the kitchen into the sitting room and put it on a low table.

'I've been enjoying the view. It's beautiful, and so is the cottage,'

Fran beamed. 'Can you imagine the sunset from here?'

Simon nodded, hoping he might even see it. 'There's a fair bit of land,' he said. 'Who looks after it when you're away?'

'Norah and Fred Yeo keep an eye on things, particularly Chuckle, and their son, Billy, gardens when necessary. He lives near Barnstaple with his girl friend and has a small farm machinery hiring business. They're a lovely family.'

Simon noticed a miniature portrait hanging beside the inglenook and bent to look at it.

'My mother,' said Fran, pouring the tea. 'She was beautiful.'

Simon agreed. 'Do you remember her?'

'Oh yes. I remember her and my father. I was four when they were killed. Miranda's always talked about them and has kept them alive in my memory. Most years we go to Jerusalem to visit their grave.'

'Why were they buried there?'

'They always knew there were risks. Dad was working there on a short engineering contract and Mum went out for a week's holiday. Dad had always insisted that if he had a fatal accident while working abroad, he'd remain in that country.'

'Wasn't that hard on the family?'

'Probably, but his wish was respected.' Fran handed Simon his tea and offered him biscuits from a tin. He took a chocolate one, thinking how Margot would disapprove. Fran sank down on a chair by the fireplace and Beamish leaned against her knees watching Simon as he sat down on a sofa.

'I'm being sized up. What if he decides he doesn't like me?'

'I'll have to ask you to leave, politely and quite kindly.'

He laughed. 'I'm not sure you're joking.'

'Well, I couldn't stand an animal hater,' she said. 'That was one of the drawbacks in Greece. I felt constantly uneasy about the treatment of the animals.'

'And other drawbacks?'

She put her cup down and made an expansive gesture with her hands.

'It was all too much. Miranda wanted me to absorb her thirty years of experience in just a few weeks. We visited islands in three major groups, the Dodecanese, Ionians and the Cyclades. I can't remember all their names.'

Simon raised his eyebrows. 'More than most people see in a lifetime.'

'Quite.' She laughed. 'Every door opened for us. I must sound so ungrateful.'

'It reminds me of a trip with my mother to Rome, Florence and Venice. I was fourteen and nearly run off my feet.'

'Miranda's now in Athens until next month; staying with friends who exhibit her work in their gallery. I'm sure she's having a great time. And I'm so relieved to be here on my own.'

'And now I come along and spoil it for you?'

'Oh no, I didn't mean that!' She looked disconcerted. 'I'm really pleased you came.' She blushed and poured more tea for them both.

'I kept wondering when you'd be back,' Simon said, 'but couldn't think of any way of finding out without coming here.'

'I'm afraid we're not on the 'phone. The Yeo's are, but you couldn't have known that. Anyway, it's not fair to keep giving away their number.'

'Well, in the end I rang the Howards who thought you'd be back in a couple of weeks. As I'd already moved into the flat in Exeter, I decided to kill time in Africa but I found it rather frustrating. I've been wanting to see you again for ages.'

Fran looked at him very directly. 'We've only met once, Simon.'

'That doesn't matter. I've thought about you almost constantly. The first time I saw you I felt I had to get to know you. Getting invited to the Howard's party was much more than luck, it was prophetic.'

Fran was now looking away from him, into the fireplace. She was very still.

'Exeter is pretty close,' Simon continued. 'We could see each other if you're not too busy. Can we have dinner together - tonight?'

She looked at him then, smiling. 'That would be fun, only I've no idea where we'd get in. There's a lovely little place looking out to sea at Lynmouth.'

'Let's try. We could go early. But what about my other suggestion? Could we spend some time together? Tell me if I'm being pushy.'

'I do have some illustrations to do but I don't have to work seven days a week.'

'Good. Six you can spend with me.'

She laughed. 'Simon, you're incorrigible. Where are you staying? Or are you driving back tonight?'

He hesitated. Prepared for any eventuality he had put an overnight bag in the car.

'Maybe I could find somewhere in - Lynmouth?'

Fran looked thoughtful but didn't reply. 'I could do with a shower,' she said, examining her paint-stained nails. 'Would you mind? There's time isn't there?'

'Plenty. It's ten to five.'

'Would you like to listen to some music, or the radio? We haven't a television.'

'How utterly refreshing. No, I don't need entertaining. May I just wander about?'

'Of course. Have a look in the studio if you like. The key's hanging just to the right of the front door. You go up the stone steps opposite.'

Fran disappeared upstairs. Simon took the key, big and heavy as if for a castle door, and walked across the cobbles, past the pony who gave him a friendly whinny. The steps were steep and without a rail. He imagined hobnailed boots wearing them smooth over decades. He unlocked the thick, heavy door and stepped into a beamed, high-roofed room about thirty feet in length. Nearly all the light came through two vast skylights operated by pulleys. The original slit of a window, at the south end, looked onto the lane. Several of Miranda's smallest sculptures stood against the walls on plinths, otherwise the room was very much a painter's studio. Beside a large easel was the usual clutter of brushes and jars on low tables and in the stone sink, and many paintings were pinned onto the cork boarding that partly lined the walls. Simon examined them closely. They were watercolours or acrylics and almost all were of birds, animals, trees and flowers.

Judging by the amount of work in evidence, Fran was busy enough. Knowing little about natural history and not having any aptitude for painting or drawing, he did not regard himself as a worthy critic, but the colours pleased him, and there was liveliness in the paintings that told him they had been created joyfully. Technically, he had no doubt Fran's work was correct or she would not have won the approval of wildlife organisations.

He glanced at his watch, surprised to see that forty minutes had passed. Carefully he locked the door and returned to the cottage. Recalling Fran's suggestion, he looked through the collection of records and selected a Hallé recording of Britten's Peter Grimes. He carefully put it on the turntable, which he guessed was thirty years old. Probably it came with Miranda when she bought the cottage.

The sound was surprisingly good and well-balanced. He reduced the volume and continued to look at record sleeves, more and more encouraged that his taste in music was reflected here. He heard quick, light footsteps then Fran entered the room preceded by Beamish. Simon sniffed. 'Mm, delicious, White Linen?'

'Simon, are you an expert on scent?'

'No, just a keen learner. You look lovely. You've done your hair differently.'

She turned around to show him. Part of her hair was combed up from the sides and plaited from the crown of her head. The rest of it flowed around her shoulders in a more orderly fashion than usual. She wore an Indian cotton dress of dark blue, with a scooped neckline and a full swirling skirt, a silver chain around her neck and small silver studs in her ears. Somehow, he resisted an urge to pull her to him.

'A sad story but such beautiful music. This bit - listen. I love it.' She stood very still. After a few bars she said, almost fiercely. 'It's become fashionable to criticise Britten. How can anyone? I'm so glad you like him.'

'Well, this I like. We seem to enjoy a lot of the same stuff. Impolite though it might be to Mr Britten perhaps we should go,' Simon suggested. 'I don't know Lynmouth or Lynton. Might be nice to have a look around.'

'Right, but first I must serve dinner.'

'What? I thought we were eating out, and it's a bit early.'

Fran burst out laughing. 'It's never too early for Beamish.'

In a tiny restaurant looking across the bay to the little tower, Simon commented that he expected to be put at a table squeezed into a corner, not by the window with this wonderful view.

'Miranda's name can be useful.' Fran grinned, shamelessly. 'She stayed here a lot one summer when friends were renting Spring Cottage.'

'Perhaps they'd find me a room for tonight,' Simon said, looking directly at Fran. Expressionless, she said that it was worth a try but, silently, she doubted it.

While they ate food more wholesome than interesting, Fran talked about Greece. Her powers of observation were matched by her powers of description. Simon, used to a level of articulation in his students that brought him close to despair,

74

listened, absorbed and enchanted. She was funny too, a quality he found lacking in most women.

'You would make a brilliant journalist,' he said, shaking with laughter as he visualised a priest washing his feet in a drinking fountain, and an old man who took his pet chicken everywhere, even to church.

Fran shook her head. 'No, I'm not really curious enough about people. I note what I see, that's all. Miranda is an honorary Greek and really loved. I was always a bit detached.'

'Don't you think she might have been the same at your age? She would hardly have been the completely confident person she is now.'

'Possibly, but it's hard to imagine her as anything but completely self-assured. Her mother, like mine, died when she was young, and she became a surrogate mother to her little brother and then, poor thing, to me. Anyway, I've talked enough about me. Tell me about your mother. Are you like her in looks?'

He grinned. 'No. Apparently, I'm the image of the father I really didn't know. He dumped my mother before I was three. Marrying too young, she wasn't trained or qualified in anything and not the type to live on State benefits.'

'So, what did she do?'

'My grandparents stepped in and were marvellous. Mum got a job with a local optician who took a genuine interest in her. He and his wife were childless and gave her every encouragement to qualify. She succeeded and was very proud of her professional status. Then, when I won a scholarship and entered private education (like the kids of the

75

local pharmacist and dentist), well, I really had arrived.'

Fran smiled. 'Was she the powerful type?'

'Not compared with her mother, but in her own way she was. She always looked marvellous, and I was very proud of her. She set great store by `good taste', and never doubted that her conception of it was definitive.'

'It sounds as if you and your mother were good friends.'

Simon smiled. 'We were. We always talked a lot, but I was largely brought up by her parents, so our times together were special. She was great with my friends, wholly accepting whoever they were, and they weren't all like Charles.'

He then described some of his early exploits, his `gang' that included Lennie, and, with some circumspection, a few anecdotes from his undergraduate days.

When he paused and poured more wine for them both, Fran commented,

'You had a happy childhood. All those adoring adults around you, two-thirds female.'

Simon laughed. 'Do I bear the signs?'

He looked around the little restaurant, at the low beams hung with mariners' memorabilia, and the walls covered with prints of nineteenth century ships under full sail. It was uncomfortably hot having been packed to capacity since six-thirty. The window beside them was wide open but there was no hint of an air current. The disappearing horizon was tinged palest orange. The moon, as if it could not wait while the sinking sun still indulged itself, rose importantly in the sky.

'It's new. We should wish,' said Simon.

'No need - I have everything I could wish for.'

Simon covered her hand with his, stroking her wrist with his thumb. Fran touched the posy of pink carnations decorating the table.

'You don't have to go back to Exeter, Simon. There's room for you at the cottage.'

'You're quite sure? After all, I've interrupted your work.'

She looked at him then, steadily, her cheeks slightly flushed. 'It's a welcome interruption.'

'Would you like the fan on?' asked the waitress from behind Simon. 'There's a little one on a ledge above the window.'

'Oh, please,' said Fran and smiled her relief as the fan twirled into motion. 'It's too ridiculously hot for England.'

Later, satiated by their locally sourced fish dinners, they walked slowly beside the sea wall, watching the lights from the fishing boats disappearing around the headland. From the harbour came the faint splash and creak of an oar being pulled.

'It bodes well for a good catch,' said Fran looking at the moon. Taking her hand Simon was in silent agreement.

Beamish welcomed them effusively then raced around the yard for a minute. Simon took his bag from the boot of the car and dumped it in the hall.

'I'll make up your bed,' said Fran. 'Help yourself to a drink, or coffee?'

'Neither thanks. How about you?'

'Oh, iced water, please. Ordinary tap water, and there should be plenty of ice.'

She disappeared upstairs and Beamish sat down firmly as if barring Simon's way. He chuckled and fondled the dog's head. In the kitchen he found a glass jug and filled it with water and ice cubes then he unlocked the French windows and stood savouring the stillness and the intense silver and black of the night sky and thinking how seldom he saw the sky unpolluted by city lights. He felt a gentle nudge in the back of his knees and found Beamish behind him, then Fran appeared swishing ice around in a tall green glass.

She stood beside him wishing for a cool night breeze to take the colour from her cheeks. In the bathroom mirror she had thought she looked thoroughly dissolute, with her trace of mascara smudged and her eyes unnaturally bright. She'd had far too much wine and hoped the water would rapidly dilute it. She wanted to remember this evening in minute detail which might be tricky with an unclear head.

'There's something weird down below. Ghost of a prehistoric creature?' Simon said in a whisper. 'Can you hear it snuffling, Fran?'

She giggled. 'It's Chuckle in his paddock. I leave the rear door of his stable open so he can come and go. He likes to commune with Ossie, the Yoe's retired Shire horse. Often, they share a paddock.'

Simon gave a long, contended sigh. 'This is an utterly blissful place.'

'So, you understand why I need to be here. This is where I do my best work. I love the solitude.'

'But you need company – sometimes?'

'Of course, but selfishly, on my terms.'

'Then should I feel flattered to be here still, but packed and ready to leave by six am?'

She laughed. 'Don't ask double questions. Must be very tricky for your foreign students.'

'They can cope. If not they shouldn't be reading English. Look, over there - a shooting star.'

'I hope so. They mean good luck, but it's probably a nasty satellite going out of control. No, you don't have to be away by six am. I like having you here.'

'Good.' He touched her hair, lifting it from her shoulders.

Beamish reared up between them putting his large paws on Simon's chest. They burst out laughing.

'No one could have a more conscientious chaperone. Down Beamish, down.'

Simon was surprised and absurdly touched when the dog obeyed him. Fran walked indoors, calling Beamish to follow then settled him on his bed by the inglenook. Simon followed her. She sat on the large sofa, eyes closed.

'Are you tired?' Simon asked.

Eyes still closed, she smiled and said. 'A bit. The heat no doubt.'

'Should I leave you, Fran? Is that what you want? I've had such a good day I don't want to spoil it for either of us.'

'Is that what you want?' Now she looked at him very directly.

'No, the reverse, that's the trouble.'

She stood up 'It isn't trouble, it's what I want too.'

He held her face between his hands and kissed her mouth gently. Her lips were cool and, for a moment, unyielding, then she was kissing him and he pulled her to him. He caressed her neck and shoulders and felt her hands correspondingly caressing him and tangling in his hair.

He drew away a little, looking at her wonderingly.

'What's wrong?' she whispered.

'Nothing - everything is right. I'm just finding it hard to believe. I've imagined this for so long. I want you, Fran, really want you.'

She smiled. 'It's all right. I feel the same way. You kept coming into my mind when I was in Greece.'

They clung together as if they had found a refuge in one another until a cacophony of noise forced them apart, a banging on the front door, a car being manoeuvred with much gear-crashing and Beamish's frenzied barking as he rushed to investigate.

Simon and Fran stared at each other, then, in spite of his disappointment, Simon grinned. 'A police raid?'

She giggled. 'More likely a mob of old friends.' She walked to the door and, pushing Beamish aside, opened it. A large, long-haired youth nearly fell into the hall. He steadied himself, then lifted Fran up and swung her around recklessly, Beamish growled then looked confused when Fran told him to shut up.

Simon, who had followed her, was effusively greeted four times as a second man and three women crammed into the hall. All were instantly recognisable as students who had been living rough for weeks. Rapidly Simon eyed the three girls and mentally dismissed them. The first man was built like a lumber jack and seemed to fill the cottage with his bulk and personality.

'Tom, our universal uncle,' Fran introduced him. 'And this is Susie - we were in the same year and so was Angie, but Jane's just graduated. What did you get Jane?'

'Oh, a two-one,' said the pale blond girl unconcernedly.

They all shrieked in mocked derision.

'Well, of course you would,' said Fran, 'or I wouldn't have asked.'

The fifth intruder, Gareth, was small and dark. In a Welsh, lilting voice he complained they had scoured half the Greek islands looking for Fran.

'I warned you not to try,' she said, laughing and hugging him a second time. 'Oh gosh, but I could have done with you all!'

'Well, here we are,' said the pert redhead, Angie. 'We've even got some nosh to show we're not going to bum off you.'

'And plenty of other stuff,' said Gareth.

Simon, feeling de trop, backed into the sitting-room and wished they'd all lost themselves in the Aegean which Susie was now screeching about.

'We were all starkers and suddenly all those fishermen appeared. Gareth, started singing in Welsh and they all fled back to their boats. They thought we were bad spirits.'

Simon, struggling with frustration and disappointment, and a simmering anger bordering on murderous, decided he'd have to leave as people swarmed past him to ransack the kitchen drawers for bottle openers and corkscrews.

'Simon, I really didn't expect this.' Fran was by his side. He gave her a rueful smile.

'I know, but they are here and I'd better go.'

'Why? I said I wanted you to stay. They'll all doss down where they can find a space – it's what they've been doing for weeks.'

Simon kissed her lightly on the temple.

'It's been wonderful, Fran, but I'll leave you to enjoy your friends. Some other time?'

She looked downcast and said in a tight, quiet voice, 'Yes, that would be nice. Thanks for the dinner and....'

He squeezed her arm, patted Beamish then found his overnight bag with difficulty, unconsciously wrinkling his nose as he shifted bundles and rucksacks.

He got into his car and as he slowly drove out through the archway, a male voice loudly said, 'Nearly a wrinkly!' It seemed to come from a smoking male standing close to Fran in the doorway

Even as he drew away up the lane, the unmistakeable whiff of grass reached his nostrils.

Chapter 7

The party host, Professor Dennis Crawford, was a middle-aged stereotype of thirty years earlier, identifying with everything tried and tested, safe and sound and, in particular, with the Establishment. A large copy of an official photograph of him receiving an OBE hung above the mantelpiece that was littered with trophies.

'Did you know there were still functions called cocktail parties? I thought the term disappeared at least a decade ago.'

Simon turned to find the questioner was a short, bearded man, possibly in his forties, and wearing a hairy tweed jacket and yellow cords.

'You won't get a decent drink here so have a drop of scotch,' he offered, producing a slim bottle from an inside pocket. Discreetly he poured a good measure into Simon's empty, sticky wine glass.

'Gerry Rankin,' he said, offering a hand. 'Archaeologist. It was that or studying the occult. Not much can be proved about either and, amazingly, I opted for the marginally more respectable trade.'

Grinning, Simon introduced himself.

'Oh, I know all about you. You're Dennis Crawford's new star. Got anywhere to live yet? I've always a spare bed in my humble shack.'

Simon was genuinely touched by such spontaneous friendliness and generosity.

'Thanks Gerry, but I'm in that property given to the university by Mrs. Benson. She's still there, in the ground floor flat.'

'Ah, lovely lady and lovely husband, Professor Benson, but sadly gone. He was hard up as a student and in his early days as a lecturer so he, with his wife's approval, willed the house to the university to provide affordable accommodation for staff members. His wife lives there freely, of course, for the rest of her days.'

Simon nodded, as if this were news. 'I was lucky the other flat was empty and fine for one person – well, quite big really.'

'So you're not married. Neither am I - not anymore. Blessed relief all round. No kids and just as well. What the hell brought you here from Manchester? One of the most stimulating cities in the world.' Gerry's directness was refreshing.

'More money. Well, a bit more.'

Gerry laughed. 'Ah, would have to be.'

'Oh, come on. Exeter is excellent academically; the city's charming and civilised and the campus is beautiful. It's hardly a backwater. If it offers a different pace of life that suits me.'

'Good, I really hope it does. To be honest the less demanding aspects of the place suit me fine. I had six years at the Institute of Archaeology, and when I no longer shuddered on hearing a female colleague had been raped or mugged five minutes from home, I knew it was time to leave. That was twelve years ago.'

'And what's kept you here?'

'Initially my wife, a Devonian, and now it's the sheep.'

'Sheep?'

'Yes, I've a small flock of Dartmoor's.'

'On the moor?'

'No, unfortunately I've not achieved that freedom. I've a smallholding near Venn. Come back and see it? We can sink a few jars there without falling foul of the constabulary. Not yet though, here's Dennis's lady wife homing in on us.'

Swiftly Gerry drank his whisky and smiled at the tall woman striding towards them.

Forty minutes later, after Simon had been assured he would be introduced to some really nice, suitable 'gels' by Harriet Crawford, and had been carefully eyed-up by the twinset and pearls brigade, he and Gerry made their escape.

Following Gerry's grubby Land Rover through beautiful, gentle countryside, Simon contrasted the view before him with the one that had held his attention a few days ago. Here the land had been tamed and cosseted, and farmed into productivity.

His thoughts veered back to the party, largely held for his benefit. Within minutes of arriving, he picked up that it was more Professor Crawford's wife's idea than his. She introduced him to more women than men and he marvelled that he'd had a chance to meet Gerry who, within minutes had quietly said he'd only been invited to swell low numbers with most of the staff being away on holiday.

Months before, on first meeting Professor Crawford, Simon had been surprised and irritated to be questioned about his political views. Had he not wanted the Senior Lectureship on offer, he would have made a formal complaint. As it was he neatly parried the questions and alluded to being steeped in enlightened conservatism from his cradle. In the next hour he was told that the staff included Liberals (both with large and small Ls), but Socialists were few.

'Exeter is not the right place for them,' said Professor Crawford, in a firm voice that still had the trace of a Liverpudlian accent although almost diluted by his student years at Oxford. Had Simon's connection with Oxford and Gerry's with Cambridge just made them acceptable?

Gerry's Land Rover veered off the road onto a track leading through an open five bar gate to a half-timbered pre-war bungalow almost concealed by rhododendrons.

'Sweetly pretty, eh?' said Gerry, with a touch of contempt as he got out of his vehicle a few yards from the front of the house that overlooked a series of small paddocks and ramshackle sheds. Only the bleating of sheep broke the stillness of the late evening. Gerry led the way up wooden steps to a verandah and unlocked the front door that sagged slightly.

'Mustn't grumble,' Gerry said, ushering Simon inside. 'My wife practically gave me the place when she went off with one of my students.' There was no bitterness in his tone.

'Are they still together?'

'Oh yes. In France - Perigord. Two kids now. She still sends cards twice a year, even remembers my birthday.'

The sitting room was cluttered with furniture and every surface was covered with books, maps and drawings. A golden retriever lay on a sofa in front of a large Scandinavian stove that spilled ash through its partly open doors.

'Meet Othello,' said Gerry, and the dog thumped his tail but made no attempt to get up. 'He's twelve and a bit arthritic.'

Beamish's exuberant presence hovered in Simon's mind, along with the light, cheerfulness of Spring Cottage, contrasting with the gloom of this beige-painted room. 'Why Othello?' he asked, amused by the choice of name.

'My ex: wife's decision. She was passionate about Shakespeare, while I was passionate about archaeology. We met when I was at Trinity and she at Somerville and all seemed well for a few years.' He stared into the fireplace for a few seconds then gave a huge sigh. 'I wasn't up to it - not all she expected. Not surprising poor Elspeth went elsewhere. Some of us have naturally low libidos, I suppose.'

Simon confessed he found such an idea difficult to grapple with even after so much whisky.

'And why would you, a good-looking chap. If you like it and can get it, good luck to you. There was even a glint in Harriet's eye. She'll have someone lined up for you in a trice.'

'I hope not, I've someone lined up already.'

'Aha, but she's not here with you. Is she following on?'

'No. She's not even a girlfriend, let alone a lover.'

He found himself describing his meetings with Fran. It was not his habit to discuss his personal life with strangers, or with anyone other than Charles, but sitting here, mellowed with whisky, it seemed the most natural thing in the world.

'And so?' Gerry filled a pipe with sweet-scented tobacco and slopped more whisky into their glasses. 'When are you seeing her again?'

'I don't know,' Simon said. 'I felt so middle-aged surrounded by her friends. Really a different generation.'

'True, but we're used to that with students.'

'Yes, but that's different.'

'So this could be important?'

'Oh, it is already. That's why I'm hesitant. It's crazy, Gerry. I've never been at a loss but now I'm worried I'm going to do the wrong thing and wreck it before it's even started.'

'Then go for it.' Gerry leaned forward in his shabby leather armchair and lightly punched Simon's knee. 'Don't let some callow, spotty youth queer your pitch. Do something tomorrow. Meanwhile, you'd better doss down on the sofa as it'll be more pleasant than the spare room which probably smells like a mushroom farm. You certainly can't go anywhere tonight after all you've imbibed.'

*

Simon rang Fran's neighbours' number. Fred Yeo seemed only too pleased to take a message. In his full-bodied Devon brogue he said, 'The young lass would've went out early in this lovely weather. Took the pony, I guess. I'll make sure she gets your message and she'll ring back directly.'

She did not. Four hours passed during which Simon drank many cups of black coffee and tried, without much success, to tidy up an article he was due to send to the BBC. He caught sight of his face in the mirror above the fireplace and grimaced. He looked pale and drawn. He was behaving like a tormented, love-sick teenager.

The telephone shrilled causing him to start, violently. His hand was not quite steady as it reached for the receiver.

Ten minutes later he rang Gerry with whom he had made a tentative arrangement to visit Chesil Beach the following day.

'She's responded so Chesil will wait. Go for it, Simon, as my ghastly students say and they're talking about sex not their overdue essays.'

Chapter 8

She had been imprecise about the time she expected him, eleven or twelve - whichever he preferred. He drove into the yard at ten past eleven. The front door was open. He called her name several times then walked through the house to the garden, where he found her picking plums. Beamish spotted him at once, barking until gently admonished then, snaking across the grass wagging his tail, he thrust a cold nose into Simon's hand.

'Is it all right to be this early?' he asked, taking in how desirable Fran looked in black jeans and an emerald polo shirt. Her hair was tied back with a black ribbon. Her tanned feet were bare. Apart from a small chromium watch on a leather strap she was unadorned.

'Of course, it's fine. We could go to a special place I want to show you. We could go before lunch unless you're starving. It's fish salad so will keep in the fridge.'

'Sounds good.'

He took the basket of plums from her and followed her to the kitchen. Every door and window seemed to be open.

'You don't worry much about security,' he said.

She laughed. 'This is Exmoor, not the inner city. Beamish is my security.'

'But Heavens - being here alone, without a 'phone even.'

She covered the plums with a clean tea towel to protect them from wasps.

'Honestly, I feel quite safe. Would you like a drink before we go? The weather's on the change. It'll rain later today.'

'How d'you know? The sky looks okay.'

She smiled. 'I can feel the change in the air. I've learnt to read the signs.'

'Then maybe we shouldn't delay.'

They walked along rutted tracks almost concealed by heather and sedge grass. Fran had put on socks and stout shoes but Simon's shoes had smooth soles and tended to slip on the heather. He walked slowly and Fran assumed he was savouring everything about his surroundings. She smiled happily and pointed out a skylark high above them, a rarity now she told him. They breasted a ridge and before them was a large plateau.

'It's hardly changed since the ice age,' said Fran. 'It's a giant sponge.'

'It's bleak enough,' said Simon. 'Wouldn't like to be caught up here in a storm,'

'Fog's worse.' Fran grinned. 'It happened to me years ago but Chuckle brought me safely home. Poor Miranda was frantic. Once, people believed dragons flew up here because of the extraordinary effects lightening can have.'

Looking around for Beamish she put a hand on Simon's arm to steady herself on a rut. He covered her hand with his and continued to hold her as they walked on with Beamish weaving around them.

'Look, ravens,' she said, pointing to three birds swooping a few hundred yards away.

'Last seen at the Tower of London,' said Simon. 'Noisy blighters. Oh, how long did your friends stay?'

'Only three days. We spent most of the time on beaches and in pubs. I didn't do a stroke of work. Look, Simon, straight ahead you can see the glint of water. Pinworthy Pond. Pinkery it's called locally. It's fed by little streams and the Barle river flows out of it. It's man made. In the last century there were great plans to build railways and canals and tame the moor. I'm so glad it didn't happen.'

Suddenly the sun disappeared behind a gathering bank of clouds. The water in the pool was the colour of slate and totally still. There was neither sight nor sound of another human being and, curiously, no evidence of wildlife in spite of Beamish's diligent searching.

Involuntarily Simon shivered.

'Are you all right?' Fran asked.

'Yes. This area could have been the inspiration for La Belle Dame Sans Merci.'

'Oh don't,' exclaimed Fran. 'It's never struck me that way. You don't like it here.'

'I find it strange - so quiet.'

Fran sniffed the air and looked at the sky. 'That's because rain's coming - partly.'

'And the other part?'

She smiled. 'Oh, your fertile and literary imagination.'

'Hm. Although Keats was writing about horrific illness, the imagery and romanticism are irresistible. Even my dullest, most prosaic students are poleaxed by him. There! Did you feel it?'

She laughed. 'Rain. A drop or two. We need it. Too short the other night. Perhaps we'd better head back. Bother, I wanted to show you a little, post medieval quarry.'

An ominous rumble of thunder that sent Beamish rushing to rejoin them followed her words. When they were a few yards along the track the clouds dissolved. The moor turned grey, the great swathes of heather darkened by the rain. By the time they reached Spring Cottage they were drenched and Beamish looked half his normal size. Simon was in far worse shape than Fran. He was shivering so she suggested he should have a hot bath.

'Yes, great.'

She went upstairs to find some towels and returned looking apologetic.

'The water's tepid. It'll take about twenty minutes to get hot.'

'Never mind. Meanwhile shall I get the fire going? We could dry out a bit here.'

She nodded and handed him matches from the mantelpiece. In a few minutes the logs were alight and crackling busily. Sheets of rain lashed the windows obliterating the view. A ribbon of lightening seared the opaque sky and was followed by a crash of thunder that seemed to rock the house.

With a yelp Beamish disappeared upstairs.

'Poor chap, it's the only thing he's afraid of,' said Fran. 'He'll be under my bed.'

'What about the pony? Does it worry him?'

'No. He'd rather stand outside in a storm than take shelter.'

Simon got to his feet and took the towel Fran handed him. 'You are absolutely dripping,' he said, and began to dry her hair.

'You're just as wet,' she said. 'And I'm used to it, anyway. I'm not a fair- weather person.'

'Are you suggesting I am? Now, keep still.'

'Well, you are a townie.'

He gently stroked her damp hair off her forehead and kissed her cool face, running his lips down to the corner of her mouth. He paused, tantalisingly, and she lifted her mouth and gently brushed his. Then he kissed her positively and urgently. Unhesitatingly she kissed him back. After a minute he drew back cupping her face in his hands and looking into her large eyes.

'God, you're beautiful, Fran. I've wanted you so much; this last week has been hell.'

She smiled holding his gaze. The logs suddenly blazed furiously and steam began to rise from their clothes. Fran took a bit of Simon's shirt between thumb and forefinger and squeezed. Water ran over her hand.

'Yours is just as wet,' he said. 'Perhaps we should both take them off.'

He let go of her and pulled the sopping garment off, throwing it through the open kitchen door onto the flagstone floor. Gently he eased her shirt over her head and threw it after his. He kissed her neck and shoulders then unhooked her bra. Her breasts were small and firm, the skin a fraction paler then her shoulders. He kissed her more urgently, exploring her mouth with his tongue. She arched against him so his desire for her was scarcely tenable.

An exceptionally loud clap of thunder made them jump. Despite their feelings they both laughed.

'A touch of deja vu,' Simon said. 'Oh, Fran, I couldn't bear that again.'

'Nor I. Don't worry, no one will arrive now. Not in this.' She smiled up at him. 'I've never made love in a storm.'

'First time for everything.'

'Yes - for me it is - almost.'

He looked at her half-amused, half-dismayed. 'You've never made love?' 'Yes, but just once. I didn't really like it. It wasn't the right person.'

He pulled her to him, stroking her hair. 'Fran, you extraordinary creature. It will be all right, I promise. Shall we stay here by the fire?'

'Yes, it's lovely here. Are you warm now?'

'Oh, I'm warm.' He chuckled and, releasing her, spread a large towel over the thick, woollen rug.

'Come, lie down.'

He settled a cushion beneath her head then shed the rest of his clothes swiftly. He knelt beside her and expertly removed her damp jeans. Her body was smooth and glowing with health and youthfulness. She trembled with excitement under his sure, gently caressing hands. He eased her brief white pants over her slim hips. She disentangled her feet from them, all the time smiling a little shyly, her eyes never leaving his. She stroked his chest and moaned as his fingers traced the triangle of dark, springy hair. He longed to follow his gently exploring fingers with mouth and tongue but resisted, afraid she was not yet ready for such intimacy.

'I've never felt like this,' she whispered. 'I want you so much - to feel you inside me.'

He kissed her as if he never wanted to stop and when at last, he entered her, he whispered, 'Home – at last.'

*

For three weeks Simon spent at least four days of each week at Spring Cottage. With all his preparation for the start of the term behind him, he had no more to do other than revise and lengthen some articles that he'd had published, possibly making them suitable for a text book.

He felt a bit disconcerted when Fran announced that Miranda was coming to stay for a few days.

'I'd better go back to the flat,' he suggested.

'Why? Miranda was born before the war but is very much a ninety sixties person.'

'Ah, the decade when sex was discovered. So, I don't have to move out?'

'Of course not. Anyway, she knows you've been staying here.'

'Fran, why has she never married? She's got everything a guy could wish for.'

'She's had the chance, I'm sure, but she's a free spirit and self-sufficient, and she put me first. She's never said so, hasn't even hinted it, but I know she has.'

'But you wouldn't have objected if she'd married?'

'Of course not. Obviously, it would have been someone pretty special who, I imagine, hasn't come along. She gets on well with men but I've never known her to become really close to anyone. What about your mother? Why didn't she re-marry?'

'Probably didn't have time, and she had a pretty cynical view of men. I'm afraid she concentrated her energies into ensuring I had a decent education and most of the things I wanted.'

'I wonder what she would have thought of me.'

'She'd have loved you. Considering I was her only child she was pretty good about girlfriends. I could tell she didn't like my friend, Margot, but it was part of her code to be polite whatever her feelings. My grandmother had no such inhibitions.'

'Had – you speak as if she were dead.'

'Well, in a way she is – for me. A totally different person.'

Miranda's visit was a success. One day, leaving Fran to complete a commission for Pharaoh, she accompanied Simon to Exeter to view his flat.

'I like it. Good position, light and reasonably quiet. You wouldn't guess it was a conversion from outside. It still looks Edwardian. The front door is solely the entrance to the bottom flat and the side one, with the steps to yours, doesn't even show from the road. Just shows how useful macrocarpas trees can be. Did you mind that it was fully furnished – sixties style?'

'No, it was a relief.'

'What does Fran think of it?'

'Overall, I think she likes it. And she raved about the campus.'

'I'm not surprised. Streatham campus is renowned for its beauty. Bit different from Leeds.'

'How did she cope there? She's such a country lover."

'The art course was great and she made friends. I think she accepted that it was just a phase in her life that would ensure she'd have a career.'

'And she certainly has. Commissions seem to be piling up,' enthused Simon. 'I'm so different from her – revelling in the creativity of others but there's not an ounce in me.'

'Rubbish. What about the articles you write and your textbooks – all so well-reviewed.'

'Kind of you but writing about another's talent isn't quite the same as having it.'

'But you are a brilliant lecturer. Charles and Anna dined with me last week and he told me about the accolades you've received.'

'Good old Chas,' said Simon. 'Now, let me take you to a really good place for lunch.'

There was an easy camaraderie between them and no questions were asked about his relationship with Fran, just a comment that it was great to see her so happy and in the right hands. It impressed Simon that Miranda treated her as a grown-up with a right to her own life. It surely would have been easy, given the circumstances, for an over-dependent and over-protective relationship to have developed. The fact that the cottage was a gift for Fran's twenty-first birthday showed how much her independence was respected by her surrogate mother, who clearly couldn't have loved her more if she'd been her natural mother.

Two days after Miranda's return to London, Simon was relieved that she was not around to witness his horse driving. She might not have been so confident that her beloved niece was in the right hands, and Chuckle certainly was not.

The sun was high above the moor but its intensity was fragmented by a strong breeze, bearing a myriad of scents. Fran put Chuckle's reins into Simon's hands and so began his first driving lesson. The pony walked unconcernedly up the lane, away from home, knowing every inch of the way. After a mile, Simon commented, 'There's nothing to it, he responds to every command.'

'Only because he's special. Driving can be very tricky. I'd never do it on a busy road, not even with Chuckle.'

'Well, as there's not a vehicle in sight, let's use him like a charioteer's pony.' He tapped the pony's rump with the long whip that Fran only used to ward off curious creatures. Surprised, Chuckle shot into a canter. The old trap rattled, the contents swivelled as did the passengers and Beamish barked in protest. Almost falling out, Simon dropped the reins as he grabbed the side rail.

'Whoa, whoa, Chuckle,' called Fran, leaning forward, trying to retrieve the reins that were flapping over the pony's rump.

'No, you'll fall out,' cried Simon.

'We both will, thanks to you. Whoa, Chuckle, whoa.'

To Simon's surprise, Chuckle responded, slowing to a trot.

'Stop,' said Fran, her voice unusually strong and Chuckle obeyed.

At once Fran jumped down and picked up the reins. Simon held out a hand to take them.

'Oh no, that's your first and last lesson. You never make a pony canter on a hard road; very bad for its legs. I see people doing it out hunting and want to shout at them.'

'I'm so sorry, darling, but it felt so easy.'

'Typical beginner's words.' Fran climbed back into the trap then told Chuckle to walk on.

'I suppose I behaved like a typical townie.'

Fran nodded but she was laughing. 'You're improving. I was impressed by the walks we did with Miranda. We'll turn off here and have our picnic.'

Minutes later Fran insisted that Simon should learn how to unharness Chuckle, put his head collar on and lead him to a reasonably grassy area.

'It staggers me that he doesn't run off. Aren't you taking a risk, given all your concerns about his safety?' Simon's tone had a slight critical edge to it.

'I wouldn't do it with any other pony but I trust Chuckle completely. Even when there are so-called wild ponies around he holds himself aloof, superior.'

Simon took the picnic basket out of the trap and seconds later there was a loud pop which caused the pony to throw up his head and Beamish to bark.

'Simon, champagne! That's why you went shopping early this morning.'

'Of course, it's a special occasion.' He handed her a glass, filled it then poured one for himself. 'Let's have a toast. May the day end even better than it began.'

They touched glasses, then drank.

'Delicious,' cried Fran, and kissed him with damp lips.

He spread a rug on the ground and unpacked the basket.

'Smoked salmon, lemon slices, bread, cheeses, olives - oh, and peaches and grapes. Simon, this is magnificent. You do believe in good living.'

He grinned. 'Certainly I do and so should you. I bet it's good when you're at home with Miranda.'

'It is, but this is home for me.'

By three o'clock the sun was relentlessly hot and Beamish lay panting beneath the trap. Fran and Simon divested themselves of all the clothes they decently could and lay sheltered by a cluster of hawthorns.

Simon leaned up on one elbow and ran a blade of dry grass along Fran's nose, tickling her. She opened her eyes and laughed. 'I wasn't asleep, just daydreaming, although that was a soporific, fabulous lunch. Oh look, Simon, wretched trippers heading this way.'

Simon glanced around. 'Not to worry. We're as dressed as we would be on a beach. Anyway, Beamish will see them off.'

'Let's go to a beach - a really special one. We could go tonight just before sundown. And it will still be hot enough to swim. It's a wonderful tiny cove, maybe nine hundred feet below the moor.'

Simon grinned. 'And nine hundred feet back.'

It was a spectacular sunset. The few unthreatening clouds were tinged with purple and gold against a band of coral pink sky. Two container ships moved slowly towards the Welsh coast, and, as the sea and sky merged into a deepening band of purple, they were discernible only by their navigation lights. The tiny beach was washed by gold-edged waves, their lapping being the only sound apart from the slight rattle of crabs scuttling away from Beamish's questing nose. Only the midges intruded; so Simon, who could smoke or not at will, repelled them with a cigarette. Fran, wrapped in a towel, leaned against him counting the slowly appearing stars.

'Such an amazing night,' she murmured.

'In every way,' Simon agreed then quoted;

' "In such a night
Stood Dido with a willow in her hand
Upon the wild sea-banks, and waft her love
To come again to Carthage".'

Delighted, Fran continued:
' "In such a night
Medea gathered the enchanted herbs
That did renew old Aeson".'

'You're a Shakespeare fan, that's good Fran. If anything activates my students' brains, it's his work.'

'I played Jessica at school, Simon; one of the easier parts. If my mother had lived she'd have been horrified. She hated The Merchant of Venice. Miranda told me that after the play finished.'

'Darling, amazing girl, you would have been perfect in any part,' Simon enthused then, in a different tone, asked, 'Did you bring your student friends here?'

'No, it would have been wasted on them.'

'Good. I'm relieved and flattered. Are you warm enough?'

'Yes thanks, are you?'

'Fine.'

Fran giggled. 'We are being formal.'

'It's a formal occasion.'

'It wasn't a little while ago. Then we were pretty abandoned.'

'Well, now it is formal. It's the occasion of asking you to marry me.'

She was very still.

'Fran?' Gently he sat upright, lifting her head and turning her to face him. 'Have I shocked you?'

'No. It's just that I didn't think you'd be the marrying kind.'

'Nor did I until I met you. It's what I want, Fran. I'm absolutely sure. I want everything with you, but you're young. Perhaps you want more time - a chance to travel - that sort of thing.'

Her lips silenced him, then, trembling, she drew back and asked, 'Why are you trying to dissuade me? I've been abroad often enough. Here's where I want to be.'

'But alone, Fran?'

'I thought so until you arrived. When my friends turned up I wanted to scream with frustration and disappointment. I wasn't sure you'd come back.'

'You should have been. I knew I wanted you last spring. You were wearing this shawl when I first glimpsed you. I was intrigued.' He draped the brown shawl around her bare shoulders.

'You hardly know any more about me than you did in April.'

'Doesn't matter. I know all I need to know. I love you. Isn't that as good a starting point as any?'

She looked across the dark sea at the diminishing lights. Simon wondered how he could bear her silence any longer, then she said, 'I love you. You're the most exciting person I've ever met. Only - I feel a bit overwhelmed.'

'You want more time? I've rushed you.'

She turned to look at him. 'No, and yes, I will marry you.'

He kissed her so thoroughly and for so long Beamish let out an anxious whine. It was effective. They drew apart, laughing.

'You know you're not just marrying me,' said Fran.

'Yes, of course. A ready-made family is the norm nowadays. The question is - will Beamish accept me?'

'Oh, he has already. He's just sampled your champagne.'

'Then we'll toast ourselves from the bottle. I draw the line at sharing a glass with him, and I expect he's emptied yours.'

Fran picked the bottle up and drank, then handed it to Simon.

'Miranda will be pleased. She thinks you're the answer to any girl's dream. Shame you haven't an older brother.'

Simon laughed. 'Thank goodness she'll approve. That means a lot to me, Fran.'

Chapter 9

'I'm still staggered. I don't mean by your choice – she's so natural and lovely, but that you've finally committed. And it took some effort. Separation for weeks, a messed-up meeting on Exmoor...'

'Chas, can't you see why I made the effort? She's the most perfect girl I've ever met. How many women are there who really fit the bill? Legs ruined by thick ankles, rotten posture and movements....'

'For God's sake, Simon, looks are an obsession with you. When we were young, I'd mention a girl I fancied and you'd always find some fault with her. Personality matters too.'

'And Fran's is perfect. She shares many of my interests and she's kind and funny. Now, I'd better get on. Fran's keen to meet Gran but she has no idea what Alzheimer's like.'

Simon left the sitting-room to collect Fran from the garden where she and Anna were playing with Beamish. His chat with Charles reminded him of the only time Fran had been critical. He'd told her that he hadn't visited Nancy since moving to Devon.

'Doesn't she deserve more than that – the person who helped so much with your upbringing?' she'd replied, looking shocked. 'She certainly must be at our wedding.'

His response was slightly cold. 'If that's your opinion you certainly must meet her, only prepare yourself for a new identity.'

Simon was right: during the nearly two hour visit, Nancy accused Fran of abandoning her, of refusing to let her walk to the park unaccompanied, then, suddenly, asked who she was. She referred to Simon by his name after half an hour of calling him Jim, and Fran lost count of the number of times he told Nancy about the forthcoming marriage. Once she beamed and congratulated him, then asked who he was and who was to be his bride. When they were preparing to leave, she said, smiling at Fran, 'You're a pretty girl. Do come again.'

In the car Fran succumbed to tears, while Simon gripped the steering wheel, staring ahead at the dismal laurels and made no move to comfort her.

'I'm sorry,' she said at last, blowing her nose. 'Let's go.'

He eased into the evening traffic, grim-faced, still silent.

'You were right. She'd have no idea what was happening at the wedding, but I think she was pleased to see you. She knew who you were at times. We can visit her after the wedding and take her lots of photographs. It seems awful that such a dignified old lady should have come to this.'

'Perhaps you'll now accept why I find it hard to visit her.'

'I do, but that just eases it for you, doesn't it? It doesn't help her. The staff said she likes having visitors.'

'Then you can visit her. It doesn't matter who it is.'

Fran lapsed into unhappy silence. Clearly Simon's feelings for his grandmother were complex. She had no similar experience to refer to and doubted her right to reprove him for his outward hardness.

At Shawfield Street, Simon pulled her gently into his arms and kissed her.

'I'm sorry. I should have known it would be upsetting for you, but let's not talk about it now. We'll have a really good evening with Anna and Chas, right?'

*

It occurred to Simon that Miranda might expect them to have a church wedding as her late father had been an Anglican clergyman. She had never forced religion onto Fran but supported her if she decided to go to Sunday school, and never argued if she opted out, but would she be like the average parent, excitedly planning a conventional white wedding? As the Best Man at Charles's wedding, Simon's slight irritation plus amusement at the elaborate fuss was shared by the groom, but discreetly.

Like Simon, Fran was agnostic but if Miranda wanted her to be married in church, he didn't doubt she'd agree out of love for the woman who had been the best surrogate mother anyone could have. When she asked him if the registry office would be acceptable, he was surprised and relieved.

'Is Miranda happy with that?' he asked.

'Yes, she said I could have anything I wanted. Of course my dad had a church wedding but he could hardly do otherwise. Apparently, he and Mum were intrigued by all religions but saw terrible flaws in all of them. Mum's father was born in England but of Jewish descent through his father, so that accounts for her passion for Israel. Shame all my grandparents have died. I just knew my father's father for a few years and Mum's parents for even less. I was eight when they decided to go on an organised holiday in Canada and were killed in an horrendous coach crash.'

The Howards offered the use of their house for the reception and, at first, Fran wanted to decline as such a public display of generosity could be misconstrued. Then, when the honed-down guest list still amounted to two hundred, she agreed, and Miranda gratefully accepted. Most of Simon's guests came from Manchester and Fran's from among her school and university friends but the party was really Miranda's and neither Simon nor Fran begrudged her that pleasure. It was the occasion for showing off her beloved niece and ward, and she spared no expense to launch her in splendid style.

Being able to pay professional organisers to do the work usually done by brides and parents, Miranda remained cool and laid back. The fact that her niece had known her prospective husband for such a short time worried her not at all. She was convinced their different personalities contributed to a successful union.

Simon was amazed and delighted at the numbers of old friends and colleagues who came to the wedding. His one invited colleague from Exeter was Gerry, amazingly smartly dressed. Having known him for such a short time Simon debated whether or not to ask him, then his words at their first meeting flashed into his mind, "Go for it".

Although, still outnumbered by Miranda and Fran's guests he didn't feel second best. He was staggered that many of Miranda's and Fallada's friends 'knew' him through his newspaper reviews and articles. During his speech, Fran's godfather, an octogenarian geologist from Scotland, spoke of Simon's successful career then referred movingly to Miranda's loving and successful surrogacy as evidenced by the beautiful bride. Fran, certainly beautiful in a cream silk dress, struggled to withhold tears.

Charles was on top form as the Best Man. 'Best Man and best ever mate', called a friend from his Oxford days at the end of his humorous delivery that earned cheers and claps lasting for minutes.

Miranda, determined not to draw attention to herself, had never dressed more simply. The effect was of such understated elegance that even close friends murmured `Who is that wonderful-looking woman?' then shrieked with delight when they recognised her inside the purple sheath coat.

After the delicious meal and cake-cutting, Simon was enthusiastically greeted by Benjamin Williams, a journalist with the Observer. 'You could be a full- time writer for any top paper,' he said. 'Your new mother-in-law − well, sort of mother−in-law - is a really good friend of mine. Here, please take my card. Let me know when you've had your fill of students.'

'Thanks.' Amused, Simon pocketed the card. 'Great to meet you. Until now we've only 'met' via phone and post.'

A second later he was face to face with Caroline who was looking as beautiful and elusive as a cheetah.

'Be a bit low key about our Mombasa jaunt,' he muttered.

'You too.' Caroline grinned. 'Tom thinks it was a large house party.'

Charles came round the side of a palm tree and gave Caroline a hug.

'Steady, you're an old married man,' said Simon.

'And very properly.' Caroline laughed. 'I've been telling Anna how you held yourself aloof from all the carousing at Oxford and refused to be led astray.'

'That's quite enough to arouse her suspicions,' said Charles. 'You're a wicked woman, Caroline. I hope you're not here to claim some kind of droit de seigneurina.'

'Oh God, here's Tom. Now shut up both of you,' said Simon.

Moments later a beautiful Chinese girl caught Simon's arm and engaged him for ten minutes in hilarious conversation. Meanwhile, Fran was circulating conscientiously. When she next bumped into Simon she muttered, 'Have you slept with all these women?'

He kissed the corners of her mouth and said, 'Only about half, darling.'

'That's a relief. I was worried. Ah, Lady Scotney, how lovely you could come. Have you met Simon, my new husband – well, only one, I hope?'

Some while later Simon caught up with Lennie.

'Shame your mum's not here.' Instantly Lennie regretted his words, seeing the pain in Simon's eyes. 'Sorry, man, didn't think.'

'Forget it. You're right though. Wouldn't she have loved Fran?'

'No question. She's got real class like my Julia. And she's so nice. She introduced me to a Tory ex: Minister but he was too inebriated to be impressed. Decadent lot, Simon. Oh look, isn't that bloke over there with the Observer?'

'Yes. Come on, I'll introduce you. I see Julia's chatting to Fran. We both enjoyed our visit to you and meeting your little one.'

'Simon, won't you even whisper where you're spending your honeymoon?' pleaded Anna.

'I'll tell you this much; it'll be a pilgrimage for Fran. Don't even say that to Chas or he'll get up to some undergraduate prank.'

Anna grinned. 'You mean like the in-flight announcement you arranged for us halfway to India? Chas hasn't forgotten.'

'Well, hush, here he comes.'

'Nice of you to invite the aged P's, but I think Dad's had the wind taken out of his sails by all this.'

Simon smiled. 'Your mother's all right, is she Chas? She's enjoying herself?'

'Yes, Fran was talking to her for ages. God, she's sweet! More than you deserve, Si.'

'I'll prove you wrong. Anna's got faith in me haven't you, darling?'

Simon kissed her fondly.

'Steady on, you've one of your own now,' said Charles.

After Fran and Simon left in one of Bernard's Daimlers the party continued into the early hours.

Leaving St John's Wood to the dawn chorus overture, Anna snuggled her head against Charles's shoulder and pulled the car rug over her knees.

'Nicest wedding I've been to next to ours,' she said, stifling a yawn.

'Are they going to be all right, Anna? D'you think they'll be happy,'

She struggled upright and looked sideways at him, quizzically. 'They seem deliciously happy. You've never questioned it before.'

'I know. And I've never seen Simon so sure about anything before, and I feel Fran is absolutely right for him.'

'So why question it now?'

'Dunno - tired maybe.'

He stroked her hand absently while waiting for a milk float to move out of the way.

'I suppose I want them to be as happy as we are.'

*

'Here they are: Elizabeth Frances and William George Shaw, my parents.'

It was as if Fran was making introductions simply and without sentimentality.

'I wonder if I fit the bill,' Simon said, seeking Fran's hand.

They stood silent for minutes, gazing at the simple headstone inscribed in Hebrew and English:

`Elizabeth and William Shaw from Great Britain, who forfeited their lives while serving a country they loved and which honours their sacrifice.'

'They were caught in crossfire, weren't they?' asked Simon, breaking the silence at last.

'Yes. It was never proved whether they were killed by Israeli or Arab bullets.'

'Why were they buried here?'

'It was something they'd discussed knowing they could be in danger. And they met here, as students working in a Kibbutz, Israel became their spiritual home, I suppose, just as Greece is Miranda's.'

'And Exmoor yours.'

She smiled and leaned her head against his shoulder.

'I want to show you Massada and the Sea of Galilee and the Dead Sea. And Hamet Gadir and ....'

'Hey, steady. You're as bad as Miranda. I'll be happy to spend the time in bed.'

He turned her towards him, tilting her face so it was bathed in the last of the sunlight.

'You outshine the Dome of the Rock.'

He kissed her lingeringly until the outline of their bodies merged into the fringing olive trees, and the moon defied the polluting lights of the city with its pure gold intensity.

For the remaining time they indulged themselves. After just two nights in a former Bishop's palace in the Armenian quarter Simon insisted on moving to the Jerusalem Hilton.

'I'd never have booked this place if I'd known what it was like. A run-down mosquito-ridden palace might have been adequate for a student but not a bride!' Luckily there was amusement in his tone.

Fran examined her swollen face in the fly-blown glass above a foul-smelling wash basin and swiftly revised her ideas on romantic settings. It had all been fun when she was a hard-up student, but now she willingly swapped Youth Hostel standards for an absence of mosquitoes, and for room service and daily-changed linen. She felt a brief nostalgic pang though, recalling how they'd all wandered about the night-still streets of the old city and played tag up and down the narrow passages and stairways like a pack of urchins.

She managed to persuade Simon to visit the Dead Sea and Massada. In the rarefied atmosphere of the ancient fortress, they lost track of time, exploring every accessible area. Frequently they stopped to drink from the strategically placed taps to combat dehydration.

They descended by the Snake Path, enchanted to hear the strange evocative calling of the faithful to prayer. They scanned the hazy distance for a mosque on the far shore of the Dead Sea but reaching the car park they collapsed with laughter to discover the Mullah's cry came from a car radio.

'Must we be assailed by the twentieth century so soon?' complained Simon.

'No, we'll postpone it. We'll go via Qumran, hiding place of the Dead Sea Scrolls.'

And although Simon did not argue, Fran sensed he would have preferred the Hilton with its king size bed.

Chapter 10

'We should have turned off,' Fran exclaimed, 'much quicker.'

'No, this route couldn't be straighter.'

'So we're going to Exeter, not to Spring Cottage. Why?'

'Darling, because I work there. I need to check a few things – just for a couple of days. Don't worry, you've left Beamish for much longer than this. He'll survive if the Yeos do.'

Fran laughed in spite of her disappointment. Leaning back in the passenger seat she closed her eyes for a few minutes, envisioning some of the amazing sights of the past two weeks. She felt emotional as she pictured her parents' grave and marvelled that Simon had secretly chosen Israel for their honeymoon. Had he not been driving she would have unreservedly embraced him. Instead, she leaned her head against his shoulder and suggested, 'Let's stop at a pub – really indulge ourselves then, later, we'll only need a sandwich.'

Two hours later, well-fed and invigorated, Fran sifted through a pile of letters, casting most aside for the rubbish bin. One she stared at, an air mail from America and addressed to her. She opened it gently – it was probably from one of Miranda's friends.

Seconds later she excitedly called, 'Simon, come and look. I've got an offer from an American publisher and not even a subsidiary of Pharoah. A British writer, living in California has written a memoir of childhood camping trips on Dartmoor and Exmoor and wants a wide variety of paintings to illustrate his book. How do they know about me? It's not as if I'm the illustrator of an international best-seller.'

'Not yet, darling,' said Simon, coming into the kitchen. He perused the letter Fran handed to him. 'Wow, a decent offer. Not a bad welcome home from your honeymoon. Chas has contacts in America and it's from a firm he knows so, I bet he gave them this address. Now, you can turn one of the spare rooms into a studio.'

Fran smiled in an abstracted way. 'I'll need to know lots more, of course. This is just asking if I'll accept the offer.'

'You can't refuse. It's a brilliant one.'

She wandered into the two spare bedrooms then joined Simon in the kitchen minutes later.

'I can't wait to get started,' she said. 'I'll ring Charles tonight to thank him.'

'Great. Which room have you decided on? We only need one spare bedroom. Here, a bit of refreshment.'

She accepted the offered glass of wine and walked across to the window.

'It's a nice flat, Simon, really nice but I can't work here. The light's all wrong.'

'Oh well, I expect we'll be able to get something eventually - near the estuary maybe, or would that be too distracting?' There was a trace of irony in his tone.

She sipped her wine, looking thoughtful for a minute.

'We don't need to find anything. I've Spring Cottage and the best studio anyone could have.'

'Yes, for weekends.'

She sat down at the table, opposite him. 'I can go to work in the week, like you, and we'll be together for long weekends.'

'Christ, Fran, we've been married five minutes! I want to be with you.'

'I know. I want to be with you but think of the money I'll earn. The American contract is staggeringly generous.'

'To hell with the money. I'm quite able to support you.'

Fran took a gulp of wine. 'I'm just getting started; not like you - you're launched. I've still got to make my way. Surely you don't expect me to give up a career just because I'm married? We're in the nineteen eighties.'

'No, of course not. Oh Christ, are we having our first row?'

She put her glass down and moved around the table to him. He pushed his chair back and pulled her onto his lap.

'Of course, you can't wait to be reunited with your beloved dog but I shan't have anyone here. I'll be all alone.'

She laughed then kissed his face.

'Think of the weekends, Simon. I promise it'll be worth it.'

'So, life begins.'

'What d'you mean? The bit we've already had has ended?'

'Well, honeymoons can't last forever but can be revisited. Bed at ten, Fran, or how about now?'

*

A telephone call came from a woman whose husband was a colleague of Simon's, a biology lecturer. 'Hello, I'm Martha Hall. I've met Simon a couple of times and bumped into him earlier today. I hear you're alone so I wonder if you'd like to come out for a pub lunch by the estuary.'

'I'd love that.' Fran was genuinely pleased. Martha sounded so nice and friendly.

'Collect you at twelve?'

'Fine, thanks.'

Dead on time Martha arrived, a pleasant middle-aged woman who worked part-time as an occupational therapist and, also, as a voluntary entertainer in three residential homes. Simon had mentioned her and her husband, Roger, telling Fran a bit about them, that they seemed really happy, and had a daughter at Southampton University. Instantly Fran felt at home with her. She was interested in people without being nosy, had a sense of humour and listened more than she talked. Fran guessed she was in her early forties. She was pretty with a round, youthful-looking face and an abundance of brown curls. At an ancient pub they sat on the terrace with a view across the estuary to the reed beds, and enjoyed a fresh fish lunch.

'This is lovely,' enthused Fran. 'I wouldn't mind setting up an easel here.'

'I'm sure you will and there's plenty more to see. I gather you've a holiday cottage on Exmoor.'

'Not a holiday cottage, a home,' Fran said, then explained how she'd acquired Spring Cottage.

'Sounds lovely. So that will be your retreat.'

Fran nodded. She would say no more about her resolution to make the cottage her base. How much had Simon told Martha, she wondered.

'You must visit the cottage. Do you work at weekends?'

'Sometimes. If there's a special event such as a birthday party or wedding anniversary, then I play the piano and everyone sings who can; some even jig a bit. Come one day and join in. My daughter has done so and loved it.'

'I'd like that. It sounds a lovely job. Shame that sort of thing doesn't happen in Simon's granny's Home.'

Fran found it easy to tell Martha about Nancy as she had come across many people with the same illness. They chatted about a variety of subjects then Martha drove back to the flat where they had tea together. Simon came in just as she was leaving and seemed delighted that they'd become acquainted.

'There, you've made a useful friend,' he said. 'She'll tell you where best to shop and introduce you to other people. You'll soon feel at home. Oh, I saw Mrs Benson as I parked. She said you helped her with a bit of gardening yesterday. Clearly, you're going to get on with her. She's really impressed.'

'Not difficult. She's so nice. And how good of her to make this house over to the University.'

'Yes, and for lecturers not students. Just a shame she's got the ground floor flat. Still, we'll get our own house, eventually.'

'We have a house – we couldn't have anything better.'

'Yes, as a retreat, but it's hardly convenient as a permanent home with my work based here.'

'Simon, it's just a short drive. Think of all the commuters who drive or travel for hours to their jobs.'

'Not my idea of heaven.' Simon sighed. 'Fran, I love the moor, all the wonderful places you've shown me, meeting red deer and those unique ponies. I'm grateful for all of it but I regard it as a holiday place.'

'Then haven't we the best of both worlds? One for work and one for leisure.'

'Yes, if you really saw it as that but you have to combine work and leisure. If only you could work here, as I do, then retreat to the moor to relax, or why don't you commute if it's so easy? No need to stay there.'

Fran didn't reply. She was sure the discussion or argument could be never-ending. The shrill call of the telephone was a welcome diversion and, after twenty minutes of chatting with Charles, Simon was relaxed and cheerful.

The following day Miranda visited them at the flat, bringing some of Fran's belongings from London. Again, Simon found he had an ally in her as she exclaimed at the attractive, leafy surroundings, the proximity to the university with its extensive grounds, and the City's excellent shops and restaurants.

Fran asked Mrs Benson to join them for tea. During one of her early chats with Fran she had enthused about Miranda's work so their meeting was a great success. She enquired about Beamish then said how much she missed having a dog but her health problems now made it too difficult. She offered the use of her garden for Beamish's early first and last thing at night 'reliefs'.

'That is so kind,' exclaimed Miranda. 'Of course, he'll leave no evidence that he's been around, will he Fran?'

'No, I've always got poo bags with me – well, not on the moor.'

'Good, so you're all organised. Now, more tea, Mrs Benson?'

'Mary, dear - yes please. I must say I'm delighted with my new neighbours.'

She beamed at Fran who laughed, saying, 'I hope you'll feel the same way in a year's time.'

A warm rapport had certainly developed between them. The fact that Fran was young enough to be Mary's granddaughter was no handicap to their friendship.

The following day, Miranda returned home and Fran prepared for the return to Spring Cottage and reunification with Chuckle and Beamish. At midday Simon answered the phone in the bedroom he'd renamed the office/studio. He returned to the kitchen looking rather perplexed.

'Sorry, darling, a slight delay. We've been invited to a dinner party tonight. A guy called Barry Field, physics lecturer. Seems nice.'

'You said we'd be here a couple of days and it's three already. You haven't accepted?'

'Yes. I'm sorry but I just felt I couldn't refuse. He was full of apologies for not being at the party Professor Crawford gave.'

'Okay. I'd better ring the Yeos. They've been so good looking after the animals.'

By seven o'clock Fran had swapped her jeans and tee shirt for a silk dress the colour of autumn leaves, a present from Miranda.

'Wow, you look beautiful,' enthused Simon. 'Not that you don't always but, suddenly you're a sophisticate.'

'Lord, d'you want me to stay this way?'

'No. You always look right for whatever you're doing. The best looking you is the one who's just shed everything. You're going to turn a few heads this evening. Lord, it is evening – we'd better get going.'

Fran was amazed, and slightly fazed by the opulence of the three other women present at the dinner party. Dripping with jewels they wore Dallas-style dresses in brilliant colours. Their make-up was lavishly applied and clashing, exotic scents wafted from them. The hostess, Jane-Anne, made heavy weather of the introductions, reciting a CV for all but Fran of whom she knew nothing, other than she was Simon's wife.

'I'm sure Frances has many talents,' she said archly but Fran, smiling politely, volunteered none.

'Such a shame we didn't meet you at Professor Crawford's but, of course, we were on cruise in the Mediterranean.'

And we weren't married, was Fran's silent response.

The pre-dinner drinks period seemed interminable and the food, when eventually it was served, looked inedible. It had been arranged, dyed and decorated so it bore no resemblance to its original form. Surprisingly it was very good as was the wine that flowed unstintingly.

Her tongue loosened, Fran chatted to her host, Barry Field. In spite of his important position as a Departmental Head (as he described it) he seemed vocally hesitant. Perhaps it was the effect of having a wife who put him down all the time. With his round, balding head, shiny face and small eyes behind thick-lensed spectacles he was unattractive, while his wife, with her bubbly light brown curls, pale blue eyes and very white, if slightly buck teeth, could, by some standards, be termed pretty.

Martine, a pert, black-haired woman with an attractive accent, informed Simon she was half French.

'Mother's French. Her contacts have helped my husband, Michael; he has a perfumery business. We live in Grasse and Paris and we've a pied a terre in Belgravia.'

For a good fifteen minutes she regaled Simon with a description of their yacht, the grandness of her daughter's recent wedding at St Michael's, Chester Square and her country house. She made it clear that they were only present because Barry's third male guest was an accountant with the English branch of their firm, and she and Michael were spending a few days with him and his wife at their Torquay apartment. Her inference that she was bestowing enormous condescension on the company caused Simon to shudder and deliberately address himself to Barry seeing that Fran had now been commandeered by Kevin, the accountant. Hardly surprising when one looked at his wife, Andrea, who could have upstaged anyone playing Cruella de Ville.

Softened up by Barry's undemanding conversation, Fran revealed that she was an artist which, said during a rare conversational lull, drew everyone's attention to her.

'Goodness,' exclaimed Jane-Anne. 'You don't look like an artist.'

Fran laughed. 'How is an artist supposed to look? Paint on the nails, filthy jeans?' Her voice was light but Simon sensed her irritation.

'Oh, you know - a bit Bohemian.'

'Ah, she can be,' said Simon. 'Thank goodness.'

'I think artists are often as conventional as anyone else,' volunteered Barry.

'Quite,' said Simon. 'You'd never guess Fran's aunt was a famous sculptor if you were looking for chipped nails and stone dust.' There was a wicked grin hovering around his mouth.

Fran wished she could reach him under the table and give him a sharp kick.

Martine asked, 'And who is this er... sculptress?'

'Oh, Miranda Shaw,' Simon said, off-handedly.

There was an over-long pause, then Jane-Anne giggled and said, 'Goodness, we are honoured.'

Surprised that she had heard of Miranda, Fran hastily explained that she and her aunt were in totally different fields.

'Ah, but a name can be so useful,' said Martine with a smile of nauseating sweetness.

'Perhaps if you are submitting work to the RA's summer exhibition, but I'm sure in the cut-throat world of illustrating you're either up to it or you're not,' said Barry, unexpectedly. Fran could have hugged him.

'Yet there are strange successes,' persisted Martine. 'If you've a name you can hang a frame on a blank wall and someone will look at it. Of course, my

124

daughter could have been an artist but she has so many talents, ballet, acting.'

'And as she's never realised those-so called talents - that's rather a silly claim, darling. I doubt if they were more than small girl's fantasies.'

As if her husband had not uttered, Martine continued: 'Of course, she'll never have to work to prove anything. She's so comfortably married.'

'How fortunate for her,' murmured Simon. 'There, darling, you should have married a rich man.'

There was uncertain laughter followed by a prolonged silence, broken at last by Jane-Anne, 'Are you fond of ballet, Fran?'

'Yes, watching it, not performing it.'

'Fran's forté is riding,' said Simon.

'Oh, I love horse-riding,' enthused his hostess. 'I always ride hunters.'

'Which hunt do you ride with?' asked Fran.

'Goodness, I don't hunt. I think it's cruel. I ride hunters at the equestrian centre I attend.'

A welcome diversion was afforded then as the unfortunate Cruella bit into a chilli and started to cough. Barry hurried to the kitchen for water.

'There's Perrier in the fridge,' called Jane-Anne, 'and do use one of the proper glasses.' To her guests she said, 'We were given a priceless set of Perrier glasses when Barry changed jobs.'

To her credit Cruella said she hated causing a fuss and tap water would be fine.

'Not in this house,' chided Jane-Anne. 'You know it's full of harmful chemicals.'

Surreptitiously Fran glanced at her watch. Oh no! Had they really been only two hours?

'Bought a place here, have you, Simon?' Martine asked.

Briefly Simon described their housing arrangements.

'How lovely, a cottage on the moor. How picturesque,' trilled Jane-Anne.

'And practical,' said Simon. 'It houses Fran's studio.'

Fran smiled at him for his generosity.

'You've plenty of time to find somewhere here,' said Barry. 'Although I must admit you'd be hard pressed to find a place like this.'

And desperate, thought Simon, glancing at fake beams and a large open fireplace in which stood a gas heater with fake logs.

'Has anyone seen the latest Jane Austin?' asked Jane-Anne, and getting no response directed her question at Fran.

'You mean the latest film – Pride and Prejudice. We were disappointed.'

'Goodness. In what way?'

'It was too glamorous. Such ostentation would have been an anathema to the author. I think she....'

'Oh, I thought the costumes were lovely,' interrupted Jane-Anne.

'Then there was the poor casting, a poor interpretation, of Mrs Bennet,' Fran continued. 'She is meant to be silly and hysterical but not downright vulgar.'

'My word, you are critical,' said Martine smirking nastily.

'Well, we loved it, didn't we, Barry?' said Jane-Anne.

Barry said he found it entertaining and was no expert on Jane Austin.

'Perhaps Fran should be joining her husband in the English faculty,' said Martine.

'Hardly, but I know Jane Austin's novels pretty thoroughly, and I can't see how vulgarising them for television improves them.'

'But any interpretation is bound to be subjective to a degree,' said Cruella, unexpectedly.

'Yes, of course, we all interpret in our own way but to deliberately alter dialogue and change something fundamental about a character seems arrogant, or ignorant. Why bother?

'Goodness me, you will be lecturing Simon's students next,' said Jane-Anne, with her irritating laugh.

'Any time,' said Simon. 'She pointed out many things I missed. She'd be a credit to the faculty.' He kept his voice light and resisted tipping his wine down Jane-Anne's cleavage.

'So we're not going to see you setting The Tempest on Mars, Simon. I've heard you like to be involved with amateur dramatics.' Barry smiled.

'I've always wanted to act,' said Jane-Anne, curtailing a response from Simon, 'but I seem to get involved with more serious issues. Committees, fundraising. that's my sort of thing. I can always find a job for you, Fran, if you're at a loose end. As one of the senior wives I feel I should help newcomers to find a niche, make friends and so on. Have you found a good hairdresser yet? I can recommend mine, and I've a marvellous little dressmaker. And Barry, you can tell Simon about your terribly reasonable little handyman.'

'Thank you, darling. You're giving our guests the impression that Exeter is populated by the seven dwarfs.'

Jane-Anne flushed unattractively and did not join in the laughter that followed his words.

'Sweet, everyone?' she shrilled. 'Bombe glacé, profiteroles, or my special cream and chocolate gateau? Must give you the recipe, Fran.'

Fran pressed the gold-coloured lavatory handle, washed her hands beneath gold taps and splashed cold water onto her flushed cheeks. In the peaches and cream bathroom, she looked at her reflection in the triple mirror without enthusiasm. Beside the numerous bottles and jars on the glass shelf above the basin, her Beauty without Cruelty cosmetics would look pathetic. Not tempted to put Charles of the Ritz, Helena Rubinstein and Dior to the test, she applied her own powder and lipstick and flipped a comb through her hair.

Jane-Anne was pouring coffee and Barry offered liqueurs or brandy. The fake logs glowed in the hearth. The warmth was overwhelming. Fran rapidly drank two cups of black coffee to combat her desperation for sleep. Andrea seemed to be well-set into an argument about the Common Market with Martine's husband. Was this wise, Fran wondered, in view of her husband's connection with the firm? Still, it showed spirit.

'Tell me who you've met, Fran,' demanded Jane-Anne. 'Sometimes you can waste time with quite awful, boring people until you sort everyone out. I like to give newcomers a bit of guidance as to who's who.'

'Oh, please don't worry on our account. I've met some interesting people. Gerry was one of the first people Simon met at Harriet's party and he's already been to Spring Cottage.'

Jane-Anne's plucked eyebrows nearly disappeared into her hairline.

'Goodness, I am surprised. Such a strange, scruffy man. I sometimes wonder if he's - well - you know.'

But no one indicated that they did know. Flustered, she dug herself in deeper.

'He lives in squalor I believe. Somewhere near Ottery?'

'Venn, actually,' said Simon, coldly. 'An old bungalow but charming. Gerry is a complete original and one of the most civilised people I've met here.'

His words had the impact he intended. Barry glanced at his wife, without sympathy then, unusually bold, took command of the conversation. Half-an-hour on the merits or otherwise of a gap year had Fran desperate for matchsticks to keep her eyes open.

'Hate to drag ourselves away,' lied Simon, shamelessly, 'but we both have work to do before Monday. Lovely evening, lovely food, lovely company.'

'Never, never again. Promise me, Simon,' begged Fran when they were safely in the car.

'Don't worry, darling. I never even want to see them again, but that'll be damned difficult.'

'We'll have to invite them, sometime,' said Fran, sighing. It was part of her code, instilled by Miranda, that one did not accept invitations one could not return.

'They can come to our flat-warming,' said Simon, firmly. 'Nothing more, ever. Anyway, we couldn't possibly have them to dinner. We haven't any Perrier glasses.'

They began to giggle. Simon swerved the car to avoid a prowling cat. 'Which of the women irritated you most?'

'Jane-Anne,' replied Fran, decisively. 'I can't bear double barrelled Christian names.'

'No, I sympathise. Double barrelled surnames are more your style. Ouch! That hurt!'

She had leaned over and tweaked his ear.

'Still, could have been worse,' said Simon changing gear. 'At least she horse-rides.'

'You mean it could have been horse-back riding? Yes, that would have been worse. You know we're snobs too, in our own way. What a way to spend time when we should be at the cottage. I know Christmas is months away but we'll spend it at Miranda's and avoid local invitations from ghastly people, and it'll be fun.'

'They're not all ghastly, think of Martha and Roger, but of course we'll go to Miranda's. She's the most marvellous mother-in-law I'll never have.'

Chapter 11

'This is a wonderful day,' enthused Fran, fourteen hours later.

'Better than the wedding – the honeymoon?' Simon asked, grinning.

'Of course, Simon. Beamish and Chuckle weren't on the guests' list and didn't have passports for Israel.'

Simon pulled her close to him. 'How do I cope with you and those creatures?'

Sadly, not for long, thought Fran, who realised they'd be back in the flat in two days!

*

Fran was not bored in Exeter but frustrated that she was limited in the amount of work she could do. She walked a lot with Beamish, appreciating the older parts of the city, particularly the Cathedral. Gazing at the wonderful carvings, she remembered a comment Miranda once made about the lack of knowledge we have of those early sculptors.

'Of course, we know the names of Bishops, Lords and Kings but not the men who made this building and hundreds more. They were regarded as inferiors. I find it upsetting,' she'd said.

Sometimes, Fran drew a sketchpad from the small rucksack she nearly always carried, and drew, or attempted to. People frequently peered over her shoulder then commented, usually favourably, and often questioned her. Was she a proper artist? On holiday? Did she sell her work?

Several times during the autumn term, she extended her stay at Spring Cottage by one or two days. It was the only way she could get enough work done so that deadlines could be met. Never lonely, she worked for hours, then walked with Beamish, relishing the wonderful sense of freedom that had been well earned. She would walk for four or five miles, observing the reddening bracken, the heather sinking into shades of brown apart from a few swathes of bell heather that clung longer to their rich purple colour. She listened to a variety of bird calls and drew in deep breaths of salt-scented air: every sense aware, every nerve alive.

She was sure that her times with Simon were vitalised by those periods alone on the moor. Being reunited with him was like the start of their relationship over and over again.

*

The weeks flew by, and Fran went to London a few days before Christmas to help prepare for a very special day – the first Christmas she, Simon and Miranda would be together.

After two hours of shopping Fran and Anna collapsed at the nearest empty table in the Peter Jones Restaurant, their many carrier bags spilling around their feet.

'Ridiculous, really,' gasped Anna. 'Not more than a few hundred yards and we're shattered.'

'That walk from Knightsbridge has never seemed so far,' said Fran, pouring coffee and passing a cup to Anna. 'Still, it's marvellous to have done all our

Christmas shopping, but why didn't we take a taxi? It's a bit late to start economising.'

Anna laughed. 'We'll do that in the January sales. Will you still be here?'

'Not sure. I hope we can get a few days on the moor before term starts. It's lovely being with Miranda, but I could do with some time down there. And it's ages since Simon was at the cottage.'

Anna looked surprised. 'I thought he was at the cottage from Fridays to Sundays.'

'Sometimes, but not when he's busy, then I'm at the flat, Fridays 'til Mondays and work three days in the week. It's the best compromise.'

'Don't you hate it, being away from him?'

Fran hesitated. 'I manage. And it's marvellous when we are together. I suppose it does seem a bit odd as we've been married such a short time. It wouldn't suit you and Charles?'

'No, but we're different people.' Anna sipped her coffee while Fran watched her thoughtfully, sensing a reticence.

'D'you think I'm unwise?'

Anna put down her cup. 'How d'you mean?'

'Being away from Simon. You've known him as long as you've known Charles. D'you think he's happy?'

Anna stared at Fran in surprise, then laughed. 'How can you doubt it? I've never known him so relaxed and happy.'

'But you think I shouldn't leave him alone so much? I know the students hang around him a lot.'

'Well, he is very attractive, and women do tend to hurl themselves at him but I don't think Simon's really looked at another woman since meeting you. He was determined to get to know you. You can't doubt that.'

'No, I suppose not. But women do seem to want to devour him.'

'They've not succeeded, have they? Isn't that flattering? I find it a real morale booster that Charles comes home to me although all the girls at Pharaoh adore him.'

Fran smiled. 'That's a good view to take.'

'There's something else, isn't there, Fran?'

'It's – well - Simon's such a strange mixture. We spent yesterday with Lennie and Julie and their lovely little boy. Simon really enjoyed it but he also has a taste for high living. Has he always spent time at Annabel's and Raffles? How could he afford to?'

Anna shrugged. 'Charles was the same. His father always gave him an allowance and Simon's mother spoilt him excessively. He seemed to have everything that Charles had.'

'Was that why she left relatively little?'

'I suppose so, but his inheritance was enough for a new car, and he paid off some long-running bills.'

'Such as?'

'Oh, the tailors and the wine merchants. They both have accounts at Hawes and Curtis, and they must have Turnbull and Assoc: shirts. There can't have been much left.'

'Maybe that's why he isn't in a hurry to buy a house although he regrets his mother never did.'

'Perhaps house-hunting will have priority next year? It could give you a local studio.'

'Maybe, but Simon has ambitious ideas. He wants something special but without a huge mortgage so the answer would be to sell the cottage but I don't want to. Why should I when our combined earnings could easily cover a mortgage? Anyway, we're all right where we are for the time being. We're only apart about three nights a week.'

'Well then, stop worrying.' Anna reached across and squeezed her arm. 'Although he implies otherwise, Charles was quite wild when I met him and now, he's almost an old stay-at-home.' She glanced at her watch. 'Perhaps we'd better go and walk Beamish before the gates are locked.'

Fran smiled. 'Yes. He likes the Royal Hospital Walk; the Pensioners make a huge fuss of him. And thanks. He'd have been alone far longer if I'd left him at home as Miranda's at an all - day conference.'

*

On the third of January London was swapped for Spring Cottage which welcomed them warmly thanks to the Yeos thoughtfulness. The Rayburn was alight, a stew simmered in the slow oven and a fire burned in the inglenook. Fran returned with scarlet cheeks and snow crystals glinting in her hair after thanking them and giving them New Year presents; Whisky for Fred and a lambswool jumper for Norah.

'Perhaps we'll be snowed up soon,' she said happily, letting an icy blast precede her through the French windows.

'Hope not. Thank goodness we're having a phone installed. Darling, please shut it.' Simon shivered violently. 'Come here, I want to kiss you. You look beautiful.' He unwound the mohair cloak he had given her for Christmas and slid his hands beneath her black jersey. 'Hmm, you're as warm as toast. How d'you withstand these appalling conditions? You thrive on them.'

She laughed. 'You can't be cold almost on top of the fire.'

But he shivered again.

'Are you all right?'

'I am now. Just needing a bit of care.' He drew back a little, looking at her as if seeing her for the first time. 'You've the most beautiful mouth I've ever seen.' He bent and kissed her, long and gently, sliding his hands around to her breasts. 'You're wearing that sexy new bra, the one Father Christmas gave you but you won't be needing it.' He slid her jersey over her head and unhooked her crimson bra. Her nipples were hard as nuts and dark against her golden skin. She locked her hands behind his neck arching her body against him.

'Dinner can wait, I think,' she said.

'Yes, but I can't, Fran. I want you now and here. Beamish will have to look away.'

She dropped her arms and let him undress her slowly, kissing every part as it was revealed. When she was naked she dropped to her knees on the hearthrug, gently pushing Beamish aside and spreading the cloak.

'We've five days on our own, Simon, and right now I want it to be like the very first time.'

When they left only a light powdering of snow lay on the moor.

'Pity,' said Simon. 'No genuine excuse not to return home.'

Ignoring the misplaced use of 'home' to describe the flat, Fran was cheered by his words but was concerned by how pale he was. Inside the warm cottage, which he'd hardly left, she hadn't noticed.

'I'll drive,' she said decisively, and surprisingly he agreed for he preferred driving to being driven, which was no reflection on Fran's driving skills.

'Simon, thanks for everything at Christmas. I know Granny was pretty confused when we all visited but it was the right thing to do, and didn't she take to Miranda?'

'She certainly did – probably thought she was the Queen. And Miranda says she's going to keep the visits going. She's a saint.'

After that Simon said little, even dozing for most of the short journey. Within a few hours of arriving at the flat he had succumbed to a feverish cold, which he refused to term `flu.

*

Dumping a heavy bag of groceries on the pub floor, Fran was about to order a cup of coffee when Gerry who'd met her in the supermarket intervened.

'A stiff drink is what you need,' he said firmly, and ordered her a small brandy.

'Really small,' Fran said. 'I'm not much of a drinker.'

'You look frozen Fran,' he said. 'I thought you were a tough, outdoor girl.'

'I am but outdoors in town doesn't count. It's unrelieved misery.'

'Oh, come now, you need a sensible occupation. Pity my sheep aren't due to lamb quite yet.'

'I'd love to help when they are,' said Fran. 'I've helped out on the farm often enough so I'm quite a competent shepherd.'

'Great. Let's sit over there by the fire.' He carried their glasses across to a table then retrieved Fran's groceries.

'Now, tell me about Simon. Has he seen a doctor?'

'No. He flatly refuses saying there's no cure for the common cold so it would be wasting valuable time. I suppose he's right provided it is just a really heavy cold or, at most, `flu.'

'Is he a well-behaved patient?'

Fran grinned. 'He's feeling very sorry for himself. I don't think Simon's type can bear to be at all ill. It's a sort of flaw which is unacceptable.'

'Well, everyone catches colds,' said Gerry.

'No, not Simon. He says he hasn't had a cold for years. He's moved into the spare bedroom because he feels so disgusting.'

'Sounds a civilised move to me. Wonder if he'll be well enough to start term?'

'Oh, I'm sure he will. He's quite determined not to lose any time. He says he only ever had two days sick leave at Manchester.'

'We're supposed to be playing squash on Friday. I'll cancel it so he's not tempted. Do let me know if there's anything I can do. Are you having to get on with your own work?'

'Not immediately, and what I have I can do at the flat. It's all drawing which I can do from old roughs, or from memory.'

'Is it time to find a suitable work-place, Fran? A house and preferably near me? We could share exotic fowl, sheep, goats or a herd of Exmoor ponies?'

138

Fran laughed. 'I wouldn't mind but Simon doesn't want to move just yet. He's hardly settled in to the job.'

'He seems pretty settled to me, but then it may be hard to tell with a confident chap like him. He'll do well here, Fran. There are too many old fuddy-duddies and I'm fast becoming one of them.'

'Rot. That's the last thing I'd call you. You're one of the few colleagues Simon really likes, 'though he appears to get on with everyone.'

'Yes, there were plenty of people at your flat-warming in October. One of them collared me in the library yesterday and asked when you were returning from your Christmas trip.'

'Who was that?'

'Jane-Anne with her daughter in tow.'

'Ah well, she's one person who is not on our hospitality list. Simon said the party had to be our sole invitation to her.'

'Well, in spite of some of the company it was a great shindig and the food was fabulous. You're a clever girl, Fran. How many blokes acquire a beauty who can cook, garden, draw and paint. Simon's a lucky devil.'

'Not if I spend much longer away from him, depriving him of his over-the-counter medicines washed down with scotch.'

Half-an-hour later Fran handed Simon a hot toddy and several pills.

'A kiss first - no, I'll give you my bug.' He swallowed the pills in one gulp. Fran shuddered.

'Don't like the stuff. I was persuaded to drink spirits by Gerry, a stiff brandy.'

139

'Dreadful old reprobate. How is he?'

'Fine, most concerned about you. He can't visualise you like this.'

'I should hope not. I'm not in the habit of languishing on sofas – well, not with a cold.'

'So what was he on about?'

'He wants me to go into business with him: rare breeds.'

'Seriously?'

Fran laughed. 'I shouldn't think so but he really wants us to move to somewhere near him. He's mentioned this before.'

'Not a bad idea. Lovely scenery. Prices would be prohibitive for a place with several acres, even a shack like Gerry's. Quite out of our league.'

'But why when we've two salaries?'

'We haven't. You're a freelance artist. The work could dry up at any time or you could get pregnant.'

'I hope so. Off the Pill in a year, we agreed. Anyway, is a senior lecturer's salary so bad?'

'No, but we'd need at least a ninety percent mortgage and think what a drain that would be.'

'It's what loads of people have - people in our situation. There aren't many couples as lucky as Anna and Charles.'

'Are we so different? Anna's father gave them a house; your aunt gave you a house.'

Fran was standing behind the sofa so Simon did not see the effect his words had. She walked to the window and absently tweaked the curtains she had made and which he had greatly admired. After a moment she turned around and sat in an armchair opposite him.

'It isn't quite the same is it? The Shawfield Street house was given as a marital home. That was never Miranda's view of Spring Cottage. It was a generous twenty-first birthday present because I've always loved it. She just wanted me to have it sooner then I might have.'

'Yes, of course, and that reminds me it is yours, not ours, so it's not part of the equation.'

'Then why mention it?'

'Because Fran darling, you seem to want to buy a house in a highly desirable area with acres of land. Be realistic.'

'You're surmising that's what I want. I simply quoted Gerry's suggestion but I've never noticed you hankering after a modern house on an estate or a semi in suburbia.'

'Agreed, but we don't have to bother to look for anywhere yet. We're extremely lucky to have this place for peanuts. Fran, we're not going to become one of those ghastly couples who argue about money, are we?'

She got up and sat on the sofa beside him.

'No, don't get too close. I don't want you to catch this.'

She sighed and returned to the armchair.

'One last question on this subject,' Simon said. 'If Miranda had given you a sum of money instead of Spring Cottage, would you have been prepared to put it towards a house?'

'That's an unfair question, Simon. I'm emotional about Spring Cottage. There's no comparison.'

'So, you would expect to use the money for a house?'

'I expect so. Yes, I'm sure I would.'

141

'I find your logic hard to understand. I imagine Miranda gave you the cottage as a valuable asset not something that could become a millstone.'

'It never will - for me. It's my workplace and my freedom.'

'Right, let's say no more about it. Your feelings are plain.'

'Simon, why do you have to be so nasty? The reason you won't agree to an equal commitment on a mortgage is that you're not prepared to modify your lifestyle. You've still got to have your expensive West End tailor and wine delivered from the most fashionable merchant.'

'So, you've been gossiping with Charles, or, more likely Anna. Well, if you think I'm altering my lifestyle completely because I'm married, you're mistaken.'

'In that case don't expect me to spend any more time here than I have to. If I need to work at the cottage I shall do so, whatever's going on here.' Fran got to her feet and, with Beamish at her heels, walked purposefully to the kitchen. She unpacked the groceries and put them away then considered what to make for lunch. She walked back to the sitting-room to ask Simon if he wanted anything in particular. He was still lying on the sofa but asleep and ashen-coloured. The room was uncomfortably warm. She lowered the gas and stood for a second looking down at her inert husband, resisting an urge to kneel down beside him and take him in her arms. He looked as vulnerable as a small boy. She sighed and feeling ashamed of her anger returned to the kitchen.

Chapter 12

Spring came late on the moor. Above the snow line the leaves could not risk unfurling at the first touch of March sunshine and the thorn trees remained stark long after trees in valleys started to bloom. The sheep dropped their lambs whatever the weather and, to watch their antics and sit quietly with her thoughts, Fran left the lane and walked to a small stand of beech trees. She let Beamish off his lead and the ewes, not knowing that he was a harmless, disciplined dog, bunched up in confusion then moved away. They called urgently to their lambs who, unafraid and curious, took their time. Fran spread her heavy mac on the damp, dark heather and sat down, calling, 'He won't hurt you. There's no need to go away.'

She laughed when the ewes checked and looked round at her, as if bemused by the unfamiliar sound of a human voice. She rolled up the sleeves of her thick jersey surprised by the strength of the sun, and Beamish, panting a little, leaned against her. Fran fondled his rough head.

'You won't mind Beams, will you? You were first; nothing can change that, first and best. Best dog in the world.'

Beamish yawned, as if he was hearing nothing new, then sank onto his front paws.

'Simon's coming tomorrow – day later than usual. We won't ring him, Beams, we'll wait. Our secret until then.'

Beamish licked his left paw, one ear cocked for Fran's voice. They sat sheltered from the light west wind for half-an-hour. Fran leaned back against her backpack, drifting from the dreamy consciousness of feeling the sun on her face and hearing precocious insects in the young gorse, to brief oblivion. Abruptly, she was awoken by the arrival of a car, doors slamming and dogs yapping. A few yards away a middle-aged couple unpacked folding chairs from the back of a Volvo estate car and admonished two Jack Russells who had sent the sheep fleeing.

'Time to go, Beams,' Fran said, reluctantly getting to her feet

Fifteen minutes later, letting herself in by the front door, she picked up a handful of letters from the mat and walked through to the kitchen. She flicked through the envelopes, extracted a flimsy one in familiar writing and put the others between two cookery books. She stood by the kitchen door, drinking apple juice and reading her letter, wondering what it would be like to work for a pittance in a Third World country. This was the lot of the correspondent, her friend Sarah, teaching in Bangladesh for VSO and, apparently, loving it. Not for me now, thought Fran, with a wry smile. She washed up her glass, grabbed a couple of apples and went across the yard to her studio, Beamish at her heels. Her appetite for work was voracious and just as well. The author of the Moorland Memoir, thrilled with her illustrations, now wanted her to illustrate another one, concentrating on moorland wildlife.

At eleven the following morning, Beamish set up a cacophony of barking. In the studio Fran laid down her brush and hurried to the open door. Below, in the yard, Beamish danced around a large, unfamiliar car from which Simon was helping a middle-aged woman. On the other side a tall, blonde girl was emerging, gallantly assisted by a stout, balding man. For a fleeting second Fran wondered if Simon's car had broken down and he'd been given a lift, then she recognised the two older people, Martha and Roger Hall. Hesitantly, almost warily, she walked down the stone steps and into Simon's enthusiastic embrace.

'Fran, dear girl, lovely of you to have us,' called Roger, warmly.

'Yes, and with so little notice,' added Martha.

With as broad a smile as she could muster, Fran greeted and embraced them.

'Let me introduce Silvia from Denmark,' said Roger. 'The dear girl was on a school exchange with our daughter some years ago, and now she's staying with us and looking for a post graduate course.'

Fran shook hands with the willowy blonde, inches taller than she was and ravishingly beautiful. She smiled with her shapely, full mouth but her green eyes looked coolly speculative.

The realisation that the entire party had come in one car nagged Fran's brain as bags were carried towards the front door.

'Come along in,' said Simon, heartily. 'Oh, Fran don't let Beamish make a nuisance of himself.'

Silvia had drawn back from Beamish as if anticipating an attack. Frowning, Fran called him away and stroked him.

'Good boy, Beams,' she said, then followed the party indoors and busied herself making coffee, while Simon put a match to freshly laid logs.

'Is the heating on, Fran?' he called.

'Of course, but it's on a timer. I'll hasten it on a bit, if you like.'

'Good. We're not all as hardy as you.'

Minutes later Fran appeared in the kitchen doorway carrying a laden tray which Roger took from her.

'I'm sorry if you find it cold in here. It shouldn't take long to warm up.'

'No, not at all, it's fine,' said Roger. 'Really pleasant as it is. Such a lovely place.'

He then helped to serve the coffee to everyone. Martha stood by the French windows exclaiming over the view, while Silvia almost sat on the fire, shivering. Fran observed this with unsympathetic surprise. Surely a Scandinavian could withstand this degree of cold? Simon was all solicitousness, even offering her a rug for her knees that she, at least, declined.

Replenishing the coffee pot Fran found herself alone for a minute with Simon.

'If I'd known she was coming I'd have left the heating on all night,' she muttered.

'But you did know. I asked you to ring me if it was a problem.'

'We're not on the 'phone. It's being put in next week.'

'Quite. It's a ridiculous situation. I rang next door. Didn't you get a note? I can't believe that Fred wouldn't have left it if you were out.'

Fran stared at him for a second, then pulled out the brown envelopes she'd shoved between books and one fell to the floor. Grimly, Simon retrieved it, pulled out a slip of paper and read quietly: '*Okay, if Martha, Roger and a visitor come down for a night? Ring me if there's a problem. Love Simon*'. I dictated it to Fred yesterday so he wouldn't have to keep looking for you.'

'Oh God. I'm really sorry. I just picked it up with the bills and circulars. I was a bit preoccupied. Anyhow, they're here and I'll do my best for them.'

'So you've no food ready?'

'Not enough, but I can get something out of the freezer. I'll manage.'

'Good. You did invite them here, you know, to come whenever they like.'

'Did I? I can't remember doing so, but it's all right. I really like Martha and Roger.'

'You invited half the world at our Christmas party.'

'I must have had far too much to drink.'

'Speaking of which,' said Simon, 'that poor, freezing girl would like a snifter before lunch.'

By early afternoon on Sunday Fran was struggling. She had managed to produce an excellent casserole for lunch on Saturday then Roger had insisted on taking them all out to a pub dinner in Exford. Now, she was cleaning up after feeding everyone Spanish omelettes and homemade blackberry and apple pie. Earlier, they had walked in the Doone Valley (Silvia uncomfortably in borrowed, too-small boots) and they'd even had a short drive in the trap. Fran's only time alone with Simon had been overnight and she'd fallen asleep before he even joined her and woke up to find he was up and dressed. Despite all those hours of sleep she suddenly felt ready to drop.

Roger, drying up and even bothering to put things away, noticed she looked drained.

'You go and sit down, dear girl. You've done us proud. I'll make some coffee, or would you prefer tea?'

'Tea, please.' She gratefully did as he suggested.

'You all right?' asked Simon, putting a log on the fire which was still being monopolised by Silvia.

'No,' called Roger. 'She's tired, poor love. She's been looking after us all.'

Simon seemed taken aback. He perched on the arm of Fran's chair and stroked her hair.

'I'm sorry, darling. Are you sure you're feeling all right?'

'Yes, I'm fine. Just felt like sitting down.'

'I shall help Roger,' announced Silvia jumping up.

It was the first time she'd lifted a finger, Fran thought, and anyway, Roger had almost finished. Then she felt rather mean. After all the girl was a guest and a stranger. She'd been amusing in the pub last night and there was no doubt she was bright. Her knowledge of Nordic folk tales was prodigious and would be the subject of her proposed MA thesis. Fran wished she could stop hoping her post-graduate course would be anywhere but Exeter. She was being pathetic she told herself and put it down to feeling unusually weary and vulnerable.

But why had Simon not brought his own car? He'd be forced to travel back to Exeter with the rest of them or take her little car which he found cramped and uncomfortable.

Half-an-hour later Fran began to feel restless. Simon and Roger were talking together, Martha's eyes were closed and she seemed to be dozing, while Silvia was immersed in the travel section of the Observer. Discreetly, Fran left the room with Beamish at her heels. She let herself out of the front door into the courtyard and looked with sudden pleasure at the thread of warming sunlight bisecting a grey cloud. Soon the clocks would be altered and the lengthening

148

days would afford more painting hours. She felt compelled to inspect her recent work for a Somerset natural history project.

She looked critically at the row of illustrations pinned along one wall. They had kept her busy and away from Exeter longer than the regular three or four days. Beamish padded to the narrow window facing the lane and growled at a robin looking in.

'Be nice, Beams,' Fran told him. A step behind startled her. She turned, saw Simon in the doorway and, at once, looked away.

'Fran, darling, something's wrong. What is it?' He came up behind her wrapping his arms around her and rubbing his face against her hair. She leaned back and, overwhelmed with tiredness and disappointment, succumbed to the emotions she'd had been struggling against all day.

'Fran, you're crying. Whatever's the matter, darling? This isn't like you. Are you ill?'

Gently, he turned her to face him, brushing her damp hair away from her face.

'No. I'm not ill. I'm p -pregnant.'

He stared at her as if he had not understood, then his face dissolved into a smile that was a mixture of pleasure and incredulity.

'Darling, that's marvellous! But how did it happen?'

She began to laugh and cry together, then, at last, was able to gulp; 'It happened the usual way. I so wanted to be alone with you to tell you and not to have all these people around. I wanted it to be special.'

'It is special - very, very special.' He held her to him stroking her hair. 'I'm sorry, darling. I too wish we were alone. No wonder you're tired. It's been awful for you having us all descending.'

'No, it's not your fault. You tried to warn me. I haven't managed it very well. I wanted to tell you every minute since you arrived so it's been a strain.'

'I know. It would have been lovely to have been alone with you. Come back with me tonight. The car needed a couple of new tyres. I'm collecting it tonight. I can come back for you if you don't want to drive your car.'

She drew away a little, shaking her head. 'I can't, I've so much to catch up with.'

'Surely it can wait. Would you have been painting all weekend if we hadn't all turned up?'

'Yes. I've lost several days through not feeling too well.'

'But you're all right? You're not ill?'

'No. I'm fine, just a bit queasy at times. It's sometimes like this for the first few weeks.'

'Oh darling, that's horrible for you. Shouldn't you rest a lot?'

'No, I'm full of energy a lot of the time, even more than usual.'

'Did you suspect you were pregnant?'

'Not until I was really late and being sick. The doctor - really ancient and stuffy in Barnstaple, thinks it happened after Gerry's birthday party. D'you remember we all went to that fish restaurant, and I was sick in the early hours?'

'Vaguely. We all had a skinful that night.'

'Well, he said probably I vomited the pill and was unprotected for long enough.'

'My God, if that's what I can achieve when half cut what about when I'm in fine fettle?'

'Don't. You make it sound cheap.'

'Fran darling, I'm sure the earth didn't merely move but positively lurched, but can you remember? Come on, lighten up.'

She laughed then, and suddenly it seemed ridiculously superficial that she'd dreamed of conceiving her first child somewhere remote and beautiful on the moor. When and where she'd conceived was of no significance; she was carrying Simon's child. A tear trickled down her cheek. She wiped it away.

'My hormones,' she said. 'They do this, I'm told.'

She drew away from Simon and went across to the sink to bathe her eyes.

'Do I look awful?'

'No, beautiful. Here, use my handkerchief, it's cleaner than that towel.'

'Don't say anything to the others, Simon. I want it to be our secret for a while.'

'Of course, I won't. You decide when you're ready. I'll have to go back with them to collect my car but I'll return immediately. My first lecture tomorrow is after lunch.'

Chapter 13

Fran reflected that she'd hardly known a day of illness. She seldom caught a cold, had shrugged off the infections of childhood and coped with minor irritations and injuries with stoicism. Falling off ponies she had regarded as excellent training for the rigours of life. Now, however, she was dismayed to be struggling with occasional early morning sickness, sudden overwhelming tiredness and an itchy skin.

The doctor, who had confirmed her pregnancy, dismissed her problems as 'normal', so she said nothing about them to Simon. As far as he was concerned, one was well, or dead; anything in between was a bore. He could hardly bear to be away from Fran so they compromised, spending the weekdays together in Exeter and weekends at Spring Cottage. She coped with this arrangement because her current work did not demand long periods in her studio but she did not enjoy it. Had Simon not been so attentive, and as proud of their mutual fecundity as if no one else had ever achieved pregnancy, she would have sought any excuse to retreat to the moor.

Miranda visited them at Spring Cottage soon after she had the news. Her excitement at the prospect of being an 'honorary grandmother' had not abated.

'D'you think I'm too old to learn to knit?'

'You're not the knitting type,' Fran said, touched and amused.

'Is there a type? Cosy d'you mean? I know some very sophisticated knitters. Well, at least let me provide a christening gown.'

Both Simon and Fran laughed.

'You know we're agnostic, Miranda. Remember the discussions before our wedding?'

'Yes, Simon, but sometimes I think one should give a child a framework. Something to rebel against.'

'Not the ideal reason for having a child christened,' Fran murmured.

'You were, you know,' said Miranda, mildly reproving.

'Well, of course with a clergy grandfather and Mum's background: missionaries, magic and medicine. And wasn't there a clergy great-grandfather?'

Miranda smiled. 'One's upbringing dies hard.'

'You know you really do have a conventional streak,' Fran said. 'You are a strange mixture.'

'I just want to do something bit special.'

'You don't have to. It's enough that you're here for me - for us as always.'

Miranda looked moved, almost to tears. 'That's a lovely thing to say, darling.'

'There is something you could do,' Simon said, a note of steel in his voice. 'Persuade Fran to be sensible about the birth. She's refusing to make any plans.'

'I've months yet, Simon,' Fran said, sighing. 'Anyway, I haven't decided what to do.'

'There's nothing to decide, Fran. You can't do better than go to a teaching hospital a stone's throw from home. I think they, or G.P's, arrange visits to groups where you learn about coping with the birth...'

'You know about that?' Fran interrupted, laughing. 'Fathers go too you know.' At that she was sure Simon shuddered. 'I don't want to get involved with a hospital. What's wrong with a check-up with a local doctor? I know you think I'm being irresponsible, but I know I'm not. At least we're now on the phone.'

'I should hope so, in your condition.

'Condition! That's an awful term for pregnancy. For heaven's sake – it's natural.'

Miranda, in a gentle tone, interjected; 'Simon's concern strikes me as quite reasonable, darling.'

Fran glared; 'I am twenty-four, in excellent health and hardly in the middle of Antarctica. I think I'm capable of judging that it's safer to be here rather than in a polluted city. If I can have the baby here I shall. I want peace and quiet.'

'Sure, at my emotional expense. While you're living peacefully here, I'll be worried sick in Exeter.'

'For Heaven's sake, Simon, why d'you have to talk as if I were a pregnant Charlotte Brontë in the last stage of tuberculosis? You're being so Victorian.'

Miranda, whose loyalties were being challenged, stood up abruptly.

'Beamish could do with a walk. Anyone else coming?'

'Yes,' Simon said through clenched teeth. 'I probably need it more than Beamish.'

Fran watched them leave through the French windows. It had been warm and still all day and Beamish had been walked earlier and was in and out at will through the open door. He didn't really need a walk. Was it Miranda's ploy to get Simon away for a while? Would she seize the chance to reinforce Fran's viewpoint or sympathise with Simon's reasonable anxiety?

They returned after an hour laughing heartily over Miranda's estimation of the Baz Lurhmann production of Romeo and Juliet. Fran wondered if her difference of opinion with her husband had been relegated to the mundane and unimportant compared with Shakespeare!

*

A few days later, shopping in Exford, she bumped into a young woman who was reaching for a packet of flour on a high shelf. The pack landed in Fran's basket and both women began to apologise then dissolved into laughter.

'No, really it was entirely my fault,' Fran insisted. 'Oh good it hasn't split.'

She handed the flour to the pleasant looking girl, not much older than herself, and said, 'I'm sure I know you.'

'Yes, you're right. We do know each other but it's all of sixteen years ago - at primary school?'

Fran laughed in delight. 'Yes, that's it! I'm Fran - now please don't say I haven't changed a bit.'

'I won't. I promise. You're even prettier. I'm Jane Horder, formerly Sharman.'

'Jane Sharman. Your parents had the garage near North Molton, but I haven't seen them in years.'

'No, we moved to Hereford when I was thirteen.'

'So, what brought you back?'

'Work and marriage. D'you remember David Horder? The naughtiest boy in the school? I married him.'

'I vaguely remember, but I was small fry. You were big people. Weren't you a prefect or the equivalent in a primary school?'

'Yes. Bossy even then. I see you're married.'

Fran nodded. 'And pregnant.'

'Great. Midwifery's my job. Look, have you time for a coffee? We could go to the pub.'

'Yes, that would be lovely. Or better still, come back for lunch and meet Simon, my husband.'

'I can't I'm afraid. In an hour I have to visit a patient in Porlock. Let's snatch a few minutes together at least.'

Minutes later they sat opposite one another at a low table eagerly trying to close the sixteen plus gap. Fran found herself warming towards Jane more and more. She was funny and bright and totally down-to-earth.

'I wish I'd known you were in London doing your midwifery training,' she said. 'We could have got together then.'

'Were you living with your aunt? I remember being terrified of her, then liking her so much when she organised a picnic and got really dirty making a barbecue table from bits of rock.'

'I lived with her except when I was at university. She always allowed me space, and I had the cottage to come to. It's mine now.'

'So, we are really close neighbours. David went into the farm at Rockbourne with his father. My in-laws moved into a cottage and gave us the farmhouse when our daughter was born. Tricia's three, you must meet her.'

'I'd love to. I've no experience of small children. Sometimes I'm terrified at the prospect.'

'Aren't we all. Don't worry, the hormones do a wonderful job of preparing us. Where are you having the baby?'

'Don't know. I hope at Spring Cottage but Simon is anti and so is the local GP.'

'Not Ron Scully by any chance? He has a surgery in Barnstaple.'

'Yes.'

'Then forget a home birth. He's sound enough but really old fashioned. Why don't we get together for a proper talk? I often work with a woman doctor in Porlock, Sonia Wilson, plus several others, as I'm an independent midwife. It really is incredible that we should meet again just at this time.'

She rummaged in her bag and found a card.

'There you are. My 'phone number and details.' She glanced at her watch. 'Crikey, I must go.'

'But you're not in uniform.' Fran looked at Jane's casual sweatshirt and jeans.

'No, I only wear uniforms for deliveries. The mothers like informality, well most of them do. Must go, Fran. Sorry to rush off, but it's been lovely seeing you again.'

Fran followed her out to her car and waved her off, then walked to her own car with a surge of optimism. Surely Simon would take to this pretty, confident, yet laid-back professional?

He was standing in the yard looking both anxious and irritable. She got out of the car and was greeted effusively by Beamish.

'Sorry to be ages but I've had a lovely surprise. I met an old friend from years ago. After I had measles Miranda decided I needed country air so I spent a year at the local school. Jane, this friend, was there too, only at the top end, quite bossy but really nice. She was always looking after the little ones and the new people. She now lives at Rockbourne, married to a farmer, and she's a midwife!'

'Well, never mind that now. I'll bring in the shopping.'

'Oh no!' Fran gave a hoot of laughter. 'There isn't much. I completely forgot to finish it. No tea, coffee or bread.'

With a look of intense irritation, Simon got into her car, jerked the seat back and, revving excessively, jolted back the way she had come.

'Just don't wreck the suspension,' she called after him. 'All well, Beamish, at least you're glad to see me.'

*

Simon slung a towel around his neck, picked up his squash racket and preceded Gerry towards the bar.

'You're puffing. What's the matter with you? I nearly thrashed you.'

Simon grinned. 'Not my usual form, I agree.'

'Maybe you should have a check-up, laddie.'

'No, I'm all right. Just a bit on edge. Fran doesn't help with her ridiculous earth-mother ideas. I worry about her, Gerry.'

'Bound to.'

They ordered their drinks then moved to a table.

'She's dead set on a home birth,' Simon continued. 'Unfortunately, she's getting support from an old friend who's a midwife, and from a female doctor. Bloody, irresponsible fools, the pair of them. You'd think professional women would have more sense.'

Gerry, whose loyalties were uncomfortably stretched having listened at length to Fran's viewpoint, patiently allowed Simon to talk himself

158

out. He felt considerable, unreserved affection for them both; he recognised he could easily feel something more for Fran but to indulge those feelings was unacceptable. His light-hearted approach to life belied his strict personal code.

Simon stared moodily into his beer

'I wanted to feel close to Fran. I imagined we'd be capable of compromising but she's quite intractable. It's so irresponsible.'

'Hardly. Another viewpoint, another way of doing things, but a bit extreme to call it irresponsible. She wants this baby very much. She isn't going to take any silly chances.'

'Isn't it rather silly to chance a first confinement in a remote cottage? Remember, the baby's due in November and that's definitely winter on Exmoor. I'd stick to sheep if I were you, Gerry. I hardly think you're qualified to judge.'

'Sorry, laddie. I didn't intend to judge, just to suggest Fran's way is medically acceptable; not against the law.' He shrugged, drying up under the hostility of Simon's gaze. He picked up their glasses and went to the bar, then called, 'Same again?'

Simon nodded. 'Got any aspirins, or something similar?' he asked when Gerry returned with brimming glasses.

'Yes. I think so.' He rummaged in the pocket of his ancient dried-up Barbour then put a small plastic pot on the table. 'There, not sure if they go with alcohol.'

Simon swallowed two tablets with a large gulp of beer.

'Thanks. Bit of a headache.'

'Where's Fran now? In London? She was telling me she's finished the American project and is about to start illustrating a children's book for a new publisher.'

Simon, grimacing, drank more beer before replying. 'She's at Spring Cottage. When she's not working in the studio, she's digging the garden or creosoting the stable.'

Gerry grinned. 'Still, it shows she's well.'

'Oh, she's well all right. So well she thinks she's invincible.'

Some of Simon's anxiety was assuaged when he met the middle-aged woman doctor, Sonia Wilson, who, with Jane, was going to look after Fran. Sensibly, Fran was absent, shopping with Norah so Simon felt he could express his fears unreservedly. He made clear his disapproval of the home birth plan but was now prepared to listen to Sonia's reasons for accepting Fran as a client, her preferred term for a patient. Surprisingly, the atmosphere was fairly relaxed, probably because Sonia had listened to his comments without once interrupting. Sitting opposite him, holding a mug of coffee that he'd made for her, she began, 'Your wife is young, in excellent health, and an ideal weight for her height, and she has the right attitude.'

'Aren't there more risks with a first birth?'

'I believe it was once thought so but, with modern technology almost all problems are discovered long before labour starts. By around twelve weeks the vital organs are forming in the foetus and then it's progress all the way.'

'I'm asking you about the mother's safety?' Simon's tone was clipped.

'We monitor our clients regularly, checking on weight, energy and all forms of discomfort – much of which is normal but we need to be sure.' Sonia paused to drink more coffee. Beamish, who had been lying at Simon's feet, got up and walked across to her, wagging his tail. She was grinning as she fondled his head. Registering that he approved, Simon thought: just the sort of daft idea Fran would have.

'The baby's position in the uterus before the birth is really important and of course the mother's blood pressure and...'

Interrupting, Simon said, 'A while back you said "Almost all problems", so what can't be diagnosed - in advance?'

'Very rarely there is a haemorrhage.'

'So you keep the odd pint of blood with you?' Simon's tone was as sarcastic as his words.

Now she addressed him formally, for the first time. 'Dr Fellowes, we have a wonderful emergency service and in the eight years I've been doing home deliveries I've had to call it once. If there is any doubt we seek immediate help. If I have any concerns about your wife I'll advise her against a home birth, I promise.'

'But why is a home birth so important to her? It seems ridiculous when everything is ready in a hospital, and all help is instantly on hand.'

'We've talked about all eventualities and she is still keen because she sees birth as a natural process, not a medical one. If she changes her mind I shall respect that.'

'And if she doesn't will you be present at the birth or will it just be Jane?'

'Midwives are highly trained specialists. I do all the check-ups during pregnancy and if I am as sure as possible that all is well the midwife attends the delivery.'

'For all you've told me, thank you, but I still want her to have a normal delivery in a hospital.'

'I understand, but I have to respect your wife's wishes. She's young but an intelligent adult who has thought a lot about this.'

'Are you sure it's not Jane selling her the idea?'

'Certainly not. She goes through all the pros and cons with patients as I do. She's a true professional.'

At that moment Fran appeared after dumping bags of shopping on the kitchen table.

'Oh good you're still here. I hope you've talked Simon round.'

'I've told him about unlikely problems. Luckily, you are a very healthy young lady and we'll be keeping a close eye on you throughout. Oh, I expect Jane's told you all about the antenatal classes. I'm sure going to those would be really helpful.' Sonia's words were now directed at Simon. 'Fathers find them a great help, too.'

His expression of disgust caused Fran to quickly offer more coffee but Sonia glanced at her watch.

'Thanks, Fran, but I'd better be off. Give me a call any time.'

Simon stood up, politely shaking her hand and thanking her for her time.

Fran accompanied her to her car and returned feeling slightly worried. 'Give him time to think about it,' Sonia had said, 'and I hope he'll accompany you to the classes.' Had Simon convinced Sonia that it would be too risky to take her on as a client? He might have

162

seemed the type who'd instantly seek litigation if anything went wrong.

Before returning to the sitting room she made more coffee. Placing the pot on the table she sat on the sofa, next to Simon, who ruffled her hair and kissed her cheek.

'Simon, why was Sonia's suggestion about going to ante natal classes so awful for you?'

He smiled. 'You are beautiful but the average pregnant woman looks like a beached whale or some kind of gargoyle. I couldn't take a roomful of them.'

'For heaven's sake why d'you reduce everything to the physical? Maybe you make me feel like a gargoyle.'

'Rubbish, darling, you still look beautiful to me.'

'What the hell have looks to do with it? Is that all you see? Suppose I got injured and became ugly to you?'

'Don't be childish.'

'No, I'm not being childish, I'm sure if I lost my looks you'd go off me.'

'Pot of my jam for you, darlin',' called Norah, from the open back door. 'I forgot to give it to you earlier.' Her arrival afforded relief for them both.

*

Nothing Fran could say persuaded Simon to accompany her to the anti-natal classes. For Fran's convenience Jane found some in Exeter with a weekday or weekend option. She attended alone on Wednesday afternoons and immediately made friends with a plump Cockney girl, Milly, who was given to giggling at inappropriate moments.

'Your bloke's not 'ere then?' she asked at the first session.

'No.' Fran grinned, thinking how out-of-place he'd be with the bearded and sandalled brigade present.

'Nor's mine. Works on oil rigs so good excuse.'

'For him or you?'

'Him. Thinks we all look like lump fish.'

This set them off, although giggling flat on one's back was not easy. Gently they were chided by the instructor whose face knotted with her intense desire to get everyone to relax.

'We'll be sent to the Head next,' muttered Milly.

Had it not been for her Fran probably would not have completed the course. She found too many of the women irritating, feeding one another's anxieties and competing for the best-equipped nursery.

'Every time they see something for babies on the telly they 'ave to 'ave it,' said Milly, who refused to be seduced despite the considerable earnings her husband received.

*

'You aren't too worried about Simon not going to the classes?' Jane asked, leading Chuckle into his stable after giving Tricia a ride on him.

'Sometimes. No not really. Would the other women be able to concentrate?'

Jane laughed. She liked Simon. Once his suspicion of her lessened it was impossible not to but she was not entirely comfortable with him. His extraordinary attractiveness was disconcerting.

'He's very pleased about the baby,' she told Fran. 'He asks me loads of questions when you're not in

164

hearing. I think he's the type to regard it a bit effeminate to reveal much interest.'

'Well, he says he's going to be at the birth,' Fran said, complacently. 'And he keeps discussing names - all boys I'm afraid.'

'Ah well, all ties up doesn't it,' said Jane. 'I'm not taken in by these macho types. They're soft as butter really. David still hates seeing the sheep go off to the abattoir and yet farming is bred in his bones.'

'Simon did say he thought Tricia was sweet,' said Fran, 'but who wouldn't?'

She took the child's proffered hand. 'Shall we go indoors now we've put Chuckle away and find something nice to eat?'

Tricia beamed her approval, said goodbye to Chuckle then hurried to the door, only preceded by Beamish.

Chapter 14

A young man walking with a rucksack on his back, wondered if gypsies had arrived on the moor. Sunlight caught the high gloss of a trap's sides as it moved along the lane below, pulled by a small pony. Interested, he quickened his pace towards a stile in the hedge. As he reached it the trap drew level with him. It was driven by young girl, her head partly covered by the slipping hood of a blue cloak. Her gaze was firmly ahead, so, unseen he stared, mesmerised by her beauty. This was no gypsy girl driving an Exmoor pony in gleaming harness, attached to a black and yellow-lined lacquered trap. She drove past and disappeared round a bend in the lane. The young man jumped lightly over the stile and headed uphill, once or twice looking back.

Fran drove her pony cautiously, pleased that the high wind was swiftly drying the wet lane and relieved it did not disturb Chuckle one jot. She had known ponies to react skittishly in the wind, but he was unfazed even when the thorn tree moaned as if tormented.

She enjoyed driving in autumn and even in winter; hardly a tourist's car was seen on the moor and, undisturbed she could relish its stark beauty. This morning the sky was brilliant with sunlight and the clouds scudded along too fast to be threatening. In the coombe below spirals of smoke arose from two chimneys, hers and the Yeo's. Beamish leaned against her, shivering; he did not appreciate the strong wind.

In the courtyard, Jane was sitting in her car. She jumped out. 'You look well, Fran. Everything else seems to shrivel on the moor except you.'

Fran laughed, got out of the trap and hugged Jane. 'Have I kept you? I'm so sorry. Only it was so exhilarating and beautiful on the moor.'

'No, I was early. I've loads of things in the car to show you. All the equipment we'll need. It's supposed to reduce your anxiety if you become acquainted with it beforehand.'

Fran laughed. 'What anxiety? How sweet. Will you go ahead and put the kettle on?'

'Yes, but only after I've helped you unharness Chuckle.'

'Jane, you know the trap's as light as a feather.'

'But you're not!'

Together they put pony and trap away then, luxuriating in the glow of a log fire, Fran allowed Jane to make the tea, then to take her blood pressure.

'Ah, tea and a blood pressure test. What more could a girl want?'

'Excellent,' pronounced Jane taking a reading. 'I'll listen to your tum when you've had your tea. You look wonderful. How can Simon stay away?'

Fran looked slightly guilty. 'I'm the one staying away. I don't want to be in Exeter so poor Simon has no choice. He's here from Friday until Monday. We've switched over now the ante classes have finished but this week I'm here to sort things.'

'Heaven's,' said Jane, grinning broadly. 'You know I think he's the most dishy man I've ever seen. Maybe a honeymoon at the weekend will make the absence worthwhile.'

But their times together were not quite as Jane envisaged. Her words reminded Fran of how her sexual desire had lessened over the past weeks. Around the fifth month she'd considered her nude reflection in a long mirror and decided she must be about as attractive to Simon as an Easter Island statue. She began to dress and undress in the bathroom and wear ankle length nightgowns in bed.

Laughing, when he first saw her so attired, Simon had slipped the straps down her shoulders, marvelling at her taut, enlarged breasts, but Fran covered his hands with hers.

'No, please don't '

'What's the matter?'

'I just don't want you to look at me.'

'Fran, you're being silly; this isn't like you. You're beautiful. More beautiful than ever as there's more of you.'

He gently but firmly pushed her hands away and eased the nightgown over her abdomen. She closed her eyes.

Later, after he had made love to her as gently and skilfully as he knew how, she turned her face into the pillow and wished she could sleep alone for the next four months.

Jane was the easiest person to talk to, and Fran was sure her professionalism and decency meant she would not reveal confidential information, so she told her how her sexual feelings had changed and wondered how Simon was coping.

'It's very common,' Jane said, not even looking surprised. 'Your hormones are concentrating on making the baby, not trying to conceive one. You'll change again once the baby's born, but it might take a little time.'

'I'm not alone, then, that's a relief.' Fran nudged a log into the centre of the fire and topped up their mugs. 'I suppose this time is quite hard for some men.'

'It can be. Quite a number have told me how excluded they feel and it can be worse after the baby is born. Simon would never talk about it, would he?'

'No. He'd be appalled to know I've said any of this.'

'Don't worry. This is between us. I'm glad you've told me as it shows you think about the feelings of both of you.'

*

The high wind persisted for days as did the sunshine. Fran was invigorated. When she painted she found she had to sit down but her capacity for work was undiminished. She was in her studio from early morning until lunchtime unless a whim, or Beamish's demands, took her out on the moor.

One morning the high wind slammed the studio door shut with the key on the outside. Beamish, in the yard, barked his concern. Fran laughed and tried to open the door. It was jammed fast. She leaned against it, pushing as hard as she could but it moved not a fraction. An iron bar, dating from a time when precious glass was first inserted, bisected the tiny window that looked onto the lane. No way could she climb out even if there was not a drop of around nine feet. She considered her situation. Eventually Fred or Norah would come to see her. Unobtrusively, they called every day, keeping an eye on her. She settled down to work and nearly two hours passed before Beamish's barking told her that the postman had been and gone.

How silly to miss him. She made herself a cup of coffee. She always kept tea, coffee, milk and biscuits by the sink. She would not starve or thirst to death but a bit awkward if she needed the loo. She stood looking into the lane, drinking and wondering if the Yeo's had gone to market, then she noticed a movement on the hill opposite. It was a figure, a man perhaps, walking rapidly downwards, pulled by the force of gravity and blown by the wind.

The wind would not carry her voice but nevertheless, she opened the window and yelled as loudly as she could. He gave no sign that he'd heard her. She waved a white paint-stained cloth, letting the wind catch it like a pennant. Perhaps she should scrawl something on it in paint and let it go like a balloon!

The figure was coming nearer. She could now see it was a man. Suddenly he stopped. He seemed to be staring in her direction. Frantically she called, `Help' and waved the cloth. again. He came on and into the lee of the hedge, waving just before he disappeared from view.

Oh God, she thought, does he understand? Perhaps he's escaped from somewhere – Dartmoor Jail? Maybe a multiple rapist! Seconds later he appeared in the lane. He carried a rucksack and had field glasses slung around his neck. Reassured she decided at worst he'd be a twitcher. He looked up at her quizzically.

'Hi. Are you in trouble?' His accent was vaguely American. He had a nice smile. He certainly didn't look like a criminal.

'Are you in trouble?' he repeated.

She laughed her relief. 'I'm locked in here.'

'Good Heavens! The Lady of Shallot, Mariana in the Moated Grange, Rapunzil?'

Oh, better and better! Confidently she called, 'The door slammed with the key outside. If you go into the courtyard you'll see stone steps on the left. The door's at the top. Don't worry about the dog. He's called Beamish and if you talk to him he'll be reassured.'

'Oh, that's a relief.' He laughed.

A few seconds passed then Beamish barked. He stopped almost at once and Fran heard the man talking to him outside the door. She walked over to it.

'There's no key,' he called, pulling the handle. 'Not that it would help. It's jammed.'

'And I'm sorry but I can't help,' said Fran.

'Don't even try. Look, could you get through the window? It's only a short drop. If I can't find a ladder you could probably reach my shoulders.'

She began to laugh.

'Are you all right in there?'

'Yes, just getting hysterical. You see I can't possibly get out of that window and not even the long one overlooking the field. I'm very pregnant.'

'Oh no! You're not about to have it, are you?'

'No, not unless I laugh too much. Oh gosh, what shall we do?'

'Don't worry. There's a house a little way along the lane, isn't there? Might there be someone there who could help?'

'I'm pretty sure they're at the market in Barnstaple today. You could let yourself into my cottage and ring the Fire Brigade.'

'Lord, you're not on fire as well, are you?'

171

Fran was almost crying with laughter. 'No,' she gasped. 'They also rescue people.' Now she felt a bit wobbly.

'Hullo, old boy, what are you scrabbling at?'

There was a pause, then a burst of laughter.

'Your dog has just found the key but it won't be the answer. Strength's what needed,' the man called. 'Hope I've got it.' He had. After a few minutes of lots of hefty pulling the door budged, then Beamish barged in hurling himself at Fran who crumpled and sat down – luckily on a nearby stool. The young man followed, extending a hand.

'Hi. Rudolph Wilson, from Philadelphia, at your service.'

Fran grinned, took hold of the proffered hand and pulled herself up, feeling clumsy.

'Frances. Fran Fellowes. Thank goodness for strong men. You're obviously Sir Galahad'

He laughed. 'Great. I've never been called that before. I'm known as Rudi. I'm glad you didn't try the window. You might then have needed the Fire Brigade. I've seen you before – three, four days ago? Driving a pony and trap.'

'Yes, I go out most days.'

'What an unusual girl, and you're a painter.' He was looking around the studio. 'Wow, almost all wildlife. Are you a freelance artist?'

'Yes, but I also work a lot on commissions. Wildlife book illustrations, pamphlets, advertising stuff - that kind of thing. Now, would you like a drink? We'll go across to the cottage.'

Rudi smiled, nodding. 'Sure you're okay?'

'Yes. I'm only pregnant. I hope you're all right after all that pulling of the door. Come on Beamish. Can't risk you getting shut in.'

'If you've the right tool I could work on the door for you. It's badly swollen so could happen again.'

Swollen like me, thought Fran, nearly giggling. 'That's so kind Rudi but my neighbour will help. I won't let it happen again.'

As Fran walked down the steps Rudi put a hand on her arm, protectively.

'Thanks.' She smiled and led the way into the cottage. She insisted he should relax in the sitting-room while she made the coffee. From the kitchen she observed he was a couple of inches shorter than Simon, well-built, muscular but not stocky. He'd flung off his anorak and was wearing jeans and a sweatshirt. Obviously not one to feel the cold. He was nice-looking with lots of springy brown hair (complimented by brown eyes) and a lovely smile that showed excellent teeth.

Fran carried the tray into the room and put it on the table. Over the next hour she learnt that Rudi was half English. His mother had married an American air force officer and he'd been brought up in the States but had family in England; grandparents in Gloucestershire, an aunt and uncle in Oxford and two cousins.

'I've spent lots of holidays over here and that's how I fell for the West Country,' he said. 'The climate suits me, the gentle pace, and I like the English. I've travelled in the Far East quite a bit; nearly expired in Borneo after getting a snake bite and after several really hairy expeditions I opted for something softer. I'm nearly at the end of a PhD. My subject is botany and, particularly, conservation. I'm hoping to find work over here eventually.'

'It sounds as if you lead a really interesting life. '

'I think so but my dad doesn't. He wanted me to join the Air Force like him. Luckily my young brother seems interested and Dad thoroughly approves of my sister who's married an army captain after training as a lawyer. Now, how do you come to be in this lovely place?'

He listened without interrupting as Fran described her situation. Beamish lay at his feet, now and then sitting for a minute, staring at him. Both of them found this amusing.

'And you've that Exmoor pony,' Rudi commented. 'I love seeing the herds on the moor. And what an interesting breed – one of the oldest known.'

The grandfather clock in the hall chimed the half hour. Fran looked at her watch.

'It's two-thirty. I think we could do with some late lunch,' she suggested. 'Will you stay?'

'I don't think I should impose and...' Rudi began but Fran firmly interrupted.

'You rescued me – it's the least I can do. Please. Something simple such as eggs on toast, tomatoes, sausages?'

He smiled. 'Lovely. Okay – as you insist. But give me a job or two. I know there are two of you but one isn't quite ready.'

Fran laughed. 'About seven weeks away.'

'Where will you have the baby?'

'Here, I hope. It's all arranged.'

'Good job you're not in America. Home births aren't approved of. Now, give me a few instructions. Cutlery drawer?'

A relaxing time was spent over lunch during which anecdotes were exchanged about their student days, travels, careers and families. How good to meet a complete stranger with whom one could feel so a at ease Fran was thinking as they returned to the sitting-room. Minutes later a voice called from the back door that led into the kitchen.

'All right m'darlin'?'

'Fred, come in. Everything's fine, I hope. Is Norah with you?'

'She is. We been at the market all morning.'

Fred and Norah entered the sitting-room then stopped abruptly.

'It's our American conservationist chap,' exclaimed Fred. 'Met you on the moor a few times.'

Rudi stood up and exchanged hugs with Fred and Norah.

'Now, please be seated everyone. I've an interesting story to tell you,' said Fran.

The laughter that followed the account of her rescue caused Beamish to give a couple of irritated barks.

'I'll sort that old door out,' said Fred. 'All wrong. Pulling it outwards and you could be knocked off the steps. Can't rely on you always passing by, young man. You deserve a medal. Fran's hubby'll think you're a saint.'

Or I'm eligible to be locked in an asylum, thought Fran and disappeared to make tea for everyone.

After drinking two mugs of tea and eating a piece of Norah's delicious sponge cake, Rudi glanced at his watch and said he'd better be getting on his way.

'Yeah, America's quite a journey,' said Fred.

'Where are you staying?' Fran asked.

'I've lodgings in Lynton, just for a few days, then home, but I'm back and forth quite a bit. Thanks so much, Fran, and good to meet you all.'

He put on his jacket and picked up his rucksack.

'I can give you a lift,' said Fran. 'It'll be dark soon.'

'Trap or car?' Rudi laughed. 'Thanks, but I'll be fine walking.'

'Distance is nothing to him,' said Fred, then he and Norah insisted on washing up while Fran walked to the lane with Rudi.

'Thanks Fran, that was good fun. How can you let me know when you're locked in again?'

Fran laughed. 'Just call in when you're in the area. You must meet Simon. He'd love to chat about America with you.'

'Ah, the university professor.'

'No, senior lecturer. I'm afraid it's Dead Men's Shoes in this country.'

'So I've heard but I'd still love to work here. Thanks again, Fran.'

'No, the thanks are for you, from two of us.' She tapped her abdomen.

Laughing, he walked away, twice turning to wave. Beamish rubbed his head against Fran's leg then looked up at her, expectantly.

'Yes, he was nice,' Fran said, 'but I suppose you now want your supper and I'd better ring the master.'

Chapter 15

Fran felt curiously light. She walked with ease in spite of the buffeting winds that swept the moor relentlessly in November. She marvelled at the colour of the landscape, yellow, purple, brown, grey, and at the wonderful intricate shapes of leafless trees. There was a purity about this season, nothing wasteful or extravagant, everything stripped to the basic essentials. Even sunshine was a luxury.

'Norah's expecting you. You'm bonny, my maid,' called Fred from the cab of his tractor, and Fran laughed and waved.

She headed for the warm kitchen where she knew a lardy cake and fresh coffee awaited her. Since her neighbours learnt of her imprisonment, they had made doubly sure they saw her every day. Knowing this, Simon was reassured but still complained at her refusal to live in Exeter.

'You need to be near people,' he said, in an authoritarian tone.

'I am near people,' she replied, struggling to be patient. 'I couldn't be near better people than the Yeos. They've pulled enough calves and lambs in their time. I'm sure they'd cope with a baby.'

But Simon was not amused. 'You're being ridiculous.'

'No. It happens the same way, you know.'

He had slammed his way out of the cottage not even bothering to call Beamish who leaned against the door ostentatiously reproachful.

*

In the second week of November strong winds arrived. Now it was hard for Fran to walk upright against their force. Simon rang her twice daily.

'I'm not due for at least another week,' she grumbled to Jane. 'He's being neurotic.'

'Count yourself lucky,' Jane chuckled. 'He's neither indifferent, nor is he underfoot. Now let's have a listen.' A few minutes later she announced all was well. 'You are prepared for this weather continuing, aren't you? You've lived on the moor long enough so, maybe, I'm being a bit over-anxious, but the forecast is awful.'

'I've enough food and fuel for weeks,' Fran said, amused. 'The house withstood the last great gales; not a tile came off the roof. All that matters is that you can reach me.'

'Don't worry, I'll ride over on a borrowed horse, if necessary,' Jane said, and Fran knew she meant it.

After she left, Fran worked in the studio until the light faded. In the last hour she shifted frequently trying to relieve her aching back.

'I'm tired of you, bump, in your present form,' she told her abdomen, and Beamish growled gently, looking around for another person.

The wind was howling around the buildings and Fran was pleased to return to the warmth and security of the cottage, having battled her way across the courtyard.

'No proper walk tonight,' she told Beamish, throwing logs on the fire. She found some old, ready-trimmed, oil lamps in the under stairs cupboard and placed one in each room she used, with a box of matches alongside. Loss of electricity during bad weather was a regular occurrence on the moor.

At ten she went to bed, tired to the bone. She talked to Simon on the bedroom extension, making light of the weather conditions.

She turned out the light a few minutes later, too shattered to read, but she could not get comfortable. She heard every hour strike on the sitting-room clock. Twice she made tea and four times went to the lavatory. Beamish followed her like a shadow, muzzle pressed against the back of her knees whenever possible. She felt well so had no anxiety, but the restlessness was new and strange. At six she let Beamish out, and Fred hailed her from the courtyard.

'You all right, Fran? We seen your lights on.'

'Fine thanks, Fred, just couldn't sleep. Is this going to blow over d'you think?'

'No, we'm in for days of it. Lucky the 'lectrics still on and the 'phone. You let us know if you'm in trouble. Tell you what, we'll see to Chuckle. Shall my missus come over d'rectly?'

'Thanks Fred. I'm fine, really I am. Just a bit tired so I might try to get more sleep.'

She ate a small breakfast in front of the fire. As she anticipated Simon rang at eight o'clock. He'd heard the forecast was bad and he was fussing. She tried to reassure him. In the last hour the wind had dropped a little and there was a patch of blue in the sky. Slightly more cheerful he rang off promising to be home before dark on Friday.

She fell asleep on the sofa and awoke two hours later, stiff and uncomfortable. She got up unsteadily, stretching and yawning, then went upstairs to run a bath. In the bedroom she bent to take clean clothes from a low drawer. As she straightened up, clumsily, she felt a strange tightening across her tummy. She backed to the bed and sank down. The room was uncannily light, everything in it was in sharp relief. She spoke to Beamish and her voice sounded distant. The tightening subsided and she lay against the pillows. Beamish whined and put a paw on her arm. The tightening came again and ran into her groin, and after experiencing this half a dozen times she rang Jane.

'Could be Braxten-Hicks contractions,' was her cheerful response. 'I'll be over very soon. Just try to relax – read or listen to music.'

*

The meeting with the Deputy Vice Principal and the Dean was informal, as casual as dropping in for a cup of coffee with colleagues. Simon sensed that he was about to be asked a personal favour. He could not have guessed it would amount to no more than being himself, as charmingly and seductively as he knew how, with groups of foreign academics in their far-flung countries.

'Of course we understand your wife is expecting her first child, so this may not be the best time to broach the subject but we don't envisage your starting until the Spring. Think about it, Simon, particularly the philosophy behind the idea.'

More like hard economics thought Simon: trawling India and the Far East for students could hardly be couched in philosophical terms, but he smiled thoughtfully at the Dean who continued,

'Of course, our plans mustn't interfere with your departmental duties. Professor Crawford wouldn't tolerate that. No, we see this as a few days overseas in each vacation.'

'Sir, I'm a little hesitant due to being so new here. I'm not sure I'm the best qualified.'

'Oh, not at all. You'll absorb all the necessary information in no time. We want someone who can put it over well and convincingly and we think you've the right manner. You have varied experience, a post in the USA, working in a more cosmopolitan atmosphere - Manchester being very different from here and you're doing the job well. We're not keen on professional public relations types. They don't always hit the right note. Diplomacy is everything, as is commitment to one's job.'

Simon's face became serious with agreement. He wondered how soon after her confinement Fran would be able to travel. There would be no objection to her accompanying him he had been assured. Of course, it would not be a holiday for him, but he'd hardly be working night and day. He'd be properly remunerated on top of his expenses. Not unreasonably, extra allowances would not be paid if Fran accompanied him. The interview ended with a mild homily about the need to uphold the high moral and academic tone of the University. The ambassadorial role entrusted to Simon would carry that reputation into the international market place. Simon managed to suppress a grin until safely outside the Vice Principal's door. He glanced at his watch; three hours of teaching and a tutorial ahead. He'd try to snatch a few minutes to ring Fran. From his office window he noticed how dark the sky had become and

181

heard the wind soughing around the building. His secretary handed him letters to sign. Her eyes were red-rimmed and puffy and her voice sounded odd.

'You all right, Shirley?'

'No, I've a rotten cold coming on. Shouldn't have come in really but there was a lot to do.'

'Nothing that couldn't wait or be done by one of the others. You look really unwell. Go home now and look after yourself.'

She looked at him with such relief and gratitude he felt quite touched.

'There you are.' He helped her into her coat. 'Not far to go, have you?'

'No, ten minutes' walk. Just as well. The weather's getting worse.'

He saw her out, telling her to rest and not hurry back, then searched for his lecture notes which she seemed to have tidied away. He opened a couple of drawers and found them, then reached for the telephone. Fran was very much on his mind. A tap on the door diverted him.

'Damn. Just a moment,' he called, dialling Spring Cottage. The line was engaged. He swore again, collected his notes and a couple of books then opened the door. A young woman stood outside, hand raised about to knock again.

'Have you an appointment? My students are waiting for me.'

The girl looked disconcerted. She was attractive, he noticed.

'Sorry, if you're busy. I'm a friend of Caroline and Tom. I've been a colleague of theirs for two years, in Nairobi.' She turned as if to walk away.

'No, hang on. I'm sorry if I was a bit short. I'm Simon Fellowes..'

She turned, smiled and shook his proffered hand. 'I know. You're exactly as Caro described you. I'm Eloise Rayner, temporary lecturer in biology. I've only just arrived.'

'Ah yes, the lecturer's off sick. Well, this is great.'

'But not a good time for you. Only I was passing your door.'

Unlikely, he thought, but said, 'I'm delighted - really, but I am in a rush now. Are you free later? We could have a drink perhaps?'

*

Jane completed her examination, grinning broadly.

'Not Braxton-Hicks, Fran, the real thing. It could wear off as you're a bit early so don't get too excited. I'll ring Sonia to keep her in the picture.'

'Right,' Fran was beaming. 'When you've finished I'll ring Simon.'

As Jane pressed the numbers she cautioned Fran not to send him into a panic. She spoke briefly to Sonia then handed the receiver over. After a full minute, Fran said,

'No reply. I expect he's teaching. Shirley must be out too. I don't really want to leave a message for him as that would be too impersonal. Was Sonia happy about me? She's not going to change her mind because I'm early?'

'About the home delivery? No, not at all. She agrees it could come to nothing this time. Now, I'll just go to the bathroom.'

'And I'll put the kettle on. Okay if I get up?'

'Yes, of course, but go carefully.'

Beamish padded downstairs after Fran and leaned against her as she made the coffee.

'Would you like a sandwich and a coffee?' she called, hearing Jane coming downstairs.

'Just a coffee please. I've got to visit a couple near Blackmore Gate and talk to them about home deliveries.' She appeared in the kitchen tying on her head scarf. 'If I was at all worried about you I'd postpone them. I'll come back once they've been seen. Is it okay if I tell Mrs Yeo that something may be happening?'

'Not just yet. I can ring her if I feel anxious, or if there's any change.'

'Right.'

Ten minutes later, as Jane got into her car, Norah was approaching.

'I saw your car, Jane and wondered if anything was wrong seeing you were only here yesterday.'

'It's all right, Norah,' Fran called from the hallway. 'I'm just having slight pains. well, not even pains really, just tight feelings.'

'I'm doing a home visit then coming back,' Jane said hastily, sensing Norah's concern that she was leaving.

'Don't you worry,' Norah said, now looking excited. 'I've been an unofficial midwife a few times. You drive carefully, Jane. It's fairly quiet now but Fred's sure the wind's going to rise directly. He's busy servicing the generator just to be on the safe side.'

'Come and have some coffee,' Fran suggested.

'Lovely, but I'm also going to make myself useful. I expect the Rayburn needs attention.'

Once Norah was happily occupied Fran retreated to her bedroom to relish a brief time alone. She closed her eyes and tried to visualise her baby as she had many times before. Beyond it being dark-haired and swarthy she did not progress. She had never wanted to know its sex, having no strong preference, but now she had a sudden conviction that she was carrying a boy.

Only fleetingly in the past months had she wondered how she would cope as a mother. She had no experience of babies or even young children but supposed it was not too different from rearing a puppy. After all, it would have similar needs. Most of the women at the anti-natal class had expressed anxieties which did not seem to be alleviated by the numbers of magazine articles and booklets they read. They discussed feeding schedules and diets and disposable nappies endlessly until Fran wondered how much more mileage could be had from these gripping topics.

'Does it have to be so complicated?' she had asked Jane who responded in her comfortable, confident way that reinforced Fran's own uncluttered views.

'Forget brand names, or better still, never learn them. Remember we all need good food so that means fresh, not bottled or tinned. Babies are meant to drink human milk until they've enough teeth to cope with something a bit more demanding, and that's months away. As for nappies, if you can afford to spend a fortune polluting the environment that's up to you. I found three dozen Terry squares, a lidded bucket and bottles of Milton far more satisfactory.'

'Jane, you're wonderful. How many midwives take your view?'

'How many expectant mothers take yours, Fran? I think we're quite a team.'

In a few hours motherhood would be a reality and, in a sense, she'd never be alone again. She'd still be biologically part of another human being with its own unique personality and separate will.

'Are you all right, my lamb?' Norah's soft Devon voice interrupted her thoughts. 'I've brought you a nice cup of tea. Wind's got up again and it's raining cats and dogs.'

Fran sat up and glanced at her watch.

'Heavens, I've been up here over an hour. Thanks, Norah, that's very welcome. Is Jane back?'

'Any minute I should think,' said Norah with more conviction than she felt.

The wind tore against the sides of Jane's car and she had to wrench the steering wheel to keep it in the centre of the road. Rain slashed suddenly and wholeheartedly onto her windscreen. She braked gently and turned the windscreen wipers on full, but they could not deal adequately with the volume of water. A flying branch hit the bonnet then caught on the roof rack.

Oh God! Where am I? she thought, then she realised she was at the start of Fran's lane. As the car bumped down the track she was afraid it would soon be off the ground.

Norah was waiting inside the hall pink with excitement.

'She's had several strong contractions. Poor lamb, she's left messages all over the place for Simon. There's been no word from him.'

'When was the last contraction?'

'Oh, ten minutes ago perhaps. Let me take your wet things. I'll hang them in front of the Rayburn. Fran's in the sitting-room. I'll make you a cup of tea.'

Jane joined Fran on the sofa in front of a huge, welcoming fire. Beamish thumped his tail but did not move. Fran fondled his head.

'He won't move an inch away from me.'

'So, what's been happening?'

'Quite a lot. Real contractions, gosh, there's one starting now.'

'Let me put my hands on your tummy, very gently. Yes, here it comes.'

Fran took deep breaths until it passed.

'Good girl. I think this could be it. We'll go up to your bedroom when you're ready and I'll examine you. Ah tea, thanks, Norah.'

Some fifteen minutes later Jane pronounced that the baby was doing fine.

'How long will it be,' Fran hugged her, close to tears with excitement.

'Can't be specific. You're not fully dilated so it could be a while.'

'Can I get up again?'

'Yes, walk about a bit if you feel like it and you can take any position you like to cope with the contractions. Keep drinking and don't put off going to the loo. Now, I'll ring Sophie and let her know the stage you're at.'

Fran was becoming fretful that she had not heard from Simon. She had even left a message on Gerry's answer phone. Maybe they were out together? The wind was howling loudly and, discreetly, Jane switched on the radio in the kitchen to get a local update on the forecast. Trees were being uprooted within a twenty-mile radius and several telephone lines were down. Jane checked the line downstairs and there was no tone. Fervently, she hoped Simon was not hurtling across the moor in a state of anxiety. As she turned to leave the kitchen Fred appeared at the back door water dripping from his oilskins.

'The generator's all set up. Should the 'lectric go I'll bring a heavy cable across as you'll need plenty of light.'

Jane thanked him warmly. She did not dampen his enthusiasm by telling him Fran only wanted candlelight in her bedroom.

Beamish was being a problem. Shut out of Fran's bedroom he paced the landing hearing every sound she made, and whimpering when she had a hard, long contraction.

'Just let him glimpse me,' Fran begged as Jane returned. 'Maybe he'll be reassured.'

Jane held the door open a fraction but he barged in and took a flying leap onto the bed.

'No, I draw the line. I could be struck off for less.' Jane, with Norah's help, hauled him off and bundled him outside. Fran was crying with laughter.

'Norah, please keep Beamish downstairs,' Jane said. 'Good job I've several sterile packs. Come on, I'll have to change the sheet.'

'Aren't babies often born onto newspaper?'

'Fran, that was eighty years ago. I expect newspapers were cleaner than some sheets, but we

188

have progressed a bit. It's the first time I've had to get a dog off the delivery bed.'

'Good experience. Oh God here's a big one. Help me, it's really bad.'

Fran leaned against Jane trying to breathe slowly but losing the fight.

'I can't. I try to remember what to do but then it gets too sharp. Oh, how much longer?'

'You're doing brilliantly, Fran. It's going so well.'

'What's the time?'

'Let's see - yes, ten past ten.'

'Where's Simon. I want him here.' Tears rolled down her face.

Jane held her stroking her hair and trying to reassure her.

'I'm being ridiculous,' she said, at last, blowing her nose.

'No, Fran, just normal.'

'I've got to go to the loo. No, I'm all right, Jane.'

Seconds later she called, 'I think the membranes have broken.'

'Sit tight, I'm coming.'

'Oh God, I'm going to be sick.'

As Jane helped to clean Fran up Norah's voice came from the bottom of the stairs accompanied by the rattle of china.

'I'm bringing you both a nice cup of tea.'

*

Eloise looked around at the giggling, chattering students, shuddered at the Spice Girls number blaring from the jukebox and wished she was somewhere quiet and intimate. Simon had apologised profusely for the venue but had promised to look in on a student's birthday party if only for an hour or so.

'Sorry, but she's one of my brightest third years.'

'Ah, and your presence may motivate her even more?'

He grinned. 'She's also the prettiest.'

'I thought Caroline was exaggerating – obviously not.'

Simon got up, chuckling, and went to the bar. In the mirror opposite he studied her reflection. Her features were narrow but extremely sexy. A determined, pointed chin, sensuous mouth and fine cheek bones. Her grey eyes were long-lashed and her fine hair (probably mousey) was blonde-streaked and just reaching the nape of her neck. A dark-patterned skirt swirled around her slim hips, and her taut, breasts hardly lifted the black polo jersey. She could pass for a boy, he thought, and would make a wonderful Rosalind, reminding him of a Head Boy with Thespian aspirations, the object of his first crush aged fifteen.

'You seem amused,' she said as he put their drinks down on a small table. He sat opposite her stretching his long legs and stifling a yawn.

'Hard day?'

'Worst day of the week. Far too much teaching. Now, tell me about yourself.'

She needed no encouragement but she was funny and succinctly descriptive. She had lived in Africa for three years and worked in Tom's department for two. Now she was staying in a flat close by. Listening and watching her Simon wondered why he always saw biologists as white-coated and lank-haired. This exciting girl didn't even have a whiff of formaldehyde about her, just a tantalising hint of *Diorelle*.

'What brought you back to England?'

'Illness. Oh, not mine. Mum became agoraphobic after my father died. She lives in Plymouth and I stayed with her for six months, then I took this job when she'd improved enough to cope. She was absurdly dependent on Dad. No one should be that dependant.'

'So, you believe in freedom, do you?'

'Yes, unless one can work out a relationship which allows a sensible balance.'

'D'you think Tom and Caroline have that sort of relationship?'

'Perhaps, but by accident rather than design. Their jobs impose separations which neither seems to resent.'

Simon was tempted to ask her if she had been part of the expedition to Lake Rudolph sixteen months ago but she continued, 'They don't trouble each other with questions and it works.'

'Or maybe Tom doesn't want to know. Anyway, I'm more interested in you, Eloise. Where did you get that romantic name?'

'From a trashy, romantic novel.'

'They have their role, then. I like it.'

'But it's hardly right for me. I'm not the wilting, feminine type.'

'Ah, that's why it's right for you; it's a conundrum.'

They were interrupted by the need to sing Happy Birthday to Simon's student who was lifted to sit on the bar, where she swayed dreamily, rather the worst for wear.

'Just as well her tutorial was today,' Simon said. 'I think we can decently go now. How about something to eat? Quite a nice place nearby.'

'You're sure you've time?'

'Of course. I have to eat and so, I imagine, do you, so we may as well eat together. I'll enjoy that. I have too many meals alone.'

Two hours later Simon let himself into the flat. preceded by Eloise.

'Make yourself comfortable,' he invited, switching on the gas fire in the sitting-room and drawing the curtains. Soon, he hoped, he'd make himself comfortable. Eloise had shed her coat and her low-cut jersey left little to the imagination. He glanced down, grinning: an erection had become a bit of a rarity.

'Nice room,' she said, wandering about looking at photographs and particularly studying one of Simon and Fran on their wedding day.

'Nice to be at tree top level with all that wild weather outside. Feels really snug.'

'Good. Fran would rather be out in it. Oh God, the answer phone. I can hear it bleeping. Excuse me a sec.' He went down the corridor to his study. Gerry's recorded voice, a little tense for him, asked Simon to ring whatever time he got in. The message was timed at 6.15pm. Uneasily he rang Gerry's number, glancing at the clock on his desk. How could it now be nearly midnight?

'Gerry. Simon here. I've only just got in. Is there a problem?'

'No, not exactly. Fran rang me earlier. She'd been trying to get hold of you on and off for hours.'

'She's all right? Nothing's happened?'

'No, fine, but the baby may have started. She sounded in great form. She didn't want to leave a message on your machine in case you panicked, so she left it on mine.'

'Oh Christ, and with Shirley off sick there was nobody to answer the 'phone. What did she say? What were her exact words?' Simon felt sick with anxiety. Gerry seemed to be taking an age to gather his thoughts. No doubt he'd had his usual skin full.

'Come on, Gerry, I must know.'

'Calm down, laddie. I'm trying to remember. She was perfectly happy, emphasised you were not to worry. She'd had a few contractions and it could be hours 'til the birth. Oh, and the weather was dreadful and you should be extra careful. Jane was with her and the doctor was expected. I think that was it.'

'Thanks. I'll ring immediately.'

'I tried two hours ago, Simon. The lines are down all over the moor. Haven't you heard the news tonight? Gales are raging across Exmoor so for God's sake be careful. Give my love to Fran.'

He rang off and immediately Simon tried Fran's number. Gerry was right. He harangued the exchange to no avail. Then he remembered Eloise. She rose to the occasion brilliantly.

'I shall go home by taxi.'

'No, I can drop you off. It's not a quarter of a mile is it? Or you can stay here and go home in the morning.' He drew the curtain back. Rain lashed the window relentlessly. 'I have to go out in this, but you don't. Really you are welcome to stay and make yourself at home.'

'I'd rather go home, Simon, but not if it delays you.'

Simon was already making for the bedroom to grab a few clothes.

*

'It won't be much longer, will it? I can't stand much more. Jane, if this is normal I'd rather die than go through a difficult birth.'

Jane sponged Fran's face.

'It should be soon now, Fran, lovey. You're fully dilated. I'll tell you when to start pushing. You're doing brilliantly.'

'My back hurts. It's worse than the contractions. Please rub it again, Norah.'

Gently Norah complied, rubbing her with warm lavender oil. For a few minutes all was peaceful. Jane had rigged up a small CD player on the landing so Fran could be soothed by some of her favourite music. In the candle-lit room no-one noticed that the Brahms Cello concerto had ended abruptly. Fran cried out clutching Jane's hand until it hurt.

'I can't, Jane, it's too much.' But she could not help it. She had no choice but to answer the demands of her body. As the contraction subsided she swore vehemently that she'd never let Simon near her again.

'That's what they all say. Now, Fran, next time try a little push down towards your coccyx. As a rider you'll know what that is. You'll have damaged it a few times. You're doing brilliantly, as if you've had a dozen.'

'God forbid.' With the next contraction Fran complied. She could not have done otherwise.

'Good girl. It's well on its way. Now, again, you really want to push.'

194

'Why isn't Simon here? Please help me, Jane.'

A commotion downstairs startled them.

'Simon!' The tension and exhaustion left Fran's face.

'I'll go,' said Norah hastening to the door.

Seconds later she returned, disappointed. 'It was Fred with the electric cable.'

Tears of disappointment trickled down Fran's cheeks. She lay back on the pillows, hollow-eyed with tiredness.

'It's much, much worse than I imagined.' She attempted a smile. 'Has anyone ever turned inside out?'

Jane chuckled and stroked her hair. 'Not in my experience but there's always a first time.'

Fran's smile contorted. 'You should be struck off for that. Oh. Christ, please not another one.'

'Yes, but hardly any-more, Fran, you're nearly there.' Jane checked Fran's blood pressure as the pain subsided. 'Excellent. You're in wonderful shape.'

'Don't be obscene, I'm in horrendous shape. Oh. this is huge, Jane.'

'Good girl, you can really go with it now. A really good long push.' Gently but firmly Jane guarded the opening of the birth canal to prevent tearing and ease the baby's head out. Fran leaned against Norah who rocked her gently as she had done years ago to make a cut knee or scratched hand feel better. She would have borne Fran's pain if she could.

Minutes later, Fran, somehow managing to do as Jane told her, heard the most wonderful words.

'One tiny push - now you can greet your baby. Here it comes. Dark hair, lovely little ears. Here he is!'

Chapter 16

Joshua William was two hours old when he met his father. In the candle-lit room Simon gazed at the seven-pound baby with his astonishing thatch of dark hair, then at Fran who, exhilarated yet reposed, had never looked more beautiful.

'Hold him,' she urged. 'He's quite solid.'

'But he was early.'

'Simon, early doesn't mean premature. He was ready to arrive. Norah said there was an amazing clap of thunder as he did so but I didn't hear it.'

'Well, it clinched the choice of name,' Simon said, drily. Cautiously he took his son from Fran's arms.

'He is solid.'

'Oh yes, I can vouch for that. Oh, Simon I so wish you'd been here.'

His eyes not leaving his son's face, Simon said, a trifle acidly, 'You didn't exactly make it easy. There are no fallen trees in Exeter. Thank God you're both all right. And he's wonderful.' Grinning. Fran said, 'Jane says he's the image of you, but I think she's prejudiced.'

For five hours Fran slept with Simon sitting beside her, dozing now and then. Half an hour later Jane arrived. She had managed to drive home to see her family and Sonia. She found Norah in the kitchen making breakfast for everyone.

'There are trees down all over the moor and several roads are closed. Sonia's coming by Landrover, as I've done. I had to bypass a tree and a heap of fallen branches. All the telephone lines are still down....'

Jane's words petered out as Simon came in from the sitting-room. His manner was rather cooler than it had been when he'd arrived at the cottage. Then his overwhelming feelings had been relief and joy. The phrase *in the cold light of day* was never more apt Jane thought, and braced herself for the attack as Norah disappeared upstairs with a tray full of breakfast for Fran.

'So, with no telephone how would you have summoned help if anything had gone wrong?'

'If desperate I could have raced off on Fran's pony or by car.'

'I'm not joking.'

'Sorry. You had every right to be concerned but very few problems crop up that aren't detectable in patients much earlier.'

'Oh! What about a haemorrhage?'

'Look, Simon, Dr Wilson will be here shortly. Why not talk it over with her.'

'Certainly, I shall, with both of you. We'll go to Fran's studio. I don't want to upset her. Now I'm going out for a bit. I'll take the dog with me. Please be good enough to tell Fran where I've gone.'

It would hardly hurt you to tell her yourself, thought Jane, but nodded her agreement, then with typical generosity of spirit handed him her cell telephone.

'There'll be loads of people you'll want to contact,' she suggested, 'but you might have problems getting a signal.'

He took it, surprised and looking almost abashed, thanked her and walked away.

Jane grinned. Not the sort of man to judge himself too harshly.

His voice came from the front door.

'Bloody dog won't come out. I'm not dragging him. I'll take the car and go 'til I get a signal.'

The door closed and Beamish bounded up the stairs.

An hour later Simon returned, his mood greatly improved. Talks with Miranda, Charles and Gerry and their delighted and effusive congratulations had done wonders for his ego. He had no wish to be unreasonable. He found Dr Wilson about to get into her car. Was she hoping to avoid him? She glanced up and at once her face broke into a smile of warm approval. She held out her hand.

'Congratulations. You've a most healthy son. And so like you! Fran's in excellent shape. Jane did a great job. Not even a stitch needed.'

He shook her hand, unsmiling. 'Thankyou. Of course I'm delighted but, equally, I'm relieved. Would you mind coming into the studio so we can talk? I'll just call Jane.'

Over the next half hour neither Sonia nor Jane became defensive but tried to answer his challenges with sound facts. They realised that much of his anger stemmed from guilt (albeit irrational) that he had not been with Fran, and some from the high emotion which often follows profound relief. Somehow, they remained calm and objective despite his relentless questioning. His controlled tone only enhanced the impact of his words and later, both agreed, they'd rather be faced by a lout shouting obscenities. Both were assured their respective professional bodies would be fully informed of Simon's feelings and opinions. At that, Sonia firmly reminded him that their patient was his wife and that she seemed satisfied with the care she was having.

'Had,' said Simon. 'I'm taking her back to Exeter for a thorough examination as soon as it's safe to move her. Clearly, you both took advantage of her youthfulness and ignorance.'

'That is going too far,' said Sonia, now with a trace of anger in her voice. 'I've been prepared to discuss matters on a professional level Dr Fellowes, but now you are becoming slanderous. Your wife is an intelligent woman, mature for her years. She was fully in the picture and was able to make a well-reasoned decision about a home birth. My colleague, here, would have been absolutely certain about that before we accepted her as our patient.'

Sonia turned to her friend and colleague. 'I think we should end this discussion. We've gone over all the important facts; you've seen the agreement Fran made with us and there is nothing else to say. If you'll excuse me, I have other patients to see.'

Simon followed them down the steps then walked swiftly into the cottage.

Seeing Jane's look of distress Sonia squeezed her arm. 'Don't worry. The greater responsibility is mine and I had no doubt Fran was an ideal patient for a home birth. Even if a last-minute problem had occurred, it could not have reflected on our decision.'

'Unless one is confronted by someone who believes a home birth should never be permitted. That's what we're up against with Simon.'

'I know, Jane, but what can we do? In future, to protect ourselves, are we going to refuse to accept a patient whose husband disapproves? Some independent practitioners do, as you know.'

Jane shook her head and sighed deeply. 'I don't want to be forced to take that stand but we could do without this.'

'Come on now, you need some sleep by the look of you, and I need to get on my rounds. I'll come back tonight so you can have a good rest.'

Although Simon had thanked Jane profusely after seeing Joshua, Fran sensed the tension between them a while later and, when he returned from the studio she realised a happy discussion about his son's arrival had not taken place.

'What have you been talking about?' she asked, making her tone as neutral as possible.

'Oh, how it all went. What care you'll need – that sort of thing.' His forced light tone was unconvincing but the last thing Fran wanted was an argument.

'Simon, your son's awake so why not pick him up again. And look – the sun's out and everything's settled. It's as if the weather heaved a great sigh of relief and so should we.'

*

Miranda arrived the day after Joshua's birth. Refusing to invade Fran and Simon's privacy she stayed with the delighted Norah and Fred. Over several glasses of champagne Norah gave her a blow-by-blow account, interrupted by hugs and tears.

'Was it really so swift and easy?' she asked, wiping her eyes. 'You make it sound so simple and beautiful.'

'It were. The little lamb coped like Fred's old mare and I mean no disrespect.'

Miranda laughed and topped up all their glasses.

For the next four days she cooked and cleaned, made Simon laugh and took Beamish for long, compensatory walks. Besotted with Joshua she carried him about and sang to him, and told him about his family. She told Fran he was the image of her and then, tactfully, added he had his father's colouring. On the fourth morning a little tension developed when she offered to stay a while when Simon returned to work.

'I don't think we'll need to impose on you. You've your own work and life to get on with. Anyway, Fran won't exactly be isolated at the flat. It is a very kind offer nevertheless.'

'Well, Simon, whatever you wish but you know you only have to ask.'

The following day she left, having ensured there were provisions in the cottage to withstand a siege.

'It was kind of you to put up with her,' Fran said. 'I too would have preferred it if we'd been on our own, much as I love her.'

'I haven't been putting up with her,' Simon said, tetchily. 'I enjoy her company but I agree, we now need to be alone.' The fire leapt high in the grate as a blast of wind hit the cottage, sending hail stones rattling against the windows. Josh, as he had become, slept like an angel in the Moses basket Miranda had given him. Alongside lay Beamish who, far from being jealous, had become his bodyguard. Fran lay full-length on the sofa reading the Guardian review section but her heart was not in it and her eyes constantly strayed to Joshua's face. Simon sat on the hearthrug leaning against the sofa, swirling whisky around in a tumbler.

'We'll need to move, Fran, once you've recovered.'

She winced.

'Obviously the flat isn't ideal for a baby. He'll need a garden, somewhere to play.'

'Well, not in a week or two.'

'Don't be silly. Who knows how long it'll take to find somewhere. We should start as soon as possible.'

'The Spring will be soon enough for me,' Fran said, firmly.

'I don't agree. Prices will go up then. Now is the time to start looking.'

It was obvious to Simon that Miranda's offer had indicated she expected Fran would remain at Spring Cottage. The sooner they got rid of the place the better. Even if kept as a holiday retreat it would continue to be a bone of contention between them.

'If you don't feel up to it I can do the preliminary looking. We can't stay at the flat, Fran. I had a word with Miranda about this place and much as she loves it she would not object to losing it. She said she gave it to you with no strings attached.'

Fran dropped the paper and sat up, eyes blazing.

'You talked to Miranda about selling Spring Cottage! But it has nothing to do with you. I know perfectly well she gave it to me without strings. That's her style. Anyway, we don't have to sell the cottage. We both earn quite a lot of money. We'll get a mortgage.'

'Yes, and have it around our necks for years. And how about Josh? How will we educate him if every penny we earn has to go into a house.'

'Simon, he's a week old for Heaven's sake! What's wrong with you? You used to be so laid back about money.'

'There was no need to be otherwise. We now have responsibilities.'

'D'you think I don't appreciate that? I shall always want the best for Josh but who knows what that will be.'

Josh began to stir and whimper a little. Fran waited, wondering if he'd settle.

'Look, darling, it's for your sake I suggest moving. You'll have space, a garden, a studio.'

'And in order to afford this mansion, a short drive from the city, you want me to sell Spring Cottage, while I would settle for something more modest and keep the cottage. I can't see any meeting point, Simon.'

Josh then decided to wake up and let out a lusty roar. Above the racket Simon said, 'I'm going to have a bath and an early night. There's no point in discussing this any further.'

Fran scooped Josh up and began to feed him, while ringing Miranda's number. Eventually she reached the real reason for the call, ending with the question:

'Am I being selfish and unreasonable?'

There was a longish pause. Oh God, Miranda was so damned fair! At last she said in a careful tone, 'Look at it this way; if Simon had inherited a house or been given one, in an area you didn't like or was inconvenient, would you expect him to sell it?'

There was a pause.

'Fran?'

'Yes. I'm thinking. I suppose I would but it isn't quite the same thing.'

'Isn't it?'

'No. The cottage isn't just a financial asset; I do my best work here. Simon's place of work is the University, mine is Spring Cottage.'

'Yes, but Simon may decide to work for another University one day. If so, would you refuse to move?'

'No, of course not, but I'd still expect to keep the cottage.'

'Then, really it's an emotional attachment isn't it? If it's so strong and so important to you I can understand your feelings. As you are both earning, and far from struggling financially, why don't you buy a house on a mortgage?'

Fran sighed. 'Simon doesn't want a large mortgage. He wants lots of money to spend. Before he met me he was used to pretty high-living. He was even a member of the Bullingdon at Oxford. And Anna described his lifestyle and Charles's night clubbing, dining expensively, having their clothes made - oh dear this sounds so disloyal.'

'No, you're not being disloyal. If you can't confide in your closest relation who can you talk to. Perhaps Simon will have to lower his sights a bit. And maybe I could help out. '

'No, I won't hear of it, Miranda. You've done everything for me.'

'But if ever there were a problem you would let me help? Please, darling?'

'Yes, I would but it's not likely to happen. We really ought to be able to sort this out.'

'What about making a bit of money from the cottage? Summer letting? Something short term like that?'

Fran grimaced. 'Well, it's one way and worth thinking about.'

They moved off the subject then, and Fran talked about an exciting commission she had received in the morning post. Overhead she heard footsteps accompanied by the sound of bath water running away. She made an excuse to ring off not wanting Simon to suspect she had been complaining to Miranda.

Josh, satiated, had fallen asleep. Fran gently returned him to his basket and sat for some minutes gazing into the fire. The thought of strangers in Spring Cottage appalled her. She'd have to remove most of her own things and store them in the attic. If it were let as a holiday cottage she'd have to visit weekly unless she found someone to clean between visits. Would it really be worth the hassle?

The following day Gerry arrived bearing gifts; an enormous teddy bear, a magnum of champagne, a giant chew stick for Beamish, and a bunch of amazing winter roses from his garden.

Fran, whose emotions were still on the surface, wiped tears away with the back of her hand, and marvelled at Gerry's skill with the baby. Cradling him against a cracked old Barbour, no doubt encrusted with prehistoric earth layers, he enthused at Josh's good looks and eight-day progress.

'He's staring at me,' he cried in delight.

Simon laughed. 'He can't focus yet, Gerry. Now let me take him while you remove your coat. Don't doubt it's seen many a plague pit.'

Gerry dumped his coat in the hall and took Josh back. He settled down on the sofa beside Fran.

'Bit of news - mixed. It's sad but good news for you.'

They stared at him, bemused. He chuckled 'You look like a pair of ancient ewes. Now, before you start looking for a house near me (which I hope you will in due course) you have the chance of taking the ground floor flat. Mrs Benson went to stay with her daughter in Sherborne last week and died there - suddenly.'

'Oh, she was a dear,' Fran exclaimed. 'Always so kind and helpful.'

'So you think we could move down, Gerry? The size and number of rooms is the same and there's the garden. It could be a useful stop gap.' Simon's tone was approving.

'Well, I hope you don't mind but I've already put in a word.'

'Of course we don't mind, Gerry. We're really grateful. If you weren't holding Josh, I'd give you a big hug,' said Fran.

A few hours later, accompanied to his car by Simon, Gerry said, in his forthright way, 'You look as if you've had the baby. Fran's blooming but you seem worn out. Still, I must admit lambing takes it out of me.'

'Hardly comparable. I think I'm having a bit of a reaction to the drama.'

'Not surprising. And the storm must have been the last straw.'

'It was so bloody stupid of Fran - a home birth here - in November. I was nearly out of my mind.'

'Still, it's behind you and they're both fine. He even looks like you, same eyes.'

'All babies start off with blue eyes. Miranda swears he's like Fran.'

'Ah well, either way, he won't have any disadvantages. How did you choose the name? I like it. Solid. Unusual.'

'The clap of thunder that accompanied Josh's arrival clinched it. But Fran was pretty keen anyway because it was the name of an Israeli friend of her parents. And William was her father's name and my grandfather's second name; so everyone is satisfied.'

Gerry opened the door of his sheep-smelling Landrover. 'Funny the knack we have of rationalising. When Elspeth and I split up I was relieved we didn't have kids. Now. I wonder. I suppose I rather envy you, Simon.'

He swung himself into the driving seat and switched the ignition on. The engine coughed into action at once despite its antiquity.

'When will you be back at work?'

'Oh, a day or two. I'll ring about the flat. Thanks for thinking of us, Gerry, it's postponed a major row about this place.'

'Right. Ring me when you get back. I could do with a game of squash. Perhaps not though, judging from the look of you. Look after yourself, old man.'

The next and final visitors were Anna and Charles. Both enthused equally about Josh, and, sensing Anna was dying for a blow-by-blow account Fran suggested leaving the men to babysit while she and Anna walked on the moor with Beamish.

'You're so lucky,' said Anna, wistfully. 'Married just over a year and with a baby already.'

'Not planned,' Fran assured her. 'Honestly, I think Simon would have preferred to wait two or three years although he's older than me.'

'But he's tremendously thrilled, and proud of Josh, and of you. Charles is so envious.'

Fran hesitated then took the plunge. 'There aren't problems?'

'We don't know. We haven't been taking precautions for at least two years. Even before we married Charles was desperate for me to become pregnant. He adores the idea of having a family and feels he missed a lot of being an only child.'

'I rather think Simon saw it as an advantage. I'm sorry, Anna, it does seem ironical that you're really trying, and I vomit the pill and get pregnant like a rabbit.'

To her relief, Anna laughed. 'You do have youth on your side, of course, whereas I'm nearly thirty.'

'That's nothing,' Fran said, silently wondering if she'd look as good in four years' time. It seemed a very long way off.

'No, I'm being silly. Lots of women wait until their thirties. It's just that we don't want to wait.' Anna stopped abruptly, her arm on Fran's. 'Look, a stag over there by the gorse bushes. He's seen us.' As she spoke the animal disappeared.

'You're lucky,' Fran enthused. 'Few people see the red deer. Visitors come year after year without seeing one. He's an old stag with a considerable harem and he still looks wonderful.'

'You know such a lot about the moor. We're all dreadfully urban or is growing up in Beaconsfield just acceptable?'

Fran laughed. 'Not really. I've only an advantage because I've spent huge chunks of time here. You're seeing it at winter's best today. Even to me it can seem very hostile on its worst days. When Josh was born, it

208

was quite a frightening place to be. Not that I was much aware of it. Poor Simon. No wonder he was so angry.'

Anna was silent for a while. A sudden burst of late sunshine enhanced the richness of the colours of the different heathers which she thought would now be brown and lifeless. Below them in the valley seagulls wheeled effortlessly above a ploughed field. At last, she said in her gentle way, 'It was probably a very poignant time. He must have been thinking about Betty and how she'd have loved being a grandmother. And maybe he was extra angry because he thought he might lose you.'

Fran stopped and looked directly at Anna. 'D'you know I hadn't thought of it in that way. Perhaps he was terrified of another loss. I've been really thoughtless.'

'Simon's not like Charles who wears his heart on his sleeve. He won't have made it easy for you to have understood his feelings. He's a much prouder man than Charles but don't underestimate the depth of his feelings. You don't mind my saying this?'

Fran smiled and hugged her.

'No. I'm grateful. You've known him so long. Being married to him doesn't mean I know everything about him. Heaven knows marriage should not mean ownership and being in an intimate relationship can make objectiveness really difficult. I knew so little of him before we married.'

'And vice versa,' Anna pointed out. 'Simon is still finding out about you and now little Josh.'

And at Anna's final words an image of her baby's face filled Fran's mind. It was the longest she had been away from him, more than an hour. Suddenly, she was anxious to get home and strode purposefully along the rim of the valley calling to rabbiting Beamish. When she saw Josh he was sleeping blissfully one and a half hours after his lunch-time feed. Yet she had to peel off her damp jersey in the bathroom and wash her sodden bras. She smiled ruefully, remembering her irritation at the intensity with which mothers were bound up with their babies, and now she was experiencing the same powerful emotions.

Chapter 17

In the university canteen Simon was pleased to be joined by Gerry who immediately enthused about Josh and Fran.

'She's a brilliant lass so I guess she's coping well. And I hope you're not overdoing the flat renovations and wearing yourself out.'

Simon grinned. 'Far from it. I've found a good handyman who's redecorating and adjusting the electrics – one of those reliable all-purpose blokes. I want it all perfect for Fran's return. She's got her aunt with her and plenty of local support, so no worries for either of us - bit different from three weeks ago.'

'I'll say. Ah, here's that friend of a friend of yours, Eloise. Hullo love.'

Eloise had arrived holding a tray with a cup of tea and plate with a sandwich on it. Gerry stood up and pulled out a chair.

'Thanks.' Eloise sat down. 'A week left then our break. Thank goodness Mum's sister is coming for Christmas and she'll take over. Cooking isn't my passion.'

'Nor is home decorating mine,' said Simon, 'I'm so grateful to Martha for finding me a good chap.'

'Into that sort of thing, is she? I must meet her,' said Eloise, grinning. 'No, I can't see you in dungarees and wielding a paintbrush, Simon.'

'But he can cook,' enthused Gerry. 'Not quite to Fran's standard but better than most. Now, I'd better get back before my students arrive.'

Eloise was smiling as she watched him walk away 'He's so different from you yet you are close friends. It's interesting.'

'Why? He's funny, intelligent and full of original ideas. Best of all he's a hundred per cent himself.'

'As you are?'

'Well, you tell me.'

'I hardly know you.'

'Let's start putting that right. You hate cooking while I don't mind it, so come for a bite tonight.'

'Great. I will,' Elise beamed. 'I was so lucky to get the use of my friend's flat and only a ten-minute walk away.'

Hours later Eloise had a sudden feeling of *deja vu*. Two feet away was the photograph of Fran and Simon on their wedding day. Behind the yellow curtains rain lashed the windows and Simon had disappeared to make coffee. This time he did not return in an anxious and excited state to announce he had to leave, but calmly reappeared carrying a tray.

'You seem amused,' he said.

She smiled. 'Bit like last time – even raining.'

'But no drama, I hope. Thank God that's all in the past. You like your coffee black, don't you?'

She was flattered he remembered. 'Thanks.' She took the cup and sat beside the gas fire.

'Will the new flat really be exactly the same?'

'Yes, apart from the fact that you'd have a nasty shock if you walked through the window from here, a twelve-foot drop at least.'

She laughed. 'So, Josh will have a garden. But will Fran have a studio?'

'No. She'll have to rent something unless she's prepared to sacrifice a room.'

'Or put something out in the garden. A summerhouse or cabin.'

'Excellent idea if permitted.' He poured coffee for himself. She noticed his hand was not quite steady.

'You okay?'

'Yes, a bit jaded perhaps. To be honest work has come as light relief.'

'Don't let Fran hear you say that when she's coping with a howling baby and night feeds. Doesn't she mind being on her own?'

'No. Miranda offered to come back for a bit. Fran agreed but she's pretty self-sufficient – already coping.'

Eloise commented that Simon struck her as being similar.

'I can be.'

'Nice coffee and that lasagne was superb. Do you compete with one another in the kitchen?'

'Lord no. I'm not in her league. Somehow, it's instinctive with her. Would you like a brandy?'

'No thanks. My ex: was a brandy drinker and that's put me off forever.'

'Mm. I'd better desist then. I didn't know you were married.'

'Less than a year. It was one of those stupid student romances. A bit of one-upmanship I think. No one else was doing it so we did.'

'Where was that?'

'Durham. By the time I was a postgraduate we were halfway to divorce.'

'And you've not come close to it since?'

'Marriage?' she sounded scornful. 'Good Lord no. The death of desire. Oh, sorry, that wasn't very tactful. You've been married such a short time.'

'So were you.'

'Yes, but I expect that was different.'

'I hope so. I didn't wait until my thirties for something mundane.'

'You really love Fran.'

'Yes, I certainly do but she isn't here. I like women in general and you in particular. I like the fact that you're a free spirit and independent. I find that very attractive.'

'But could you stray - so soon?'

'I wouldn't be straying. I'm committed to being Fran's husband but that doesn't mean total fidelity.'

'Well, you're nothing if not forthright. At least one would know where one stood.' She drank her coffee slowly. She could set down her cup, thank Simon formally for an excellent meal, and leave. There would be no embarrassment or unpleasantness and they'd be comfortable together when they next met. They were sophisticated and civilised people. On the other hand...

She stood up. Instinctively, public school training behind him, Simon did likewise. She made the move, crossed the few feet that separated them and offered herself in smiling silence. After a few minutes she asked, 'How long since you had sex with Fran?'

He drew back, amused and a little surprised. 'You think I'm using you?'

'Yes, but I'm also using you. We have a certain, obvious need.'

'You're very direct. I like that. I like you. I want you.'

As he led her down the corridor to the bedroom, she stopped abruptly, saying, 'You don't think it's a bit insensitive - being in the room you share with your wife, if that's where we're going?'

'No. She won't be sleeping in here again. There's nothing to worry about. Well, only one thing. Are you safe?'

'On the Pill? Of course!'

'Then we'll be doubly safe. Since Fran fell pregnant, I don't solely rely on that rubbish.'

*

No way was Fran going to deprive Simon of his son by insisting on staying at Spring Cottage all the time – much as she'd have liked to for her own sake. To wander about the moor on foot, or in the trap with Josh safely in his basket, would be wonderful but she had to be firm - to relish these moments when they came and not long for them daily.

Consoled by spending Christmas and New Year at the cottage, she resigned herself to the prospect of being in the city for most of the Spring. The move to the ground floor had been slower than expected as Mrs Benson's son had removed a few of the contents from the flat so they had to be replaced. At least they now had a garden, appreciated by Beamish, but working in a cramped space was irritating. She declined a commission that would have meant spending time on the Devon and Cornish coasts, liaising with a well-known ornithologist, David Handley, who had suggested to his publisher that she should illustrate his book.

'It's a shame but I must let it go,' she'd said, rashly, to Simon who was feeling edgy about the volume of work he was having to cope with.

'Why can't you just do copies of sea birds and sea scapes. You could draw a seagull with your eyes shut,'

Simon had said. 'Why all this rubbish about being shown nests and special sites by him. Tell him to photograph them and send them to you.'

'That's not the way he wants to work and if I can't immerse myself in the project, it's only fair to let it go.'

'Well, of course you can't wander at will now you're a mother. Thank goodness you accept that.'

Crossly. Fran had responded that she had no doubt that her main duty was to her son; hadn't she shown that by restricting her lifestyle, by putting up with living in the town and cutting down her work to a minimum?

That row happened weeks ago she reflected. Spring, thank goodness, had arrived with a burst of sunshine in time for an open-air production of Shakespeare's Coriolanus.

Simon was co-director with Roger, and they had received two standing ovations after the cast had been similarly rewarded.

'Not only does he pull off a difficult play. I mean really, really difficult and he's got scorching days after weeks of rain.' The speaker, an intense-looking student in a glittering catsuit, swigged red wine as if it were coca cola. 'Whew, I needed that. I'm pretty steamed up.' She was standing a few yards from Fran.

'Trust Simon to pull it off,' said her companion, very differently dressed in a strapless ball gown

From the tail of the queue for the bar (a striped marquee) a third girl turned towards them, grinned broadly and said she'd always trust Simon to pull anything off.

Girlish giggles rippled along the queue.

'Come off it, Allie, you're fantasising again.'

'What are you on, Allie? If it's that good, can I have some?'

'Better not let her drink as well. She'll strip him down to his codpiece.'

The giggles grew hysterical. Fran edged away holding her programme like a fan to conceal her face. Simon, not Dr Fellowes, she mused. She had never called a lecturer by his or her Christian name. It surprised her that Simon allowed such familiarity but perhaps the students were showing off.

An inviting arc of grass flanked by shrubs would deter intruders she considered; so positioned herself carefully seeming to give all her attention to the outsize programme which was as familiar as if she had designed it herself. The actual designer, Georgia, a beautiful fine arts student, was equally familiar to her. To ensure she was meeting Simon's exacting requirement she had visited him at home a number of times.

'I'd have been happy to design the programme and the poster,' Fran had said, a little petulantly, when it was already underway.

Surprised, Simon said he thought she'd be too busy and, anyway, as she showed no interest in anything to do with the university it hadn't occurred to him to ask her.

'Sorry,' he said, 'another time I'll expect your help,' and he put his arms around her only to release her abruptly as the doorbell rang and Georgia's voice called:

'It's only me. I've got the finished design for your approval.'

What an absurd fuss, Fran had thought. Anyone would think the production was going to be at the Old Vic.

Surreptitiously she glanced around for a familiar face. She had arrived late, due to Phyllis, Josh's babysitter being delayed and had sat far from the row of reserved seats where she would have been with Simon's colleagues and friends. She enjoyed her anonymity and the chance to quietly observe and absorb the atmosphere. The evening was warm and full of luscious scents, from flowers and newly mown grass. The majority of the guests were middle-aged and conservatively dressed while the students were wearing multifarious styles, from evening dress to casual gear. A tall Nigerian girl wore her splendid tribal costume while her very different escort was straight from an old classic movie in his white American tuxedo.

'Fran dear gel, what are you doing here? Wasn't it a triumph? Why aren't you with your clever husband?'

Hell! The programme wasn't sufficiently outsize. She lowered it to be confronted by Harriet Crawford.

'I know there was dissent about the production – not a favourite but in these lovely grounds and with this amazing weather it really has paid of. What a clever chap Simon is. You must be basking in his glory, my dear. I gather he's going to be our student recruiter overseas. I'm sure Josh is a tough little chap so will you be taking him abroad. Could you leave him with a granny? Is he weaned?'

Fran was about to respond but, scarcely drawing breath, Harriet rushed on. 'Breast feeding beyond six months seems rather unhealthy, even self-indulgent don't you think? Wasn't the casting brilliant? Where

218

did he find that lovely gel to play Virginia? Such a difficult part as so little is said, yet the strength must come through.'

'I don't like the play, I'm afraid. Technically all right I'm sure, but not a good choice.' Only a braying fellow Valkyre could stop Harriet in full flow. Now one stood beside her in a long brocade dress, almost identical to hers.

Barely disconcerted Harriet took the interruption in her stride, introducing Fran with quite a flourish. Jennifer Ashley-Cohen shook Fran's hand and. unabashed, continued to criticise Simon's choice of play as being subversive and too overtly political.

'I think Coriolanus is one of Shakespeare's least attractive plays, and why choose it when all is quiet and settled. We don't want trouble to stir up as it did on campuses in the sixties; sit-ins, rejection of chancellors and goodness knows what. It was appalling.'

Fran perked up and opened her mouth to respond but Harriet upstaged her.

'Well, we've a right to our opinions,' cried Harriet, 'but I'm sure you'll concede it was brilliantly done. Ah, here's a familiar face. Eloise – you must know her.'

Jennifer walked away and Fran turned to the woman who had been walking past before Harriet caught hold of her arm, detaining her. She was slim, attractive and elegant, in a sheath-like blue dress.

'You were at university with Simon, I hear, ' said Harriet.

'No, I met a contemporary of Simon's when I was in Kenya and worked with her husband.' She turned to Fran, smiling. 'Caroline was at Oxford with Simon.'

She and Fran shook hands. Strange they hadn't met, Fran thought, as there was that distant connection.

'Are you working here or visiting,' Fran asked.

'Working, temporarily. Filling in while Mike Woods is poorly.'

'He's a biologist. I doubt if you've met him,' said Harriet. Her tone indicated she wanted to dominate the conversation so, hastily Fran said,

'It must have been really interesting working in Kenya. I heard a bit about it from Tom at my wedding.'

'Oh yes, they came over and loved it. I gather you spent your honeymoon in Israel.'

'Now, what did you think of the play? That's the important topic today,' said Harriet. How can you be so rude, Fran wanted to say and noticed Eloise was frowning. A familiar voice called, 'Fran, Simon's been looking for you and there's a marvellous supper. I was quite worried - thought you'd gone home.' Martha was approaching.

'Excuse me, I must go,' said Eloise. She walked away, turning to add, 'See you again, Fran.'

. 'Of course you will. We're like a family – we lecturers' wives,' called Harriet. 'Hullo Martha, what's your opinion of the play – the choice, the directing, the acting – of course your husband was involved so you might find it difficult to be objective.'

'To me objectivity amounts to honesty and that's what my response will be,' was Martha's reply that brought a brief look of annoyance to Harriet's face.

A minute later Fran and Martha managed to extricate themselves. Arm in arm, giggling like schoolgirls they wandered towards the marquee that housed the refreshments.

'So you know Eloise,' Martha commented. 'A life-saver to the science department.'

'No, I've only just met her: a bit surprising considering she knows a couple of Simon's friends. He's never mentioned her.'

'Too busy, I expect, what with the drama group and his writing on top of the lecturing.'

'I've only been able to glimpse Simon since the play finished. He's been surrounded by adoring admirers showering him with praise.'

'The only praise that matters is yours, Fran. Look, there he is, he's coming over.'

Seconds later Simon was beside them and, after much effusive hugging, he drew back a little looking at Fran appraisingly.

'You are the only thing the play lacked, my love. But I know you dislike Coriolanus and his vicious brat so thank you for enduring it.'

'I didn't endure it – I enjoyed the acting and presentation. It was really well done.'

Fran's words gained her another hug.

'Combining directing and acting is a bit of a feat,' said Roger, appearing at Martha's side, 'but it worked like a dream.'

'Largely the credit is yours,' Simon responded, warmly. 'You provided the material - the easiest bunch I've worked with, and it was generous of you to give me a free hand.'

'My pleasure. Now let's reward ourselves before the students devour the lot.'

Minutes later, juggling a plate of food, a glass and trying to keep Josh in the back of her mind, Fran

221

realised the party was likely to extend into the early hours and Simon fully intended to stay.

'Surely Phyllis is staying late,' he said, when Fran put her plate down beside her chair and glanced at her watch. 'You can't do a Cinderella on me - not tonight.'

'It's not that: it's Josh's feed. You know he now has a later feed then sleeps through the night.'

'Can't Phyllis give him a bottle,' suggested Martha'

'No, he's never had one. I don't possess one. He's always coped with a spoon for drinks of water you see.'

'Well, I admire you for keeping it all so simple,' Martha began but irritably Simon interrupted:

'Simple! I'd say the reverse. We can't move without that baby. I'm amazed you didn't bring him with you. I'll run you home, you feed him, then come back.'

Fran shook her head. 'I haven't asked Phyllis to stay later than eleven. She can't anyway. She has her own family to consider.'

'Oh for God's sake. There are dozens of people who'd babysit for us and stay the night; half my students for a start.'

'Look, why don't I go home with you Fran, and stay there so you can come back. I'd love to see Josh again.'

'Why should you, Martha. Fran should get herself organised. She can bring Josh back. That's all right isn't, Fran?'

Martha intervened calmly, 'Josh is about four months, isn't he? A bit too big to be carted about to parties and a bit too small to join in.'

Fran nodded, grinning. 'I'll stay a bit longer, then I'll go home alone. It's not fair to drag you away, Martha. This is Roger's success too.'

Half an hour later Fran left. Simon, his good humour seeming to be restored, hardly noticed her departure. He was surrounded by the cast who had pooled their meagre resources and bought him a bottle of Bollinger on which they had stuck a personalised label.

Josh did not wake up for his late feed and Fran, miserable and cross with herself (although not sure why) sat in the kitchen with Beamish, her hands cupped around a large mug of tea.

The city, never quiet in Fran's terms, hummed outside, intrusive even at one in the morning. It had been a beautiful, triumphant evening for Simon. She was sure he was still thoroughly enjoying himself and why shouldn't he? She should have arranged things better. Maybe, even trained Josh to feed (breast milk) from a bottle. Was her passion for a natural way of life becoming an obsession?

Maybe, if Josh were weaned by the time Simon's Singapore trip came, she'd leave him with Miranda, who was brilliant with him and would care for him willingly. Even if she were really busy, she'd insist; if necessary, she'd employ extra help.

After two o'clock, Fran was still wide awake and restless although she'd had a warm bath, rather than a shower, hoping it would relax her. She heard Simon arrive but he didn't come to the bedroom. Soon water was running so she assumed he'd undressed in the bathroom. Of course, after a gap of nearly three hours he'd expect her to be asleep.

He slipped into bed beside her, not touching her. She stroked his shoulder tentatively and he turned towards her.

'Sorry, did I disturb you?'

'No. I wasn't asleep. I'm sorry, Simon. I feel I spoilt your party.'

He leaned up on one elbow and ran a finger along her cheekbone.

'You didn't, Fran. It was a great party. I wish you could have stayed on but perhaps I was a bit unreasonable. Josh will have to be weaned one day, I imagine.'

She giggled and snuggled against his shoulder.

'By the time you go to Singapore.'

There was just too long a pause.

'Ah, someone's mentioned that?'

'Harriet.'

'It's only an idea for a recruitment drive. A long flight. Anyhow, Martha has recommended a small hotel on a lovely beach in Brittany. They've stayed there often since their daughter could toddle. How about that for a proper bucket and spade holiday for Josh?'

Chapter 18

The summer was one of the hottest and driest for years. By August leaves were fading and shrivelling, blackberries ripened early, and hips glowed, intertwined with cream honeysuckle. Fran made rose hip jelly and pureed fat blackberries for Josh. At nine months he was a good-tempered and sturdy child, continually pulling himself to his feet and babbling in his own language which Simon was sure included `Dada'.

'He probably will say "Daddy" first,' said Fran complacently. 'I use the word all the time to him when you're not here.'

'What a pity you have to,' said Simon smiling but with an edge to his voice. Fran did not respond. She considered she had been sufficiently dutiful spending weeks in Exeter until a particular commission necessitated the use of her studio. She even availed herself of the pleasure the city offered spending hours in the Cathedral listening to the choristers while Josh lay quietly in his pram usually wide awake, apparently listening. The estuary was a continual joy. She even joined an organised trip to look at avocets and from memory and photographs she painted a picture that came close to pleasing her.

'Just shows you didn't have to do it all from life. Have you ever seen skies quite as furious and filthy as Turner's? He made them up.'

Fran burst into laughter and threw her arms around Simon.

'Would you like it? I'd have it framed properly.'

Simon was delighted and hung the painting in his office at the university.

*

The holiday in Brittany gave rise to no problems for Simon enjoyed using his fluent French, eating simply but superbly and spending lazy hours on the beach while Josh played so contentedly that other parents commented that they envied the couple with their smiling baby. More active times were spent exploring the large Parc d'Amorique, where they both enthused about the areas that were like Dartmoor. Fran took dozens of photographs, particularly of the wildlife. Excitedly she called the names of birds she recognised, Fan-tailed warblers, Spoonbills, Ospreys and Cirl buntings.

'We won't be able to access the flat in a few weeks,' Simon said, watching her load yet another film into her camera.

'Why?'

'The place'll be littered with your paintings of these squawking creatures.'

Fran laughed. 'I guess I'd better take some of you – forestall your jealousy. Now, one of you alone, then one with Josh.'

The hotel was small and run by a friendly French couple. They had a poodle who formed an instant affinity with Josh.

'We should have brought Beamish. I bet they'd have got on all right,' said Fran, stroking the dog's head.

'Not if that pooch got too close to Josh,' said Simon, laughing. 'Did you choose this place or did I?'

'You did, after discussing it with Martha and Roger.'

'Good, so I've got something right for once.'

'Certainly you have. It's nearly as good as our honeymoon.'

'Only nearly. Why is that?'

'I just think there was added rare excitement.'

Simon glanced at his watch. 'Give it a couple of hours and I'll perk up the excitement.'

*

Back at Spring Cottage, Fran described the holiday to Anna.

'We couldn't have had a better time. The people were so friendly, lots of lovely scenery and Simon was so relaxed and happy. He looks as if he's been away for months.'

'Tanned and gorgeous,' Anna said. 'I can picture him. He hasn't always looked well in the past few months. Well, you've been a bit worried at times.'

'I have but he's fine now. You know he's now on his way to Singapore, recruiting students but he'll be back on Friday so you'll see for yourself at the weekend. I'm so glad you're both coming down.'

Minutes later Fran replaced the receiver and decided to spend the rest of the day luxuriating in the late afternoon sunshine. Weeks before she had a baby's safety seat fitted to the trap enabling her to drive safely to her favourite haunts with her two most regular passengers. Now she would go to a tiny, remote stream, loved by Josh and Beamish.

227

High on the hillside, Rudi stood clad in shorts and plimsolls with binoculars around his neck. Attracted by the sound of laughter he looked downwards where parts of the bank of a small stream were swathed with white flowers, then he glimpsed a naked tanned figure sitting in the water, supporting a much smaller one, splashing and shrieking with excitement. Occasionally a bark punctuated the laughter.

It was – it had to be! The colour of the hair was right, both on the girl and the dog. Sweat gathered along his brow and trickled down his nose. He wiped his face with the back of one hand, while fingering the strap of his binoculars with the other. Resolutely he turned away and purposefully retraced his tracks.

'You are Sir Gallahad,' he told himself, sighing deeply. 'You deserve the Holy Grail.'

Two days later Beamish had occasion to stand guard, hackles lifted, a low moaning grumble coming from his throat. Approaching his precious charge was a man, albeit familiar but the dog was taking no chances. Moving from the shade beside Josh's pram he padded slowly towards the intruder.

'Hey boy, you know me. I mean you no harm.' A movement to his left at the top of the steps attracted him but he kept his eyes on the dog yet not looking directly at him.

'Beamish, he's a friend. It's all right boy.'

Fran's voice reassured the dog. He sat down, not entirely convinced but he stopped growling.

'Would he go for the jugular?' Rudi asked, trying not to laugh at the dog's commendable diligence.

'I don't think so; only if you hurt Josh.' Fran came down to the courtyard and patted Beamish who then walked across and licked Rudi's hand.

'Good fella.' Rudi made much of him, then with a smile and nod of approval from Fran, approached Josh's pram. 'So he was the bulge.'

'He was indeed.'

'He's beautiful.'

Josh, brown as a hazelnut, naked but for a white terry napkin, lay snoring gently.

'How old is he?'

'Eight months. Born in the November gales.'

'Oh yes, we heard about them.'

'They certainly added to the drama of Josh's arrival. Come inside and have a drink. Tell me what you've been doing.'

'I'll be interrupting your work.'

Rudi glanced at the brush in Fran's hand. She laughed and put it down on the step.

'A welcome interruption. I'm having to meet some exacting requirements and I'm finding it a bit irritating.'

'Well, if you're sure.'

Fran led the way into the cottage beneath a swathe of scented clematis.

'Beautiful,' said Rudi, breathing deeply. 'This is a lovely place.'

Fran beamed her approval. 'Coffee, tea or something cold? I've beer or fresh orange juice.'

'Beer would be great.'

In the kitchen Fran took a tin of Worthington from the fridge and poured it for him, then an orange juice for herself.

'The courtyard is quite cool until the sun tips over the roof,' she said. 'Shall we join Josh there?'

Rudi nodded his approval, and they sat on a rough bench watching house martins lining up on the telegraph wires.

'They'll be away all too soon,' Fran observed. She gave Beamish the ice from her drink. He held it in his mouth, runnels of water seeping from the corners.

'Funny old boy,' said Rudi, and his tone encouraged Beamish to lean against his knees.

'Well, how did the thesis go?'

'Okay. I got my doctorate, now all I need is a permanent job. I'm pursuing a couple of things in conservation. One, linked to Cardiff University, is based on Exmoor but it's only temporary.'

'And that's what you'd like? You seem to be as keen on the moor as I am.'

'I think I am. It's miraculous it hasn't been more spoilt as it's relatively small and accessible. The long winter rescues it I suppose, when only the residents disturb it. It's quite a short tourist season, but really the hard nuts are the landowners with their ideas on land improvement.'

'Starting with the Aclands who once owned this farm,' agreed Fran. 'Although it was with the best intentions that they set about irrigating and clearing. At least they did a lot of good for the ponies. Chuckle descends from an Acland line.'

'There's a small herd only a few hundred yards away,' Rudi told her. 'I suppose you know all the owners.'

'Most. There are still families around who've bred the Exmoor for generations. It was a lucrative business when the ponies were used in the mines.

Now they're valued as a rare breed, thank goodness. I hope you'll be around for the Drift.'

'What's that?'

'The annual round-up of ponies. They're driven to a holding farm and inspected, then branded if they meet the stringent requirements for a pure-bred pony. Doubtful ones may be sold away, but few are nowadays because the breeding is so well controlled. It's probably the purest native pony in the country.'

'So when is the Drift?'

'In October.'

'I'll be here, somehow.'

'Can you stay for lunch? Josh will be awake soon and demanding his.'

'Great, that's really kind. Where's your husband? He never seems to be here.'

'He's in Singapore recruiting foreign students.'

'And you couldn't go?'

'I couldn't leave Josh and he was a bit too young to go with us. I decided it would be too long and tiring for him, also I have an important commission. And, perhaps I'm a bit insular.' She sighed.

'I don't think so, though having only met you twice that may sound presumptuous. You're interested in too much to be insular.'

'Well, an Anglophile maybe, although I think I could live in Israel.'

'Nothing wrong with that. I'm an Anglophile.'

Fran laughed. 'Ah, but that's more acceptable. You weren't born here so a definite choice – not inbred. Oh Lord, the Kraken wakes.'

The pram was rocking as Josh on hands and knees struggled to be free of his safety harness. Fran helped him out and introduced him to Rudi who said. 'Hi, how are you doing?' which elicited a shriek of delight from Josh.

'Was it something I said?'

'I think it's your accent. Shall we go and find some food? We'll eat indoors don't you think. It'll be cooler.'

Fran settled Josh in his high chair, giving him a rusk to chew while she put salad, bread and cheese on the kitchen table.

'Another beer?'

'No thanks but I'll help myself to water please. What a joy to drink tap water. You English are so sensible about these things.'

Fran grinned thinking of Jane-Anne.

'There's a vogue for bottled spring water here as everywhere else.'

She took a basin of cold cooked carrots and potatoes from the fridge and mashed them for Josh then put them in the small, electric oven for a few minutes. Josh was convulsed with giggles trying to play pat-a-cake with Rudi.

'You're good with babies,' Fran remarked. 'Have you any brothers or sisters?'

'I'm the oldest of three. I was always having to babysit, and I didn't always appreciate it. My next sibling, Eleanor, will make me an uncle by Christmas.'

'Simon and I haven't any siblings. I wonder if it shows.'

'Well, it hasn't stopped you being kind to strangers.'

Fran laughed. 'You've not come as a stranger. You were my knight in shining armour; remember?'

'I'll never forget it. What did Simon think of that little escapade?'

'He wasn't amused. He hated my being here alone. When Josh was born a bit early and he couldn't get here due to the storm, he was furious.'

'Got to see his viewpoint. I guess a man feels pretty helpless and scared at such a time.'

'Yes, and I was pretty stubborn I suppose.'

Fran put Josh's lunch on the tray in front of him and gave him a spoon.

'Pretty good,' said Rudi, impressed.

'He can't really use it but he tries with the help of his fists. Do help yourself, Rudi.'

She took ham from the larder and a selection of home-made pickles.

'The ham is home-cured from next door and wonderful.' She sat beside Josh giving him a hand now and then. 'How long are you staying, Rudi, and where?'

'Depends on whether I get a permanent job, then I'll have to find somewhere to live as I can't afford the pub at Brendon for more than a week or two.'

Fran was thoughtful for a minute.

'I'm just wondering if my friend Jane could help. She lives at Rockbourne Farm and sometimes has paying guests.'

'Oh, I know it. I've seen the signpost. Sounds ideal.'

'I'll ask her if you like. She and her husband are really nice. I'm sure you'd all get on.'

'Great. Maybe you could help me locate important sites on the moor, if you're not too busy of course.'

'Things should ease off after next week but I've a deadline for my current project.'

'And I've interrupted your work.'

'No, I'd done three hours. I needed a break. Oh, that's the phone. Better answer it in case it's Simon.'

Fran hurried to the hall and minutes later returned looking really pleased.

'Amazingly that was my friend, Jane. If you want to go down this afternoon, she'll show you around. The room for guests – well, really a tiny flat - is above the garage. A bedsit with a shower room and kitchenette. Really nice.'

'Thank goodness life is full of coincidences. What time should I go?'

'Did you walk here?'

'Yes.'

'Then I'll run you there. We'll leave in an hour as Jane's got an appointment at four.'

Fran dropped Rudi at Jane's and within two hours he rang Fran to say he would be moving into her flat the following day and staying for two weeks while completing the temporary job. He then asked her if they could do a moorland walk, visiting some of the special places she had mentioned.

Fran agreed happily and two days later, with Josh in a back carrier and Beamish roaming freely, they strolled on narrow, heat-bleached paths that looked like white string dropped between swathes of purple heather. Enjoying the extensive views and multifarious colours around the Badgworthy area, they exchanged more appreciative looks than words, then Rudi surprised and pleased Fran, by saying, 'Below must be the church where Lorna Doone was shot but luckily, she survived.'

'So you've read Lorna Doone. That's great. Let's go there'

'Fran, I'm half English, remember. Mum introduced us to her favourite books from an early age. Long ago I decided I had to visit R.D.Blackmore's Exmoor and Hardy's Wessex.'

'Brilliant. You're a literary scientist. What a combination.'

As they descended towards the river valley tall stands of foxgloves appeared. On one a beautiful silver fritillary caused them to stop, exchange smiles and stand watching until the butterfly, having had enough of lounging, fluttered away.

'The foxgloves are hanging on,' Rudi commented. 'I thought they'd have shrivelled by now.'

In places the riverside path was stony and uneven. Although Fran had walked it many times, she was the one who stumbled and nearly fell. Rudi grabbed her arm and steadied her.

'Careful, You've something of great value in your backpack. Let me carry him for a bit. I expect his weight unbalanced you.'

Fran nodded, smiling. Rudi's hand felt warm and firm giving her a strange, momentary sensation; she wanted his touch to remain. Gently, he eased the pack off her shoulders, sat on the ground with Josh on his lap, and lengthened the straps. Josh was dozing but Beamish watched every move. When the pack was in position, Josh chortled.

'He likes the extra height,' said Fran. 'And I like feeling light. Thanks, Rudi.'

Arriving at the tiny St. Mary's Church, better known as Oare Church, Fran impressed a large number of tourists when she pointed to the window through which Lorna was shot. The majority present were German and French but the words Blackmore and Lorna Doone were frequently spoken.

'I love this little place,' said Fran. 'Miranda brought me here to a Christingle service when I was really young.'

'Were you married in church, Fran?'

'No, Simon and I agreed to a registry office as we're both agnostic – 'though sometimes I think I'm a reluctant one.'

'Bit like me. Now, I want to treat you to a pub lunch. Okay, we've drinks and snacks in my bag but I'm starving. Please agree.'

'I'd love to but isn't Josh a bit young? Will he be allowed in.'

Rudi laughed. 'Come on, this is England, not the States.'

They were all welcomed at the pub including Beamish. Josh, sitting contentedly in a highchair seemed to be taking in everything, returning smiles that came from everyone else in the pub.

'This is one of the best things about life in England. I'm so lucky having so much freedom to come and go, belonging to two worlds. Thanks, Fran, for coming today – showing me the lost medieval village, the monument and the church.'

She grinned. 'They're all quite traceable. How about your temporary work? I bet I've interrupted.'

'No more than I've interrupted you, Fran. I'm meeting a fellow from the university tomorrow to compare notes. He's been checking on the spread of rhododendrons. A lovely, popular shrub but can be very invasive and damaging to native plants.'

Fran then noticed Rudi was grinning and sniffing, eyebrows raised.

'What's wrong?' she asked.

'Nothing – well not with me but Josh may have a problem.'

'You've an acute sense of smell! Right - off to the loo, lad. Must get you sorted.'

Fran picked up the small backpack and carried Josh to the Ladies. After changing him she tightly wrapped his old nappy in a thick plastic bag and pushed it to the bottom of the pack. While washing her hands she noted that her cheeks were unusually pink; clearly a bit sunburnt. She combed her hair then retrieved Josh who was inspecting every part of the small room.

Already, Rudi had removed Josh's lunch from his large rucksack and, minutes later, watching the child eating with relish, he enthused about his contentment and sociability.

'Yes,' said Fran, 'but will he be like this when he's two? Jane described her daughter to me at two and I could hardly believe it was the same child.'

'Ah, don't anticipate the worst. Josh, you wouldn't play your mum up, would you? A lovely chap like you.'

Josh screwed his eyes up as if contemplating the question and his minders burst out laughing.

'I love him so much,' said Fran, feeling really emotional.

'A two-way thing,' said Rudi. 'Ah, our fresh fish has arrived.'

During the meal Fran was amused and impressed by the number of smiles and nods Josh directed towards Rudi. His mumbled response to Rudi's question, 'Is your lunch nice, Josh?' sounded more like mice than nice but, managing not to laugh, Rudi enthused that his was mice too.

'He's talking, Fran. Saying the odd discernible word. That's brilliant.'

Beamish's good behaviour was rewarded with a biscuit from the landlady when they exchanged their farewells, and assured her they would be back.

'Thanks, Rudi, that was lovely. You've entertained all three of us excellently,' said Fran, as they walked towards the rising valley.

'No, my thanks to you three,' Rudi replied. 'A brilliant day and still a way to go.'

Back at Spring Cottage, refreshing themselves with tea and the snacks not consumed on the walk, Rudi commented, 'Walking longish distances doesn't trouble you, which is great. I've an older cousin who's a doctor and he believes it's the finest way to keep fit. Does Simon enjoy it?'

'He does when he feels like it. He's a bit vulnerable to infections. He had several colds last winter while I didn't have one. I do hope you'll be able to meet him soon.'

'So do I.' Rudi glanced at his watch. 'The chap who's meeting me tomorrow is going to ring about five so I'd better get going. It's been a great day, Fran. Thanks so much.'

'No, thank you. The lunch was really good. Drop by any time. Rudi.'

He beamed, nodding, and they both stood up and hugged which elicited not even a bark from Beamish. Fran accompanied Rudi to his hired car and, reluctantly waved him off.

A morning's work in her studio convinced Fran she needed a break, so she walked a short distance with Josh and Beamish, then she lounged against a

238

rock, with her two companions snoring beside her. Now and then she closed her eyes, shutting in rather than shutting out the beauty around her. The various colours of the three heathers, purple, amethyst and pink intermingled with gold and green were painted before her. Close by a Painted Lady sat on a spray of heather while a variety of smaller butterflies fluttered around her. There had to be male Painted Ladies so what were they called, Painted Laddies? A buzzard hovered well above her for minutes then swiftly flew lower, attracted to something edible – a lizard, rabbit? With its extraordinary eyesight it could even be homing in on an insect. It disappeared behind some gorse bushes then rose again, giving a cat-like call which attracted a companion and together they scanned the area, frequently dropping swiftly to seize a succulent morsel.

Their activities reminded Fran it was nearly time to feed her companions. She glanced at her watch and realised she must have dozed a bit. As if compensating for her slightly reluctant return home, a young deer preceded Fran for a few yards as she entered the lane to Spring Cottage.

She bathed Josh and put him to bed early after giving him the last of his now three times daily breast feeds. It had been a good day; progress achieved with her commission, and the afternoon on the moor had been a reward for hard work but now she was feeling the effect of the relentless heat. She fed a listless Beamish, showered, slowly turning the dial to cold, then wrapped in a huge towel, lay on her bed looking at the reddening sky.

'A few minutes, Beams, then I'll have to get a bit of supper. Maybe Rudi will drop by later.' She yawned. 'We haven't seen him today, have we?'

Beamish grunted from the rug and Fran gave a long, contented sigh and turned her face into the cool pillow.

Chapter 19

Simon telephoned from Heathrow but there was no reply. Needing a petrol top up he rang again from Fleet Service Station. Damn. She'd have to get an answering machine. He had no doubt Fran was at Spring Cottage because she was expecting him home tomorrow. The chance of an earlier flight had arisen and, with the business brilliantly concluded, he had no wish to linger in a city disappointingly soulless after the initial excitement had worn off. He enjoyed meeting fellow academics, particularly a professor of English, a Magdalen graduate of the early sixties with all the charm and courtesy of Eastern fame. Hard-hitting questions about finance were asked; he was expected to converse knowledgeably about domestic and world politics and predict the behaviour of the pound sterling. A visit to Raffles, unchanged he imagined from decades ago, had lightened things a bit but Fran and Josh were constantly in his thoughts.

There were several delays on the A303. Simon calmed his impatience by pushing a tape into the cassette players. `I'm not crying over you' sang Chris de Burgh, a wry reminder of Melanie who played him incessantly, deeming his songs excruciatingly romantic.

He glanced at queuing holiday drivers with a mixture of pity and exasperation. Pale, tense, weary and irritable, their faces told the tale of long drives from Scotland and the North. Was it worth it, he wondered, to spend one or two weeks in some dreary guest house with whining kids? Doubtless they'd be happier in familiar surroundings, with familiar toys, and the assurance that the telly lasted from breakfast until bedtime. Holidays in his childhood were predictable and, usually, lonely. For years his grandparents rented a cottage on the Pembrokeshire coast, but after a couple of visits it held no interest for him. Occasional holidays with his mother, which included Charles, became a high spot but nothing could compare with school trips to Paris, Venice, Germany and Austria always with crowds of friends and all the rules in the book to be broken. He and Charles came close to expulsion after a skiing trip that ended a day later for them than the sixteen other fourth formers. Simon smiled at the memory. Good, he's seeing Chas in a couple of days. Maybe, they'd fit some surfing in. The tape ended. He turned the radio on and heard there were traffic jams all the way to Land's End. He switched off and inserted another tape, Mozart's Clarinet Concerto, evoking exquisitely one of his earliest times with Fran. He avoided the Minehead road with its crawling Somerset World traffic, and found himself behind a huge tractor, a more tolerable obstruction. Beyond the pink fringe of willowherbs, he looked across the Brendon Hills and felt a rare, intense pleasure that he was coming home. The sky was already streaked pale orange and indigo. All this, he thought, all this and Fran too.

The cottage looked deserted. No lights were on. Simon drove into the yard and switched the engine off. He reached for his Duty-Free bag, bulging with gifts for Fran and Josh, and for his suitcase, full of grubby clothes. He started when a slightly American voice said:

'Hi, I'm Rudi, a friend of Fran's.'

He noticed then, the figure standing close to the car. There was just too long a pause before he said drily, 'I'm Simon, Fran's husband,' and shook the extended hand.

In spite of the dusk, he could recognise the pleasant smile, and the tone of voice that sounded genuinely pleased to meet him prompted him to add: 'Ah, you're the rescuer of distressed damsels.'

Rudi chuckled. 'I expect she'd have got out somehow.' There was a pause, then Rudi suddenly thrust a bottle into Simon's hand. 'A thank you for Fran. She's helped me to find temporary accommodation. I really must go. Nice to have met you, Simon.'

Privately wishing him across the Atlantic, Simon amazed himself by his words:

'Don't you want to come in? Fran must be around as Beamish is here and her car's in.'

He realised, then, that Beamish was standing beside the American, and not leaping about effusively greeting `The Master'.

Rudi said lightly, 'Thanks but I was just passing on my way to meet a student. Nice to meet you, Simon.'

Say it again thought Simon, and I'll believe it. He watched the man walk swiftly under the archway and disappear. There was no sound of a car starting. Was he setting out across the darkening moor on foot?

A pang of conscience troubled him, but fleetingly. He'd asked the chap in, what more could he do? He found the front door ajar and felt a moment's irritation at Fran's carelessness. He went through to the kitchen, switched on the light and put his bag on the table. An unwashed lettuce lay on the draining board, the table was not laid, and there were no signs of a meal in preparation. Why did he find this reassuring? Where was Fran? In the bath perhaps? Asleep?

As he turned the bend in the short staircase, he smelt Fran's lemon bath essence. He looked into Josh's tiny room for a second. His face softened at the sight of the sleeping child, whose scruffiest, best-loved toy was clutched in a chubby hand against his face. Now and then he made a gentle snuffling sound but not a flicker of response when, softly, Simon spoke his name.

He found Fran as soundly asleep as their son. She lay wrapped in a cream bath towel, her hair spread across the pillow and half concealing her face. Her chest scarcely moved.

He felt an intense mixture of tenderness and desire. His excitement was almost painful. He glanced downwards grinning ruefully. Not yet! He was travel-stained and disgusting.

He left his clothes where he dropped them and showered rigorously, turning the handle to cold for a second as was his habit. He towelled himself, shaved and cleaned his teeth. The window looked across the coombe where distant lights were coming on, tiny pinpoints like grounded stars. He opened it to dispel the steam and the air was heavy and still with the day's heat. He breathed in the scent of a hardy honeysuckle that swarmed over the warm stone of the house.

On the tiny landing he switched the nightlight on for Josh's comfort should he awaken and returned to the bedroom. Fran had shifted a little and the towel had slipped away to reveal her smooth, flat tummy, only a shade paler gold than the rest of her.

She sighed, turning her face into the pillow. Her left leg flexed; the skin inside the thigh pale also. Afraid of startling her he resisted the strong impulse to bury his face in the dark triangle. Instead, he knelt beside her and spoke her name quietly but persistently. She stirred at last, opened her eyes then gave a small, startled cry. He moved swiftly, reassured her, and drew her into his arms.

Some while later, replete and lying with her head on his shoulder, Fran said,

'You might have been a complete stranger, a multiple rapist. The beast of Exmoor on two legs.'

He chuckled, then remembered Rudi standing quietly in the courtyard, gently fondling the ears of an unusually quiescent Beamish. He felt a surge of irrational jealously.

'Don't joke, Fran. You are vulnerable here alone. You must learn to lock doors.'

Sensing his sudden tension she leaned up on one elbow and stroked his face.

'Beamish is my protection.'

'Not tonight he wasn't. He was very chummy with your friend, that American. He was in the courtyard when I arrived. He left you a bottle of wine.'

'That was kind.'

'He knows your taste.'

'He's had a meal here once or twice. I've been helping a bit with local knowledge.'

'Lucky chap.'

'Simon, you're not jealous! He's so nice. I want you to get to know him. He's. different, really interesting.'

'Good. Right now I'm only interested in you and being alone with you. Not that I mind a few days with Chas and Anna.'

245

During the remainder of Simons' vacation, Fran avoided mentioning Rudi. Simon was relaxed and happy, lounging in the late summer heat, then walking on the moor in the cool of early evening with Josh, and with Beamish doing his hopeless hunting. Most evenings Fran stayed at home, cooking the best meals she could devise. With Simon in this happy mood she was finding it easy to indulge him. Three times Jane brought Tricia to ride Chuckle and, out on the moor, discreetly kept Fran up to date with Rudi's activities.

'He seems really set on working here. He's had interviews and seemed pretty upbeat after one at Bristol.' Jane stopped suddenly, halting Chuckle. 'Look Fran, a couple of deer. Can you see them, Tricia?' Jane pointed to a stag and hind a couple of hundred yards away.

'Yes, Chuckle showed me.'

Now seeing that Chuckle's head was raised and ears pricked Fran and Jane laughed.

'We'd better divert our attentions to the task in hand, away from a gorgeous chap – well, not quite as gorgeous as yours, Fran. I'm amazed Rudi hasn't been snapped up. No girl friends around but, maybe, he's got one back home.'

'And speaking of home, we'd better get back,' said Fran, looking at her watch. 'We've each got a chap to feed, well two in my case.'

Chapter 20

Simon was looking pleased, even excited. Following Fran into the kitchen he said, 'Another special visit – just four days in India this time.'

'Goodness, the first one must have impressed your boss!' Fran exclaimed. 'When are you going?'

'In a couple of days – if that's all right?'

'Of course – oh gosh, it's Miranda's birthday in three days. She's expecting us in London.'

'Sorry, but attracting wealthy foreign students must come first. I'm sure she'll understand.'

Simon was right. Miranda was impressed by the importance the university was placing on his visits and, just with Fran and Joshua, enjoyed a simple birthday.

*

On the sixth day of Simon's absence after a morning at London Zoo, Miranda and Fran relaxed on the sofa while Josh had a much-needed snooze until the loudly-ringing phone roused all three.

'Keep resting. I'll answer it,' Miranda said, disappearing into the hall. Minutes later she was back. 'It's for you, dear. Simon's poorly and in hospital.'

Gasping, Fran rushed to the phone.

'Yes, I am Mrs Fellowes. Please tell me what's wrong.'

Minutes later she turned to Miranda who was close by. 'It's pneumonia, they think. They're keeping him in for a while to do some tests.'

She concentrated on the phone again, then said, 'Thank you. I'll come very soon.'

She replaced the receiver. 'I can visit. I'm so relieved.'

'Fran, I'll drive. We can settle Josh comfortably in his special seat and you can be next to him.'

Fran had only once entered a hospital. Years ago, she visited a school friend who'd had her appendix out and it had seemed rather a lark. The friend took on an aura of importance and distance, having travelled in the strange world induced by anaesthesia. In a private room, bulging with pink balloons, huge polished-looking black grapes and bunches of flowers, she had queened it over her school friends who regarded her with awe, bordering on envy.

It was very different this time. The hospital seemed overwhelmingly large and impersonal. Everyone was in a hurry. The receptionist who directed Fran to the lift, was conducting a telephone conversation at the same time. A doctor, looking no older than Fran, was in Simon's room when she entered, after being instructed by a nurse to put on a plastic apron and gloves.

'Just a precaution,' he'd said. 'We don't yet know what sort of bug Dr Fellowes has picked up. I understand he's been in India?'

The doctor, a woman, smiled and shook hands. It seemed a bizarre ritual in plastic gloves. Fran looked at the shape in the high metal bed, with apprehension.

'Don't be put off,' said the doctor. 'The mask is helping him to breath more easily, and the drip is giving him fluids. He was quite dehydrated. We're doing some tests - all quite routine. I'm surprised more people don't get ill on 'planes. All those bugs breeding for hours in recycled air!'

Fran grinned. The down-to-earth words were reassuring. Tentatively she approached Simon.

'Is he. conscious?'

'Drifting. He may respond when you speak to him. I'll leave you now. Please ring if you're worried or needing anything. The staff nurse will be back in a minute.'

Simon's colour was grey. Not that she could see much of his face which was almost obscured by the mask attached by a tube to a cylinder on which hung a placard saying; 'No Smoking. Highly Inflammable'! That would strike Simon as funny. She sat down and pondered on whether she should speak then, emboldened by the doctor's words, she spoke his name with normal volume. There was no flicker of response.

'It's Fran, Simon,' she continued. 'You're safe, in hospital, in England. You were taken ill on the 'plane.'

'Don't worry if he doesn't respond, Mrs Fellowes.' It was the male nurse again, coming into the room quietly. 'It's early days.'

'Days!'

He grinned. 'Hours then.'

'I hope it won't be days.' Her voice became unsteady. 'He won't even open his eyes.'

'Don't worry. Really, he's very stable. The body needs to rest to deal with the infection. He has surfaced a bit and muttered something. I expect his high temperature is making him a bit delirious.'

'D'you think it could be something tropical?'

The nurse hesitated. 'Bit too soon to say but it seems he has a chest infection. It'll be a while before the doctors can tell you anymore.'

'My aunt and my little boy are somewhere outside. I'd better find them and then, if it's possible, I'd like to....'

'Stay? Of course you can. We may not be able to make you very comfortable but I can promise lots of tea or coffee. I'll be here with him while you're away. There's a bag by the door for the plastics.'

Fran gave him a grateful smile and removing the apron and gloves, left the room. A little way along the corridor Miranda was waiting, a sleeping Josh in her arms. Fran hurried to her.

'Let me take him, he's such a weight.'

Fran gently took the child who grunted and snuggled against her shoulder.

'Simon's not really aware of anything. He's barely conscious but they say he's going to be all right. He could just have a nasty chest infection, perhaps something tropical. They're not sure yet.'

'Darling, slow down. Let's sit over there for a minute.' Miranda indicated a small reception area.

'No. I'm fine. But I'd like to stay here with Simon.'

'Of course. I'll take Josh home and we'll talk again in the morning. You mustn't be concerned about anything, or anyone, but Simon. And if you're at all worried you will ring me?'

'Yes, of course. Thank you. It's ironical isn't it, the way we were talking about Simon's health? It seems you were right, and I hadn't even noticed.' Fran struggled to withhold her tears as she began to walk towards the exit.

'Darling, you've nothing to reproach yourself with. Simon's a grown man. If he won't take advice there's nothing you can do. Anyway, if he has a tropical illness, it would be the sort that could strike any traveller, run down or not. I've picked up odd infections travelling around and I'm pretty tough.'

Fran smiled then. 'Yes, you are. You're amazing.'

At the car she gently lowered Josh into his safety seat. He opened his eyes, looked puzzled, then closed them and gave a little sigh.

'Contentment, or resignation?' whispered Fran.

'Oh, he's such an easy child,' Miranda said, then in a less steady voice, 'He's so precious. You mustn't worry, darling. I'll take the greatest care of him.'

Fran hugged her. 'I shan't worry - not about Josh. You're always here for us. I must seem to take it all for granted.'

'You should, Fran darling. That's one of the functions of families. Now before I get silly you must go back to your husband.'

Apart from the night of Josh's birth it was the longest Fran had endured. A nurse gave her a pile of magazines but she turned the pages unseeingly. Endless cups of tea and coffee were offered and she encountered nothing but kindness from the busy staff, who looked in at ten minute intervals. The oxygen had been turned off once Simon's breathing improved but the drip had to be checked frequently. Whenever his blood pressure and temperature were measured Fran resisted asking questions, too fearful of the answers.

She found herself endlessly reviewing their life together. It was a pretty volatile relationship; he,

251

flaring quickly to anger but never sulking, she more patient, deflecting his anger with humour, occasionally, but she had a stubborn streak which, he admitted, often defeated him. He still complained at her absences but greeted her with such pleasure on her returns that she considered the mild arguments were worth it. Theirs was not a marriage that would fall into complacency.

Simon's gradual compliance with their unusual routine had been reassuring. He was certainly not at a loss on his own. He spent his more active times with Gerry, and involved himself with Roger's drama group, but now seeing him so vulnerable, and even helpless, she began to torment herself with doubts: should she have spent so much time away? Had she neglected him, failed to see signs that he was unwell? Was this what Miranda had implied? But how could she look after him? Frequently he'd teased her for even trying, telling her if he'd wanted a domestic little body, fussing around him, he would have chosen one. Occasionally, he accused her of being too wrapped-up in Josh but this she ignored. Men do get jealous of their offspring; she'd read about it. Once or twice she'd discussed this with Jane whose response was robust: 'If you employed a nanny and saw Josh twice a day, Simon would still find something to be jealous about. David's the same.'

.Jane spoke sense so she was reassured. Anyway, she was not like those mothers who continually drag their children into conversations, never leave them with a babysitter, and make their needs as obtrusive and unattractive as possible. All these thoughts trundled around in her mind until, worn out and tearful, she dropped her head on the white cellular blanket beside Simon's harnessed arm and slept.

When Simon became restless trying to move the arm attached to the drip and muttering incoherently, she awoke. She moved as swiftly as possible, recognising the change in Simon, and found a widely yawning staff nurse in the corridor. Nurse James became alert instantly and in minutes had rearranged Simon's arm, checked his temperature and sponged his face.

'Do this whenever you like,' she suggested. 'It'll cool him down and soothe him.'

As she spoke Simon opened his eyes, looked at them both in bewilderment, muttered something then drifted off again. Fran's look of distress that he still didn't seem to know her moved the nurse to suggest she should have a break. Grateful but reluctant Fran smiled and shook her head.

'Then how about a cup of tea?'

Again, she declined. 'No. thanks. Anyway, you've betters things to do.'

When the door closed, she sank into an armchair and wept with tiredness and frustration. She supposed she must have dozed because, when awareness returned, light was penetrating the Venetian blinds.

She got up, stiffly, to investigate. Dawn, a ragged, muddy orange, was breaking over the uninspiring skyline. In the shower room she splashed cold water on her face then found Simon's toilet bag in the smaller of his two cases, and rubbed her teeth with toothpaste squeezed onto her forefinger. She rinsed her mouth several times but the taste and feel were still horrible. All that tannin, perhaps!

Simon seemed peaceful. His skin was cooler and slightly damp. She wondered if he could be sleeping normally and a nurse, appearing to do the early morning observations, confirmed her hopes.

'It's amazing how quickly the patient responds once we get the fluids going in. And it's helped having you here, but you look all in. Why don't you go to the canteen for a break and some food? We'll make him comfortable.'

Fran followed her suggestion and ate ravenously the kind of breakfast she normally avoided, bacon with eggs, tomatoes and fried bread, then buttered toast.

She longed to see Josh. She had never been parted from him for more than three or four hours and her need for him was physical. She wanted his solid weight in her arms and the softness of his face against her cheek.

When she returned to Simon, he looked much more comfortable. He was sitting up against a bank of pillows and was wearing his own pyjamas. As she approached the bed he turned and looked at her, the heavy, vagueness gone from his eyes, and he smiled.

'Darling Fran. You're early.'

She kissed him but he moved slightly and murmured, 'No, I'm so revolting.'

'Don't be silly. They've given you a wash and spruced you up. They've even dabbed you with Paco Robsane.'

He grinned. 'My mouth is disgusting. Could I clean my teeth, d'you think?'

'I expect so. All your luggage is here. That was thoughtful, wasn't it? It could so easily have been left behind, or lost.'

'I don't remember much, Fran, just getting on an early flight due to a passenger's cancellation. I felt so rotten I didn't even think to ring you. I didn't think it was possible to feel so ill and still be alive.'

He was discharged home after seven days. Miranda was shocked.

'He can't possibly be ready,' she protested. 'He's been dangerously ill. He's had pneumonia.'

'It isn't like that nowadays,' Fran said, patiently. 'The danger period may be very brief due to the antibiotics. He just needs to rest and he can do that anywhere.'

'Well, he'll come home of course but I still think they're pushing him out.'

'They do need the bed, I'm sure. They seem hectically busy.'

'But he's in a private room!'

'Doesn't make any difference. There's pressure on all beds. I'm sure they wouldn't discharge him if they thought there was a serious risk.'

Fran did not tell Miranda that Simon charmingly put pressure on the consultant to discharge him. In Miranda's largest guest bedroom he settled down to a swift and trouble-free convalescence.

'I thought he'd be quite awful,' Fran told Anna, who visited with a bunch of freesias, a bottle of Bollinger and a copy of Simon's latest book to be autographed for Charles.

'He's being really sweet. Not picky and impatient as I imagined and very tolerant of Josh who has practically moved in with him.'

'It is impressive as he's never enjoyed ill-health,' Anna said. 'If he even just got a cold when he was a student he was furious. It was as if he felt he was above getting the bugs the rest of us had to tolerate.'

'D'you think his mum and gran regarded him as a superior being?' Fran asked.

Anna nodded 'They didn't spoil him, exactly; he had to behave well but it was clear they thought he was marvellous.'

'I guess that can be overdone – especially in a female-dominated household,' said Miranda. 'We'd better be careful with Josh; we could utterly wreck him.' She picked up the loaded tray to take to Simon and, grinning, Anna followed her with her arms full of gifts,

Chapter 21

The relief at Simon's rapid recovery did not completely obliterate Fran's memory of the soul-searching she'd inflicted on herself. Less dependent on her studio she had more time to socialise so gave more dinner parties for local friends and accepted their invitations with good grace. Simon was pleased. He even commented that her adult, independent life had only just started when he met her and now, in less than three years, she was both a wife and a mother. She'd experienced a minimum of adult freedom compared with him.

One of the biggest surprises for both of them was Fran's involvement with a Mother and Toddler group where she found a few like-minded women and learnt to grit her teeth and smile blandly at the others. Simon took on a little more child-minding allowing Fran an hour or two of freedom several times a week. Jane, who dropped in whenever a need to do major shopping brought her to the city, commented on Simon's involvement with Josh.

'He's really good with him, isn't he?'

Fran noted the surprise in her voice and grinned. Loyally, she did not say that he usually attracted an admiring following of female students, all dying to get their hands on Josh if only to get his dad's attention. His progress with Josh in his pushchair was second only to the Pied Piper's! Never mind, she and Beamish could visit the estuary, the cathedral, do a bit of self-indulgent shopping, or she could pick up a pen or paint brush and work on the less demanding commissions her good friend Thomas now found for her. Having fathered three children in the early days of his career he was very understanding of her need to avoid frantic deadlines or jobs requiring research. Her current commission was to illustrate a humorous story about a cat. Samples had resulted in encouraging phone calls from the writer, a middle-aged woman who was quickly becoming well-known and respected.

'An ideal job,' Simon enthused. 'No need to spend time researching, staring at wildlife on the moor, and splattering yourself with paint.'

*

Within the next four months Fran had commissions to illustrate three more books for children. She was interviewed on the local radio which pleased Simon greatly.

'You're on the road to fame,' he enthused, 'not just being recognised by moorland sheep and ponies.'

Her visits to Spring Cottage were now limited but Fred kept an eye on Chuckle, often letting him graze with his long-retired Shire horse and Jane took her daughter out riding at least once a week. There was no sign or news of Rudi then a postcard arrived at Spring Cottage addressed to Dr.& Mrs. S. Fellowes. Simon found it and studied it for a minute before handing it to Fran.

'From Brazil. Must have taken weeks to get here.'

The front of the card showed a view of a mountain rising above an expanse of forest, and on the back were the words;

Hi, hope all is well with you. I'm involved in a project with students from Pennsylvania University, researching rare floral species. The Rain Forest is the most amazing place I've visited and constantly under threat of exploitation. Thank goodness Exmoor is better protected.

Rudi.

''What a place to visit,' Fran enthused.

'So you'd like to go there – for our next holiday?' Simon had got up to refill the kettle so Fran couldn't see his expression but his tone told of a grin. She giggled.

'I've always imagined you'd opt for trips to the Caribbean when not in Venice or Rome.'

'More tea?'

'Please. I was surprised that a beach holiday in Brittany was so acceptable.'

'Well, when Josh is older we'll go a bit further, but not to Amazonia. You're right. I have travelled a lot but I'm not very keen at present, three long distance trips in under a year are enough. I don't think flying suits me anymore. How about going back to Josh's beach in Brittany? Now he's quite a walker he'll get even more out of it.'

Fran beamed her approval, got up and gave Simon a hug which brought a chortle from Josh, watching from his highchair,

*

In early July Jane rang just two days after spending time in Exeter with Fran. She sounded excited.

'It's just that I've heard from Rudi. He's back in Pennsylvania, staying with his parents but, in the Autumn, he's starting a job at Bristol University, a research project on Exmoor and part time teaching. I wish he could stay with us – remember he spent a couple of weeks with us last year – but we're booked up. As you're not at the cottage so much I wondered if you'd let it to him. It would be ideal for him and there'd be some advantages for you. Of course, I haven't said anything to him.'

Fran sat on the bed and considered this for a minute. 'I don't know. I do miss my times at the cottage. It's not entirely my choice to be there less often.'

'I gathered that, Fran.'

'You know Simon's always hated the way it draws me. I imagine he'd be pleased if I let it. The trouble is once I start, he'll expect it always to be let. I'll think about it, but don't raise Rudi's hopes.'

'No, I won't and you've plenty of time to consider it. I gather he's had an amazing time in Brazil. I feel quite envious. Make our lives seem a bit mundane!'

*

The second holiday in Brittany was as successful as the first. Fellow visitors were impressed and amused when Josh responded to the arrival of an ice cream with the word, 'Messy.'

The waitress burst out laughing, then said, 'Il dit "merci," le petit gentilhomme.'

Simon agreed with her and left her a large tip.

An hour later, with a sketch book and camera to hand, Fran watched Josh and Simon playing along the edge of the beach, kicking the frothy waves. Simon was tanned and gorgeous as ever but had lost weight. Over several weeks Fran had mentioned this as tactfully as possible but the response was always the same. He was still eating well and had energy so what was she worried about? When, once again, she suggested he should see a doctor and he had told her not to be stupid – he wasn't going to waste any doctor's time.

Whatever he said she was sure he tired more quickly than usual. If she mentioned letting the cottage would that buck him up? Or wasn't it an appropriate time? She decided to wait until they were at home, wherever that was! Holidays should mean a complete cut off from day-to-day life.

Ten days later, when they were staying at Spring Cottage for a few days, she decided to broach the subject. With Josh in bed they were relaxing on the terrace at sunset after a spending the warmest part of the day on Combe Martin beach. The low tide had afforded them plenty of sand for castle building. For Josh the best part of the job was flattening the 'building' seconds after it was made.

'Demolition expert rather than builder,' Simon had commented. 'Let's treat ourselves to ice creams after all that hard work.'

The day had gone so well the last thing Fran wanted was to spoil it so Simon's reaction to her letting plan came as huge relief.

'Commonsense at last, Fran, and better for you if it's an acquaintance living here rather than a stranger,' he said. 'You can relax and enjoy the other part of your life. Thank goodness your current work allows for the distance and for our closeness. I think a toast is appropriate.'

Was their rapturous lovemaking that night stimulated by Fran's decision? The thought flashed into her mind at a highly inappropriate moment.

Simon's good mood continued. He even accompanied Jane and Fran when they took Tricia for a ride on Chuckle. Josh seemed intrigued and happy, particularly when Tricia said, 'Put him on too, Mummy. I can hold him.'

'No room on the saddle for two so will you swap for a bit?' suggested Jane and was pleased and surprised at the response - a beam and nod. Fran helped her to dismount then lifted Josh on and held him for safety as they continued.

'Lord, it'll be Beamish demanding a ride next,' said Simon.

'Sadly, not you,' said Fran. 'Exmoor's are really strong. Chuckle could cope for a while.'

'No. I've never understood how men can cope with riding. Our anatomy's all wrong. Shouldn't we be the ones riding side saddle?'

Fran and Jane were joined in laughter by Tricia but they guessed/ hoped she didn't fully understand the joke.

Above the Doone Valley, Fran recalled the day when Rudi had treated her to the pub lunch and had pleased her with his knowledge of Lorna Doone. She was so relieved that Simon had approved of the letting to Rudi. The garden would be cared for, she was sure, as he'd enthused about it on his visits and Chuckle would have two carers, Rudi and Fred. A few times she had wondered if Rudi's research would irritate Fred whose forebears had contributed to the clearing of great swathes of bracken and gorse from the moor to increase grazing areas for their livestock. The result was that, due to overgrazing in certain areas, there was a greater increase in bracken growth as if the plant had aggressively re-established itself. On the steepest slopes bracken stabilises the soil, preventing erosion, so a lesson had to be learnt as to where and how clearance should be carried out. Miranda had spoken often of the various rules imposed on farmers, the arguments between them and organisations committed to preserving the moor. Fran then remembered that on the day of her rescue Fred commented that he'd had chats with Rudi when coming across him on the moor, so he knew about Rudi's passion for conservation. The atmosphere between them had seemed relaxed and friendly.

Jane had once mentioned that she'd had reservations about how David would get on with Rudi but they'd had several chats, often over a few pints at their local pub.

No, she had no reason to worry as Simon's agreement was assured so all she had to do was discuss matters with Rudi. A phone call resulted in an enthusiastic response and an arrangement to meet at Spring Cottage in two weeks' time.

Chapter 22

'Can you come to the cottage with me, please? I'll be sorting things out about the letting and your input would be helpful.'

'I can't, Fran. There's that important meeting on Monday about some changes in funding. You know how the bloody politicians are interfering all the time. If we didn't have an increase of self-funding students from the Far East we'd really be feeling the pinch.'

'You'll be free for your birthday?'

'Of course. You're not taking me to Israel, are you?'

'No, bit soon for a second honeymoon.'

'Well, I hope it all goes okay. When will you be back?

'Tuesday. Bit of cleaning to do.'

'Why don't you get the Yeo's to help?'

'I don't need their help. Anyway, they're always busy and they refuse to charge for any job that isn't structural.'

'Not many like them these days.'

'No, and I'm not taking advantage of them.'

After making sure the cottage was as pristine as possible for a two hundred years old building, Fran amused herself by making a card for Simon's birthday: a pen and crayon drawing of an astonished looking Exmoor pony congratulating herself on the arrival of her foal.

'Now Josh, what will you make for Daddy? How about a model of Beamish?'

Josh, sitting beside her, was fully occupied pushing a miniature toy tractor up and down the table. Ten minutes later he looked delighted when Fran showed him a tiny clay model which could have been anything between a wolf and a Dachshund.

'Not quite Auntie's standard, Josh. Now, we'd better go for a walk before it warms up and we must be here when Rudi arrives.'

From the terrace Fran looked across the combe to the purple-coated hills. Occasionally birds appeared, single buzzards and more socially minded smaller birds, too far away to identify. Apart from them there was no sign of movement. It was as if nature was having an afternoon nap. The light was hazy, softening the tops of the hills so they looked endless, suggesting the moor went on forever

Beamish wandered in the garden, surprising Fran that he was still active as he'd struggled on their morning walk, keeping close to her and Josh. She reminded herself he was eighty-four in human years so, maybe, she should restrict his walks. Although he was physically less active than usual, he was still mentally alert. Eyes bright, staring at her, he gave a short bark, at the sound of a car arriving.

'Good boy, it must be Rudi,' Fran said and walked through the house to the yard where Rudi was getting out of a small Ford.

'Great to see you,' he said, and they hugged. Fran was surprised that Beamish didn't bark but gave Rudi a welcoming lick.

'You look well,' she said. 'Your Amazonian trip must have been wonderful.'

'It was. I've photos to show you if you've time?'

265

'All the time in the world. Let's have some tea.'

Josh, who had been dozing in a small chair by the French window, scrambled to his feet and beamed a welcome to Rudi who scooped him up. Josh laughed and plonked his head on Rudi's shoulder as if he was about to doze off again.

'You know who he is, don't you, Josh?' enthused Fran and was sure he nodded.

They sat on the terrace for at least two hours hearing each other's news. Fran was amazed by the photographs; they were of plants, birds, insects, amphibians and reptiles. She counted a hundred and forty photographs and was not surprised to hear he had hundreds more.

'I didn't take them all. I was with four other leaders, all researching different aspects but my students, bless them, thought our research was the most important. We were studying the dependency of tree-living species on the survival of the forest. The scientist in charge was my tutor when I started at university and a brilliant guy.'

'So don't you want to stay out there, doing that vital work?'

'I'm one of many, Fran. That research attracts people world-wide, so I was really lucky to get the chance to spend months there. Not that camping there was easy. Our faces hands, arms and legs were constantly covered with insects. Anyway, I like your little country.'

'Mine? It's also half yours. Your English roots are as deep as your American ones, aren't they?'

Rudi laughed. 'Deeper according to my grandparents. They're thrilled I'm back here and about to rent this place.'

'Maybe, we'd better get down to business. You haven't even seen the whole place – you don't know what you'll be getting.'

'Fran, are you leaving the records here?'

'Yes, I can't clutter the flat with them and that old gramophone. D'you mind?'

'No. I 'd love to play them. Is that okay?'

'Of course. I'm pleased they'll be appreciated.'

While showing Rudi over the cottage Fran told him there was no need to supply a thing, towels, sheets, duvets were all included in the rent.

Back on the terrace, Rudi commented, 'What you're charging is so reasonable. Are you sure it's correct, Fran and is Simon happy with it?'

Luckily Josh who was studying a rose leaf as if he was considering eating it took her attention.

'No Josh, a prickly thing.' She picked him up and sat with him on her lap.

'Simon is really pleased you're going to rent the cottage and he's leaving all the details to me.'

'So once again he's not here with you.'

'No, there's an important meeting at the university to do with finance. A number of staff are still away so Simon felt he had to go.' Fran said, silently adding, Thank goodness.

'How long are you staying?'

'I must be back for Simon's birthday on Wednesday, but when do you want to move in?' 'As soon as it's convenient for you, Fran.'

'Tomorrow if you like.'

'Really? That's great. Now, I'd better run over the instructions about Chuckle. And what about Beamish?'

'He's staying in Exeter if you can bear it.'

Rudi laughed. 'I'll cope, somehow. Fran, if you want to come down to check on Chuckle or anything, I could move into the studio. Luxury after the Amazon.'

'Thanks, I'll remember that. More tea or something stiffer?'

'Tea will be fine, thanks, but have you the time?'

'I certainly have. The dear Yeos are insisting on feeding me tonight with one of their sheep. I shall take Josh in his carrycot and hope he sleeps throughout.'

'Fran, I've copies of all the photos so would you like these? I've had visions of you making paintings of some of them.'

'Gosh, yes thanks. May I select some as I'm not too sure about the insects and snakes.'

'Take whatever you like. I'll look forward to seeing the results.'

In a few years, thought Fran, suddenly longing for time in her studio.

Another hour was spent chatting then Rudi said he'd better get back to the Bed and Breakfast in Malmsmead or they'd think he didn't want to be fed.

'You don't have to walk this time. Is the car yours?' Fran asked.

'Yes. I bought it in Barnstaple a couple of days ago. Pretty good for a six-year-old. Honestly, Fran I can't believe I'll actually be living here. I'm so grateful to you.'

'And I to you. I'd hate to let it to a stranger.'

Leaving Josh and Beamish dozing in the late warmth they went to the courtyard. Rudi put his backpack in the car then gave Fran a hug.

'Oh, the keys,' she exclaimed 'I haven't given them to you. Just a sec.' She ran inside then back with the spare keys and handed them over. 'Fred has some too so you'll always have access. Turn up whenever you like tomorrow. I might still be here or I might not.'

'Well, I hope to see you soon, Fran. Thanks again. Please say goodbye to Josh and Beamish.' Rudi got into the car and, waving, drove slowly out of the courtyard and down the lane. Fran watched until the car disappeared then, hearing the phone ringing hurried indoors.

'Jane, great news – it's all arranged. Rudi's moving in tomorrow.'

'That's fine. Lucky chap and lucky you. He's looking wonderful. He's dropped by a couple of times to Tricia's delight. First crush?'

Laughing Fran said, 'I trust David's not around. I've explained to Rudi about Tricia's rides and the farrier's regular visits so nothing has to change.'

'Except, I'll miss you, Fran. Before you go can you come for a meal? My parents are here for a few days and it's years since they've seen you.'

'That would be lovely. I'm planning to leave tomorrow but it doesn't matter when.'

'Then come for the day. They're still keen on swimming so we could fit a lot in. David's parents are away for a funeral in Gloucester or they'd be with us.'

A few minutes later Fran rang off, feeling elated. With Jane, Fred and Norah so close and Rudi installed, the cottage couldn't be more secure.

Chapter 23

'Thanks so much, it's been a brilliant day, Jane,' Fran hugged her friend and waved to her parents and David, then drove away from the farm where an early supper had been supplied, even for Beamish. So much had been achieved, a picnic lunch on Saunton Sands and loads of entertainment for the children provided mainly by the grandparents. Jane's father had driven them all in the newly purchased motorhome in which he and his wife were aiming to spend much of their retirement. Taking a rare day away from work David was also present. Everyone swam or just dipped into the sea, apart from Beamish who chose to lounge on the sand under a sunshade.

'He's getting on a bit,' David commented, 'but he looks well.'

His words had reminded Fran that she wanted to get an appointment with the vet, so it was better to go home a day early as the practice she used was popular and busy.

It was almost dark when she reached Exeter. She swung gently into the drive, noting the garage doors were shut and no lights were on. Simon could be with Gerry, downing a few drinks after playing squash. As Josh was fast asleep, she decided to first unload Beamish and their belongings. With her hands full she pushed her way into the kitchen dumping bags on the table. Beamish checked that all was in order then reared up putting his paws on the sink. Fran laughed and gave him the water he wanted. She flipped through a pile of post on the table all addressed to Simon, mainly birthday cards she supposed, recognising Miranda and Anna's handwriting. How restrained of him not to open them in advance. She glanced around smiling her half-amused appreciation at the tidiness. Much as he disliked domesticity Simon hated squalor more. Beamish whined softly and walked to the door looking back at Fran enquiringly.

'Yes, we must fetch Josh, or do you want more supper?'

She found an open tin of dog food at the back of the fridge and turned the contents into the now empty water bowl, adding a few biscuits.

'Hardly cordon bleu,' she told him, 'but adequate if you're hungry, although you shouldn't be.'

She left the kitchen, closing the door behind her then paused, sniffing. She hoped Simon hadn't started smoking. It was more likely he'd had a friend around who smoked but this wasn't the smell of Gerry's pipe tobacco. There was a hint also of a musty scent. She could dismiss her curiosity and get on with the activities that called, but she had a strange feeling, reminiscent of childhood moments of indecision before pursuing an action that usually got her into trouble. The moment passed and her curiosity took charge; she checked the sitting-room, unused, it seemed, since Phyllis's visit, for the cushions were poised on points and the undrawn, carefully pleated curtains bore her stamp. The study door was open and the room was empty. The next door was shut. The mingling scents were stronger here. Just for a second Fran hesitated, then she opened the bedroom door. The room was in darkness but the light from the hall made the intertwined shapes on the bed visible.

*

The sound of a door slamming jolted Simon from a satisfying, post coital doze. Christ! Not Fran! She wasn't due back 'til morning! The open bedroom door and the light on in the hall were a sufficient answer. Clutching a towel around his waist he reached the juddering front door as Fran's car was jerkily reversing into the road.

He could hardly run after her, nearly starkers, so he went into the kitchen where Beamish was whining anxiously.

'God, what am I going to do?' He sat down and slumped across the table, head in hands. What could he do, or say, to lessen the enormity of his behaviour? He'd sailed close to the wind before, maybe had become blasé, but to be caught out at home was unbelievable. How long he sat, running the gauntlet of every emotional brick he flung at himself, he didn't know. Gradually the shock subsided into self-pity. How could Fran expect anything else when she chose to stay away so much. He wasn't a monk! Finally, when fear took command, he realised he'd given no thought to the needs of his son. He looked into the empty nursery and came close to panicking. Where had Fran gone - driving off in such a state? To London. Exmoor. even perhaps to Gerry? The latter was unlikely. She'd confide in a woman, surely? Anna, Jane, Miranda or one of her student friends? All the possibilities were hammering inside his head, then a sound called his attention on the present; a girl's voice calling unconcernedly from the rear of the flat.

Fran drove aimlessly for an hour. When shock gave way to tears, she could scarcely see. Once she found herself in the lane leading to Gerry's house although she had not consciously been heading his way. She pulled up, desperate for the relief of unburdening herself but would male solidarity temper his reaction, and did she want to put their friendship to such a test? Perhaps he knew Simon slept around, for now she had no doubt this was not the first time. There had been plenty of clues; dropped telephone calls, wrong numbers, late tutorials or rehearsals but she had not been suspicious. Now her imagination ran riot to add to the torture.

At last, remembering Josh's needs, she drove away, hoping Gerry had not heard the car or glimpsed it. The sound of a police car's siren on the A30 awoke Josh rudely. Bewildered, he vented his distress at the top of his small but powerful lungs. Fran talked to him, then sang, The Ugly Duckling, Jack and Jill and Baa Baa Black Sheep and the effect almost made her laugh; a few snuffling sounds but no more crying.

The garage was open and empty. There was a light on in the hall but nowhere else. Thank goodness the tenant of the other flat was away. Beamish barked furiously behind the kitchen door and hurled himself at Fran when she released him. Josh, confused to be up at this hour, demanded food and sensing his mother's distress, regressed by a year, smearing mashed banana over his face and chest. Fran gathered him onto her lap and spooned the rest of his food into him, then she gave him a quick bath. The moment she tucked him into his bed, he pushed his face into the thin pillow and, clutching a blue velvet rabbit, fell asleep.

Fran let herself into the garden and walked up and down the narrow lawn with Beamish at her heels. Her arms were wrapped around her shuddering body and tears collected into the hollows of her neck. High above the polluting city lights the pale moon was sitting. She glanced at it without her usual appreciation as she longed for daylight. At last cold and exhausted, she returned indoors and lay for nearly half an hour in a hot bath. She considered sleeping in the spare room but, instead, tore off the sheets and duvet cover, remade the bed and flopped onto it. She craved for sleep but knew it would be hard won and could hardly bear the thought of lying awake listening for Simon. Would he even return? Overwhelmed with misery at this thought, she finally sobbed herself asleep.

She awoke at seven and for a second wondered why she was alone in the king-size bed, then reality hit her. Only Josh's needs gave an urgency to her movements, but she found him sleeping soundly and resisted an urge to gather him to her for comfort. There was not a sound in the flat. She returned to the bedroom, dressed rapidly in jeans and a shirt then went to let Beamish out. As she approached the kitchen the door opened revealing Simon holding a tray.

Not meeting her eyes, he said, 'I was bringing you some breakfast. How are you?'

She walked past him, let Beamish out then sat down. 'How am I? How can you ask that?'

'I've been desperately worried. I searched for you for ages.'

'I was back before midnight. Josh had to be looked after.'

'Well, it was the early hours when I got back. I thought you'd return for your beloved dog if nothing else and here you were. I slept in the spare room.'

Simon lifted the teapot from the tray and poured tea into two mugs. Adding milk, he passed one of them to her. 'Darling. I so want to explain.'

'Explain! I look forward to hearing how having some tart in our bed can be explained.'

He flinched. 'She's not a tart. She's Eloise.'

'I thought she'd gone away.'

'She's has, she's living with her mum in Plymouth. She rang me because she was upset about a problem at work. Foolishly, I said she could come over and talk about it.'

'I didn't see her car and yours must have been in the garage - out of sight.'

'It was. You're right. I fetched her from the station.'

'And if you're giving someone a lift back shortly, why would you take the trouble to put the car away?' She smirked.

'I did it automatically. Fran, I know it all looks and sounds terrible, but I just intended to provide a shoulder.'

'Is that what you're now calling it?'

'Don't be crude - it isn't like you. Honestly, I just meant to comfort her.'

'And you expect me to believe that? Why can't you just admit you're having an affair?'

'I'm not, Fran. I don't want an affair. I want you. I've only wanted you ever since I first met you but you don't make it easy. You spend half your time buried on that wretched moor and you're more interested in your work than in me.'

275

'If I were a man that would be seen as normal. How much of your time do I get?'

'Be honest, Fran. Ever since we married you've insisted on being away for days on end.'

'Not since Easter. I've spent far more time here than at the cottage.'

'Yes, that's true but you still have odd days away and there's no need for it. You don't have to work so much. Certainly not since you've had Josh.'

'Oh, I'm neglecting Josh for my work, am I? That couldn't be more untrue. I've always fitted work around Josh. His needs come first.'

'Of course.' Simon's tone was cold.

'You're jealous of the time I spend with our son. I've heard of men like that. They're pathetic.'

'Now you're being ridiculous. What I meant was you're trying to do too much. There's little room left for anything except work and caring for Josh.'

'And for you it's work and whoring. How could you bring another woman here - in our bed? It's the cheapest, most cruel thing you could do.'

'I'm not proud of it, Fran. I didn't want to hurt you.'

'There's no excuse for what you've done. It's on the level of sleeping around while your wife's pregnant.' She stopped abruptly, staring at him. 'You did that too, didn't you? You met her just before Josh was born.'

'Yes,' his voice rose. 'We did meet then. You were out of touch and out of reach. I'm not saying another thing. I've a job to do.'

He pushed back his chair with an ugly scraping sound and got up. Beamish snaked his way into the room and whined, shivering and leaning against Fran's legs under he table. He hated raised voices.

At the door, Simon paused. 'I've some free time this afternoon. We'd better talk.'

Only when the front door slammed ten minutes later did Fran give way to tears dropping her head onto her folded arms. Beamish pressed his muzzle into her lap and whined as if sharing her distress.

Josh's needs forced her to face the day in as normal a state of mind as possible. She was surprised by the size of breakfast she ate, even bacon and sausages. Remembering her resolution to have Beamish's health checked she rang the vet to hear there had just been a cancellation for ten o'clock. Good, with no pressing needs at home she could get a good walk afterwards and hope the light, freshening wind would help to clear her head...

The vet's verdict was a heart problem that required medication, probably for the rest of Beamish's life. 'But what an otherwise fit dog,' she enthused. 'I bet he enjoys his walks, but you might have to limit them.'

Fran left feeling anxious yet grateful. The effects of the medication had been fully explained and advice given about diet. They then walked by the estuary, enjoying the salty air, the sight of numerous birds which Beamish never attempted to chase. The walk was just for half an hour which Fran suspected caused Beamish to give her a slightly reproachful look

Back home she warmed up a casserole and, just as she withdrew it from the oven, Simon appeared.

'Hm, smells delicious as always,' he said, and once the dish was safely on the table, he hugged her. 'It's been hard to concentrate. I feel so awful about yesterday. Please, forgive me, darling.'

'I want to but it's hard.'

'Darling, I've seen Gerry.'

'You mean you told him?' She stared, astonished.

'No. He thinks the world of you and Josh. I don't know if he'd ever speak to me again. He wants us all to go for tea this afternoon. He's got a new young goat to introduce to you and Josh – his words, of course.'

Fran came close to laughing. 'I'd like that more than anything. Have you forgotten it's your birthday tomorrow? Is there something special you'd like to do?

'There is but it's a secret. A surprise.'

Different from the last one, let's hope, Fran thought.

During their drive to Gerry's house Simon was quiet. Was it because he was concentrating or wary of starting a discussion that could become a row? Fran risked no more than a few words directed at Josh and Beamish. Lunch had been easier than she'd expected with Simon concentrating on Josh, chatting to him and helping him spoon up his food when necessary.

The sight of Gerry's house caused Beamish to give one bark of excitement and, at once, Fran felt a great weight had been lifted. Gerry was one of the easiest people to be with, always relaxed and full of humour. Within minutes Josh was introduced to the new goat, called Charlie, and delighted all by saying over and over again, 'Chalee goat, Chalee goat.'

'I love it here,' Fran enthused, looking at the paddocks where sheep contentedly grazed and at the small but highly productive vegetable garden. 'It must be such a relief to return here after days spent on digs with students.'

'Well, I'm lucky as the whole lifestyle suits me and, with my neighbour stepping in whenever I'm away, I've no worries. Like you Fran with your good friends, the Yeos.'

Simon was about fifty yard away talking to Josh about the unusually friendly sheep who hurried across to the fence to say hullo and have their heads stroked. As he was out of earshot Fran asked Gerry if he knew she'd let the cottage.

'Yes,' he replied, smiling sympathetically. 'Brave girl but the cottage will still be there for you.'

Simon had turned towards them and to Fran's delight was laughing as he swung Josh up in his arms and approached. 'Gerry, I don't think you ride your ram so, I guess, Josh can't. What about the goat?'

The whole afternoon was like a great slice of therapy to Fran. The men hardly mentioned work, putting every other aspect of the world to rights. Josh trotted around followed by both dogs, one protectively, the other a bit like a sniffer dog, intrigued by this small, active person. Every now and then Othello sat down and stared at Josh, head to one side.

'Have your ex-wife's children ever been here,' Fran asked, as Gerry had just shown her a card sent from Cyprus where they were on holiday. It was so good that they were friends.

'Two years ago they were over and visited me. The kids are great, a girl now seven and boy of four. They speak a mixture of French and English. They're mad about the countryside and animals, like your lad.'

'So far but, remember, he's not yet two.'

'Easy to forget as he's such a bright lad. Now, tea d'you reckon? Time to replace a few calories.'

It was still warm enough to eat outside on the verandah. Scones with cream and raspberry jam, biscuits and lemon drizzle cake were soon laid out on a floral-patterned tea set that had been Gerry's grandmother's.

'Delicious,' said Simon after eating two slices of cake. 'Your own recipe, Gerry?'

'Mum's. She was a brilliant cook.'

'You made it?' exclaimed Fran. 'How do you find the time?'

'I made it. Not digging all Summer.'

'There, something else you two have in common,' said Simon, grinning. 'Passion for animals, the countryside and cooking.'

'Yeah, shame you haven't an older sister, Fran. Speaking of age, Beamish is looking a bit more like Qthello. Taking it easier than usual.'

Fran described her visit to the vet's and Beamish's medication.

'Similar to what my dad's on I guess. He's seventy eight and, I hope, will go on for years. He and Mum were down here when you were in Brittany. They'd have loved to have met you. Now let me top up your tea.'

Anecdotes of happenings on digs highly amused Simon and Fran for the next hour while Josh snoozed in a deckchair having gorged himself on the delicious food.

'That was a lovely time,' said |Fran as they drove home at nearly six o'clock.

'Always is. Gerry's so easy to be with. Let's hope tomorrow works out as well as today.'

Simon opened his birthday cards, then his presents. The jersey Fran had found in Harrods earned her a hug and the model of Beamish brought a shriek of laughter which Josh took as strong approval. Miranda 's present was a gift voucher for two tickets for *Les Miserables* over which Simon enthused. 'Miranda's gift is perfect. Remember that rotten write up in the Observer? Well, numerous people disagreed, many I know, and I want to write my own review.'

The table was littered with bottles of wine, whisky and boxes of chocolates.

'Loads of people know it's your birthday,' said Fran.

'Yes, but not my age.'

'Why? To be in your thirties and in your position should make you proud.'

'I'm ten years older than you, Fran. I don't want everyone to know that.'

'I know and I don't care. You're you and that's all that matters. Now, as I don't know where we're going, I don't know what to wear. Should I smarten up?'

'No, stay as you are. Just bring towels and a swimsuit. I'll put Josh, Beamish and their necessities in the car now.'

Fran was delighted when she realised they were approaching the small, historic village, Beer. Still a fishing village but, presumably, no longer linked to smuggling. She put her hand on Simon's arm and squeezed it.

'How did you know that I love it here?'

'Just guessed it's your sort of place. Mum brought Chas and me here years ago. The pebbly beach isn't the best for Josh but plenty of other attractions.'

Simon was right; Josh had to be restrained from jumping into the stream running beside the descending road. High excitement for him was seeing colourful fishing boats being winched up the beach and the pebbles didn't worry him a bit. The small, sheltered cove still offered warm bathing in September and all except Beamish (restricted to one area of the beach) took advantage.

'Gerry loves the Jurassic Coast,' Simon said, as they sat enjoying lunch in a beach café. 'I reckon he's as knowledgeable about geology as archaeology.'

And wouldn't Rudi like him, Fran thought. Great if they could meet. One of the things she loved about Simon was his friendship with Gerry. Sometimes it seemed ludicrous, this younger man, usually smart and always in good quality clothes and regarding the countryside as somewhere that afforded occasional holidays, while Gerry often looked like a happy farm worker of decades ago. He hadn't yesterday, however. His jeans and cotton shirt had been pristine, and the tea had been set out perfectly. Fran felt a huge surge of affection for them both. grinning as she mentally positioned them, one to the left and one to the right.

The excellent lunch was followed by a visit to Jubilee Gardens and the adjoining playground, again providing excitement for Josh. As they drove home Fran enthused that it had been a perfect family day. 'But more for all of us than you although it's your birthday. What d'you want to do this evening?'

Turning to her and smiling, Simon said, 'I'll tell you after Josh is safely in bed and we're about to follow.'

*

It was just after 11am when the phone rang.

'Hullo, dear girl. Hope yesterday went well. I didn't ring then as it was a special time. Is Simon there?'

No, he's out with Josh, doing a bit of shopping. Gerry, thanks so much for that lovely time on Tuesday and yesterday went really well too.'

'Good. I forgot to give Simon a message on Tuesday. It's about the finance meeting that was going to be held last Monday and was cancelled. It's now going to be at 3pm tomorrow week.'

Chapter 24

The doubt came insidiously over the next days. Had that whole weekend been spent with Eloise? Was it pre-planned? Fran struggled with the possibility of questioning Simon or burying the whole horrible event in a recess in her mind if she could even find one. Was Simon's attentiveness, helpfulness and demonstrated affection no more than an attempt at reconciliation or was she seeing the real man, the man she loved and could never imagine losing? A change in the current atmosphere would affect their whole situation and she hated the thought of being responsible for that.

Keeping her doubts to herself was a strain but at least it was affecting her only. She busied herself with domestic chores, cooking more than usual and working on her current art project.

On the third day Martha arrived, collecting for the RNLI.

'I hope you don't mind but you're on my allotted patch and I know you support it.'

'Of course I don't mind. Good to see you I was about to have a coffee break and even more welcome now. You will join me?"

'I'd love to. We've had some busy weeks. Our trip to Italy was a great success and I'm so glad your Brittany trip went well.'

In the kitchen Fran took cups from the dresser and filled the kettle.

'No Josh or Beamish?' asked Martha.

'Phyllis has taken them out. She loves to do that. I'm so lucky having her help. I can concentrate wholly on my work. She comes a couple of mornings a week and babysits when needed.'

'Have you been working this morning? If so I mustn't take up your time.'

'No, really. I've nearly finished a simple drawing project – not even requiring the studio. Now, I must make a contribution before I forget.' Fran raided the small-change tin she kept in a drawer and put several coins in the boat.

'Thanks. I've a cousin who's a volunteer so it's one of my favourite charities.'

Fran poured water into the coffee pot, placed a plateful of biscuits and cups and saucers on a tray then suggested, 'Let's go to the sitting room. Bit more of a view there.'

Martha insisted in carrying the coffee pot to lighten the tray and they went to the comfort of the room that caught any sunlight. There was quite golden tinge on the small trees and bushes in the garden. They say down, enjoying the warmth that penetrated the French windows.

'I think we're having an Indian Summer. The moor must be looking lovely with early Autumn tints. Yes, milk but no sugar Fran. Thanks.'

For a few seconds they drank then Martha commented, 'Lovely coffee, but I'd better ignore those delicious looking biscuits.' She patted her stomach. 'I'm far too comfortable-looking and I mustn't forget that Roger is surrounded by lissom young women.'

Fran smiled. 'Roger wouldn't look at anyone but you,' she said, 'He adores you.'

'I think he does now.'

Fran felt a little uncomfortable. What was Martha hinting at? Was she about to become confidential and, if so, could she be the impartial listener?

'It's the biggest mistake to take any man for granted, and I did in the early years. Then, when our daughter was quite little, Roger had an affair.'

Fran nearly dropped her cup. Surely not Roger with his short legs, slight beer gut and receding hair?

'Oh yes, I know it's hard to visualise but he's always had a certain attraction. Obviously I thought so or I wouldn't have married him, and he really has a way with him.'

Hastily, Fran said 'He's an inspired listener, and incredibly kind.'

'Yes, and insecure young things can get the wrong idea. But this was as much my fault as Roger's and the girl's.'

'You blame yourself?'

Martha hesitated. 'Not blame exactly. I made it too easy for him. It was his first lectureship and I was preoccupied with motherhood, and not giving him much support. I suppose the young woman made him feel wonderful. It only lasted five minutes. He was devastated at the effect it had on us. As far as I know, he hasn't done it again.'

Fran got up to pour more coffee.

'Thanks, dear. I will have another cup. Are you off to Exmoor for the weekend?'

'No, Rudi's there so that limits my visits and that's why I'm not painting much. I'm trying to adjust. but I'm not finding it easy.' Her voice was unsteady.

'Was it Simon's idea?'

'No mine, but it was what he's always wanted. I think it was the right decision. You see, I've made it easy for him, Martha.'

'Are you saying it's happened to you, Fran?'

'Yes.'

'My dear, I am so sorry.'

'D'you mind if I tell you, Martha? I haven't talked to anyone about this, not even to Miranda. Least of all Miranda as she thinks so much of Simon and I don't want to disillusion her.' Then she poured it all out, sparing no details, and Martha sat for a minute in silence, looking away. Was she shocked? Fran wondered. Did she question the story? At last Martha looked at her and said,

'One hears rumours but one doesn't want to listen. They were very thick of course, he and Eloise, but colleagues often are. Nowadays one tries not to consider their sex. Why should men and women colleagues not be as close as people of the same sex? And there was some student day connection, wasn't there?'

'Only that Eloise worked in Nairobi with the husband of one of Simon's past girlfriends. But there were rumours?'

'Yes. She's been gone a while, now working in Falmouth, so one hopes the talk has died down. If he's still seeing her it will only cause harm.'

'He said that she came to see him because she was distressed about something at work. He tried to help her and it just happened. He swears it never will again.' Calm until now, Fran dropped her head and tears trickled down her cheeks.

Martha got up and sitting on the sofa beside her put an arm around her shoulders. 'He loves you, Fran,

I'm sure of that. You should see the proud way he looks at you. And he adores Josh. I can't see him jeopardising this marriage. It's so important to have faith in its success.'

'How did you survive it, Martha? I think I'm strong enough then, suddenly, I just slumped.'

'I know. It'll take time. You've had a dreadful shock. One gets over it, Fran. I did and I've no regrets.'

'I try to think of other things then it creeps back'.

'It does take time, I'm afraid. Sometimes I lost control and said every dreadful thing I could and, even when it was obvious that he was contrite and wanted us to remain together, I couldn't stop. It went on and on. I lost weight, looked terrible and really let myself go. A friend took me in hand eventually. She made me go to stay with her for a week and got me sorted out. Lots of heart-to-heart talking, hair-do's, face packs and a splurge around the dress shops.'

Fran patted her damp eyes then blew her nose. 'I want Simon. I'm sure of that, but I can't share him.'

'If he says it was just a fling this time I think you've got to believe him, Fran. After all she is some distance away now.'

'How long did she work here?'

'I think a couple or, maybe, three terms.'

'So at least she's not round the corner. But what about all the students who drool over him. Might he have slept with some of them?'

'He'd be putting his job in jeopardy, Fran. He's stunningly attractive and I know what you mean about the students' behaviour but, when I've seen him at rehearsals with Roger, he's been quite professional, although he's friendly.'

'When you first came to the cottage, long before Josh was born, there was that Swedish girl, Sylvia, with you. Do you think he had an affair with her.'

Now, Martha looked shocked. 'Dear girl, she was our guest, remember. Oh, she fancied him, that was obvious but there was no way they could have got together.'

She took the last sip of her coffee then, gently, suggested that a man like Simon for all his outward confidence and sophistication, still needed attention and flattery.

'It's the nature of the beast,' she added. 'Sometimes I wonder if men ever fully recover from being weaned.'

At that Fran laughed. 'I hope Josh copes.'

'But seriously, I don't think there's a man alive who doesn't thrive on attention. Perhaps it's good you're staying here a bit now.'

She voiced what Fran was thinking but any response was curtailed by sounds of Phyllis and Josh returning. They both stood up and Fran gave Martha a hug then braced herself for Josh and Beamish's effusive greeting.

The talk with Martha was cathartic. If a couple could survive the effects of an affair and end up as relaxed and happy as Martha and Roger obviously were then there had to be hope for her and Simon. With an unusual surge of energy Fran made chicken and almond mayonnaise salad and raspberry fool for dinner.

'This is marvellous, darling. Just the job after a frustrating day.' Simon pulled her close to him and kissed her. 'So much to come home to now.'

He was relaxed and much chattier than usual, telling crazy stories about his students so they spent plenty of time laughing. It was as if the previous days had disappeared and they were back in wonderful times, holidaying, having days out with Josh, Miranda, and Anna and Charles.

Chapter 25

At Josh's second birthday eleven children shared jelly, ice cream, biscuits, savouries and birthday cake, washed down by a variety of juices. The majority of grown-ups were friends Fran had made at the Mother and Toddler group. Simon arrived late carrying a huge bunch of balloons. His rather unrealistic intentions to conduct such games as Pass-the-Parcel and Pin-the-Tail-on-the-Donkey, fled at the sight of so many cream and crumb-smeared children. He pressed the balloons' strings into Miranda's hands and fled to his study. Milly, whose twin pregnancy was ill-concealed by multi-coloured dungarees, said, sounding almost breathless, 'He's gorgeous. Like a film star.'

'Hmm. I'm afraid he sometimes behaves like one,' muttered Fran. 'He's not too keen on toddlers *en masse*.'

'In mess, more like, said Milly, giggling. 'Can't blame him. Now then, stop it you little monster.' Her son, angel-faced Jakey, was bashing the arm of the small girl next to him with a paper cup. She positioned herself between them.

'Don't fret. Tricia probably deserved it. She's already got the makings of a bossy midwife,' said Jane.

Half-an-hour on, fortified by a stiff drink, Simon was lured from his den by the ever tactful and charming Miranda, and soon had the children shrieking, playing musical cushions. Sensibly most of the mothers remained in the kitchen.

'Your Simon's brilliant with them,' enthused Milly.

Jane who had visited often enough now to assess the limits of Simon's parental involvement, exchanged a meaningful, private wink with Fran. She glanced appreciatively around the kitchen whose clinical look had been softened by displays of local pottery, dried flowers, bowls of fruit and a basket of brown, speckled eggs from the Yeo's hens.

'You've made this place really lovely,' she enthused, and picked up a framed photograph of Josh at a few hours old. She smiled. 'I can't believe it's two years since his dramatic arrival. Still, it didn't do him any harm and Simon seems to have forgiven me for my dubious involvement.'

Fran laughed. 'Hardly dubious- really vital. He likes you. No, really. He doesn't suffer fools gladly and you're definitely outside that category. And you amuse him.'

He terrifies me,' said stout Barbara, busy with a dustpan and brush. 'But he was ever such a help at the check-out on Thursday. The older kids were playing up and a bag of rice got spilt all over the counter. I felt such a fool. Anyway, your Simon got me another bag and made the kids help him pack the groceries. And all the people behind me stopped muttering and pretended they'd all been about to help me too.'

Fran was bemused but impressed. Neither of them enjoyed shopping and tended to do it separately and, in Simon's case, sporadically. Being in a supermarket surrounded by yelling kids was one of his worst nightmares.

'I noticed he wasn't doing the weekend shopping.' Barbara grinned. 'It was all booze, wine, whisky, vodka. All for Josh's birthday.'

Fran joined in the laughter then suggested 'Let's have tea, shall we?' and turned to switch the kettle on. The off licence account had arrived that morning and was huge. What was Simon doing buying all that extra drink in the supermarket?

'I'd love a cuppa. It'll clear my head. I'm no good at drinking in the afternoon, much as I like it,' said Barbara.

'Don't worry. If you're a bit muzzy I'll run you home,' said Miranda, coming in carrying a small girl. 'This little thing is decidedly damp.'

The child's mother took her from Miranda.

'Thanks. I'll sort her out. It's down the passage, isn't it?'

Fran walked ahead to show her the way and look in on the party.

Miranda put cups and saucers on the table. Diana, a lecturer's wife, pretty and outspoken, said, 'I wish I had a mother-in-law like you. Mine just sits and expects to be waited on.'

'I'm not the mother-in-law. Sadly, Simon's mother died before he met Fran.'

'Oh, you're Fran's mother. Well, of course, you're so alike. Lucky Fran.'

Miranda began to pour the tea. 'No, I'm afraid I'm not that either. I'm her aunt, her father's sister.'

'Oh gosh,' the young woman looked embarrassed.

Miranda passed her the first cup of tea. 'Don't worry. In a way you're right. I'm a surrogate mother. I brought Fran up. She was only four when her parents died.'

The mothers murmured sympathetically and nodded their approval of her. She knew several of them. Over the past two years, as word got around that she was visiting, the kitchen filled with young women drinking endless tea and coffee, their arms full of their offspring. All agreed that Miranda was a marvel. No one would think she was a famous sculptress as she was so down-to-earth. She knew about removing stains and how to bake perfect bread and coax delicate plants to thrive in a hostile climate. Even the children thought her wonderful. In seconds, she would have them absorbed with bits of dough to knead, or exciting pictures to make. Today, she was in her element.

'How long are you staying?' Jane asked.

'A couple of nights then I've students coming. I'll give Simon a bit of help now – relieve those mums, I expect they need some tea.'

After Miranda left the room, Jane said, 'If Miranda's staying a bit longer, wouldn't it be a good time to visit the cottage? Everything's fine of course but you must want to see Chuckle.'

'Gosh, it's weeks since I was there. It was so kind of Rudi to give Josh a present and thanks for bringing it Jane. If it's okay with Miranda, I'll pop down tomorrow. I'll check with Rudi tonight.'

The day ended well with Simon taking ages bathing Josh and blowing strings of multi-coloured bubbles to amuse him. He then tucked him into bed and read him Rudi's present, a story about a dog called Buster who is lost and then found. It elicited shrieks of joy from Josh who shouted the triumphant last line with Simon `Buster is found'.

Overhearing in the kitchen, Miranda and Fran laughed and hugged. 'Oh, it's all going so well, darling. I'm so pleased for you.'

The weather was surprisingly calm, in contrast to its welcome to Josh's arrival two years before. The sun was tentatively appearing behind misty clouds but even that was not needed to intensify the late autumn colours. Beech trees had reached their final zenith of colour, hanging on to their crimson, orange and golden-brown leaves while higher on the moor several trees stood naked and dark against the sky. Large patches of dark purple dominated the moor as if keeping it cosy in preparation for approaching winter.

Fran drove slowly, relishing the sights she had taken for granted for years. It was as if she were now reclaiming them, locking them into her mind. Despite the journey being short she stopped and, with Beamish, strolled for ten minutes, breathing in the fresh air and enjoying the proximity of a small herd of ponies. One or two glanced at her then continued to graze while the only really interested ones were the foals, not quite yearlings, who stared, intrigued and unworried.

Had Rudi made it to the Drift this time? Fran wondered. Well, soon she'd know.

The sound of quiet music was drifting into the yard, Elgar's Seranade for strings in E minor, one of Miranda's favourites. The front door was open a fraction and in a second Rudi appeared. In jeans and a long sleeved sweatshirt he was more warmly dressed than usual, He hurried across and opened Fran's car door.

'Great to see you. You've even brought better weather. And Beamish.'

Fran laughed, stood up and they hugged then Rudi let Beamish out. He greeted Rudi effusively.

'Thank goodness he approves of your tenant; not that he's checked the place out yet, of course.'

'I'm sorry it's been so long, Rudi.'

'So am I, but everything's fine here and I couldn't have nicer neighbours.'

They went inside the cottage and Rudi turned music down. 'One of your records, Fran. I must be wearing them out. Now, coffee, tea, or something stronger?'

'Bit early for that. Coffee will be fine. And play the records as much as you like.'

Fran was surprised and pleased to find the fire was alight. Instantly Beamish slumped onto the hearth rug.

'He's showing his age a bit. He's on pills for some minor heart problem,' Fran said.

'He still looks good. Milk and a little sugar – right?'

'Yes, well-remembered. Thanks.'

'I hope you've time to stay for lunch. I've a beef casserole I just need to reheat, and all made from best local stuff.'

Thanks. That will be lovely.'

While Rudi made the coffee Fran looked around the room. It was no different from usual apart from photographs on the sideboard and different books and magazines on the table. She looked across the terrace to the garden and down to the paddock where Chuckle was grazing alongside Fred's old horse.

'Did you get to the Drift?' she asked as Rudi returned with a laden tray.

'I certainly did. Jane and Tricia were there and there was great excitement. I learnt lots about Exmoor ponies and their uniqueness. Not that there was one to equal Chuckle, according to Tricia.'

Fran laughed. 'She's lovely. Josh calls her Trish and she was so sweet to him yesterday, although she did emphasise her superior age a few times.'

'I've a photo of my niece, Joanna. She's a year old on the twenty-second of December. I guess I'll have to go back for her first birthday if that's okay?'

'Of course, With Jane and the Yeos around you can come and go as you like,'

Rudi got up and fetched a couple of photos from the sideboard and handed them to Fran. One showed the baby with both parents and the other showed her alone, holding a teddy dressed as Paddington Bear.

'Your sister's really like you. She's lovely.' Instantly realising what she'd said Fran blushed, looking away, but not before seeing Rudi was grinning.

'Thank you, I'll tell her that. She's heard quite a lot about you so your opinion will count. I think we'd better top up our coffees, don't you?

'Please. And thanks for putting a water bowl down for Beamish.'

'Well, it's his home.'

Fran put the photos back while Rudi went to the kitchen. Next to what she assumed was a photo of Rudi's whole family she noticed a small portrait photo of a pretty, young-looking girl with long fair hair. She picked it up to see if anything was written on the back of the small frame but there was nothing. She replaced it as Rudi returned.

'You've found Rosemary's photo, I see,' he said as Fran sat down. 'She was a friend from Fresher Ball days.'

'She's really lovely, too,' Fran said.

Rudi poured more coffee, drank some then leaned back in his chair. 'She was lovely – in every way.'

'She was? So is she no longer a friend?'

Rudi was looking at the smouldering logs. In a tight sounding voice he said, 'She's no longer here, Fran. She died in a skiing accident three years ago. I would have been on holiday with her but I had some urgent research to do.'

'That's awful. How terrible for her family.'

'It was the most dreadful shock.'

'Is that why you came to England, Rudi?'

'Partly. I love the U.K. as you know but I also felt the need to get away, have a complete change. We were together for four years and it would have gone on.'

'I'm so sorry, Rudi. To meet someone so special and then lose her must be hardly bearable.'

'It's such a cruel loss in many ways. She was a biologist, and could have done so much good for this planet. The director of a small, film company, specialising in Natural History, wanted her to do some research for their next film. She was about to start it when the accident happened.'

The phone rang and, perhaps, Rudi's expression told of relief at the interruption.

'Sorry, better answer it,' he said, and went to the tiny hall.

'Hi Jane, yes she's here. Shall I call her? Fran, Jane would like a word.'

Fran took the receiver from Rudi, who looked more relaxed.

'Fran, that was a great time yesterday. Would you mind if I come over with Tricia this afternoon. She'd longing for a ride, only I don't want to interrupt. You get so little time at Spring Cottage.'

'Jane, please come. I haven't even said hello to Chuckle yet. About two o'clock. Okay.'

She returned to the sitting room. 'Jane's coming over so Tricia can have a ride,' she called as Rudi was in the kitchen.

While Rudi organised their lunch Fran brought Chuckle in from the paddock and brushed the mud from his thickening coat. She nearly cried when, at first sight of her, he whinnied a greeting. As she left the stable Rudi appeared, offering the key to the studio.

'Please check it. I want you to be sure that everything's okay.'

Everything was. The paintings lining the walls were unchanged. Piles of books, papers and a typewriter stood where once had been the clutter of paints, brushes and palettes. All the painting gear was on a long shelf where Fran had put it, to leave the table clear for Rudi's use.

'If you ever need this place, I can shift my gear indoors in seconds. It was so thoughtful of you to include it. In here I lose myself in my work, the stuff I usually struggle with, resenting the fact that I'm not out on the moor but in here I feel quite different.'

'There is something special about it. It's so odd; I shut myself in, become absorbed in my project, yet never feel trapped and.... What's so funny?'

Rudi was shaking with laughter. 'Come on – be honest. There was one time. Now let me help you down the steps and back indoors for some lunch.'

Out with Chuckle, Jane, Tricia and Beamish, Fran inhaled deep breaths of air.

'This is bliss, Jane. So good to be back and find everything unchanged. What a brilliant tenant you found for me.'

''It makes it all a bit easier for you, doesn't it, and it's helping Rudi. I'm relieved you know about his girl friend's death. A few weeks ago Tricia was being nosey, going through his photos, and that's how it came out.'

'Now we know why there isn't a girl-friend around. Yet it's been three years.'

'I thought it odd as he's so attractive, but there are a few men who don't flit around and he's one of them. She must have meant the world to him. By the way, Fran, and this is between us for the time being, I'm....' Jane cupped her hand around her mouth and turned away from Tricia and Chuckle. 'I'm over two months pregnant.'

'Oh that's great news, I hope.'

'It is, and David's really pleased. I'm not telling the world for a bit. Nine months can seem a long time and delaying telling too many people can seem to shorten it. What about you, Fran. D'you want another one?'

'I do. I don't want Josh to be an only child but I haven't broached the subject yet with a vital person.'

Jane laughed. 'I guess it could be a major topic but now Spring Cottage is taken care of might it be a good time?'

'Could be. Simon was an only child so he too knows what it's like. You told me a while ago you hoped it would happen so the gap wouldn't be too wide. I must think that way, after all, even if it happens soon there'll be nearly a three-year gap'

'You could just come off the pill.'

'No, it doesn't work like that in our relationship. I might broach the subject soon as I get back.'

'How is he, Fran? He was great with the children yesterday, but I didn't think he looked very well.'

'He does have bad days when he seems really tired but he won't admit it, as you know. Since that awful bout of pneumonia he hasn't once seen a doctor and I can't....'

'Mummy, can I trot,' interrupted Tricia.

'Yes. Time we all got a bit more exercise. All right, Fran?"

'Yes, fine. When we get back, I'll call on and Fred and Norah then I'd better get going.'

Chapter 26

Fran was surprised when Simon announced he'd be spending a couple of nights in London, staying with Charles and Anna. They'd seen them only a month ago.

'What's the urgency? We'll be with them in a short while. Miranda's invited them for Boxing Day.'

Miranda nodded. 'I certainly have, We all enjoy their company.'

'Fran, this is about business. I'm seeing Matt, my publisher and there are people he wants me to meet.'

'Okay, Give Chas and Anna my love.' Fran refrained from adding that she'd had a long, interesting chat with Anna only three days ago, similar to one she'd had with Jane a few hours ago.

Over an early pre-dinner drink in the Crossed Keys Charles, having heard about Simon's new, highly lucrative contract with his publisher, decided it was time for him to dominate the conversation now rather than over dinner at home.

'Simon, Josh is two so isn't it time to think about a mate for him?'

'Why? He's happy enough on his own. He goes to toddler groups and is as sociable as any kid his age can be.'

'Wouldn't you have liked a sibling?'

'No – never gave it a thought. What about you? You never said anything.'

'I had a mate, remember - you, but when I was younger, I envied friends with siblings. What about Fran, did she regret being an only child?'

'She's never said so. Brought up from the age of four by a loving, famous and very comfortably off aunt I can't imagine she had yearnings for anything different.'

'She might feel strongly about having another baby. I think you should mention it.'

'I don't. I'm really happy with Josh but I'm not sure if I want any more.'

'Ironical isn't it – you can toss off the idea while we're struggling to have one. That awful IVF's been mentioned and if we have to we'll go for it.'

'Well, good luck. I really hope you succeed. It obviously means a lot to both of you. I was thrilled when I knew Fran was pregnant although it was unplanned and a bit soon.' Simon paused, frowning slightly then, after taking a long swig of whisky, continued, 'You know, it's not just the upheaval when they arrive you have to face. There are months when you need to be a cross between a monk and a psychiatrist. Believe me, life's never the same again and.... there's the lack of sex.'

'Six weeks, isn't it.'

'No, it bloody isn't. More like six months. And Fran went off it long before Josh was born. I don't want to go through that again. And she'd have to be sensible and have a hospital delivery - not a repeat of that last fiasco.'

'So if she agreed to that would you consider another one?'

'Chas, you've a house you own outright, no mortgage, and in a desirable area. I want to find a house I can afford and it's ridiculous that we can't sell Spring Cottage. Until I get everything sorted I don't want any more responsibilities.'

'I can understand how you feel but I also see Fran's viewpoint. Now the cottage is let that could be a useful income towards a mortgage so, maybe, you wouldn't have to sell.'

'Except that it's let for peanuts.' Simon drained his glass. Again, he was frowning as he eased himself into his overcoat. 'We might have to buy a house quite soon, Chas as I'm not sure if I want to spend my life as a lecturer. This is between us but other opportunities are looming ahead, besides Anna's delicious dinner.'

'Right. Tell me more as we drive home.'

*

Simon glanced at his reflection the long mirror. Hell, he was losing weight. If he'd been overweight, he'd now be delighted but never had he needed to lose an ounce. A perfect body was important to him: he exercised sensibly, ate well, thanks to Fran, so why was it happening? 'Get a check up', were words he heard too often and they never failed to irritate him. His lack of faith in doctors started when his grandfather died. He'd been having check-ups for years due to high blood pressure but the fact that he had an embolism hadn't been diagnosed and, once the reason for his death was discovered, his daughter's health should have been monitored.

While he dressed, Simon reflected on how little he knew about genetic inheritance in his family. His colouring was certainly inherited from his father but what else had been passed on to him? His gran's side of the family were tough survivors and Grandad had been well into his eighties and still active mentally and physically when he died so suddenly.

No, he had more relevant and immediate problems to think about – not health issues. When he was treated for pneumonia, his heart was found to be fine. Anyway, other heart issues were more pressing.

A final brief glance at his now clothed reflection was reassuring. He joined Fran in the kitchen where she was encouraging Josh to eat his breakfast. She smiled and gave him a hug.

'Good, you're up. You were flat out when the alarm went off. Are you all right? Did you have an exciting time with Chas and Anna?'

'Of course I'm all right, and it wasn't that sort of visit. I told you about the new contract with my publisher. What are you doing today?'

'It's the toddlers' swimming day. My turn this time.' Fran grinned, knowing how much Simon approved of Josh's aquatic progress, revelling in the kudos it gave him.

She passed him a plate of toast and poured tea into a large mug.

'Thanks love, I'll have cereal as well. I'm quite hungry. Sometimes this bloody teaching is exhausting.' For a while he concentrated on eating and talking to Josh then, pushing his plate aside, he leaned back in his chair looking at Fran with a serious expression.

'I've had enough of teaching and I've a chance to get out of it.'

'But you've only been here for just under three and a half years.'

'Yes, but this wasn't my first teaching job. I've been at it for nine years. Miranda's friend, Benjamin, has said I can work for him – well the Observer – whenever I'm ready.'

'That would be brilliant. Far less exhausting than being a lecturer and, I suppose, you can do a writing job from anywhere.'

Fran was beaming and Simon guessed what she was thinking.

'We couldn't stay here; we'd have to rent or buy something.'

'But if you wouldn't be tied to an area, couldn't we move back to the cottage?'

'No, it isn't in London.' Simon's tone was hard.

'Oh no! Why there?' If Fran hadn't spoken her expression alone would have told him how she felt at the prospect of living where she had mainly been brought up.

'If I accept the job as a regular reviewer and writer I'll need to be on hand.'

'But our way of life here is pretty good. This is a lovely city with access to beautiful country....'

'Fran, for most of our time together you've resented living here. Okay, you're a bit more resigned to it but I'm not an idiot – I know where you'd rather be.'

'Yes, provided we'd be together much more, and if you didn't have to go to work each weekday it would be perfect.'

'It probably couldn't be like that. Look, love, I haven't accepted a new job, or mentioned leaving to the bosses – it's an idea I'm toying with. Now I must be off.' Simon stood up, kissed Fran's cheek then Josh's brow.

'Enjoy your day, both of you,' he said then left the room.

Somehow Fran did enjoy her day, concentrating on Josh., chatting with fellow mothers and chatting with Jane, who was anxious to know if she'd had a chance to discuss the important issue with Simon.

'Not yet, but he's pretty preoccupied with work issues. I hoped his visit to Charles and Anna might have made a slot but not so far.'

'Don't give up, Fran. We deserve two each. Shame you won't be coming home for Christmas as Rudi's going to America for a couple of weeks.'

'I know, but we'll have a good time at Miranda's and I want to visit Granny with Josh. She loves seeing him. I'm hoping we'll be able to grab a few days at the cottage after Christmas.'

'I hope so too. Ah, Trish is calling as her friend's arrived. Lovely to talk, Fran, and good luck.'

And luck is what I really need, Fran thought, as she replaced the receiver. Christmas and, possibly, a decision about Simon's new job opportunity would take precedence in the immediate future.

She was right; on Christmas Eve, after discussing the job change possibility with her, using a gentler tone than the previous time, Simon broached the subject with Miranda whose reaction was positive

'You couldn't have a better boss than dear Benjamin,' she enthused. 'Honestly, you'll have international recognition. I'm not surprised; he's talked about your books and reviews many times.' They both stood up and hugged, then Miranda turned to Fran who was sitting on the sofa with Beamish leaning against her legs.

'Isn't it wonderful? We'll be reading Simon's piece every weekend.'

'So you've decided to accept,' Fran said, keeping her voice as neutral as possible.

'Yes, unless you're totally against it.'

'I'm not but there are things to consider. Giving up the flat, living somewhere else ....'

'We've time,' he interrupted. 'I have to give a whole term's notice.'

'Is there any pressure on you to start soon?' Miranda asked.

'No. I'll be replacing that chap, Edward Vaughan, who wants to retire this year. For my students' sakes I'd prefer to complete the academic year, but Benjamin has mentioned April.'

'In a way that would be ideal, Simon. You see, after Easter, I'm going to Canada, then North America for at least twelve weeks so you could stay here.' Miranda turned to Fran. 'That would give you time to decide where you want to live, wouldn't it.'

The question was clearly rhetorical, but Fran nodded then thanked Miranda. The fact that her aunt's reaction might have clinched the matter for Simon would have angered her but she had to resign herself to the fact that he had decided weeks ago. That was why he hadn't discussed it with her.

Five days later, driving to Exmoor, Simon commented, 'Christmas went really well. And thanks, Fran, for accepting the new job decision.'

No choice, Fran thought, but smiled. The eight day break had been a happy time. Simon had even visited his grandmother with Fran, Miranda and Josh. A visiting pianist and singer was present so, in the large sitting room, the residents and their visitors joined in many of the carols, and songs dating from past decades. Josh stood up and jogged with a little girl a bit older than him, to the delight and amusement of all present. Simon was clearly moved when Nancy called to Josh, 'Clever boy, Simon.'

Nobody corrected her; her confusion would have been increased and her happy expression and frequent smiles would have vanished.

.'I'm glad we did so much,' Fran said, putting her hand on Simon's arm. 'Good walks with Beamish and lots of fun with Charles and Anna.'

'And now a reunion for you with Chuckle.'

'And with Norah and Fred. We've got their presents, haven't we?'

'Yes, darling. Everything's on the back seat. I'm not, am I?'

She laughed. 'Never. 'Specially as we're going to the cottage.'

As always, the Rayburn was on, even the fire was alight and a healthy-looking poinsettia sat on the kitchen table. Sprigs of holly and ivy sat behind pictures. Within minutes of arriving Fran ran down the paddock with a treat for Chuckle then called on the Yeos who invited them to dinner that evening

'Before we go next door, I must ring Gerry,' Simon said. 'I want him to hear about the job change from me.'

'He'll be sorry,' said Fran

'We won't lose touch. You'll want to come down still, so we'll meet up pretty often.'

Fran nodded, relieved. She fed Beamish and tied a net of hay in the stable where Chuckle had constant access. Bathed and asleep, and luckily now sleeping for hours, Josh would be guarded by Beamish and regularly checked by his parents.

'Gerry's in so I've told him,' Simon called ten minutes later as Fran fetched Beamish in from the garden. 'He's not surprised, and he's pleased for me. We'll see him soon.'

Happily settled in the Yeos' large kitchen/diner, enjoying a delicious lamb casserole, Fran felt she had returned to real life. However different Simon was from his hosts he and they could make conversation and create much humour. Often, he deliberately asked naive questions about farming that had his companions collapsing with laughter. As ever he enthused about Norah's cooking and remembered that she had taught Fran to cook when she was really young.

'That was a special year,' said Norah, beaming at Fran. 'A wonderful chance to get to know her and her aunt really well.'

'And very special for me,' said Fran. 'I even had my first rides and that told me I had to have a pony.'

The grandfather clock chimed the half hour. 'Excuse me. My turn to check Josh, 'she said, and hurried out of the room.

Beamish was waiting at the bottom of the stairs as if he'd been sensing her arrival. He followed her up to Josh's room. She stood for minutes beside the cot, somehow resisting scooping Josh up and cuddling him. He was fast asleep, cheeks lightly flushed and the hint of a smile on his lips. If he was dreaming it was clearly of something lovely. Reluctantly, Fran returned downstairs, and her hand was on the door handle as the telephone rang. She picked up the receiver and, instantly recognised the voice of the speaker.

'Rudi! What a lovely surprise. Where are you?'

'With my grandparents for a few nights – back on the eighth if that's okay.'

'Of course it is. We're leaving at the weekend. And thanks so much for the presents, Rudi, and everything was perfect here. How did Christmas go?'

'Brilliantly. And my little niece is lovely. Wide eyed and smiling – well most of the time. We were all together, even my brother had leave, and my cousin was with us – the doctor chap. He's doing vital research work. Now, how did your Christmas go.'

Briefly, Fran told him, then explained what was happening that evening. If she stayed away much longer, Simon or Fred would come looking for her.

'Then I mustn't delay you. Please give my best wishes to them all and I hope we can meet soon.'

'So do I. Good to talk to you.'

After Fran hung up she wished she could have told Rudi about the forthcoming changes. She knew they could have talked for an hour or longer.

'Is there a problem with Josh? 'Simon asked as Fran entered the kitchen.

'No, fast asleep and fine. I'm sorry for the delay but the phone rang. It was Rudi; he's in England, staying with his grandparents. He sends his best wishes to you all.'

'There's plenty of pudding, love.' said Norah. 'We didn't eat it all. Help yourself. So glad Rudi's all right. If he weren't a scientist he'd make a good farmer.'

You're right. Brilliant with sheep 'e is. You're real lucky, Fran, getting stuck in your studio like that.'

Everyone laughed except Simon. Clearly, any mention of Rudi irritated him although he had every reason to be grateful to the man who was a rescuer in more than one way.

Chapter 27

The majority of Simon's colleagues were dismayed to hear of his Notice of Resignation, and Professor Howard's surprise and disappointment was tinged with anger. Gerry, grateful that he had been warned in advance, enthused about the opportunities that would go with Simon's new job although he was sorry to lose Simon's close company. He confided his feelings to Fran, meeting her one morning when she was walking with Josh and Beamish.

'I understand why he's so keen on the new job; he's a natural at writing reviews and textbooks. I gather he can write instructions for students that fire them up; well, more suggestions than instructions that encourage them to search for their potential. Only a few days ago I heard a student enthusing about his latest book. "Most textbooks are dead boring, but not Doc Fellowes's", he said.'

'I think lots of students will be sorry to see him go. As he's such a good lecturer it seems a waste of his skills to give up, but he seems really positive about the change,' Fran commented.

Gerry was quiet for a moment. He glanced down at Josh who was trotting alongside his buggy, always preferring to walk rather than ride.

'Tough little chap, Fran. Does you both much credit. It seems unfair that his dad who believes in exercise isn't too well. I wonder if that's his main reason for taking a less demanding job.'

Fran stopped and facing Gerry, said, 'You see changes in Simon, don't you, probably more than I do. Living with someone one notices far less.'

'You're right. He often has to really force himself to complete a game. Swimming suits him better. Will he talk to you about how he's feeling? He certainly won't to me.'

'No. I've tried to get him to have a check-up whenever he gets one of those nasty viruses but he always refuses. I wonder if he was affected by his mother's sudden death. He hardly ever talks about it but, I know it was a shock and made him angry.'

'Trouble is, Fran, there's no way of persuading Simon that I've discovered. He's a strong-minded chap which is good if it's about important issues but, sadly, his health doesn't come into that category.' He paused, smiling as he accepted Josh's proffered hand.

'Okay, so you're in charge of me and Beamish is in charge of your mum. Fran, we'd better behave ourselves.'

After a good half hour of playing with Josh and Beamish, Gerry left to give a lecture while Fran, enjoying the early Spring sunshine, was in no hurry to go home. She relaxed on a bench while Beamish dozed and Josh wandered around no more than a few yards away, happily watching every human and animal with the intensity of one doing a survey.

Over the past year Fran had grown to love the parks and playgrounds in Exeter. Knowing that the coast was near, and that two moors were a short drive away made the neat, manmade acres tolerable. Of course, London had huge open areas, and she knew most of them well but how could they ever compensate her for losing close contact with Exmoor?

Don't ruin the day by being negative, she told herself, there's work waiting for you at home.

The following morning was not one of Phyllis's usual working days but she had rearranged her hours so Fran could meet up with a writer and retired teacher, Jennifer Green, and start planning the illustrations for her book. The meeting was arranged for nine-thirty at Jennifer's cottage near Maidencombe, so Fran decided to take Beamish as there would be time for a walk on a dog-friendly beach.

'Well, no shortage of jobs,' Simon commented as Fran said her goodbyes, but he had not asked her for details of the commission. Too busy with his own work, Fran assumed, with the date of his resignation looming. He hugged Josh, then Fran and thanked Phyllis for her extra help.

There was plenty of traffic but all moving so the journey was almost relaxing.Fran felt a surge of warm gratitude towards Phyllis. Once again, she'd willingly taken Josh on. Would such amenable help be available when they moved? She would miss so many good friends, but she was determined not to lose them. Her visits to Spring Cottage would be occasions for meeting up again, and she was determined there would be plenty of those. What would Rudi do, she wondered, as she was sure Simon would refuse trips home if the cottage were still rented. As far as she was concerned Rudi could stay as long as he liked if he could bear their visits. She could offer Rent Free days/weeks for the times she visited.

Better concentrate on finding Jennifer's cottage, she told herself as the dashboard clock showed she was going to be nearly ten minutes late.

The friendly reception she received was an instant relief and a good hour of walking in the area where much of the story was set was really helpful. Notes and photographs would be invaluable.

'This is exactly what I was hoping for,' Jennifer enthused. 'You see I feel an illustrator needs to get the essence of the story and that's what my publisher said you would do.'

'I hope so. I love the text. I've read it to Josh, although it's aimed for slightly older children.'

'And did he fall asleep, Fran?'

'No, but I'm afraid Beamish did.'

Laughing, Jennifer patted Fran's shoulder. 'Maybe I could ease him into the story – there's plenty more work to be done, Now, time for cake and coffee. I know you've got to get back but can we fit it in?'

Back at the cottage, with its lovely sea view, Fran enjoyed a half hour chat then took leave of this delightful woman whom she knew was an immediate friend. Never mind the fact that she was old enough to be Fran's mother.

'You're under no pressure,' called Jennifer, as she waved Fran away. 'My publisher has said it'll be at least six months.'

Again, there was plenty of traffic, but it was all on the move. She'd be back in time to give Phyllis lunch, if a bit late. Not fifteen minutes from Exeter the oncoming traffic was slowing down. In the line of cars, doing about twenty miles an hour, she saw a grey BMW driven by a dark-haired man with a girl beside him. It was Simon- there was no question. A man of his looks doesn't have a double. Instinctively Fran lifted her foot off the accelerator and only the blast of the horn from a following car alerted her to her sudden loss of speed. She pressed down and jolted forwards then she saw that the car ahead was about to turn off. Seconds later she could have driven into it but she braked in time. There was a loud bump in the boot area and a strange cry. Beamish must have been thrown forwards. Again, the rear car driver hooted, probably wanting to race on but unable to overtake. There was nowhere she could pull off the road so she had to keep going. It was a struggle to concentrate on driving; not a sound was coming from Beamish so he'd probably just had a bump. In her state of mind the sooner she got off the road the better. It wasn't just her mind that was in a turmoil – her heart was thumping and she felt uncomfortably hot.

Somehow, she arrived home safely and within seconds Josh and Phyllis were beside her.

'Did it go well?' Phyllis asked.

'Yes, very but Beamish has had a bump. I had to stop suddenly – well, almost stop and I think he was thrown forward.'

She lifted the hatch door and saw Beamish lying against the dog guard. She leaned inside and stroked him but there was no response.

'I think he's unconscious,' she said.

'May I touch him?' asked Phyllis and, as Fran nodded, she reached out and ran her hand all over him.

'Fran, there's no movement – no heartbeat. I'm not a vet but I've done a first aid course for humans and I don't think the symptoms are very different for dogs. Please let me lift him out.'

Fran nodded, tears coursing down her cheeks.

With difficulty, Phyllis managed to lift Beamish but she had to put him down on the drive. There was no question that he was dead. Sobbing, Fran knelt beside him, stroking him while Phyllis took Josh indoors, telling him the dog was having a long sleep. She settled him in his highchair with a rusk then returned to Fran.

'It was my fault – the way I was driving. Perhaps he's broken his neck.'

'Fran, go to the vet. I can stay and get some lunch for us, or I'll bring Josh and come with you.'

'But you've done so much already.'

'No. I can stay another hour or two. Let's get Beamish back in the car.'

Together they managed to lift him onto the soft bed that was always in the boot.

'Phyl, I don't think Josh should come. I'd rather go alone if you're sure you can stay.'

'Of course I can but you take care. Shall I ring your vet?'

'Yes please. Her number's in the book by the phone.' Fran hugged Phyllis then got into the car and drove away.

*

Turning down the six o'clock news, Fred picked up the telephone. 'Hullo – Fran, good to hear you....Lovey, what's wrong? Oh no! I'm goin' to help. Whatever you want I'll do it. Tell me where.'

. Ten minutes later he hurried next door, relieved to see Rudi's car in the yard.

'Hi, where are you, Rudi?'

Almost instantly Rudi appeared on the studio steps.

'Lad, I've bad news. Fran's much-loved dog is dead. A heart attack.'

'Oh no, she'll be heartbroken. She adored him.'

318

'Well lad, she wants him buried in the garden, below a hawthorn tree he liked to rest under. She's bringing him down tomorrow morning. I'm going to dig his grave,

'Can I help, Fred?'

'Yes, thanks lad. Please bring me a beer.'

*

It was nearly nine o'clock when car lights showed in the drive. No meal awaited and Fran was watching television which was unusual for her. Simon entered the sitting-room .

'Sorry to be late, love. It's been a hectic day. How's your day been?'

As he moved towards her Fran switched the television off and jumped up.

'How can you ask? Thanks to you Beamish is dead.'

'What? Oh darling...' He hurried then, arms outstretched but she moved away.

'Don't touch me. I saw you on the A34. Is that your idea of a hectic day – off with another woman?'

'For God's sake, I was only giving Eloise a lift. She came up to see one of her past students then realised she had to rush home. Anyhow, what's that got to do with Beamish dying?'

' When I saw you, I suddenly had to brake. He was jolted forwards and had a heart attack. The vet confirmed it.'

'Well, good job Josh was with Phyllis.'

Fran stared at him, her feelings bordering on hatred.

'I'm sorry, Fran, but obviously you overreacted. The past's gone and I was just helping a friend.'

'So it took about eight hours to help her? You weren't at work. You haven't been seen all day.'

'You've been checking up on me? Well, think what you like. I'm getting something to eat.'

Simon left the room and seconds later sounds came from the kitchen of the fridge and oven doors being slammed. Fran went to the bedroom where, seeing a photograph of Beamish standing guard beside Josh on the moor, she dissolved into tears. Whatever Simon said she'd be at Spring Cottage in the morning, the last decent thing she could do for Beamish. She showered then got into bed, thankful that Simon seemed to be in no hurry to join her. The next time she was aware of his presence it was seven o'clock. Amazed that she had slept for hours she concluded it was due to stress. 'There are few things more draining than stress', she remembered hearing Miranda say many times. Simon was asleep; not stirring an inch while she dressed then she got Josh up and ready for his breakfast.

'Where's Beams?' he asked, twisting around in his highchair.

'He's having a very long sleep, darling. He hasn't been well, so he decided he'd had enough.'

Josh stared, eyebrows raised. 'He need b'kfast?'

To Fran's relief and surprise Simon appeared. He was wearing his dressing gown.

'What are you up to today?' he asked, after giving Josh a kiss.

'I'm taking Beamish to be buried at home.' Her tone was cold and determined.

'What? Where is he? You said you'd taken him to the vet.'

'Yes, for a diagnosis, not for disposal. He's in my car.' She glanced at Josh who was busy eating. 'Please remember we're not alone. You'll be looking after Josh. You're free today.'

'Oh, so you really did check up on me. Fran; please, put this behind you. '

'I want to but how can I when you say it's over and then I see you together again. How can I believe you.'

'I married you, for God's sake. Isn't that enough to prove you're special to me?'

'Only it isn't enough, is it?' Fran retorted, then left the room.

Chapter 28

The moment Fran drove into the courtyard Fred and Rudi appeared. They each gave her a hug then she opened the car boot and Fred lifted Beamish out.

'We've done just what you said, lovey, so he'll be in his favourite resting place. D'you want to come with us?'

Fran nodded, struggling to withhold tears as she followed them round the side of the cottage, down the sloping lawn to the grave, perfectly sited as she'd requested.

'Do you want him to stay wrapped in the blanket?' Rudi asked.

'Yes, please.' Fran's voice was wobbly and, as they lowered Beamish into his grave, she began to cry. Fred put an arm around her.

'He had a wonderful life, Fran. Couldn't have been better. More'n many humans get, now, shall we cover him up?'

Fran nodded and moved away so Fred could pick up his spade. She stopped after a few yards and glanced back. Rudi smiled at her, his kindly expression saying he understood all that she was feeling.

'I don't want to see this part. D'you mind?'

'Lovey, you go to my Norah. She's expecting you. And we'll do everything right.'

'Thankyou – both of you. I so wanted him to come home.'

Fran left them to finish the job and walked round to the farmhouse where the smell of coffee and fresh baking wafted through the open door.

'Oh love, I'm so sorry.' Norah hurried towards her. They embraced. 'Come inside and warm up. The weather's not cold but you're a bit shivery.'

Fran sank onto a thickly cushioned chair in the always warm kitchen and Norah poured coffee for her then cut into a sponge cake.

'Norah, I'm so grateful to you and Fred.'

'Well, we care about you, Fran. You and Miranda have been very good to us over years. Best thing that could have happened was Miranda buying the cottage. And Ossie agrees – he's got a dear companion.'

Fran smiled. 'For life, I hope.' She drank then started to eat. 'Norah, this cake is delicious.'

'Good. I wish it could be lunch, but we must go to the market. I'm really sorry we can't stop but Rudi's not working today. Why isn't Simon with you, Fran, at such a difficult time?'

'He's looking after Josh. We agreed it didn't seem right to bring him today.'

'No lovey, of course not. He's lost a dear friend too.'

After Fred and Norah left, Fran returned to the grave to find Rudi standing beside it.

He was looking down towards the paddock that Chuckle was sharing with his large friend. He turned to Fran, smiling. 'I was wondering, Fran, if you might want to plant something special – to commemorate Beamish.'

'That's a lovely idea but I don't know what to choose. I must think about it. I'll just go to see Chuckle now.'

'Well, lunch is ready when you are - a simple salad. I do hope you'll stay, Fran.'

She really smiled then and, thanking him, walked to the paddock. If tears could cause shrinkage would Chuckle end up looking like a miniature Shetland she wondered when, ten minutes later, she left the patient rock.

She walked into the cottage via the open French windows and Rudi came out of the kitchen.

'I'll close them now if you like. The Spring sunshine isn't very warm. In a few minutes there'll be soup, thanks to Norah,' he said. 'Would you like a drink?'

'Just water, please. Chuckle is looking great.'

'His hooves were trimmed last week, and he's being ridden at least twice a week. According to Trish I should mount Ossie and accompany them.'

Fran grinned. 'I think you'd be the first person ever to ride him.' She shed her jacket and sat down, facing the fireplace, grateful that the logs were slowly burning. The subtle glow was comforting. Rudi joined her, handing her the glass of water. She took a few sips then placed the glass on the coffee table.

'Beamish was only ten. I expected him to go on for a few more years.'

'That's not a bad age for a dog, Fran, and he did have a heart problem.'

'But it shouldn't have happened. It was my driving that caused it.'

'How d'you mean?'

'I was returning from meeting a writer and on the A 38 I saw Simon approaching in his car....' she tailed off, struggling not to cry.

'Fran, please don't upset yourself.'

'No, I want you to know.' She took a deep breath. 'Beside him was a girl he'd had an affair with. I suspect it started before Josh was born but I only found out about it last year. He told me it was over but it can't.....' Her words tailed off again and she felt in the pockets of her jeans for a tissue. Rudi jumped up and fetched a box from the kitchen. As he handed them to her she could no longer withhold her tears and he sat beside her, gently putting an arm around her and stroking her hair.

'It was the shock – I lost concentration and nearly drove into a car ahead. I braked and poor Beamish was thrown against the dog guard. The vet said that the sudden jolt might have brought on the heart attack but his heart was in a bad way.'

'You mustn't blame yourself, Fran. If Simon hadn't behaved badly this wouldn't have happened. How could he cheat on you? You must be the best person in his life.'

Fran leaned against him, now sobbing.

'I've stayed here a lot, leaving him alone for days.'

'But he's a mature man, not a lust-driven teenager. Surely marriage means commitment? And you've been living in the flat for more than a year. Has he admitted to still having an affair?'

Struggling, Fran related the conversation she and Simon had after his late arrival home. 'If he is still having an affair then it's been a long time – Josh is well over two,' Rudi sounded shocked. 'You always seem so happy, Fran, and talk of Simon lovingly.'

She sobbed again then, struggling, said, 'I do love him. I just wonder if something's missing. I've asked him to talk about it but he won't. I'll do anything to put it right.'

'Fran, some men can't resist having affairs. I'm not assuming Simon's one of them but .....' he tailed off, looking away.

'I know. A friend once suggested that. Girls surround him in his job and I know many fancy him. I've overheard them talking about him.'

Rudi sighed. 'Lecturers have to be very strict with themselves. Surrounded by late teenagers, tasting freedom for the first time - it can't be easy.'

'But you know,' said Fran, suddenly sounding normal and even smiling.

Rudi grinned. 'I'm pretty new to the game, Fran. Luckily, I'm out on the moor more than in the lecture room.'

Fran then laughed. 'Escaping to the moor – a perfect solution.' She straightened up and squeezed Rudi's hand. 'You've helped me again. I can't talk to friends in Exeter, unless they broach the subject. It's too close.'

'Fran. I wonder how many people know. When I was a second-year student a very attractive lecturer was suspended, and the story was that she'd had several affairs with students. I don't know if it was ever verified because she left of her own accord. Tolerance levels for those kinds of relationships are pretty low in the States.'

'At least Eloise is a lecturer and now works in Plymouth and we'll be moving in a few weeks.'

'Oh no, where to Fran? But I'd better rescue the soup.' Rudi jumped up. There was a bubbling, hissing sound coming from the kitchen. 'Please tell me over lunch.'

Fran went upstairs to the bathroom to wash her face and tidy herself up. She stared at her red-rimmed eyes and wished she could conceal them with makeup she but hadn't any with her just a purse inside her handbag. Afraid that Simon might change his mind about looking after Josh, she'd left in a hurry.

The kitchen table was set with bowls of Norah's parsnip soup over which Fran enthused while accepting a second helping.

'Half my meals are provided by Norah,'Rudi said. 'I find bags of fruit and vegetables hanging on the door handle or she drops in with a bowl of something she's cooked. And she won't let me pay her.'

'But she's told me you often help out on the farm. I bet you earn it, Rudi.'

'Maybe, just a bit. Apparently, she told Jane I should drop biology and become a sheep midwife.'

Fran laughed. 'Some day you must meet Gerry. You'd really get on. I'll miss him so much.'

She then told Rudi about Simon's job change. He was clearly impressed by the opportunity it would give Simon but questioned how Fran would cope with city life.

'I'll have to. One consolation will be closeness to Miranda and some old school friends but how I'll work up there I don't know. Will you mind my being a rather more absent landlady, Rudi, assuming you want to stay?'

'As long as you want to let the cottage I want to be your tenant, and it looks as if my job is really secure. Do you want any changes here?'

'No, with Jane and Tricia using Chuckle that needn't change as long as you don't mind. I gather you clean the paddocks up sometimes. Jane said she sets out to poo pick and finds it's often done. And is the gardening okay? If it gets too much, please say. There's plenty of help around.'

'All is fine, Fran. I'm just so happy to be here. Now, how about ham and salad?'

Surprised that she had an appetite, Fran gratefully accepted everything that was put before her.

Later, completely relaxed and enjoying post lunch coffee, she described her latest art project and for a couple of hours their chat was general. Only when the clock struck four did she speak of Simon and Josh.

'I'd better get back. Simon's good with Josh but he finds him a bit taxing,' she said then, in the kitchen, began stacking dishes onto a tray. Rudi blocked her way to the sink, taking the tray from her.

'No, Fran, that's my job. I've got the rest of the day. I only wish you could stay longer and have a good rest. Please, come here whenever you need a break.'

He put the tray on the draining board and turned towards her, his expression confirming his words. 'I miss you, Fran. I know I don't see you often but it's so good when I do.'

'I enjoy it too. Rudi. I shall try to visit, but it will be harder. Again, thank you so much.' She moved to him and they embraced. Instinctively she sensed it could have lasted much longer but the ringing phone forced separation.

'Hell, I'd better get it,' Rudi said. 'Could be work.' He walked to the hall and Fran collected her jacket from the sitting room.

'It's Simon,' Rudi called. 'D'you want a word?'

'No. Please tell him I'm just leaving.'

She joined Rudi and together they went to the courtyard.

'How did he sound?'

'Quite normal. Asked if you were okay.'

'I wondered if he'd be annoyed because I've been a while.'

'Fran, you matter. You've had a bad time. Please look after yourself.'

'Rudi, I haven't let Jane know about Beamish. Please will you tell her when you next see her.'

'I will. It will probably be in a couple of days.'

'We catch up on the phone about once a week and whenever she comes to Exeter we see each other. She's looking really well.'

'She certainly is. Trish seems pleased to be having a little brother or sister. She informed me as if I didn't know, then turned to her mum and said, "We'll need another pony".'

Fran laughed. 'Oh dear, we could go on talking for ages but I must go.' She opened the car door, hesitated, then got in.

Rudi waved her off and, as he disappeared from her view, Fran's face became damp with tears.

Surprised to find an evening meal was being prepared, she felt better than she had expected. Josh was delighted to see her and Simon hugged her.

'I'm sorry, darling. I know how much that dog meant to you and I was fond of him. A bit of cheering news. Gerry is holding a party next Sunday, a barbecue lunch so Josh is included. He asked me who

I'd like him to invite among local friends. That was thoughtful of him.'

And who will be there, Fran wondered.

Simon had made it clear, as politely as possible, that he wanted no official farewell function. What could be more embarrassing than a conventional party, attended by colleagues who were either angry or disappointed that he was leaving. Professor Crawford had spoken to him a few times since receiving the official notice and his manner clearly indicated that he considered Simon was letting him and his students down.

On the telephone Charles had tried to persuade him to change his mind about a leaving party.

'Can't you see that it's embarrassing for the boss and his contemporaries? Almost as if you're being sacked or, at the worst, leaving 'under a cloud'.'

'Don't be so bloody ridiculous. I want it this way and I'm not changing my mind. A small party given by a good friend is enough.'

'Okay, I'll say no more except prepare yourself for a Welcome to London dinner. That's my boss's idea of course – still, you know she can cook really well.'

Chapter 29

Presiding over the barbeque, Gerry was in his element. The chicken he was cooking was provided by his next-door neighbour, who was present, the vegetables were home grown by Gerry and the excellent wines had been a gift from a French landowner whom he had met on his recent archaeological dig on the Continent.

'He's even got the weather sorted,' said Martha. 'Great that we can be out of doors.'

'If anyone can sort the climate it'll be Gerry,' said Roger. 'His neighbour, Joe's been telling me he's a genius at everything. He's the guy who takes over when Gerry's away. Ah, thanks, lad. I'll have a red wine and one for my missus.'

A student called Mike, who had taken the role of wine waiter, had appeared beside them., holding a tray of drinks. 'I can serve Pimms if you prefer it. Too big a tub to circulate with, so it's on the verandah.'

'Please, that's my favourite,' said Fran, so she followed Mike to get one, then hesitated. The tub was made of grey metal. Was it sometimes used as a mini trough? She openly laughed at the thought and Mike asked, 'What's the joke? Me?'

'No, just a daft idea. I'd love one of those please.'

'Right, Mrs Fellowes. I'm one of your husband's third year students. Really sorry he's leaving.'

'Thanks. I'm Fran – well, Frances. I'm sorry too. I've grown fond of Exeter. Now, weren't you in Coriolanus?'

331

'I was - that scheming Sicinius. Not the most popular of Shakespeare's plays but that's what was so surprising – all the reviews so enthusiastic. Of course, Doctor Fellowes is a brilliant director.'

'Thanks, Mike. Quite a number of people were really critical, calling it a bad choice. I have to admit it's not my favourite play, but I agree it was very well produced and acted.'

'Last year The Tempest was equally well reviewed, but I wasn't in that. Your husband likes a challenge, doesn't he? That's what keeps us alert – ooh, what next? That's a frequent question.'

Fran smiled. Mike was just the sort of student Simon liked. Not just accepting challenges but most likely offering some.

'The drink is lovely. Thanks Mike. Now, I'd better join my son.'

When not chatting to the sheep, the goat and Othello, Josh was circulating among the other guests, guided by Joe's grandchildren, a girl of around six and a boy of four. Fran was pleased to see Josh was spending time with them. She'd sometimes worried that he wouldn't be a sociable child as he had spent so much time alone with her at Spring Cottage. Joining the Mothers' and Toddlers' Group and the swimming club had been a godsend and, certainly, at his last birthday party he had shown he was totally at ease with his contemporaries.

Remembering a comment Simon had once made, 'He probably thinks he's a dog, sheep or pony as he sees more of them than his own kind', she smiled and looked around but there was no sign of Simon.

'Food's ready,' Gerry called. 'Plates, cutlery and everything you need on the verandah. Just bring a plate over and I'll serve you delicious chicken and sausages.'

'And they will be,' said Roger, arriving beside Fran. 'What a turnout – nearly all the drama group. Simon's a popular chap. And so is Josh. He now appears to be dancing with that charming young lady.'

On the lawn below Josh and the six-year-old were pirouetting to the tune, Summertime. Half a dozen of the younger guests joined them, causing laughter and clapping.

'Come on, food before frivolity,' called Gerry.

'Absolutely,' said Roger, and seconds later was well to the front of the queue, caressing his considerable paunch. Martha, catching Fran's eye, grinned broadly and shook her head. Fran put her glass on a nearby table and went to disentangle Josh from his dancing partner.

'That's right, lunchtime lovies,' said Joe, joining her and taking his granddaughter's hand. 'Aren't we lucky, Fran. How often do we get Spring sunshine like this.'

For a few minutes they chatted then Fran took Josh to the table where, from a bag, she extracted a plastic box that contained his lunch.

'I'll see to him,' said Martha. 'You go and get your meal. Where's Simon? I haven't seen him for a while.'

Fran shrugged. 'Overwhelmed by attention, I expect. Thanks, Martha. You enjoy your lunch, Josh. I'm just going to get mine.'

Standing beside the barbecue Fran felt a sudden overwhelming wish to stay in the area forever. Willow, hazel and hawthorn trees, afforded the residents of the small paddocks protection in all weathers. Except in his kitchen garden Gerry did not plant conventional choices, preferring almost self-managing shrubs and small trees that required attention only once or twice a year. The land sloped gently away from the bungalow, disappearing into a copse. Close to the boundary were two figures moving forwards, a tall, slim man and a smaller girl wearing a floral-patterned pink dress. Simon and the girl who had played Virgilia.

Fran's gaze was fixed. She felt her whole-body tense. Only her mind was active. Why were they so far from the rest of the party? Had they completely disappeared for a while? How long had Simon been away – out of sight?

'Your turn, Fran. Chicken and sausage?'

She started then turned towards Gerry who, luckily, was looking down at the food.

'Both, please. I'm hungry.'

'Good, not that you need building up. You're perfect.' The implication of Gerry's words was clear. She'd lost count of the number of times he'd expressed his concern about Simon's weight loss.

'You choose your vegetables, Fran. Isn't Josh enjoying himself? He's a winner with Joe's grandchildren.'

Fran relaxed, smiling. Had she have not been putting her safety and Gerry's at risk she'd have leaned over and hugged him.

'Where is Simon? Surrounded by his admirers? They're devastated that he's leaving. I'm sorry, as you know, but I'm mature enough to cope. Ah, more customers. Enjoy your lunch dear girl. The pudding will be on the verandah.'

Fran joined Josh, Martha and Roger and John, the older man who lived in the flat above Simon's, and minutes later she saw her errant husband standing by the barbecue, sharing a laugh with Gerry

'Ah, there he is,' said John. 'I'll miss you and Simon, Fran.' He turned to Martha, who was sitting next to him. 'Wouldn't one expect a couple with a small child and a dog to be noisy neighbours? Yapping dog and screeching kid? Well, I couldn't have had better or quieter neighbours and a lovely garden to look on to.' He smiled across at Fran, lifted his wine glass then, looking uncomfortable, said, 'Oh, I'm sorry, Fran. Beamish has gone, of course.'

'That's all right, John. Let's hope the new neighbours live up to our standards.' The words were spoken by Simon who had arrived, holding a plate of food and a glass of wine. Apart from Fran, everyone laughed and shifted to make room for Simon to join them.

The party continued to be a success, with no diminishing warmth in the weather and endless food and drink.

Driving home, Simon commented, 'That was perfect. Exactly what I wanted – good friends and my best students giving me a send-off. Now it's all about making a fresh start and I want it to be good for both of us.'

And how fresh will it be, Fran wondered; will adoring colleagues replace adoring students?

Chapter 30

June 1988

'Anna, I can't believe over two months have passed and I haven't been to Spring Cottage. We've been so busy – Simon settling into his new job and I've had work to do for Jennifer. She's started a new book and already I'm committed to illustrate it. I'm so pleased as she's a lovely person and her books are selling well.'

'That's great. It must be a help having Miranda's studio.'

'It's a compensation up to a point, but I miss the cottage and the moor so much.'

'You're in touch with everyone down there, aren't you?'

'Yes, by phone every week and Simon's regularly in contact with Roger and Gerry. Oh, Gerry and Rudi met up on the moor a couple of weeks ago and are already firm friends. Gerry fully approves of Rudi's projects.'

'When is Miranda back?'

'Next month. We spoke on the phone yesterday and she told me how well everything's going out there. She wants us to take our time to find the right property. She knows I'm not very keen, but I've got to do it. We've looked at a couple of houses, but they weren't right for us.'

'It would be great if you could find a house near ours. I could babysit for you.'

'Josh would approve. How are things with you and Charles? '

'We've had the test results and we've been told IVF should be okay. It's all been explained to us and some of it sounds pretty unpleasant. Lots of injections to stimulate the ovaries and the removal of eggs can be really painful.'

Josh who, having been happily kicking a ball around the lawn, suddenly fell over and gave a screech, interrupting the conversation. Fran hurried to him but he got to his feet unaided.

.'All right, darling?' she asked.

'Yes.' He patted his stomach. 'Hungry.'

'Right, time for lunch. Let's go to the café in the gardens. It's warm enough to sit outside.'

Anna smiled her agreement, then quietly said. 'I'm surprised Josh hasn't demanded a trip to the zoo. He certainly knows where he is.'

'We come so often maybe he wants a slight change, people rather than animals. He enjoyed kicking the ball with that lad a while back.'

'He certainly did.' Anna put a hand on Fran's shoulder. 'Do you ever consider having another child, Fran.?'

'I'd love another one – maybe more, but Simon isn't keen. He loves Josh so much it's as if there wouldn't be room for another one.'

'That's a shame, for you and Josh. I bet he'd love a brother or sister.'

'But it's much harder for you. It seems so unfair...'

'Well, I have to think about what I have got; the only man I've ever really wanted to be with.'

And have I got the same? Fran wondered. 'Josh, slow down. You're not starving.'

Anna laughed. 'He'd order for us if he could. He gave me a sweet when I arrived. Are you free tomorrow evening? There's a concert on at Kenwood House which is ideal for you and Simon, a mixture of classical music, Elgar, Chopin and Mozart. Charles can't come as he won't be back from a conference in time.'

'I'd love to come and, I'm sure, Simon will.'

*

Fran was disappointed when Simon declined to go to the concert.

'You know we have no problem about a babysitter,' she said but he shook his head and shuffled the papers on his desk.

'I've plenty to do. You go and enjoy yourself.'

Enjoy herself she did, loving the music and the view across Hampstead Heath.

'Have you time for a drink,' she asked as Anna drew up her car outside Miranda's house.

'Much as I'd like to I'd better not as Charles will be back and he might be wanting a bit of sustenance.'

Fran laughed. 'One thing or another. Thanks so much for suggesting this. I've loved it.'

They hugged then Fran let herself into the house feeling elated, having enjoyed music in conditions that caused her to shrug into her old brown velvet wrap only for the last twenty minutes. The lake had mirrored the orange and indigo sunset and a family of ducks, intent on roosting, announced their arrival loudly so the audience and even some musicians, dissolved into laughter. It had been a magical evening.

Simon had forgotten to leave the hall light on. The whole house was in darkness. She put her bag and keys on the table, glanced up to the half-landing where the study door stood ajar then went downstairs to the kitchen where she was met by emptiness. The fridge door was open. Irritated she shut it. A bottle of Delamain and a used glass were on the table and an unwashed plate, knife and fork on the draining board. She returned to the hall, picked up her bag and mounted the stairs lit only by the streetlights showing through the fanlight above the front door. If Simon had gone to bed she didn't want to disturb him as he slept so fitfully. Quietly, she checked Josh who was snoring gently, surrounded by soft toys, then she looked around the half-open door of her room. It was empty but a thread of light showed beneath the door to the en suite bathroom.

'Simon, I'm back,' she called, switched on the lights beside the bed, discarded her shawl and shoes and drew the curtains. It was strangely quiet. A horrible sense of foreboding took hold of her, reminding her of her return home one March evening ages ago. That was a ridiculous line of thought. There had been no hint of another woman in Simon's life, no changed behaviour, no absences that couldn't be explained. He was enjoying his work, seemed less tired and was better-tempered than he'd been during the last weeks of their move.

There wasn't a sound from the bathroom. Had he fallen asleep in there? She went to open the door and found it yielded only a few inches.

'Simon, are you all right?' she called. There was no response. Gently, she pushed the door until something flopped behind it and enough space appeared showing that Simon's arm had been the obstruction. He was lying on his back behind the door.

'What's happened? Are you drunk?'

She eased herself through the still narrow gap. and knelt beside him. Fully dressed, apart from his shoes, he appeared to be deeply asleep. He was breathing noisily. She thought of the brandy bottle and used glass. He was drunk! She felt a moment of intense fury, then realised she was mistaken. He looked deathly, his face the colour of putty; he was ill, not drunk. Swiftly, she knelt to feel his brow. Despite his pallor he was hot and clammy. Urgently she cried, 'Simon, it's me, Fran. Please wake up.'

Gently she touched his closed eyelids, and a lack of a response told her he was unconscious. His chest was barely moving but he was breathing. She called his name again then jumped up and, painfully banging her cheekbone on the edge of the bathroom door, rushed to the bedside telephone. She'd never dialled 999. Struggling against panic she wondered what she'd do if there was no reply or a queue, then an efficient-sounding voice answered and took charge. An ambulance would be with her within minutes. She returned to the bathroom and knelt beside Simon pleading for him to wake up.

Had he fallen, concussing himself or breaking something? The ringing doorbell prevented more questions and, seconds later, two paramedics were kneeling beside Simon, listening to his heart and checking his pulse rate.

The older one, who introduced himself as Rob, smiled up at Fran and said, 'We'll get him to hospital but don't worry – it's usual when there's unexplained loss of consciousness.'

With confident, gentle deftness the two paramedics eased Simon onto a stretcher and carried him down to the waiting ambulance. When he was safely in the vehicle the younger man gave him oxygen through a face mask.

'Where are you taking him?' Fran cried more than said.

'St.Mary's, love, quite close' said Rob. 'Are you coming with us?'

Fran stared. It now dawned on her that her only way of accompanying Simon was to awaken Josh and bundle him off with her.

'My little boy - I can't leave him. I'll bring him in my car.'

The man patted her shoulder. 'Don't worry. Your husband'll be in good hands. Seems to be chesty more than anything.'

Fran, feeling excluded and useless, hurried up the steps and closed the door, reducing the awful noise of the siren. She had better fill a bag with essentials as Simon would certainly be kept in overnight. The first small case that came to hand was an expensive, monogrammed Vuitton bag and seemed an appropriate token of Simon's style and dignity. She found silk pyjamas, a cashmere dressing gown, sponge bag and travelling brush set. After carrying the case to the car she gently roused Josh who whimpered then fell asleep.

*

'My husband, Simon Fellowes, has just been brought in.'

'Yes. That's right. Just wait over there, would you. Someone will come and see you as soon as possible.'

With Josh lolling against her shoulder, Fran sat in the waiting area in the company of two snoring drunkards, a man with a bandaged head and a dozing bag-lady. Their presence scarcely impinged. Even when the younger-looking of the drunkards became noisy and obstreperous she sat numbly preoccupied, like a patient awaiting dreaded treatment while the injection takes effect. A security guard led the offending man away and the other leered in Fran's direction. Several young people in evening dress came in, noisily escorting a girl with her ankle bandaged with a silk scarf. They all giggled helplessly and draped themselves around the reception desk, giving conflicting stories.

'Stoned,' muttered a female staff nurse, then, scanning the waiting area, called, Mrs Fellowes?'

Fran turned and stood up.

'The doctor will see you, bring you up to date. Can you cope with the child? Need any help?'

'No, but thanks. He's a heavy sleeper.'

'Good. I'll show you the way.'

Fran nodded and followed her into a cubicle-lined corridor.

'Your husband is along here. They're just finishing putting up a drip. It's routine really and he's on oxygen.'

As they reached the last cubicle on the left the concealing curtain was twitched aside and a tall, white-coated woman blocked their way.

'Ah, you must be Mrs Fellowes. I'm Dr Hall. Perhaps you could give me a bit of history while we're having a slight lull. There's a room in the next corridor we can use.'

Fran hesitated. She wanted to see Simon to reassure herself he was no worse.

'Oh, don't worry, your husband's in good hands. You'll be with him in a few minutes.'

She had the air of authority of Fran's old headmistress. Docilely she followed her to a small room already occupied by two nurses drinking tea and looking ready to drop. They nodded at Dr Hall and left the room.

'Do sit down,' said the doctor. It was more of an instruction than an invitation. Fran did as she was told.

'How is Simon? It's all been such a shock: so unexpected.'

'He's poorly. Has a nasty chest infection which we're already treating. Has he seemed unwell lately?'

Fran struggled to marshal her thoughts.

'I suppose he's been more tired than usual, but he hasn't been sleeping well. He moved into the spare room because he's restless and sweats a lot. But he's been working as usual.'

'And what is his work?'

'He's a journalist.'

'I see. So a sedentary job, not demanding physically?'

'Yes, but he's always been a physical person, playing squash and swimming. He's taken a pride in keeping fit but not so much lately.'

'Normally you'd say he was a healthy man?'

'I don't know. He did have pneumonia about fourteen months ago. It was a bit like this. It happened very suddenly on a flight from India. He was taken straight to the Middlesex Hospital from Heathrow.'

'And did he make a good recovery?'

'Yes, he came home quickly but, I wonder if he's really been well since then.'

'I see. What does his GP think?'

'He never sees a doctor. I registered when we moved to London a few weeks ago but he didn't.'

'So there's no up-to-date history beyond what you've told me.' Her tone was reproachful. She sighed. 'You say he's taken a pride in keeping fit and yet it appears he's been neglecting himself. You must have been concerned.'

Fran took her words as criticism. With a touch of asperity she replied, 'If you knew my husband you'd appreciate why he never sees a doctor. He finds illness rather repugnant. Of course, I've been worried about his lethargy and weight-loss but I've no influence on him. He doesn't listen to advice from anyone.'

Dr Hall's thick eyebrows rose above her spectacles. Clearly she was unused to anything but docility from patients and their relations. She shifted forward in the chair, preparing to get up.

'I'd like to know what's going to happen next? What treatment Simon will have?'

Fran's questions forestalled her. She gave a tight smile. 'Of course. We'll keep him in and do some tests. We're treating the infection and getting fluids into him. Now I expect you'd like to see him.'

Fran followed her to the cubicles where she was handed over to a nurse who gave her the first real smile she'd seen since arriving.

'Hullo, I'm Nurse Freeman,' she said. 'Don't be worried by the technical stuff. It's all routine treatment for a chest infection. We'll be moving him soon to a medical ward.'

'Oh, could he have a private room? He'd never tolerate a ward. He pays into an insurance scheme.'

'Of course, I'll find out for you. And I'll get you a cup of tea. I'm sure you could do with one.'

For half an hour Fran stayed beside Simon, then when Josh became restless, she decided she had to put his needs before her own. It was amazing that he'd remained asleep for most of the time. As she walked away Nurse Freeman approached.

'You look all-in, Mrs Fellowes. Sensible to go home and get some rest. Don't worry, we'll look after your husband and, if there's any change, we'll ring you'.

'Thank you, and for the tea.' Fran smiled at her gratefully. She was shattered and no use to Simon. And the nurses had better things to do than worry about anxious wives. Not that there was a hint of that in Nurse Freeman's tone, just real concern and friendliness.

Chapter 31

Rushing to answer the phone close to midday, Fran was relieved to hear Miranda's voice.

'How are you all? I hope Josh is finding the zoo animals a bit of a compensation for Chuckle and Beamish.'

'He is. We nearly live there. Are things well with you?'

'Fine, and how are you and Simon?'

Fran hesitated, reluctant to load Miranda with her troubles.

'Come on, darling, tell me if there's a problem.'

'I'm so sorry but there is. He's got that awful pneumonia again. He was admitted to St.Mary's yesterday.'

'Then I'm coming back. I don't want you to cope alone.'

'But you've another month. It's not fair on you.'

'No, I can't stay here knowing what you're coping with. I really want to come home and help you. I should be back in a couple of days.'

Five minutes later Fran put the phone down and sank, crying, onto the sofa. There could be no real mother better than Miranda. Never possessive or over-protective she had been a true supporter whenever Fran needed help.

Josh's needs forestalled more tears and providing a simple lunch then talking to Simon's boss strengthened her.

'There'll be no pressure for Simon to return to work. We've masses to use already and the important thing is his full recovery. I'm so sorry for you, Fran but it's great that your aunt's returning. Please give my best wishes to her and to Simon. Goodbye, dear girl, and thanks for your prompt call.' Benjamin's gentle voice was a comfort as much as his words. How different might the pressures be if Simon were still a lecturer.

At three o'clock Margaret arrived and when Fran told her that Simon was in hospital, she offered to care for Josh for as long as was necessary.

Fran entered the corridor leading to Simon's ward. There was no one about to ask if she could see him; so she walked with all the confidence she could muster.

'Oh. Mrs Fellowes? Your husband's been moved. He's in ITU.'

Fran stared at the Staff Nurse who had arrived behind her.

'It's all right, don't worry. We tried to ring you but the line was busy. Dr Fellowes was moved about four hours ago.

'Why? What do you mean, ITU?'

'It's the intensive therapy unit. Sometimes it's easier to nurse patients there if they need constant monitoring.'

'You mean he's worse?'

'Not necessarily. He is poorly, of course, you know that. Now, I'll tell you how to get to the unit.'

Fran followed directions until she arrived at a closed door bearing a notice saying `Restricted Entry'.

'Can I help? Are you a patient's relative.' A friendly looking male nurse had opened the door.

'I'm Frances Fellowes. My husband's in there, I'm told.'

'Oh yes. Try not to worry, Mrs Fellowes. He's just needing a bit of extra help. Come with me. I'm Richard. Just to the left is where visitors must clean their hands and we cannot let people in who have colds and I'm afraid little children are mostly banned.'

Fran did as she was told then followed Richard to Simon's bedside. His eyes were closed. She was sure there were more tubes attached than when she last visited.

'Do sit down, Mrs Fellowes and I'll explain it all, if you like.'

Tentatively, Fran sat down close to the bed and quietly said Simon's name.

'Can he hear me?' She was controlling her voice with difficulty.

'I don't know but it's good to try.' Richard drew a chair alongside hers, checked a monitor against a sheet of hieroglyphics on a clipboard, and began to explain the treatment; which tubes were providing oxygen, medication and nutrition. She warmed towards him and felt confident enough to ask questions.

'Yes, he did become distressed. We weren't sure if he was rejecting the treatment and here we can keep a constant eye on him. The smallest change is noted. We're almost dealing with the cause before the patient feels the effect.'

'There isn't much I can do, is there?' Fran said.

'Oh yes, just being here could make all the difference. He might be aware of your presence. You're the most important part of the treatment. The rest is just impersonal technology.'

'But not the people behind it,' said Fran, smiling warmly. 'Thank you. Richard. You've really helped.'

348

He told her where the public telephone was, the drinks' machine and the loo.

'We have to restrict visiting times because there isn't a lot of room.' He indicated the other patients, each with an attendant nurse. 'And it is important to keep it quiet; so that's why children can only come by prior arrangement.'

'Yes, of course. Our son isn't yet three so he'd find this all very bewildering. My aunt, Miranda Shaw, will want to visit Simon. Is that all right? She's more like his mother-in-law really. She brought me up.'

'Of course it'll be all right. Now I'm going to get you a proper cup of tea not one in a paper mug.'

That was too much for Fran - the sudden switching from high technology to tea-making! Tears of relief and fright mingled on her pale cheeks.

'There.' Richard passed her a box of tissues. 'Best to let it all out. You'll need that cup of tea to replace the fluid.'

She came close to leaping up and hugging him.

Twenty minutes later a woman doctor arrived to check Simon. Not the tall, austere Dr Hall, to Fran's relief, but a round-face Eurasian girl, perhaps in her thirties. Briefly, she explained that Simon's body had seemed to reject the first drug used but with a different one there could be a real improvement.

'It may take a while and, as he has had this nasty pneumonia before, we need to find out why he is vulnerable.'

Fran picked up nothing from the doctor's tone.

'You mean he could be anaemic or have that strange thing called M.E.?'

'We'll find out, don't worry.' She moved away to talk with a couple of nurses and Fran became aware

of the time she'd been away from home – away from
Josh.

*

Miranda's return was a huge relief for Fran. Josh was
thrilled to see her and even more with the presents
she gave him.

'He'll think it's his birthday,' Fran said, as a
battery-driven bus travelled around the kitchen floor.
'And thanks so much for my dress and necklace.
They're lovely.'

'Simon's presents will be waiting for him; a
welcome back, I hope. I wonder how long he'll be in
hospital.' Miranda sighed, looking worried.

'The last thing I was told was that further
investigations were being carried out.' Fran said. She
picked up two mugs of tea and put them on the low
table in the sitting area. She sat opposite Miranda who
now had Josh on her lap plus the toy bus. Slowly she
drank, wishing she had something positive to say. In
five days nothing had changed. Simon was still being
helped to breath and having fluids put into him. No,
something had changed: yesterday he'd smiled,
mumbled a few words but the mask made them
unintelligible.

Josh slid off Miranda's lap and set the bus
travelling again.

'I wonder if an underlying problem could be
cancer. It's awful when it's in the lungs, isn't it?' Fran
struggled to keep her voice steady.

'I believe it is a bad one but try not to think along
those lines, darling. It's amazing what progress has
been made in the last decades. Fallada has an uncle

350

who was cured of stomach cancer five years ago.' Miranda drank her tea then suggested it might do them good to go for a walk. 'The weather's good, Josh is full of energy and mine seems to be coming back. If you're planning to visit Simon later, I'll look after Josh.'

Fran smiled gratefully. A walk would be relaxing, preparing her for the visit and, certainly, fun for Josh.

A week later Simon was breathing without help and was moved to a private room. He felt weak but at least he was no longer on the verge of extinction – the words he used when Charles visited him.

'I haven't been told anything definite – why and what's caused this but God knows they've done enough tests. One was so bloody painful.'

'Thank goodness they're really conscientious. You've been poorly for a while – over a year so let's hope that's all behind you.'

'I suppose I've been in denial; refusing I could be anything other than fit. I realise now it can't have been easy for Fran. Apparently, she's visited me every day but half the time I wasn't aware of anything or anyone.'

'She's certainly been worried. Must be such a relief that she can now have a talk with you. and Josh has seen you're still in the land of the living.'

For the first time in thirty minutes, Simon smiled broadly and said, 'He had to be stopped from bouncing on the bed. Shame I couldn't respond to his last command.'

'Come home, I bet.' Charles said, laughing. 'I gather he's been asking about you daily. Ah, well once you're well enough he'll be taking you to the zoo for a treat. Anna's told me how much....' his voice trailed off. A tall, white-coated man had entered the room, accompanied by a similarly attired younger man.

'I'd better go. It's been great to see you,' Charles said, reluctantly standing up. 'I'll ring Fran and tell her I've seen you. Okay?'

'Fine. Give her my love.'

'I'm sorry we're interrupting,' said the older man, 'but visiting is a lot easier now so do come again.'

Which says Simon's not about to be discharged, thought Charles as he left the room.

*

The registrar who occupied the consultant's chair barely shifted as Fran entered the room. He glanced at her then down again at the file in front of him. Fran wondered if she should go out and come in again but decided it would be a waste of time. He probably wouldn't notice. There was an easy chair to the right of the desk. She was considering whether to sit in it when he jumped to his feet, apologised and invited her to take the chair.

'We have met, haven't we?' he asked.

Fran hesitated, trying to remember. 'I'm not sure. I think so.'

'Well, I'm Dr Wren's registrar, Dr Grierson.'

'Oh, I thought I was going to see Dr Wren. His secretary said the appointment was with him.'

The youngish-looking man seemed slightly disconcerted. There was a pause then a shade defensively, he said, 'I'm afraid Dr Wren was called away to er - an emergency.'

He was looking away and Fran sensed he was unhappy with his delegated task. She took the plunge as much for his sake as hers.

'Dr Wren wanted to talk about Simon's future care. He seems to be quite back to normal but he's very low-spirited. Yesterday he hardly talked at all.'

Dr Grierson nodded, still looking away. 'Dr Fellowes is still poorly. He will need special care.'

'But he's getting better. I don't understand.'

'The type of pneumonia he had is called pneumocystis carinii. Have you heard of it?' She shook her head, suddenly afraid. 'Is it a form of cancer?' Somehow she kept her voice strong.

Still not looking at her directly, Dr Grierson replied, 'No. It's a particularly nasty, recurring illness caused by a virus that resists treatment. I'm afraid it is HIV and Aids defining.'

Fran felt as if her life was draining from her. Then she heard an intake of breath, tried to moisten her lips so she could speak but no sound came. She was aware that Dr Grierson had got up and was calling to a nurse to bring her a glass of water. When it arrived she held it as if she didn't know what to do with it. At last she took a gulp and nearly choked. She drank again slowly while, with effort, Dr. Grierson continued,

'I'm sorry to have to tell you this, Mrs Fellowes, but the tests we did were conclusive.'

At last Fran found words. 'You're wrong, you must be. Simon's not gay. He's a normal, married man. You must have made a mistake.'

'I'm afraid not. We have to be very exact. And this infection is not limited to the gay community.'

'But he's never had a blood transfusion or taken drugs. Not injected drugs, I mean. I expect he tried

LSD and pot as a student as most of us did, but never anything like heroin.' Her voice rose in panic.

Dr Grierson looked around the small room as if desperately searching for reinforcement.

'I'm afraid it's quite possible to be infected by a heterosexual relationship. It probably happened some years ago, eight or ten.'

'Before we met, you mean?' Fran's voice was now little more than a whisper.

'Yes. The symptoms sometimes take years to show, and with a strong, fit man may be masked. I don't know how much you've read about HIV and Aids.'

'Enough,' said Fran. 'We had one talk at university.'

'Right. Well, a reaction may occur shortly after infection, but may not. The person may stay well for years but the virus is there. The rate of progression varies greatly and we don't fully understand why. In your husband's case we think the earlier attack of pneumonia may have been the first serious sign. Aids is the final stage and that is what your husband has.'

'What do you mean – final? He'll get better, won't he?'

'We have a variety of drugs to treat the symptoms but not yet one to eliminate the virus. We do our best to give patients a normal life.'

There was a protracted silence, then, with effort, Fran asked, 'Josh, our son, he's safe isn't he? He's very well and sturdy, he can't have been infected.' Her composure fled, and her body shook with tearing sobs.

'Your son may be perfectly all right but we'll need to test him and you. Please, come in at ten tomorrow.'

Fran blew her nose and pushed her hair back from her damp face. She lifted her chin and looked at him steadily. 'We could both be infected?'

'You could but you might not be. I wouldn't want to speculate. I understand your husband took precautions.'

'Only because he didn't want me to get pregnant again. He didn't trust the Pill. Does he know all of this? Why are you telling me this without him?'

'I'm sorry, Mrs Fellowes, but he refused to allow that. He insisted one of us should tell you.'

'He knows you're talking to me now?'

'Yes. I think he would now like to see you but, first, I'd like you to have a talk with one of our specialist nurses. She'll explain about aftercare, minimising risks etcetera.'

The nurse's manner was so different from Dr. Grierson's; gently confident she explained how life should be as normal as possible for the patient.

'Physical contact, apart from unprotected sex, is not a risk. Blood is a means of transfer so great care must be taken if an infected person gets cut – while shaving, for example. Never touch the blood and use diluted bleach to clean up.'

'Does Simon know all this?'

'Yes, we talked yesterday.'

'Our son, like me, is being tested. If he's found to be infected will he be unable to start nursery school.'

'No. He'd be able to have normal contact with other children. The only risk comes from grazes and cuts – again the blood problem.'

'So the school would have to be told. Suppose they banned him?'

'Efforts are being taken to educate people in all levels of society about HIV/AIDs. I'm afraid there is ignorance and prejudice but it is being worked on. There are some wonderful supportive groups and our social worker and counsellor, Clare Barnes, will do all she can to help.'

'Thank you, Nurse Wilson. You've been a real help too. Poor Dr. Grierson. I think he was hating his job earlier.'

'He's nice but a bit baffled. Poor man's only been here six weeks. Now, I gather your husband is expecting you.'

Fran felt nothing but compassion for Simon. Now no longer cluttered with a mask and tubes his thinness was shockingly obvious. How could she not have guessed he was so ill?

She sat on the bed, stroking his shoulder, longing to take him in her arms but he remained firmly leaning back against the pillows.

'You know don't you. Oh God, Fran, what have I done to you? I may have contaminated you. You're so young and beautiful and I've wrecked your life.'

'Simon, it was a terrible accident. It could have happened to almost anyone we know. It's all been explained to me. I still love you no matter what's happened. Dr. Grierson told me the treatment could make you well again.'

'For how long? It's really advanced. And I'm a danger to you. I'll always be a danger to you. Oh Fran. I can't begin to think what I may also have done to Josh. If I've infected you it could have been passed to him in utero or by breast feeding.'

'We're being tested tomorrow. It wouldn't be your fault Simon, honestly. They've only known about that virus for about eight years and still not everything.'

For the first time ever Fran saw Simon's eyes were watering. She held him as close as she could until a tap on the door drew them apart.

'Supper,' announced a nurse carrying a tray.

Fran bent to kiss Simon but he turned away.

'Don't, Fran,' he muttered. 'You don't have to.'

'You don't have to go, Mrs Fellowes,' said the nurse. 'I could get you tea or coffee?'

'Thanks, but I must get back to our little boy.'

The nurse put the tray on the bed-table and, smiling, withdrew.

'She seems nice'

'Mostly they are, and they're not treating me any differently, thank God.' For the first time Simon smiled. 'Give my love to Miranda.' Then his expression changed. 'Oh God, what are we going to tell her?'

'The truth, Simon. It would insult her to do otherwise. She loves you and that won't change.'

'Don't tell anyone else, not even Charles and Anna. The rest of the world will be told I've a rare form of cancer. That's a bit more acceptable. You'd better get back to Josh, love.'

He blew her a kiss, and that told her no closer contact was invited.

Chapter 32

The following morning Gerry telephoned sounding high-spirited. 'Again I've met up with Rudi on the moor. Yesterday, we had a good two hour natter in the pub at Simonsbath. That's enough about me – how are you all?'

'Simon's pleased with his new job, Gerry, but he's not very well. He's had that awful pneumonia again. He's in hospital.'

'Oh no. Have they found the cause? He's been poorly on and off for ages.'

'They're doing tests. It seems his lungs are in a bad way.'

'Oh Fran, love, I'm so sorry. Is he allowed visitors?'

'Very limited, Gerry. Just family.'

'I understand. Please tell him I'm thinking of him.'

For a few minutes they talked about more general things and when their chatting ended Fran was close to tears. Like Charles, Gerry would be such a support to her and Simon. He'd be so understanding and totally non-judgemental.

'Another good friend being kept at a distance,' Miranda commented, when Fran rejoined her and Josh in the kitchen. 'Thank goodness I'm allowed to know the truth.'

'You were so good to me last night, but it must have been awful for you. I just offloaded.'

'And thank goodness you could. No way could you bear this alone. I'll respect Simon's wishes up to a point but not if they're causing you more distress.'

'I'm taking Josh out in a bit, then we'll both go in to see Simon, if Josh is allowed.'

Fran had said nothing about their double appointment at the hospital. She assumed Miranda's knowledge of HIV/Aids was more limited than hers and giving her yet more to worry about was unthinkable.

After Miranda, Fran's main support came from an attractive thirty-ish woman, Clare Barnes, the social worker and counsellor mentioned by Dr Grierson. She met Fran after her and Josh's tests and a couple of days later made a home visit. For an hour Fran spoke of her feelings concerning Simon's diagnosis. Clare's method was to listen and explore, not to question and advise – unless advice was requested. After she left, Fran felt as if a fresh wind had blown cobwebs away. She would see her again – the offer was open. However, Miranda was the stoic supporter when, a day later, the information came that Nancy had suffered a major heart attack and had died in the Home.

'I can make all the funeral arrangements,' Miranda offered, 'but with Simon's approval, of course. Remember, I've done it before, for my parents and a great aunt.'

Simon fully approved of Miranda's offer. All he suggested was that his grandmother should be cremated, like her late husband and daughter, then her ashes should be mingled with theirs in the family grave.

'May I put a piece in the paper – after all she was a councillor and highly respected,' Miranda asked, at her first visit to Simon.

He smiled, nodding, even looking quite emotional. 'Of course you may. In many ways she set me and Mum on the right road.'

*

Simon was to be discharged two days after his grandmother's funeral. His tone, when he told Fran, was indifferent. She guessed he would not have gone to the funeral anyway, but wasn't he relieved to be coming back to his temporary home?

'If it's okay with Miranda I'll go back to the top spare bedroom. If I don't need to, or can't go into the office, I can work in there,' he said. 'Miranda showed me the piece that's going in the papers. It does Gran proud. I'm really pleased. Incidentally, I trust she's keeping all the funeral bills. I'm not letting her pay for anything.'

'You can deal with all that when you come home. Now, she just wants you to concentrate on getting better.'

'A kind thought but hardly relevant. You know there's no cure. You've had it all explained.

'Miranda hasn't. Anyway, please don't feel you've no future. You're on good medication.' Fran's voice was shaky

'I'm sorry, Fran, but we all have to be realistic. I don't want to lose you and Josh, of course I don't but I feel as if life's drained from me already. Now, remember, no one is to be told the real diagnosis. Be careful at Gran's funeral as there might be a few old friends there.'

There were some friends present, Charles and Anna, Lennie, and handful of carers and patients, perhaps at Matron's request, and two ex: councillors who looked as old as Nancy and claimed to have visited her regularly. The voices singing Nancy's favourite hymn, *'The Day Thou Gavest Lord is Ended'* struggled reedily, then a deep masculine voice sounded from behind Fran. She made a half-turn and glimpsed Lennie, hymn book held high, valiantly injecting a bit of enthusiasm into the occasion. Later, she was so relieved that Miranda was with her when, at the end of the simple service, all the close friends enquired after Simon's health and nearly everyone else asked why he was absent.

Hours later, after they had settled Josh in bed with his teddy, Miranda said, ' 'Lying for the sake of ones loved one is hardly wicked. Come on, darling, let's get replenished – the Wake was pretty small and you could do with a bit of building up.'

*

The weeks that followed Simon's discharge from hospital were the hardest Fran had ever experienced. She had expected to take the role of home nurse and general helper but Simon distanced himself from her. Apart from sometimes joining her for main meals, he shut himself away, resting or working in his bedroom cum office. Twice he accepted visits from Charles and Anna but, as Miranda had invited them to lunch and

361

again to tea, he had little choice. An unexpected visit from Fallada infuriated him. He refused to see her. Luckily, she accepted Fran's apology. 'Of course, he's too poorly. Anyway, I should have phoned first,' she said, and pressed a gift into Fran's hand, a bottle of best quality champagne.

*

After emptying Nancy's room, Miranda and Fran had put appropriate photographs in Simon's bedroom; lovely ones taken with his mother and grandparents at a variety of ages, funny ones taken when he acted in school plays and impressive ones of his three University awards' ceremonies. Hoping he'd be pleased, Fran was disappointed when he glanced at them and made no comment.

'Everything else belonging to Nancy is stored in the attic,' she said, but again he said nothing. She decided he was too sad to speak of Nancy so she said no more, apart from telling him that the funeral had gone well but what could she say when his response was, 'Good, a bit of practice for you.'

She had retreated to her bedroom and sat on the bed, her head resting in her hands and tears dampening them. Thank goodness Josh was allowed into Simon's room. Hearing them talking and laughing was an uplifting event for Fran and Miranda and just about the only one. It worried them that Simon hardly ate a thing but when they tried to persuade him to eat more, he blamed his drugs for his poor appetite.

'It's disgusting stuff,' he said, almost angrily.

'Tell them when you go for your check up,' Fran suggested. 'Maybe, they'll change it.'

'For what? Some other poison? God, you've no idea what it's like. I feel disgusting and I look disgusting – well I bloody am disgusting.'

'Please, talk to Clare. She'll help you to cope.'

Don't talk bloody nonsense. She hasn't got this so what can she know and why should she know anything? What have you been saying to her?'

Simon's anger was such that Fran left the room.

At her next session with Clare, she began to understand how many people react when diagnosed with a life-threatening illness. Anger is a normal reaction and verbally laying some of the intolerable burden on loved ones can give temporary relief. Denial is perhaps even worse and that had been Simon's problem for years before he was diagnosed. Gradually, she came to understand he was not being intentionally malicious; his eyes betrayed his horror at his cruel words and she knew his apologies were sincere.

One thing moved her greatly: Simon insisted on being with her when she was given the test results. He hated to be seen in public so it was not easy for him to return to the hospital as a visitor but, while they sat in a waiting room, Fran noticed he was the one receiving sympathetic looks from fellow patients. His smart suit did not disguise his thinness and his face was ashen. When called in by Dr Wren she was aware that Simon was walking a good two yards behind her.

'Hullo, please be seated.' Dr Wren was smiling. ' We'll be seeing you for a check up next week, Dr Fellowes. Meanwhile, some hopeful news for you.'

He then looked directly at Fran. 'Yours and your son's tests were negative. You've certainly got a healthy little boy. Although it is good news just now, I want to do more tests in three months time.'

'So it could be there – lurking,' Simon said, his voice quite shaky.

'We can't rule it out but we are optimistic. Let's try to keep a positive attitude.'

*

Miranda had known there was a possibility that Fran and Josh could have the virus. When Fran told her the result of the tests she struggled not to cry her relief. 'I couldn't mention it, I was so scared. It was cowardly of me. You might have wanted to talk to me.'

Fran hugged her. 'Please, don't worry. I could barely face it also. I just shut down. And how much worse for Simon it must have been.'

'I'm so pleased he was with you, Fran. He can hardly bear to be seen in public.'

Fran nodded and sat down at the table where tea and cakes awaited her. Josh, in his high chair, looking so well and contented, was already happily munching. Watching him, Fran felt a great surge of emotion. Her hand was wobbling when she lifted her cup and tea splashed onto the table.

'Naughty,' said Josh, causing Fran and Miranda to dissolve into laughter.

'He's bringing you up well, Fran,' Miranda said. 'Better job than I did, d'you think?'

'Much stricter. Oh, I wish Simon were here. He and Josh can be so funny together. He went straight to his room – looking shattered.'

Take him tea and cakes when you're ready. He's always devoured my ginger cake so let's hope.'

A little while later Josh and Fran were tea-time visitors and Simon did eat and drink with obvious satisfaction while Josh ran his American bus around the floor.

*

The elevation that the test results had given Simon's spirits lasted a few days, then awful bouts of sickness and diarrhoea dragged him down. He refused to allow a call to a nurse or doctor and insisted that only water, no food, should be left outside his door. Even Josh was barred.

'We can't let this go on – he must have some help,' said Fran..

'Remember, he's due to go in for a check-up tomorrow, and we can't let him refuse. If he does I'll call an ambulance.'

Luckily, Miranda did not have to dial 999. It seemed a relief to Simon to be back in hospital, but not when he was told there would be an investigation into the diarrhoea and vomiting.

'Investigate! That's a strong word when the cause is due to that bloody pill,' he said to

Dr. Grierson who was staring at the medical notes.

'The medication can cause side effects but we're not sure in your case and I'm afraid your temperature is up.'

'So I'll be in for a bit. Please make sure my wife knows or she'll be waiting for me.'

'Of course. It will be best if you have no visitors for a day or two.' Dr. Grierson turned to the nurse standing nearby. 'Please find Mrs Fellowes and inform her of the delay.'

Fran was reassured by the nurse that the delay was precautionary, not serious. She explained this to Miranda who was looking worried when she arrived back home alone.

'They're really conscientious,' she said. 'Fran, you look as if you could do with a few days in bed. Won't Simon be needing the usual overnight stuff – tooth brush, soap and so on? I can drop it in for him.'

'No, the nurse said they'd supply everything, Oh, the phone's ringing. Shall I answer it?'

Miranda nodded and minutes later intrigue by Fran's ripples of laughter and happy exclamations.

'Who was it?' she asked when Fran joined her in the kitchen where lunch awaited.

'Jane, she has a little boy. He arrived at seven yesterday evening. Born at home with Sophie in charge.'

'Oh. that's great news. Why don't you go down to see her? You could do with a break. I'll take care of Josh so you'll really be free.'

'You'd really be happy with that?'

'Of course, darling. Josh is so easy and Margaret's always on hand. You've been advised not to visit Simon for a few days so take the opportunity.'

Chapter 33

Rudi picked up the phone. 'Fran, you've heard the news too. Great. I'll see you about four o'clock. Of course I don't mind. It'll be great to see you. 'Bye.'

What luck he was working at home for a couple of days. An earlier call had informed him that a New York publisher had enthusiastically accepted his book, a mixture of his research and travels. That, and now Fran's call, just about elevated him to a level that made him feel superior to the buzzard flying high above the hill from where he'd noticed a strange white 'flag' waving nearly three years ago!

He drained the coffee pot, leafed through a few papers but was suddenly too restless to get on with his writing. An incident from his Amazonian trip flashed into his mind. He'd had a brief fling with a fellow botanist, an event that, for him, had been no more than the easing of a physical need and he'd been honest from the outset. But she'd written to him and even telephoned from her Australian home when he returned to England. This had worried him. Was celibacy the only decent way for him until or unless he met a girl who could obliterate his longing for Fran? There had been times when he thought there had been a reciprocated sensual awareness. Their physical contacts had been no more than the lightest brushing of lips, touching of hands and a hug when meeting so perhaps it was wishful thinking. Was it enough for her that they could spend hours rambling on the moor in companionable, mutual enjoyment, and they could talk animatedly or be silent, yet at ease together? Did she have all this with Simon and love-making too. He didn't doubt her love for Simon. Her devastation when she discovered his affair said it all.

It was absurd to ponder along these lines, when all Fran was looking for at this time, was a bit of space. He just happened to be occupying that bit of that space. He forced himself into a practical frame of mind and well before four o'clock had vacuumed and made up the bed in Fran's room (allowing no self-indulgent fantasies).

Fran's appearance shocked him. Tired eyes, lank, dull hair and skin almost translucent. For a second, as she stepped from the unfamiliar car (Miranda's), he wondered if a stranger had arrived. They hugged and Fran said, 'The baby's lovely. Have you seen him?'

'No. I'm going to meet him tomorrow. David rang yesterday. He's thrilled and so is Trish. I could hear her happily chattering. Is that your bag on the back seat? I'll get it.'

'Thanks, I've enough stuff for an overnight stay if that's all right.'

'Fran, don't be daft. This is your home. Norah and Fred will be thrilled to see you.'

'You haven't told them I was coming?' From the cottage doorway, Fran turned. She looked worried.

'No, I haven't seen them. It's their Barnstaple day but they'll be back soon. Is there a problem?'

'Not with them.' She went inside and when she reached the sitting room's French windows, called, 'I must see Chuckle. Excuse me for a minute.'

She was gone about ten minutes and returned looking more relaxed.

'Chuckle's fine and he whickered his usual greeting, and Beamish's rowan tree has really taken off. Thanks so much, Rudi – oh, and tea's all ready.'

She sat down on the sofa, leaned back into the large cushion and stretched her legs.

'It's quite a drive from London. You must be tired, Fran. Have you had anything to eat?'

'Yes, Jane insisted I stayed for lunch.' She bent forward and picked up the mug of tea.

'Good. I've a large pork casserole we can have this evening. Shall I ask Fred and Norah to join us?'

She was drinking and swallowed hard. 'I think I'm a bit too tired, Rudi. I can see them tomorrow.'

She looked around, smiling, as if silently greeting all the familiar objects in the room.

'You're domesticated, Rudi. Everything's in order.'

'But you Fran, you seem a bit shattered. Has Simon been ill again?'

She opened her eyes but was looking away. 'Poorly, on and off, and his grandmother died recently. It's been quite a strain. He couldn't even go to the funeral. He was in hospital at the time

'Is he better now?'

'No, he's back inside, having more tests. There's a problem with his lungs and it's best if he doesn't have visitors. That's why I was able to come here.'

'I'm so sorry for what you're going through. I often wonder how Jake, my doctor cousin copes. His patients aren't relations but it must still be hard seeing so much suffering. He isn't just doing research but he also works voluntarily with a group that's trying to educate the general public and make life easier for patients.'

'Are they handicapped - mentally ill?'

'No, they have HIV/Aids.'

Fran gasped, staring at Rudi and frowning, then she looked away. 'So you know quite a lot about his work.'

"Yes, and about all the prejudice and downright cruelty many sufferers are subjected to. Jake works at San Francisco University and they're streets ahead of all the others.'

"Why did he choose that particular research?'

'For ages he's been aware of prejudice against gays. His wife's brother, Andy, is gay and they were schoolmates. Andy's a writer and university lecturer and in a really solid relationship. When Jake learned of the horrible idea that gays were the perpetrators of Hiv/Aids he was appalled - and not just gays but black people are blamed. He's taken part in demonstrations, spoken on radio and TV.'

'But straight, white people with it are often despised, aren't they?'

'Yes, many sufferers are shunned, even by friends and families. There are ideas that the infection can be caught by hugging and handshaking, and in the way we catch colds, which is ridiculous. There are even plenty if ill-informed medics. Jake says the prejudice is less here than in the States.'

'Rudi, I can tell you....'Fran's voice was shaky. 'I don't have to pretend it might be cancer; Simon has Aids.' As she said the word she looked directly at him, meeting his eyes, unflinching. Shock and immediate compassion registered in his expression; any spoken response had to be banal. What words could anyone use to describe the enormity of feeling evoked?

'Oh God. Fran, dear girl, I'm so sorry.'

'It probably happened years ago, that's why it's so advanced. It had gone beyond the HIV stage when it was discovered. He's always kept himself fit, eaten well, not overworked; all of that masked it, I suppose. And he's intolerant of illness so ignored symptoms. It couldn't go on, of course, and a few weeks ago, he collapsed. He feels so ashamed.'

'It could have happened to any of us – wild students living life to the full and ignorant of possible dangers.' Rudi genuinely wanted to make it clear that the infection could be picked up by anyone meeting his/her sexual desires.

'Fran, you're getting support, aren't you?'

'I am, from a counsellor. I can say anything to her but she is a professional. To be able to tell you means so much and I had no idea you'd have all that knowledge. Thank you, Rudi.'

She dropped her face into her hands and began to cry. Instantly he was beside her, his arms encircling her.

'Fran, I'm here for you – always.'

She sobbed then, her body shaking. All the desire he had ever felt for her was nothing compared with his yearning to ease her distress. She tried to speak but was crying too hard. After minutes her sobs lessened and, jerkily, she said, 'Thank goodness Josh is fine but I can't love anyone ever again. I'm not infected now but they're going to keep checking.'

'Fran darling, there are many ways of making love. Sex may not be the most important.'

For minutes he held her until she seemed more in control, moving so she was sitting upright. She mopped her face with tissues that were never far from hand. She'd cried more in the last weeks than she had over years.

'He hates his medication. He says it makes him feel worse not better.' She looked down at her tightly clenched hands and took a long deep breath. 'I think he wants it all to end.'

'Fran, things could improve. Research is going on all the time to find better medication and, hopefully, a cure. And he has you and Josh so everything to fight for.'

'He sees Josh most days, even plays with him if he's not feeling too bad but I'm kept at a distance. He's so appalled by the way he looks.' Fran was quiet for a moment, then said, 'The first time he had pneumonia, why didn't they diagnose it? That was well over a year ago.'

'All I can suggest was that he's the wrong class and colour. Suspicions wouldn't have been raised. Fran, would you like me to get Jake to contact you? He could give you all the most recent information and he'd be a real support.'

Fran smiled. 'Once again you want to help, too.' She leaned her head against his shoulder.

'I'll think about it. Simon would be very angry if he knew I'd told you. Even his closest friends can't be told the truth.'

'That leaves a huge support gap for him and you. I understand, now, why you don't want Norah and Fred to come round. Thank goodness you've got Miranda. I imagine she knows it all as you're staying with her.'

'She does and I don't think I could manage without her. She suggested I should have a break –

come back to the best place in the world. It means so much.'

'I know. If you're up to it, would a walk be a help, before we eat?'

The smile Fran gave Rudi was her reply; she stood up, stretched and put on the light gilet she'd left on an armchair.

The purple of the first bell-heathers was intensified by the late afternoon sunshine, even dominating the patchwork of summer colours. Fran drew deep breaths, smelling a mixture of scents from flowers that she hadn't seen for months, even a year. She and Rudi walked in companionable silence or exchanged enthusiastic comments about the environment. Sheep and ponies glanced at them, unconcerned by their presence, while high above, ravens, kestrels and buzzards soared in the cloudless sky.

'Just two absentees,' Rudi commented as, after an hour, they returned to Spring Cottage. 'Josh and Beamish. Are you going to get another dog?'

'We discussed it when we moved and decided we'd wait until we bought a house. Now I don't know what we'll do. Josh still mentions Beamish. He really misses him.'

'How could one not – remember, he was your co-rescuer.'

Fran laughed, feeling happier than she had for ages.

Once they were inside the cottage Rudi announced he was taking charge as chef, and waiter. 'You relax. The short walk's been good for you but you are tired. I've only got to warm the casserole up.'

'Thanks, I'll do as I'm told – for once.' Fran removed her plimsoles and gilet and stretched full-length on the sofa. She closed her eyes and images arrived of times on the moor. Beamish was hunting alongside the trap, then a red stag attracted his attention and he barked until it tore away. A herd of Exmoor ponies were amazed at the sight of one of their kind attached to a large piece of mobile wood.

Fran jumped into reality as the phone screeched in the hall.

'Damn, you were having a good doze,' said Rudi, going to answer it. Seconds later he called, 'It's Miranda, Fran.'

He smiled as he handed the receiver to her and murmured, 'Nothing bad.'

'Darling, are you having a good time.'

'Lovely. Miranda. The weather's gorgeous and so is everything here. Any news of Simon?'

'I rang the hospital a short while ago and, to my surprise they accepted that I'm a relative and told me he's stable. No real change but at least he's no worse.'

'Is he conscious?'

'Barely, but the medication is partly responsible. Josh is fine and has had a busy day painting in the studio. Well, that's what he called it.'

For five minutes they talked then Fran returned to find the delicious smelling casserole was waiting for her.

'Wine Fran, red or white?'

'A small red, please.' Fran sat down. 'To be looked after like this is wonderful.'

'And not just for you. I wish you could stay.'

The way Rudi was looking at her told her far more than those words had. She concentrated on the meal, then discussion flowed between them, tales of crazy childhood events that had them laughing.

'I'd better drink water, not wine, in future,' Fran spluttered, as Rudi concluded an account of a holiday in Florida when, for nearly two hours, he wandered away to search for an alligator small enough to put in his schoolbag.

'Dad wasn't the hitting kind of father but I got one that day, and poor Mum was in such a state of panic he was sure she was going to have a heart attack.'

Two hours had passed unnoticed during which Fran had eaten more in one meal than she normally ate in three. Firmly told to return to the sofa while Rudi cleared up, she didn't argue and only the gentle rattle of coffee cups awoke her ten minutes later.

'You could do with a long break, Fran, but I know it's not possible. I hope when the treatment is sorted things will get easier for you both.'

'I'll really think about your offer to contact your cousin. I just wish I could talk about it with Simon. If he would have talks with Jake it might help him a lot.'

'Well, he's helped loads of people but they do have to be willing. God, it's so difficult for you.' Rudi sighed heavily as he poured the coffee then passed a cup to Fran – a cup not a mug, she noticed, Miranda's old set. Nothing had to be removed, apart from Fran's personal possessions, when Rudi moved in. It was as if he were more the guardian of her beloved home than a tenant.

Coffee was a stimulant, surely? Not for Fran. Within half an hour she was struggling to stay awake.

'Bed, Fran. You really must get some sleep. You've coped so well.' Rudi's tone was gentle but firm. He was sitting opposite her, smiling. He stood up, leaned forward and touched her shoulder. 'Up you get. Your room's all ready for you.'

She stood up a bit shakily. He put his arms around her and kissed her cheek. 'Remember, Fran, I'm always here for you.'

'I know. That means so much.' She drew away reluctantly and walked slowly from the room.

The hall clock chimed eight times. Rudi awoke and took a few minutes to orientate himself. He glanced at his watch. Yes, it was eight o'clock, at least an hour later than he usually awoke. In case Fran was still asleep he decided a reviving wash would be quieter than a shower and fifteen minutes later was dressed and in the kitchen. He filled the kettle and switched it on then noticed a piece of paper on the table, anchored by a plant pot.

He picked it up and read a pencil-written message.

My dear Rudi,

Again you rescued me. Thank you has never sounded more inadequate. I can never equal your kindness to me.

Your loving friend,
Fran.

Chapter 34

'I thought - hoped you'd give yourself a longer break, Fran. A few days even.' Miranda's comment surprised Fran.

'That would have seemed so wrong, leaving you with Josh and not being close if anything awful happened with Simon.'

Miranda put glasses of fresh orange juice on the garden table and called, 'Nice drink and cake here, Josh.'

He was higher up the garden, kicking a large ball around. 'Mummy have it,' he replied, and concentrated on getting the ball out of a flowerbed.

'That's generous of you Josh, but there's plenty here.' Fran laughed and felt emotional. 'Can I visit Simon later? Is he allowed visitors?'

'Yes, but very few and only if they are well, so you can go. Honestly Fran, a longer break would have been sensible. There's nothing you can do here as he's still barely conscious.'

'But he might be aware of my presence; that's important. I came back so soon, partly because I felt guilty. I was happy there - where I should always be. I really wanted to stay as Rudi was so understanding.'

Pausing several times, Fran told Miranda about Rudi's cousin's work.

'That's such a coincidence. I'm sure contact with him would help but I can't see Simon allowing it. But if it's helpful for you don't hesitate. You're both having to live with that awful illness.'

Fran nodded. 'Being shut out – not being allowed to talk with Simon and hardly to be with him is so hard. I feel utterly useless.'

'Darling, I wish I could do more to help.'

'You do so much, already, and it's hard for you not able to talk to friends. It's meant so much to be able to tell everything to Rudi, and he's not even an old friend yet I feel he's so close.' Fran leaned back in the chair so the sun could caress her cheeks. 'It's so awful of me but I feel I share more with him than I do with Simon. I love Simon but... it's different.'

'He may not be capable of the sort of friendship you have with Rudi. I understand that, darling.'

'I so want to forgive and forget those times when he was unfaithful.' Fran stopped, and frowning she stared at Miranda. 'Oh, I haven't told you, have I?'

'No, but you don't have to. If telling me helps you that's okay, but I've never expected you to divulge things you want to keep private.'

'I know, that's why I love you.' Fran's tears flowed again. Miranda moved, sitting beside her and stroking her hand.

'I only know of one affair with a fellow lecturer but there might have been others. I thought our relationship was so special; the way we met at the Howard's party, the weeks apart then ending on the moor and, quickly marrying. I suppose I just wasn't adequate.'

'No, that's not true. He could have had any woman – you've said that several times. He was determined to marry you. He loved you and still does. Darling, many men have to have more than one sexual partner. It's probably a hormone thing.'

'But they're not all like that. Charles isn't, I'm sure.'

'No, there are exceptions, of course, but I've met plenty of the other sort.' Miranda noticed Fran was looking at her, quizzically and half-grinning. She smiled, and tightening her hold on Fran's hand, said, 'Please don't think my life's been spent having affairs with married men. The only one I really cared about was married so I turned him down.'

'I know, and that's what so decent about you but why couldn't life have been kinder? You deserve so much more.'

'I don't look at it like that. I have the career I wanted and a daughter and grandson without all the physical difficulties...'

At that Fran laughed then, glancing up at the sun-tinged, late afternoon sky, called, 'Come on down, Josh. Let's all go for a nice stroll before you wear yourself out.'

Over the next few days Fran and Miranda took it in turns to visit Simon. This was a help to Fran who could spend more time with Josh, chat on the phone with Jane and Martha and explain to Gerry why Simon still hadn't been in touch. 'I so want to see him,' Gerry said. 'Do let me know when it's possible.'

Would it ever be? Fran wondered. If he continued to refuse to see Charles it was unlikely he'd see any other friends. Poor Charles and Anna; did they feel as if they'd been cast aside? It was a huge relief for Fran when Anna rang with exciting news that, at last, she was pregnant.

'Do tell Simon. He'll be so pleased for Charles. We can't say more as we deliberately didn't ask the sex. I

379

wouldn't want to miss that final bit of excitement. Charles would love to tell him himself, but we realise he still can't have visitors, other than family."

Thrilled with the news Fran went to the hospital within an hour only to find Simon was having an examination with a consultant, so her visit was delayed.

'He's conscious so things have improved,' said a male nurse. 'Why not pop to the canteen for a cuppa then come back in – say– half an hour?'

Her spirits lifted, Fran followed his suggestion and sat in the busy canteen, completely shut off from the noisy chatter around her as she pictured Simon returning home, regaining strength and leading a normal life again. Perhaps, he would even agree to have contact with Rudi's cousin.

'Scuse me, all right if I sit 'ere?' Fran started and looked up to see a smiling, middle-aged man standing beside an empty chair – the only one it seemed.

'Yes, of course. It's a busy afternoon.'

The man put a tray on the table and sat down. 'I wondered if you was asleep. Sorry if I woke you.'

'No, I was just thinking. I often close my eyes when I'm doing that.'

'Well thanks, love. Got a bit of time to kill as my partner's bein' x-rayed.'

The man had the sort of cockney accent that Fran loved and a kindly expression that was as much in his eyes as in his smile.

'I'm waiting too. My husband's being seen by the consultant.'

'I've seen you before. A regular visitor like me. Been in and out for ten months has Ronnie.'

'That's hard for you both. Are you pleased with the treatment he's getting?'

'Couldn't be in a better place but there's limits. No definite cure for what e's got. It's called Karposi Sarcoma. 'Orrible skin problem along with other things.'

At once Fran realised that he was talking about Hiv/Aids and was amazed that he was so open about it. He drank for a few seconds, then said, 'The x-rays about 'is chest. That's a problem too.'

'My husband's problem is mainly chest and the drugs don't seem to suit him.'

'My Ronnie's met 'im in one of the clinics, Dr Fellowes. Ronnie's a bit up market, see – a teacher. I'm a cab driver.'

Fran smiled. 'An indispensable service. Do you live locally?'

'Fulham. Ronnie was lucky to be cared for 'ere, but 'is GP chose it. 'E knew what was what. Oh, I'm Bill, by the way.'

'And I'm Fran. My husband is Simon.'

'Aye, and been to Africa, like Ronnie. 'E worked out in Ghana, 'elping to establish a school. That's where 'e caught the infection, long before they knew about it 'ere.'

'But black people aren't to blame for it, are they?'

'No, that's a cruel idea. The bug thrives in the African weather and, mainly inside green monkeys. But Ronnie never met a green monkey and who'd 'ave sex with one anyway.'

By now Fran was laughing. She gulped the rest of her tea and decided to have another one.

'Would you like another?' she offered but Bill shook his head.

'Thanks luv but three's enough.'

Thank goodness there were people like Bill in this world and, she guessed, Ronnie and Simon must have talked sometime. That could have been a help to him. She bought the tea and returned to the table. Bill had picked up a copy of The Guardian. He put it down, sighing.

'I 'ope my son don't go in for politics. There's so much rubbish. 'E's off to university in September, to study geography. 'E's been greatly helped by Ronnie. My ex-wife's thrilled.'

'That's lovely. I suspect my nearly three-year-old is aiming to be a zookeeper.'

Bill grinned, reached across and squeezed Fran's hand. 'I bet e's a lovely little fella.'

They chatted for a good half hour, much of the time laughing, then Bill glanced at the large clock on the wall, facing them. 'Guess I'd better go and check on Ronnie. Lovely to meet you, Fran.'

'And you, Bill. I hope all goes well for you both.'

I'd best drink up then check on Simon, Fran said silently and ten minutes later was relieved to find that he was alone and looking relaxed as if having a doze. A horrible-looking breathing machine was close by but he seemed to be breathing normally.

Almost whispering she said, 'Simon, I'm here.'

His eyelids flickered then opened. He was looking directly at her and smiling. She stood up and leaning over kissed his cheek.

'Lovely to see you. Thankyou, Fran.'

'For what? I've been longing for this – you being able to speak to me. I've missed you so much.'

'Not much longer. I can be discharged in a day or two. They've adjusted the drugs again. How's Josh?'

382

'Fine, just wanting his dad to come home. He'll be so pleased when I tell him the good news.'

'Good news for him but not necessarily for you or me.' Simon was looking away, frowning.

'What d'you mean. Of course I want you back home.'

'How long will it last this time 'til I'm back here again?'

'Don't think like that, please.' Fran closed her hands around his and he smiled.

'Well you're nice and warm. Half the time it feels like winter, even in here. My weight loss is appalling.'

'Simon, I've some good news. Anna is pregnant, at last.'

Simon stared at Fran, frowning. 'I hope it's Charles's child. That IVF treatment can use anyone's sperm.'

'It definitely is his child and he's thrilled.'

'Oh well, give them my congratulations.' Simon's tone was flat and he was not even smiling.

Surely, he should be pleased for his old friends? Fran risked suggesting he could phone but he didn't even respond. He closed his eyes but his fingers tightened slightly on Fran's hand.

'That part of our life is over. You understand that don't you?'

'Everything's been explained to me – professionally. If you hadn't cared about safe sex I'd be infected. Honestly, the doctors are really optimistic.'

'I know. They've told me.' Simon sighed. 'But I've no energy and my body is fast degenerating,.'

'Simon, you're being treated. You'll get stronger. I met a nice man, Bill, in the canteen and he told me his partner was diagnosed a year ago and they've even had a holiday abroad since then.'

'I know. Don't compare them with us. Ah, here's Nurse Jenkins.'

The door had opened and a tall, male nurse entered. He introduced himself to Fran then told her that Simon's discharge was imminent.

'We'll arrange for a nurse to visit you at home so we can check up on the drugs. That's so important.'

To Fran's surprise Simon forced himself to sit upright as if he'd suddenly been injected with energy.

'If I've sufficient medication and instructions why should I need a nurse checking on me?' he asked. His tone was firm and, luckily, not aggressive.

'It's to be sure the dose is right for you, so we like to do regular tests. You'll be living at home when you leave?'

'Oh yes, and not far,' said Fran, hastily.

The nurse smiled at her. 'The support system is good in this area so please don't hesitate if you need help.' He then left the room.

'I'm not having visits at home.' Simon said. 'I bet they turn up in plastic overalls and face masks.'

'As long as they look after you that's all that matters.'

'Yes, but we don't want the street cordoned off.' Thank goodness he was now grinning. Fran wished she could seize the moment to tell him about Rudi's cousin. It could be a real help for him to talk to such a committed expert. Maybe, once Simon was stronger they could even go and meet him. If only he would see that discussing his illness showed how much she cared but he would see it quite differently, as disloyalty.

'I don't suppose you've been able to work much,' he said. 'Anything in the offing?'

'A bit for that nice writer, Jennifer Green. Working for her is great as I never feel under pressure.'

'Well, I've got to complete a piece for the Observer in a few days.'

'But you're off sick.'

'No. In a day or two I'll be fine as far as they're concerned. I can work from home.'

Fran had no doubt that Simon would meet his commitment but for how long would he be able to delude his boss that he was well enough to work?

'Ah, supper's arrived. They feed us so early here as if we're kids,' Simon said as Nurse Jenkins entered, pushing a trolley.

'Good that your husband can eat again,' he said, but Simon's expression said otherwise.

'I'd better get home and start planning menus,' Fran said. 'Nothing but your favourites, I promise.'

Chapter 35

When Simon had been at home for four days Charles rang, hoping to visit him. Simon was sitting in the kitchen where Miranda picked up the phone. After a minute she covered the receiver and said, 'We haven't seen Charles and Anna for a while. Let's ask them to lunch on Saturday or Sunday. With their news a good reason to open a bottle of champagne.'

Simon nodded. Surprised and pleased, Miranda handed the phone over and walked away, leaving him chatting.

"No argument about the lunch suggestion,' she said to Fran who was weeding at the top of the garden. 'Maybe it shows his attitude is changing.'

'I hope so. It's as if he loathes the person he's become. Never mind, Josh and I still love him.'

'I wonder where the idea came that everything and everyone must be perfect,' Miranda said. 'I'm sure Nancy was very proud of him, and Charles has told me about his excellent relationship with his mother. Now, I'll give Josh his bath and put him to bed to give you a break.'

'Thanks. I love being out of doors as you know and hate to think that we've only about eight weeks of summer left.' Fran gave Josh a hug then watched him walk down to the house. At the door he turned and they exchanged a wave. Emotional and, suddenly tired, Fran sat on the grass and leaned back, resting on her elbows and narrowing her eyes against the late sunshine. Swathes of heather nestled close by, transporting her imagination to the moor. Would they, could they ever live there again? There had been some wonderful times, walks, rides in the trap, picnics and even dips in local rivers. Although Simon saw himself as a townie he still enjoyed the countryside. Their holidays in France had been as perfect as any could be. Togetherness was the vital ingredient for their relationship so as soon as Simon was well enough they'd have a holiday in a place of his choice.

Lunch on Sunday was a success. Fran cooked a traditional roast beef with all trimmings. Simon ate about half his usual amount but more than she's seen him consume in ages. She'd been afraid that his thinness would be mentioned but she should have credited Charles and Anna with more tact. They spoke of anything but the illness, eagerly hearing about Miranda's time in America and Canada, talking about their thrilling news and how they had been firm about not being told the sex of the child.

Around three o'clock Miranda suggested having a walk. 'How about Hampstead? One of Josh's favourites.'

Anna and Fran nodded and jumped up, instantly followed by Josh but Simon, who looked very tired, declined and Charles agreed with him.

'Let's give the girls a chance to natter alone. Josh can fill us in later,' he said. Anna laughed and hugged him.

After 'the girls' and Josh left, Simon lifted his legs onto the sofa as if he was anticipating a doze, but he asked Charles to pour more coffee as it would keep him awake.

'Sleep if you want to,' Charles said, carrying out the request.

'I want to talk. Thank goodness we're alone.'

He sipped the coffee for a moment. 'I want you to know the truth. It's only fair as you are my closest friend.' He drank again.

'You're talking about the illness?' Charles said.

'Yes. It isn't cancer but one of the effects is like lung cancer: It's Aids.'

'Oh no.' Charles gasped. 'That's so wrong.'

'It's probably just. Remember my wild life eight or ten years ago.'

'No worse than mine; we were in competition. I should have it too.'

'You didn't spend weeks in Africa.'

'Is that where you caught it?'

'Nobody can be sure but it's thought that's where the infection originates. Loads of people, particularly soldiers based in Africa, returned to the States with it. I've spent time in both places, remember.'

'.But for years you've been fine, fit, active; so it can take ages to develop.'

'Yes. And for ages I kept well. That so-called pneumonia when I returned from India was probably the first outbreak.'

'Fran knows, does she?'

'Yes, and Miranda but no one else other than medics. Fran and Josh have been tested. For now they're okay but will be checked regularly. It's appalling what I might have done to them.'

'You can't blame yourself. Even five or six years ago what did we know about the disease. The newspapers were full of articles for months because it was such a mystery.'

'Chas, it's up to you if you tell Anna but no one else must know. Benjamin thinks I'm being treated for cancer like everyone else who knows I've been ill and they'll go on thinking that. Imagine how it would be if the truth got out: journalist and former university lecturer, married and father of a son, recently diagnosed with Aids. The papers would have a field day. Think of the social stigma.'

'Would they be that cruel?'

'Of course, that's their forte.' Simon sighed and closed his eyes.' How awful it would be if Mum were still alive.'

'Would she have had to know the truth?'

'For God's sake, she'd probably have outlived me. I could have weeks, months, or a year or two.'

Charles blanched, staring away. After a short silence he asked, 'What's the treatment like?'

'Bloody awful. The medication often makes me feel worse than the illness. Nausea, diarrhoea, a dry mouth. Anyway, it's useless as the virus is beyond control. It's killing decent cells all the time. Because my main problem is my lungs I've got to have a procedure about every two weeks which means having an antibiotic straight into my lungs via a face mask. I didn't ask any questions as I don't want to know any more. I don't know how long I can let this go on.'

For minutes Charles had hardly moved as if transfixed by the news, now he shifted uncomfortably. 'There's frequent information about drug research. All the time they're trying to find a cure.'

'And meanwhile our bodies shrink, everything deteriorates. I can't bear the thought of Fran seeing me like a skeleton. It's bad enough in front of medics,' Simon sounded really depressed now.

'She loves you, Simon. Her feelings aren't going to change.'

389

'But our relationship has to. We're not a functioning couple any longer and I doubt if we can ever be again. Anyway, let's change the subject. What's been going on at Pharoah lately?'

Chapter 36

The meeting with Anna and Charles seemed to improve Simon 's spirits. He played with Josh as often as he could manage, spent time on the phone to his boss and, to Fran's surprise and relief, to Gerry and Roger. If he rang anyone else from his Exeter days, she didn't care. What hadn't changed was his unwillingness to leave the house.

'Josh loves going to the parks and the zoo, particularly if you're with him. How about now? The weather's lovely,' she suggested one morning.

'Well, he'll just have to go with you. I'm not being seen looking like a scarecrow.'

'You're thin but nothing else has changed.'

'You don't know half of it, Fran. And what about my feelings? I'm disgusted with my looks and I'll be surprised if you aren't too.'

'Oh, don't say such things, please. Why can't you accept that I love you and want us to be as normal as possible.'

'Things aren't normal. If you can't accept it talk to your precious Clare.'

He was sitting by the desk in his bedroom and swivelled the chair so his back faced her. His words tormented her acutely. It was as if she was a stranger to him, no one he could trust. She left the room and sank onto her bed. He wouldn't change Already she had talked about his attitude with Clare. She learnt that plenty of patients loathed themselves but many accepted help, even coming to counselling with their partners.

'If Simon would talk to me I'm sure it would help, and if you were there it would be even better. The trouble is, the wish to do this must come from the patient,' Clare had said. They talked for nearly an hour and Fran felt less burdened. If constancy and support were all Simon would accept from her, what more could she give?

Simon's return to hospital for treatment to his lung was a setback in his view. If Fran hadn't been able to drive him there and back, he would have refused to go.

'But it can be done at home,' she said. 'They've told you that.'

'Then for Christ's sake don't you tell me. I'm not having this place turned into a hospital. I've been pestered by a physiotherapist and an occupational therapist in hospital; d'you think I'm allowing them to come here? Not bloody likely.'

'But they do things for you that I can't. I'm useless compared with them.'

'Rubbish, if ever I reach a stage of needing their help I hope I'll be off this planet. They've even told me I should contact the Terence Higgins Trust.'

'They're wonderful helpers. I've read lots about them.'

'Maybe, but I've a home and family. If you can't cope just tell me. Well, we'd better go.'

A pleasant middle-aged woman, Nurse Saunders, told Fran the treatment would take about an hour, then suggested, 'Why have a drink and snack while you're waiting?'

Feeling the need for a drink, cake or biscuit Fran followed her suggestion. In the queue at the canteen's counter she found herself standing next to Bill. She was pleased and he beamed and said, 'Share a table shall we, do a bit of catching up?'

They found a two-seater and Bill asked if Simon had been admitted. Fran explained he was just in for a short treatment.

'Ah, bit different from Ronnie. 'E's been in for days. Things 'ave got worse in a short time.'

'I'm so sorry. He'd been doing quite well when I met you.'

'Don't last, love. I don't think the drugs 'elp much. Them awful viruses can't be killed but sometimes they 'ave a bit of a rest and we get all excited. Radiotherapy 'elped a bit when the Karposi was on 'is skin but it's now inside, in the gut and liver, and I don't know what can be done.'

Bill was looking away as he spoke, his hands tightly clenched. From what Fran had read it sounded a very poor prognosis. For a minute they were quiet, drinking tea and Fran started to eat a large slice of chocolate cake.

'I miss 'im so much. Thank God I got I our dog. 'E even comes to work with me and I don't care if anyone complains. Anyway, e's got a special area in the boot, separate from the luggage.'

'It must be a very large taxi,' Fran said, amused and thinking of Gerry who sometimes took his dog on archaeological digs, or did when he was younger.

'You got a dog?' Bill asked and Fran told him about Beamish.

'Get another one,' Bill advised. 'They're such a comfort, although I guess you got a lot to put up with. D'you get any 'elp.'

Fran explained that Simon was still self-caring and Bill looked pleased. 'I 'ope it goes on so that you don't need 'elp, love.'

They talked about all manner of things for nearly an hour.

'We bin puttin' the world to rights,' Bill said, then Fran glanced at her watch.

'I'd better collect Simon. It's been really good to meet again and I do hope Ronnie improves.'

Bill stood up and kissed Fran' s cheek. 'Your bloke's a lucky chap. Goodbye, Fran.'

Although Simon didn't complain about the treatment when Fran collected him, he was angry the following day.

'It's left a disgusting taste in my mouth and I coughed all night. Didn't you hear me?'

'Once or twice but I slept pretty well.'

'Lucky you. Fran, thanks for going to that trouble with the lunch but I've no appetite.'

Simon had opted to eat in the bedroom and the plate on the tray was almost full.

'We've been given information about diets – the need to eat plenty of protein to build up your weight. Please try, Simon.'

'Written information isn't much help when food quickly shifts out at both ends. I'm having a bad day so please give me some peace. Best keep Josh occupied elsewhere.'

Fran picked up the tray and left the room. Words that would sound normal to most people in Simon's situation, such as, 'Let me help', 'Tell me what's the immediate problem', irritated him; so Fran felt she was neither of practical nor emotional use.

That evening she felt so low she rang Rudi. Thank goodness he was at home and ready to give her all the time she wanted. After asking after Chuckle and the Yeos, Fran told him about Simon's current condition and his feelings.

'It's so hard to hear him speaking of rubbish drugs and useless treatments. He has such a pessimistic view. Nothing anyone says will convince him things can improve. That isn't right is it?'

'No, although there's still no positive cure, but Jake was telling me a few days ago that he knows people who have improved no end after treatment and even lead normal lives. Fran, I hope you won't mind but, without disclosing Simon's name, I described his symptoms to him and he said that when the desease has developed to a stage where it's termed Auto Immune Deficiency the damage done to cells can't be rectified but there's increasing evidence that progress of the illness can be slowed.'

Fran gave a huge sigh and stretched her tired-feeling legs on the large sofa. Miranda was out, dining with friends, and Josh asleep in bed. To be able to talk freely gave her a sense of release.

'The treatment he's going to have regularly to aid his breathing he's already very critical of that.'

'That's really important with PCP. Jake asked me if my friend was having it and sounded pleased. One of the hardest things for patients to tolerate is that they often feel they're being experimented on. If one drug has no effect, another is tried and some cause awful symptoms.'

Their conversation went on for at least half an hour but not all about Simon's illness. Fran was pleased to hear that between Gerry and Rudi an easy, casual friendship had developed. They would have talked even longer but the ringing of the doorbell forced Fran to end what had been like a therapy session.

Anna was at the door. 'D'you remember I said I was coming this way and I'd pop by?'

Fran didn't remember but concealed her surprise and soon they were sitting by the French windows, enjoying Chardonais.

'I wanted to tell you that, with Simon's permission, Charles told me about the diagnosis. I'm so sorry for you both. Thank goodness you and Josh are okay. When Simon is up to it could we all go on holiday together? I'm fit as a flea and not due until January and we thought if we all went it would be support for you.'

'That's a lovely suggestion. I'd be all for it but I've a feeling Simon wouldn't agree. He won't go outside unless it's for an appointment at the hospital. He can't bear to be seen. What did you make of how he looked when you came to lunch?'

Anna frowned. 'To be honest I was shocked; he's lost so much weight. He was always slim but never skinny. All the years I've known him he's always looked wonderful.'

'And his looks matter to him more than anything,' Fran said.

'Not more than you. Before he met you, Charles and I had never known him so determined about anything. You were a hundred per cent the one for him.'

'But he doesn't see himself as the man I fell in love with. I can't be close any more. I'm like a chambermaid, allowed in to tidy up, bring meals and take away the dirty clothes.'

'That's awful. Does he know how that makes you feel?'

'I've tried to tell him but he gets angry. Miranda tried to talk to him but he almost shouted and yet he really respects her. Has he changed mentally as well as physically?' Fran gave a huge sigh. 'You understand about mental health problems.'

'Fran, I work with children with learning difficulties. I don't think Simon comes into that category.'

For the first time that evening they both laughed. The atmosphere lightened as Anna described the moment she was informed of her pregnancy, the excitement of the prospective grandparents and the way she'd been showered with treats from family and friends.

'There'll be a bit of a gap between he/she and Josh but I do hope they'll be friends.' Anna said.

'He likes babies. He peers into prams and buggies and sometimes imitates the sounds they make.'

'Is he doing that now?' Anna said, looking upwards.

'Oh, he must have had a bad dream.' Fran got up.

'Won't Simon go to him?'

'I doubt it. He's been rather unwell today. Please top your glass up.'

'I'd better go but it's been lovely to see you.' They hugged and Anna let herself out while Fran hurried up to Josh's room to find he was worried because his

Teddy had disappeared and, a second later, Fran found him under the bed.

'What the hell was that about?' called Simon. 'First chance I've had of a sleep all day and he had to ruin it. No more interruptions, please.'

When Simon's second treatment appointment was due he was feeling really ill. Weak and nauseated, he'd just managed to reach the lavatory in time, then collapsed half way back to his bed. Arriving with a clean set of towels and sheets, Fran dropped everything and knelt beside him.

'I must get help,' she said, and was relieved when he responded, showing he was conscious.

'No. Give me time. I'll get up when I'm ready. I've told you this treatment is no bloody good. Don't call anyone.' He struggled to his feet and managed to reach the chair beside the bed.

'Please understand I would never have wanted to leave you but now I have no choice.'

'What d'you mean?' Almost breathless with anxiety Fran sat on the bed as close to him as possible.

'I'm not with you now – the man you married has gone already.'

'No. You've said such things before and it's so wrong. I love you – the person beside me now. Please believe me.'

'I do and I love you, but I loathe myself. Fran, please try to understand my feelings.'

He was looking at her, even smiling. She leaned forward, resting her head on his shoulder, then he moved, slumping. She jumped up, and realising he was again barely conscious, rushed downstairs to consult Miranda.

'What can I do? He doesn't want me to get help but he's not fit to go in the car.'

Looking very anxious, Miranda left the room without replying. Only minutes later she returned, close to tears.

'I've called the hospital, Fran, so he can't blame you. You're right, he's barely conscious.'

Chapter 37

Had Simon been fully conscious he would again have refused help. Two hours after his admission to hospital Fran returned home with a sense of relief.

'Margaret has taken Josh out. She worships him,' Miranda said. 'She wanted to turn out Simon's room but I said 'no'. He can't stand anyone but you and me going in so I've done it.'

'Oh no. I could do it now. You do too much.' Fran gave Miranda a hug then sat at the table gratefully drinking tea.

'Darling, I've been agonising whether to tell you but I feel I must as the medics should know.' Miranda was looking worried, even close to tears.

'What is it? Not signs of self-injury?'

'No darling, self-neglect. I was cleaning in the bedroom and found lots of packets and bottles of medicines in the cupboard.'

'Oh no. If he hadn't kept me at a distance I might have found them.'

Miranda nodded. 'That's how I felt, but if we had found them and confronted him how would he have reacted? However ill he is, he's in charge.'

Fran sank her head into her hands, eyes closed.

'I love Simon, no matter what's happened I don't regret marrying him. If only he'd accept that.' Fran's voice was shaking. 'It's as if he thinks the present has blotted everything out for me. A week ago, when I told him Fallada had phoned to enquire about his health, he said the most regrettable thing he'd ever done was to go to the party where he met me and started to ruin my life. I begged him not to think like that but he wouldn't listen.'

'It's guilt that's speaking, Fran, and quite irrational. You've had some good times; lovely holidays and his professional life couldn't be better.' Miranda hesitated, looking thoughtful, then said, 'I was surprised when he gave up his lectureship. I suppose he felt he needed less demanding job but it must have been so disappointing for his employers.'

'It was a shock but I'm not sure if it was also a relief,' Fran said.

'A relief. How could it have been? His work, writing etcetera, is universally respected.' Miranda looked astonished.

'Nothing to do with that, but about his private life. I wonder how many people knew about the affair.'

'D'you know when it started?'

'I suspect just before Josh was born but I didn't find out for months. I found them together at the flat. He seemed really sorry, but I suspect it went on.'

After a pause for a top-up of tea, Fran described the incident that contributed to Beamish's death. Miranda looked horrified and close to tears.

'I so wish you'd told me then. You know I'd have supported you.'

'I do know but think of all you've done for me.'

'Family care is unending, Fran. That's what love is all about.' Spontaneously, they stood up embracing one another for minutes, until Josh and Margaret's return separated them.

The early morning call preceded Josh's regular seven o'clock awakening. Half-awake already, Fran picked up the receiver to hear the highly anxious voice of a nurse she remembered, Richard.

'Mrs Fellowes, please can you visit really soon. Your husband regained consciousness last night but things have changed and he is now very poorly.'

'I'll come straight away. Thank you, Richard, and I'm Fran.'

The doctor who was waiting for her was not familiar, presumably because he was part of the night shift. He looked about forty and had a kind expression.

'I'm Dr. James. Please come in,' he said, opening the door to a small, empty room. He sat opposite Fran but not behind the desk, which seemed ominous.

'Simon is still alive, isn't he?' Fran's voice rose, shaking.

'Yes, but he is very poorly. I'm so sorry but he has refused all treatment.'

'But you can't allow that. You've got to help him.'

'I'm afraid we can't if he refuses to let us. He has said this and has written it down. It is so hard for you, Mrs Fellowes.'

'It shouldn't be allowed.' Fran started to cry. 'To let this happen should be a crime, it's wilful neglect.'

'But to force treatment onto an adult patient is an assault. It must seem so wrong, but it is the law. I'm so sorry.'

'Can I see him? I'll persuade him to keep going. We have a son - he must go on for his sake.' Fran was barely in control now.

'I'll get a nurse to go with you.' Dr. James left the room for a minute, returned with Richard then, apologising to Fran for stress his information had caused, left them alone.

'I'm so sorry, for the way things are. I've got to know your husband over the weeks he's been in and out. He's so clever and still has lots to offer.' Richard sat next to her

'But the diagnosis came late, didn't it?'

'I'm afraid it did. When he was first diagnosed with pneumonia, even if further tests had been done it would have been found to be advanced, but we do all we can.'

'I know and I'm really grateful, but he's lost the will to....' Fran started to cry. More like a friend than a professional, Richard stroked her hand.

'It seems awful, I know, but we have to respect our patients' feelings. Shall we go soon so you can talk to him?'

'All right, and thank you for all you've done.'

'I just wish it could be more.' Richard walked to the door and held it open, but the doctor appeared as if blocking their exit.

'Please sit down, Mrs Fellowes.'

'Why? I'm going to see Simon.'

Doctor James looked away for a second than back at Fran. 'I am so sorry, but your husband has just died.'

As if shock delayed her tears Fran managed to say, 'No, he can't have. I haven't seen him. I wasn't with him. I want to see him now.'

'Yes, Richard will go with you.'

Gently taking her hand, which earned him a slight look of disapproval from Dr. James, Richard took her out of the room and within yards, into the private room where Simon lay.

'Please stay with me, Simon, I love you.' Fran cried, leaning across the bed so their faces touched.

She longed to gather his body against hers, to feel warmth and movement.

'Fran, please may I ring your aunt?' said Richard. 'I don't want you to be alone.'

It was a minute before Fran could respond. 'Yes, please.' She stood upright, looking at Simon as if transfixed.

'Fran, dear, he's at peace. His expression tells you that.' Richard left the room, but a female nurse came in, silently standing by the door until he returned.

'Your aunt is on her way. She'll be here in minutes.'

A pair of men appeared, hovering in the doorway beside a trolley. Richard walked across, spoke to them and they moved away a short distance.

When Miranda arrived, Fran sobbed onto her shoulder, unable to speak. At last, controlling herself, she turned towards Simon.

'Is he at peace? Is he where he wanted to be?'

'Darling, there's almost a smile. We must respect his wish.' Miranda leaned over and kissed his cool cheek. 'We'll always love you and we'll care for your son. You're there, in him, for always.'

The weeks following Simon's death could have brought Fran to a complete collapse without the loving support of Miranda and her closest friends. Aware of this she struggled to be strong and, most importantly, to give Josh as normal a life as possible.

Coping with his almost daily questions, such as, 'Why doesn't Daddy come home?' and 'Is he with Beams, Mummy?' were the toughest, far worse than the general ones and comments about the cancer treatment failure, or had the hospital let Simon down?

The instructions Simon left for Fran limited her to arranging a secular cremation, attended by family only and not mentioned in the press, a carefully drafted obituary for the Observer, Times and Telegraph, then she found a separate letter, written when he must have been very poorly as she could hardly read it.

Darling,

Can you ever forgive me? I cannot forgive myself. I've wrecked the life of my most loved person. Please scatter what's left of me in the place you love, where you should be. I don't want anyone else to be with you when you do this; you are strong enough to be alone.

Can my love stay with you? I don't know, not being religious, but I'll do my best for you and our darling son.

Simon X X

Never would she be without the letter.

It was early October when she decided she had the strength to go the moor.

'I'll ask if I can stay next door for a while. I'm sure Norah will allow it,' Rudi said when she rang him.

'There's no need. The cottage can contain all four of us.'

'So Miranda's coming?'

'No, she's going to Rome for a couple of weeks: another exhibition. Number four is a new friend.'

'Oh, who is that?' Rudi sounded a little guarded.

'He's called Scamp, and he is a bit of one.'

'Oh, a dog.' Rudi laughed. 'Tell me more.'

'He came from Battersea Dogs' Home two weeks ago. Really, Josh's choice. He's thought to be about two and is a mixture of collie and some kind of terrier. He was dumped on Hampstead Heath about three months ago and was in an awful state.'

'He's okay with Josh?'

'Yes, they've bonded already.'

'That's great. I look forward to meeting him and, of course his companions.'

'Rudi, please don't feel you have to leave the cottage, I really mean it. The only thing is, can we share the studio?'

'That won't be a problem. I do most of my writing at the campus now and the job is fully secure.'

'Oh, Rudi, that's good news. I'd better go as Josh is needing his supper. So, Saturday will be all right?'

'Of course. I look forward to it.'

*

'I wish I could be with you, Fran. Expecting you to carry out his last wish all alone seems hard,' Miranda said, as she helped Fran to pack the car.

'But I must do as he asked me. That was a decision for my benefit, I'm sure.'

Miranda nodded. 'He wasn't a sentimentalist. The choice of the moor was certainly for love of you. Although your passion for it annoyed him at times, he did understand it.'

'I hope your visit goes well. When you come back can we have a holiday together – anywhere in the world?'

'Of course, Fran darling. Travelling is never too much for me as you well know.'

A while later, Fran struggled not to cry as she and Miranda exchanged their goodbyes.

Considering it was past conventional holiday time, there was plenty of traffic on the roads. Fran was pleased she'd left early, eight o'clock, which was no hardship for Josh, still an early riser. He hadn't been to Spring Cottage since Christmas and kept asking questions about it. She dreaded any mention of Beamish but, luckily, only Scamp's name came up.

'Mummy, will he like Chuckle?'

'I hope so, darling, but it might take him a while.'

'Can we take him swimming with us.'

'Not sure if with us, as Summer's gone, but he can swim under our watchful eyes.'

'What are those, Mummy?'

'Our normal eyes, darling, but watching him to be sure he's safe.'

'Will Auntie Norah be there?'

'Yes, next door. You'll be with lots of friends.'

Thank goodness for the company, thought Fran, on what was a pretty boring drive until the first moor came into view, Dartmoor. Soon, it would be even better, Dunkery Beacon and the promise of moor to come. Maybe Autumn was the best time to be on Exmoor; already it was tinting the foliage and, probably, rutting calls from stags could be heard. The company she'd be getting would be the best anyone could have; in a few days she'd catch up with Jane, Gerry, Martha and Roger and almost daily she'd see Norah and Fred and, daily....No, she must concentrate on driving as, apart from a brief comfort stop for the benefit of all three travellers, she hadn't allowed herself a break for hours.

As she approached Spring Cottage, with two windows lowered for Scamp's benefit, she heard quiet music, Elgar's Serenade for Strings in E minor, a lovely, relaxing piece she often played when working.

'We here, Mummy?' Josh asked, trying to shift in his safety seat.

'We certainly are, darling. Now, I'll get you out.'

Fran lifted Josh on to the courtyard then noticed Chuckle looking over the stable door. Above his head was a banner saying, 'Welcome Home'. As if saying the words Chuckle whinnied and Josh ran over to him, calling his name. At once Fran felt a surge of emotion. She lifted Scamp out of the boot and was about to remove the luggage, when a familiar voice called, 'No, I'll do that, please. Hullo, all of you.'

A second later Fran was encircled by the arms of her very best friend and rescuer.

THE END